"What do you th

"Is it possible? Poss

"How the hell do I k̶n̶o̶w̶?̶ ̶I̶'̶m̶ ̶a̶ ̶l̶a̶w̶y̶e̶r̶,̶ ̶n̶o̶t̶ ̶a̶ ̶s̶c̶i̶e̶n̶t̶i̶s̶t̶.̶"

"Now *that* is the right answer," Wade said, then reached for Holcomb's hand and shook it. "It's been a pleasure speaking with you. One of us will be back in ten minutes for your decision." Then he released Holcomb's hand, glanced at his companion. "Ben?"

"Yeah, we're outta here."

They didn't walk away, didn't move at all. One moment they were there, occupying space, breathing the air Holcomb breathed, and the next moment they were gone.

Impossible.

RUNNING TIME

T.J. MACGREGOR

PINNACLE BOOKS
Kensington Publishing Corp.
www.kensingtonbooks.com

PINNACLE BOOKS are published by

Kensington Publishing Corp.
850 Third Avenue
New York, NY 10022

All Kensington titles, imprints, and distributed lines are available at special quantity discounts for bulk purchases for sales promotions, premiums, fund-raising, educational, or institutional use. Special book excerpts or customized printings can also be created to fit specific needs. For details, write or phone the office of the Kensington special sales manager: Kensington Publishing Corp., 850 Third Avenue, New York, NY 10022, attn: Special Sales Department; phone 1-800-221-2647.

This book is a work of fiction. Names, characters, businesses, organizations, places, events, and incidents either are the product of the author's imagination or are used fictitiously. Any resemblance to actual persons, living or dead, events, or locales is entirely coincidental.

ISBN-13: 978-0-7860-1833-8
ISBN-10: 0-7860-1833-X

First printing: November 2008

10 9 8 7 6 5 4 3 2 1

Printed in the United States of America

For Rob and Megan,
con mucho cariño, siempre.

*Today I felt pass over me a breath of wind
from the wings of madness*

—CHARLES BAUDELAIRE

Prologue

Key Largo, Florida, Thanksgiving Day, 2006, 7:10 P.M.

Just as Eric Holcomb entered his living room, the floor lamp winked on and the recliner swirled around, revealing a tall, muscular man with a diamond stud glinting in his right ear. He wore an expensive suit, shiny Italian shoes, and his hands were folded on a briefcase in his lap. His buzz cut said ex-military, but Holcomb flashed on a scene from a Mafia movie where the loan shark wore brass knuckles and a sidearm and threatened to bust kneecaps unless money was forked over.

His mouth went dry, his heart thumped and throbbed like an engine badly in need of an overhaul.

"Fantastic view, Mr. H." The man stabbed his thumb over his shoulder, indicating the moonlit view of the Gulf off the back deck. "New dock, fruit trees all over the property, metal roof, three thousand square feet of hardwood floors and tile, every upgrade imaginable. And a foreclosure notice." He clicked his tongue against his teeth and shook his head. "It'd be a shame to lose all this."

Holcomb didn't see a weapon or brass knuckles and relaxed a little. "I don't recall borrowing money from you. And since I don't owe you money, get the hell out of my house."

"I may be the answer to your financial woes, Mr. H. Please, have a seat."

"I'll stand." He whipped out his cell and was punching 911 when someone behind him snatched the cell from his hand and pushed him down onto the couch.

"You'll sit." A black man stepped out in front of him, gun aimed at Holcomb's chest. Dangerous eyes, broad shoulders, arms the size of tree trunks. "And you'll listen to our proposition." He pocketed Holcomb's cell.

Holcomb's eyes flicked from one man to the other, anxiety eating like acid through his stomach. He willed his son to stay in the apartment over the garage, which he was cleaning in anticipation of his girlfriend's arrival tomorrow.

"Your gun is making Mr. H nervous, Ben," said the white man.

"That a fact?" Ben's arm dropped to his side, the gun still clutched in his hand. "Better, Mr. H?"

"At the moment, 'better' is relative," Holcomb said.

The white guy laughed. "A sense of humor. Good. I admire that in a man."

"And you are : . . ?" Holcomb struggled to keep his voice even, to mask his emotions, his fear.

"Wade."

"Wade and Ben." Like a vaudeville team. "Okay, and how are you going to be the answer to my financial woes, Wade?" *And how the hell do you know about my finances?*

Wade sat forward, his face entering the circle of light cast by the lamp. Holcomb now saw the sharp angles of his face, the cruelty of his mouth. The veneer of a businessman was as phony as Holcomb's courage. His panic deepened.

"In return for perhaps six months of your time, your terrible credit rating will be wiped out, the foreclosure order on your house will be canceled, the existing mortgage will be paid off, and what you owe to the IRS will disappear. In addition, you'll be paid a million dollars."

Holcomb exploded with laughter. "Right." Wade and Ben didn't laugh. They watched him the way an entomologist watches bugs. "Who the hell *are* you people?"

Wade calmly popped open the lid of his briefcase and removed stacks of bills that he arranged neatly on the coffee table. "Here's an advance on that million, Mr. H. Fifty grand."

Holcomb stared at the stacks of money, each bundle perfectly symmetrical, neat, bound with a rubber band. *Jesus God, is that money real?*

"If you agree to work for us, the foreclosure process on your beautiful home here will be stopped with the touch of a computer key. . . ." He tapped a computer case next to the chair. "The back property taxes and back mortgage payments will be paid off, and the next six months of mortgage payments will be paid as well. You have ten minutes to decide. And all of that and the fifty Gs happen tonight."

"Ten minutes," Holcomb repeated, his thoughts racing, stumbling over themselves. "I don't even know if that money's real."

"Ben, if you'll do the honors," Wade said.

Ben went over to the coffee table, reached out to pick up a bundle of cash, but Wade touched his arm. "Let Mr. H choose. Just so he knows we're on the up-and-up."

"That one and that one." Holcomb pointed.

Ben picked up the bundles Holcomb had selected and handed them to him. Thanks to his job as a bank clerk when he was in law school, Holcomb could spot a phony bill in a heartbeat. Granted, the bills—genuine and bogus alike—had changed in the years since then, but as Holcomb riffled through the bundles, he knew the money was real. He tossed the bills back onto the coffee table.

"And for all these fantastic benefits, just whom am I supposed to kill?"

"Now why would you automatically assume you have to kill anyone?"

"Why else would you offer me this kind of money?"

"We'll get to that. Right now, rest assured that you only have to use a stun gun."

"A stun gun," he repeated, and laughed again. "C'mon, you guys break into my house, one of you is armed, the other is carrying a shitload of money, and you're offering me the deal of a lifetime. What's the catch?"

"How's your memory these days?" Wade asked.

"As far as I know, it's excellent. Why?"

"Would you say your memory is still as good as it was when you took the Florida bar exam and placed second in the state for that year?"

They obviously had some very personal information about him, the kind of stuff you could get if you worked for the FBI, CIA, Freeze, NSA, or any of those acronym spook agencies. "Since I took the bar twenty years ago, it's hard to say for sure, but I'd say my memory is still good."

"Eidetic, that's how one of your professors described your memory."

"It sounds like you probably know my cholesterol level and the last time I got laid. Okay, I'm impressed."

"We know you're up shit creek, my friend, that for months now your life has been a seven forty-seven in a nosedive. We know that four years ago you were charged with misappropriation of funds in a land deal, got fired from the law firm where you'd worked for ten years, and became an untouchable in Dade County legal circles. Even though the charges were dropped, the damage had been done, Mr. H. Wife divorces you, gets custody of son and the house in Miami, and you get this place and a pile of legal bills. Now you're a legal consultant here in Key Largo, but let's face it, the pay is shit." Wade threw open his arms. "And now the seven forty-seven has crash-landed."

True, all of it. Holcomb just sat there in a kind of horrified trance wishing Wade would shut up. But he wasn't finished yet.

"We know that your ex-wife's new husband has nearly as much money as ExxonMobil, that your seventeen-year-old son lives in the caretaker's cottage on the stepfather's Palm Beach estate, that he hates Palm Beach, but remains rooted in his mother's custody because of his lovely girlfriend. In fact, young love and hormones can't compete with wealth and privilege, the yacht and the private jet, the endless parade of celebrities and their groupies. We know this house is your last refuge as father and son and now the bastards at the bank are planning to foreclose and . . ."

"I get your point," Holcomb finally managed to say, his voice tight.

"We're just offering you an alternative, Mr. H. If you accept our offer, training starts on Monday and lasts for about a month. It's vigorous, exhaustive, but if your memory is half as good as they say, you'll do fine. At the end of that month, you get another two hundred Gs regardless and you have the opportunity to opt out. If you opt out, you keep all the benefits for just signing up. If you're still in, you get the remainder of the million when the mission is accomplished. But in one respect, you're in for good."

"I thought you just said you need only six months."

Wade's slow, creeping smile chilled Holcomb. "You'll be given a security clearance so high that if you ever betray it, you'll pay with your life."

It was such a ludicrous line that Holcomb felt certain he was on a reality show filmed in secret, like the old-time *Candid Camera*. But then he caught something in Wade's eyes that whispered of a childhood spent jamming lit matches down inside anthills, teen years pulling petty crimes, a young adulthood pretending he was Brando in *On the Water-front*. And he suddenly knew that the ridiculous line Wade had uttered was true.

CIA? Was that it? Was Wade part of some black op group with the ultimate spooks? The kind of person you read about in spy novels but never met personally? Never mind that he lacked the class of Bond, that he didn't hold a candle to any of the spies in Graham Greene's novels. He was the new breed of maverick spook—and proud of it.

"I need more information before I can make a decision like this in ten minutes. Other than vigorous training and the stun gun, what else is involved?"

"I'm not at liberty to say, Mr. H."

"How convenient. Just who do you think I'm going to tell? My ex? She can't stand the sight of me. My son? He's got his own life and couldn't give a shit. A lover? I'm in a very dry spell. My former colleagues? I'm an untouchable to them. This is for *me*."

Wade and Ben traded a sly, knowing glance that made Holcomb distinctly uncomfortable. "Maybe you're not the morally compromised cripple we think you are," Ben re-marked, with a smirk.

"Really, Ben." Wade clicked his tongue against the back of his teeth and smoothed one hand over his jacket. He gripped the briefcase in the other. "That wasn't nice."

Ben shrugged. "Hey, it was truthful."

"Now *that's* important," Wade said, holding his index fin-ger in the air, as if testing for the direction the wind was blowing. "Ben is our honesty barometer."

"And *you* two think *I'm* a morally compromised cripple?" Holcomb laughed again, that quick, staccato laughter that came out when he was nervous or had had too much to drink. He hated the sound of it, but couldn't stop himself. "Then what's that make you?"

"Oh, make no mistake about it, Mr. H.," Wade said. "We're corrupt, but . . ."

". . . you have scruples. Honor among thieves and all that. Yeah. Save your breath."

Ben snapped his fingers. "Wade, he reads minds."

Wade came around the side of the coffee table and leaned down, his face so close that Holcomb could smell mint on his breath. "What do you think about time travel, Mr. H? Is it possible? Possible in a tangible, practical way?"

"How the hell do I know? I'm a lawyer, not a scientist."

"Now *that* is the right answer," Wade said, then reached for Holcomb's hand and shook it. "It's been a pleasure speaking with you. One of us will be back in ten minutes for your decision." Then he released Holcomb's hand, glanced at his companion. "Ben?"

"Yeah, we're outta here."

They didn't walk away, didn't move at all. One moment they were there, occupying space, breathing the air Holcomb breathed, and the next moment they were gone.

Impossible.

Holcomb shot to his feet and ran for the sliding glass doors that opened onto the back balcony. Still locked and closed. He spun around and raced for the front door, threw it open, and loped out into the driveway. No cars speeding out of the cul-de-sac, no sound except the rustle of wind through the trees, the chatter of palm fronds as they rubbed together.

He trotted to the end of the driveway and then up the street. Nothing unusual. The parked cars that hugged the curb were fewer than usual, probably because of Thanksgiving, and he recognized them, knew to whom they belonged. They were parked in the street because the houses lacked garages, carports. Besides, when he and Mike had turned onto the street half an hour ago, nothing had caught his attention. And he was accustomed to checking. A man whose credit card debt hovered at a hundred grand, who hadn't paid a mortgage or property taxes since summer, whose home owner's insurance had been canceled months ago, whose car insurance was barely at the legal level . . . well, he had to be vigilant, a man like that.

He ran back into the driveway and nearly collided with his son. "You okay, dad? You look spooked."

"Did you . . . see anyone leaving?"

"When? Just now?" Mike's large, soulful eyes fastened on Holcomb, as if he didn't quite know what to make of his father's question.

"Uh, yeah. When I went into the house, there were two guys who . . ." *Who offered me the deal of a lifetime and then disappeared.* He couldn't bring himself to say it. "Never mind. Just some wacko calling my cell. What do you need for the apartment?"

"Nothing. Everything's in there. I'm still cleaning. Listen, you'll love Ann."

The girlfriend, heiress to nothing.

"We'll go fishing," Mike rushed on. "Maybe we can get the old Harley up and running."

"Right. You bet."

"I'll be over in half an hour so we can watch the movie."

Which movie? Holcomb couldn't remember. "I'll make some popcorn." *And hide that money.*

He hurried back inside the house, those last few moments with the two men playing in his head, an endless loop of images.

People don't just disappear.

But he knew what he had seen. And he was sure of it when he went over to the coffee table and started counting out the bundles of cash.

Ten minutes later, Wade simply appeared just inside the sliding glass doors, a laptop tucked under his arm. "Hope your wireless service hasn't been cut off, Mr. H. You ready?"

"How . . . how'd you do that?"

"Do what?"

"Disappear and reappear."

Wade set down his laptop, flipped open the lid, went on-line. "I told you."

"Actually, you didn't tell me. You asked if I thought time travel was possible in a tangible, practical way."

He rolled his eyes. "You're splitting hairs, Mr. H."

"I need to know what I'm getting into."

Another roll of the eyes, an exaggerated sigh. "All right. I'll give you a taste. Fair enough?"

"A taste. And what's that me—"

Before he finished his sentence, Wade clasped his shoulder, and Holcomb felt a mounting pressure at the back of his skull, as if something were jammed up against it, something with weight and a blunt edge. A piece of concrete, a block of wood. His ears rang, nausea gripped him, the pressure at the back of his head exploded, and suddenly he was on his hands and knees in brilliant sunlight, vomiting onto the largest flower he'd ever seen. A flower the size of his head, with bloodred petals and velvet leaves half the size of his arms that twisted and curled at the edges. Rich, fecund smells assaulted him—of earth and water, sky and green, every odor excessive. The air around him, the ground against his hands, vibrated, trembled, shook.

Holcomb rocked back onto his heels, blinking against the brilliance of the light, the staggering blue of the sky. And there, against all that blue, all that vivid color, loomed the impossible, the incomprehensible. He scrambled back on his hands and knees, a stream of unintelligible sounds spilling from his mouth, his hands grabbing at the gigantic flower, as if to cover himself with it. But the dinosaurs continued to stampede toward them, their long necks bobbing in the brutal light. Shrieks and cries exploded through the air, the earth kept shaking, rumbling. Overhead, skimming the tops of the trees, flew tremendous birds with wingspans that stretched several dozen feet. They emitted strange, shrill songs that echoed across the savannah. His head spun, more sounds ran from his mouth, he thought he was about to pass out.

"Shit," Wade hissed. "Somewhere in the Jurassic era. Seen enough, Mr. H? Can we go home now?"

"Jesus," he whispered and toppled sideways, into Wade, his vision blurring, all the colors melting together like hot wax.

"Stay conscious, man. You've gotta stay conscious." Wade struck him across the face, grabbed the front of his shirt, and shook him like a dog with a bone. "C'mon, stay with me. Or you won't get back."

Conscious, conscious, the word slammed against the walls of his skull, ringing, vibrating, and then he was on his kitchen floor, stomach churning, the taste of bile surging in the back of his throat. He clutched bits of bright red flowers, silken grass, black earth.

"Drink some of this, Mr. H."

Wade, crouched beside him, pressed a bottle of Gatorade to Holcomb's mouth and he clasped it with the awkwardness of a toddler. He guzzled, coughed, drank some more. His vision began to stabilize, the nausea ebbed. Wade handed him a wad of paper towels and Holcomb wiped his mouth, his hands. He stared at the clump of vegetation on the floor beside him, petals and leaves from that gigantic flower. Then he raised his eyes. Wade looked amused.

"Well, Mr. H? Was that enough of a taste?"

"Sign me up," he said hoarsely.

PART ONE
REFUGEES

*For much of our lives, time moves within us
like a circle.*

—JAY GRIFFITHS, from
A Sideways Look at Time

1
Kincaid & McKee

The biochip will transform life as we know it.
—Mariah Jones, 1980

Aruba, March 15, 2007, 3:33 A.M.

Alex Kincaid bolted upright, listening hard for the noise that had awakened him. But all he heard was the island's music, that strange, rhythmic beat that played here 24/7—wind shaking the trees like tambourines, then strumming the branches as though they were the strings of Jimi Hendrix's guitar.

His fingers twisted around a corner of the damp sheet and he swung his legs over the side of the bed. Even though the window was open, the air conditioner was also on, his and Nora's concession to his need for fresh air and her insistence on comfort at night. The apartment's AC unit hummed and clattered, and he had to concentrate to find the noises beneath and behind this sound and that of the wind. The soft cries of the parched earth, the sad and lonely howl of a stray dog, the crash of waves against the nearby beach, the squeal of tires against the road: business as usual.

Any messages or codes preserved within nature's undercurrents were apparently meant for senses more sharply honed than his. The wind ruled, end of story. Just as he started to stretch out again, the dog growled, low menacing growls that signaled danger. And it was close.

Kincaid quickly joined Sunny at the window. The golden retriever's paws rested on the sill, her ears twitched, she kept growling. He ran his fingers through her fur, which stood straight up along the length of her spine. "What is it, girl?" he whispered.

She whimpered and licked his hand and kept staring out into the moonlit field one story below. The misshapen branches of the diva-diva trees swayed in the wind like hula dancers. Off to the right stood an abandoned school bus, windows busted out, the front squashed in like an accordion. Beyond the field lay the road that looped around the island. On the other side of the road rose the first of the resort hotels, grand, sprawling places, most of them American, that were the heart of the island's economy.

At this hour of the night, there wasn't even a car in sight.

Kincaid started to turn away, but Sunny barked, an event rare enough so that he glanced back, frowning. "It would be so great if you could learn to speak English," he said.

She dropped her paws to the floor and trotted over to the bed, waking Nora, Sunny's version of a dog snub. Who needed English?

"You have to go out, Sunny?" Nora murmured sleepily.

"I'll take her out," Kincaid said, even though he doubted this was about a need to pee.

Whimpers, another bark, then the dog seemed to be staring at something in the hall and suddenly shot through the bedroom doorway.

Now Kincaid was spooked. He peered through the window again, and *saw* what Sunny had sensed, several figures making their way through the moonlight, toward the old bus.

Kids? Not at this hour.

Thieves? Possibly. But thieves would target lone houses

in neighborhoods, not a cluster of apartments that catered to windsurfers.

"What is it?" Nora whispered.

"I'm not . . ."

Something tore through the open window, eclipsing the rest of his sentence. "Grab Sunny!" he shouted. "They've found us!"

Nora vaulted out of bed and sprinted through the bedroom door. Kincaid lunged toward the dresser, snatched up his and Nora's packs, and raced after her, one hand covering his mouth and nose as a canister rolled across the floor spraying tear gas everywhere. He kicked the door shut, ducked into the bathroom and snapped towels off the rack, then pressed them up against the crack under the door.

It might buy them a few moments.

Already, the tear gas seeped into the towels, and in minutes the front door probably would burst open. Fortunately, they were in the process of moving out of Waverunner, the apartment complex where they had been living these past months, and most of their belongings were in the new place they had rented in Santa Cruz, thirty minutes inland. They also had cleared all the syringes out of the freezer and taken them inland as well. So whoever had shot the tear gas canister, he thought, was welcome to whatever remained in the apartment.

The glow of the night-light plugged into the wall under the living room window provided enough illumination for him to see Nora checking the dead bolt and chain on the front door, her cell pressed to her ear. She spoke in a hushed, urgent tone, warning the others, telling them to get out of their apartments now. Sunny had found her Frisbee and was carrying it in her mouth as she moved closer to Nora. She knew the drill. They all did.

Kincaid swept Sunny's leash off the coffee table and paused long enough to part the blinds with his fingers and peer outside. From here, he could see the moonlit parking lot, the lush vegetation that surrounded the swimming pool off to the left, and the row of hedges that ran along the wall on the right, marking Waverunner's property line. The figures came from that direction, materializing from the shadows with the stealth of the assassins they were.

He counted half a dozen of them, all wearing dark clothes. No telling what agency they were from, which country, which rogue group. It didn't matter. They ran, hunkered over, through the moonlight, crossing the parking lot and vanishing into the trees around the pool.

"Here they come," he said, and hurried over to Nora and Sunny, both of them crouched now against the far wall. He passed Nora her pack, and she slung it over her head, then adjusted it so the pack rested against her hip.

"We'll meet the others at the house three hours ago," she whispered as she wrapped one arm across Sunny's back.

The front window shattered. The explosion of glass tinkled like wind chimes when it struck the tile. Three tear gas canisters rolled across the living room floor. The stuff spread so quickly that within seconds, Kincaid's eyes watered, his lungs burned, the dog wheezed, and Nora stifled a violent spasm of coughing. A heartbeat later, a fourth canister slammed into the wall behind the couch, spewing tear gas that spread quickly through the air pouring out of the AC vents.

Kincaid grasped Nora's hand and flung his other arm across the dog's back. "We're outta here."

An excruciating pressure seized his head. The darkened living room of their apartment at Waverunner vanished and the next thing Kincaid knew, his knees hit a hard surface, he fell back onto his ass, his stomach lurched, his head spun, and everything listed to the right. His eyes still burned, his lungs ached. The faint stink of tear gas lingered in the air. But he also recognized the smell of fresh paint and the sweet scent of the flowers that Nora had bought at the market yesterday. Roses.

The pressure in his head eased, the fluid in his inner ears stabilized, and his vision returned to normal. There, right in front of him, was the kitchen clock, hands at twelve twenty-two. The window beneath it was dark. And in front of the windows stood the wooden kitchen table, six chairs around it, each with a pumpkin-colored cushion that matched the color of the walls. They had bought the cushions from a local woman who made them by hand.

In a vase in the center of the table stood the roses, each one a different color. A light over the sink was on, casting just enough illumination to give the room a soft, fuzzy texture, as though it were a room in an old photograph.

His pack slipped off his shoulder, and he managed to stand. He still felt weird, as though his legs were made of warm rubber, and he lurched over to Nora with the gracelessness of Frankenstein's monster. She rocked back and forth on her heels, face pressed into her thighs. The dog was huddled beside her, breathing hard, as though she'd been running, Frisbee on the floor just in front of her. She wagged her tail when she saw Kincaid, then struggled up, weaved over to her bowl, and lapped up water.

"Rough, I know," Kincaid murmured as he rubbed the back of Nora's neck.

"I feel sick. Can you get me a damp towel?" She kept her face pressed to her thighs as she spoke. "With ice cubes rolled up inside it?"

"Sure."

The sink seemed very far away, though, and he moved toward it at a snail's pace, his hands constantly seeking something to hold on to. The back of a chair. The edge of the counter. Every transition was different, some tougher than others, but this one struck him as particularly debilitating, perhaps because of the tear gas. Or the suddenness with which they were forced to act.

He splashed water on his face, then ran a towel under the faucet and rolled ice cubes into it. By the time he made it to

Nora with the ice pack, she was sitting back on her heels, her face as pale as her hair was dark. He handed her the towel and she pressed it against the back of her neck. After a few moments, she struggled to her feet, lurched toward the fridge, opened it, and removed a bottle of ginger ale. She fought with the top, apparently too debilitated to open the bottle quickly. She finally sank onto one of the chairs, got the cap off, gulped from the bottle.

Kincaid pulled out one of the other chairs and collapsed into it. He felt totally wasted, spent, used up.

"Who *are* they?" she finally asked.

"It doesn't matter *who* they are. How'd they find us?"

She shook her head and pushed the bottle of ginger ale toward Kincaid. "Drink some. It'll help."

As he grasped the bottle, even his hands felt strange to him—his but not his, fingers clumsy, joints popping. He tipped the bottle to his mouth and sipped. And sipped again. She was right. The ginger ale settled his stomach. His equilibrium seemed almost normal.

"Are we safe here?" she asked. "Will they find us? Can they trace where we went?"

He heard the anxiety in her voice, the uncertainty, and it hurt him. He felt as if he had failed her, failed all of them. Then again, they had been living with this possibility for nearly five months, constantly perched at the edge of anxiety, always alert, prepared, ready for the unexpected. They were all so paranoid after the events of last fall that everyone was suspect: the cleaning women at Waverunner, the Dutch couple who rented them the house into which they were nearly moved, the waiter at a restaurant in downtown Oranjestad, the workman who had installed their wireless system, the satellite TV guy. Their suspicion of everyone and everything was an insidious thing and had begun to infect the ways they related to each other.

"I don't know," he admitted.

Nora rubbed her hands over her face, nodding. He didn't

know what the nod meant. Acceptance? Denial? Suppressed anger? She, like Kincaid, still wore the clothes she had slept in, gym shorts and a T-shirt. Her feet were bare, her jaw-length black hair uncombed. He remembered her best as the long-haired brunette in the Blue River College library, a graduate student in psychology who had devoured books the way other students devoured meals. Their three-year affair had been the most intense of his life, had ended through no fault of their own, and she subsequently had married Kincaid's close friend, Jake McKee, an English professor.

It astounded Kincaid that for the five years of that marriage he had been able to keep his feelings to himself. But at some level, he had known that sooner or later McKee would slip up and Nora would see him for what he was, a bright and seductive charmer who couldn't keep his pants zipped when it came to his young, lovely students. In fact, the day she intended to tell McKee she wanted a divorce, he was arrested, hauled away for alleged subversive activities, just as Nora's mother had been when she was ten.

Now they knew, of course, that Catherine Walrave, mother to both Nora and her older brother, Tyler, had been disappeared by a black ops government agency—Special Operation Temporal, SPOT—that for more than thirty years had been disappearing subversives, dissidents, and other undesirables into the past. Catherine supposedly had been dropped on a deserted road in Blue River, Massachusetts, in January of 1695 and had either perished or survived.

McKee had been sentenced to Vietnam—specifically My Lai—but had been spared through a series of events that ultimately had brought Kincaid and Nora back together. Now, here they were, a group of six humans and one dog who had brought down SPOT and were trying to build normal lives for themselves. But *normal*, he thought, watching the golden retriever sink to the floor, apparently wasn't their karma.

Tyler Walrave, Nora's brother, and his wife, Diana, suddenly emerged near the couch in the living room. Kincaid could see them through the doorway, their heavy packs bulging from their backs like tumors. Sunny's head snapped up, her tail started wagging, and she struggled to her feet and made her way slowly into the living room to greet them.

The dog divided her time among the six of them and apparently considered all of them her charges, as though they were sheep she was supposed to herd, or Frisbees she was supposed to retrieve. Of them all, Sunny had been chipped the longest, since somewhere back in the seventies, when the chip's inventor began her experiments on animals. As far as Kincaid knew, she was the only dog that was ever chipped. Her longevity brought up speculations and questions about the chip and aging that none of them had been able to answer. The biochip that made time travel possible was like the dog herself: the ultimate conundrum.

Kincaid pushed up from the chair and went into the living room. As he neared, he could see that Walrave, wearing pajama bottoms and a wrinkled T-shirt, was doing okay. But Diana's head was tilted back, her hands pressed to her nose, blood seeping through her fingers. The sight of the blood alarmed Kincaid. He knew what it meant. Her body was rejecting the biochip.

Sunny licked at Diana's arm, her leg, trying to comfort her, to heal her. "It's okay, Sunny," Diana murmured. "I'm okay. Really."

"Keep your head back," Walrave told her as he helped her to her feet. Then, to Kincaid: "Who the fuck *were* those people?"

"I don't know." And he was sick to death of being asked. "Nora," he called, "we need ice. Di's got a nosebleed."

"It's not just a nosebleed," she said, drops of blood hitting the floor. "My body's getting rid . . . of the chip. Oh my God, I can feel it . . . moving in my sinuses."

"That sensation will pass, hon," Walrave said, his voice gentle, loving.

They steered her into the bathroom, where Kincaid jerked a towel off the rack and pressed it up against her nose. She took it and crouched in front of the toilet and when the towel dropped away from her face, the blood poured from her nose.

"Keep your eyes shut," Walrave told her. "So you don't get nauseated."

And you won't have to see the chip, Kincaid thought, then stepped out of the way as Nora hurried in with an ice pack.

"When did her nosebleed start, Tyler?" Nora asked.

"I'm not sure. Maybe with the first whiff of tear gas, maybe as we were emerging."

In the moments that they spoke, Kincaid looked from brother to sister and marveled, as he always did, at their physical similarities. It was as if they were supposed to be twins—both of them six feet tall, dark haired and dark eyed, but born seven years apart. When their mother had been disappeared, Nora had been in elementary school; Tyler had been a college freshman.

Nora knelt beside Diana, pressed the ice pack to the back of her neck, and started talking her through it—that she should breathe through her mouth, that it would be over soon, that she should try to remain calm, centered. Kincaid touched Walrave's arm. "C'mon, Tyler. Leave her with Nora." Once they were in the kitchen, he added, "She's going to need a new chip."

"She's done with chips." Walrave jerked open the fridge door and helped himself to an apple and a bottle of local beer. "She's pregnant."

"Pregnant." The word rolled off Kincaid's tongue with a gross unfamiliarity, as if he'd never heard the word before. "How do you know?"

"She took a pregnancy test, Alex. I've never seen a damn thing written about the chip and pregnancy, but I'm pretty sure that's why her body is rejecting it. Three months pregnant, all those new hormones pumping through her, the white cells rallying around the invader, and *poof*, there goes the chip."

"Christ," Kincaid whispered.

"Yeah. It means doctors, hospitals."

"But *you* were a paramedic. You've delivered babies."

"Not for years."

"But you *can* deliver a baby."

"Sure, I can do that—if the birth is normal. But I'm no OB. Who the hell is going to monitor her pregnancy? I'm not qualified to do that."

"She won't be the first woman to give birth, Tyler."

"No." He guzzled down half the beer. "But as far as we know, she'll be the first who has been chipped for at least three months of the pregnancy. And she'll be the first in our group to give birth. And what's that mean, Alex? How're we going to keep running if we've got a baby?"

"We've got another six months to figure it out." Right now, he was frankly more concerned about how they had been found.

"But you can see what this transition just did to her," Walrave said. "What's it doing to the baby? What's it going to be like when she's six months pregnant and we have to escape?"

"Hey, we've been safe for nearly five months. That's longer than I thought we had."

Walrave pressed the beer bottle to his forehead. "I'm thinking that Di and I will pick a spot in the past, transition there, and just stay until the baby is born."

Maybe this, maybe that, Kincaid thought. Their entire lives now seemed to be predicated on maybe, what if, suppose. "Do you have a spot in mind?"

"Not yet." He set the bottle on the table. "We've pretty much been going day to day, just like you and Nora. We do the training with Ryan and Kat, study up on whatever era they want us to target, and then we transition, get a brief taste of what the era is like, and they evaluate our precision. I mean, the whole point of this training is to get us up to speed so we can retrieve Mom. But now that we know Di is pregnant, everything has changed."

"You can still go, Tyler."

"Sure, and Di can, too, if one of us transitions her. But I think that's too risky. Aside from the effects it might have on the baby, it means that Di wouldn't be able to get back unless one of us transitions her." He shook his head. "The whole game is different now, Alex. I think you and Nora are going to have to do the retrieval by yourselves while Di and I look for a spot to live until the baby is born."

Before Kincaid could reply, the door to the garage burst open and Kat Sargent exploded into the kitchen, her eyes stricken, her clothes bloodstained. "I need help getting Ryan inside. He's hurt."

Kincaid and Walrave shot to their feet. Walrave said he'd get the medical supplies and clear an area in the house for Curtis. Kincaid threw open the cabinet door under the sink and grabbed a handful of dish towels. He hurried after Kat, into the garage, where Ryan Curtis sat on the floor propped up against the freezer, sucking air in through his clenched teeth, his pale face bright with sweat. His left hand clutched the upper part of his right arm, where bright red blood bloomed against his T-shirt. It rolled down the underside of his arm and seeped into the long, white drawstring pants he wore.

"Bastard sliced me . . . just as . . . we . . . were transitioning," he said, his voice thick and soft.

"Move your hand, Ryan," Kincaid told him. "Let me wrap this towel around your arm so we can get some pressure on it."

As soon as Curtis took his hand away, Kincaid grimaced. If this were his arm, he would want to see a doctor, get an X-ray to make sure the knife hadn't struck bone, have it stitched up professionally. But when he suggested as much, Curtis shook his head.

"It's midnight. There's only one hospital on this island

and I'm not going to the ER. These guys know they sliced me. I'm betting the word has gone out to the hospital and the island doctors."

Kincaid thought of the doctor in the Dominican Republic who had inoculated them, provided them with antibiotics, and asked no questions. In return, they had donated ten grand to help build his new clinic. But before he could mention it, Curtis said, "Just help me inside."

He and Kat propped Curtis up between them. At six five, he towered over them both, this man who had spent seven years with SPOT. In the beginning, Kincaid had hated him. He had turned their lives upside down and inside out the day he had arrested McKee. But during their months on the island, he had come to admire and trust him.

They got him into the living room, where Curtis collapsed onto the couch, which Walrave had covered in a plastic tarp and towels. Thanks to his paramedic experience in Boston, long before he had started his computer software business, Walrave was the closest thing they had to a doctor. But he didn't have an X-ray machine, couldn't perform any kind of surgery.

After washing up and snapping on latex gloves, Walrave unwrapped the towel from Curtis's arm and cut away the sleeve of his shirt. Kincaid nearly passed out when he saw how deep the slice was. Walrave didn't look any too happy about it, either.

"Jesus, Ryan. I don't know. This looks deep. If the knife nicked the bone, you're going to need surgery so the bone doesn't get infected."

"The bone's not nicked," Curtis said through clenched teeth.

"You don't know that."

"Yes, I do" he hissed. "Just clean it up and stitch it shut, Tyler. Please. We have penicillin, right? I'll need a shot of penicillin and then I'll start Augmentin tomorrow. It'll be fine."

"The blade may have sliced through muscle, Tyler," Kat said worriedly, biting at the edge of her thumbnail, shifting her weight from one foot to the other, over and over again.

"We've got some other problems, too," Walrave said.

When he told Curtis why he and Di wouldn't be part of the retrieval for his and Nora's mother, both Curtis and Kat looked stunned. "When will the baby be born?" Kat finally asked.

"In the fall," Walrave replied.

"How far back are you going to go?" Curtis asked.

"I don't know," Walrave replied. "But I think all of us should be giving some serious thought to finding a haven in the past where we have supplies and a place to live and establish identities."

"I thought that was what we were doing here," Nora said as she and Diana came out of one of the bedrooms.

Diana had changed clothes and although she looked unsteady and spent, her nosebleed had stopped. "I thought that's what this house was about," she added.

"Whoever these people are, it won't take them long to track us down," Curtis said. "The island's too small for us to hide here for very long. I'm surprised we've lasted *this* long."

"So we, *what*?" Kat exclaimed. "Run again?"

"*He's* not running anywhere for a couple of days " Walrave gestured at Curtis. "For all we know, if he transitions too soon, he could hemorrhage." He was cleaning the cut now, squirting Betadine over it, then preparing his needle. Curtis turned his head in the other direction.

"Is that true?" Nora asked, directing her question at Curtis. He knew more than any of them about the parameters of the chip and the logistics and dangers of transitioning.

"It might be," Curtis admitted. "With the older versions of the chip, SPOT lost Travelers who got injured in the past and died when they were trying to get home. But we've got the newest versions of the chip and we just don't know enough about how it works to say that anything is certain."

"But we just rented this place," Diana said, throwing out her arms. "What do we do about that?"

"We're paid up for six months," Kincaid said. "The only people who know we're here are the owners, and they're in the Netherlands now. We paid them in cash, they filed the paperwork. No Realtors, no middlemen. We give them notice now, that gives them five months to find other tenants. For the next few days, we disguise ourselves when we go out. We shop somewhere other than Santa Cruz. We can extend our stay here long enough for Ryan to heal, for Nora and I to go back to retrieve her mother. In the meantime, Kat and Tyler can start looking for new havens. Sound like a plan?"

Sunny, sitting at the edge of the group as if she were listening to everything, suddenly barked—no growls, no teeth bared, nothing menacing.

Nora laughed. "I think Sunny just cast her vote for your plan, Alex. You've got my vote, too."

"Okay, that's three out of seven," Kincaid said.

"Do you feel you're ready to transition back more than three hundred years, Alex? Just you and Nora?" Curtis asked.

"We managed to live for a while in 1968 and did pretty well for a couple of amateurs," Kincaid replied. "We even nabbed you, Ryan."

Curtis winced as Walrave finished stitching and began to bandage his arm. "It's not the same thing. Nineteen sixty-eight is recognizable, okay? We're talking about the darkest period of Blue River's history, when three women were executed for practicing witchcraft, when women were chattel, didn't learn to read, and were basically suspect if they weren't married. We're talking about the fucking *Puritans*, Alex. The era of Bible-thumpers and hell-and-brimstone preachers. Can you immerse yourself in *that* culture? Because that's what it's going to take. Immersion. For a few days, a few weeks. You simply won't know until you get there and start looking for Catherine."

Kincaid and Nora exchanged a glance. *Are we ready?* his eyes asked.

Absolutely, her smile replied.

"We're ready," Kincaid said.

"Then your plan has my vote," Curtis said.

"And mine," Kat echoed.

"Ditto," Diana said.

"Yeah," Walrave added, then tapped an imaginary gavel in the air. "The vote is unanimous."

2
Prison

It may well be that every action we take, every thought we have in the present, alters our entire history.

—Lynn McTaggart

He came to with shocking suddenness, gasping for air as if he had been held underwater. He couldn't see. Couldn't move. His mouth fell open, but the scream that raced across his tongue stumbled out as a dry rasp. *OhGodohGodwhat's- happenedwhereamIwhat . . .*

His mind emptied of everything except fear and it drummed through him, hurling open adrenaline floodgates until his heart hammered and sweat poured off him and tears streamed down his cheeks. Shudders tore through him. *Where's my dad?*

The floodgates slammed shut, and Mike Holcomb's body went still. An image leaped into his head and danced across the screen of his inner vision. *I am backing out of my step- father's estate one evening when three cars shoot out of nowhere, blocking me in. Five men leap out and drag me from the car and inject something into my neck.* Then: nothingness, blackness.

When did that happen?

He had no idea.

He noticed that the air smelled of ocean, desert, heat. He focused on that, on the odors, and gradually his heartbeat stabilized, and his panic dove underground. He sniffed at the air, following the threads of other scents—the flatness of the air around him, the faint tendrils of food, the stale stink of cigarettes. He realized he wasn't blind, that something soft and thick covered his eyes, a blindfold of some kind. And he felt cuffs around his wrists, ropes around his ankles, and knew he was tied to a bed. Memories now rushed through him, popping into his consciousness like air bubbles as he surfaced from some deep, underwater place.

He had been kidnapped, taken to a place where the wind blew relentlessly, swallowing other sounds—a dry, greedy wind that smelled of water. That narrowed the geographical choices considerably. Island? Yes. That was his first guess.

In his sweat, Mike smelled the weak residue of the drug that had knocked him out and stolen some of his memories. Small doses, administered in short periods of time. Not enough to kill him, just enough to keep him confused, groggy, *controlled*. He could see the face of the man who had drugged him, a black man with homicidal eyes and impeccable clothes. Ben.

He moved his tongue around in his mouth, struggling to work up enough spit so that he could shout loudly. He cleared his throat and bellowed, "Hey, someone. I need to take a leak."

Silence. Mike counted silently to twenty. Then the door creaked, he heard footsteps. A man said, "Next time you scream, I gag you."

Ben. That was Ben. Jailer. Caretaker. Asshole. "I'd like to use the bathroom."

"I think we can arrange that."

"And I'd like something to eat."

"Sounds fair. What day is it, kid?"

"I don't have any idea. You tell me."

Ben laughed. "You're a bright kid. You'll figure it out."

The blinds clacked together as Ben raised them. "Okay, I'm removing the blindfold first. Lift your head."

He raised his head and Ben untied his blindfold. Mike blinked hard, his eyes adjusting to the soft glow of a nearby lamp, to the starlight that glinted through the huge wall of glass. He didn't see moonlight, so either the moon hadn't risen yet or it had set already. His gaze slipped to Ben, standing beside the bed, wearing his creepy smile and his fastidious clothes, the pants with perfect creases, a silk guayabera shirt. His dark eyes glistened like marbles in his even darker face. The muscles in his biceps seemed to ripple, as if he had just worked out.

"You know the rules, kid," Ben said. "You pull any shit and you end up gagged and bound inside a closet. We clear?"

"Yes. Did you already do that to me?"

"You don't remember?"

"You give me so many fucking drugs, how can I?"

"We give you drugs to keep you calm. If you stay calm, there won't be any drugs."

"Not even in the food?"

"Not even in the food."

"And I'm supposed to believe you just because you say it?"

"I don't lie."

Well, then, how comforting.

Ben reached down under the cuff of his pants, pulled out a knife, and sliced through the ropes around Mike's ankles. His muscles screamed and twitched simultaneously, making the release nearly as painful as the restraints. "Can I sit up now?"

"Sure thing, kid."

"I have a name, you know."

"To me, you're nameless," Ben replied.

Mike snapped forward, swung his legs over the side of the bed, and held up his cuffed hands. Ben unlocked the cuff from his left wrist and it dangled against his right forearm. "When do I get a shower?"

"Now. You'll have five minutes. Clean clothes are in the linen closet. Everything you need is in there. I'll be outside the door."

He stood on legs that felt rubbery, not quite real. "Am I going to get to eat or do I just get the shower?"

"Your food will be here when you finish." Ben gestured toward the picture window. "Don't even think about leaving through there. We're fifteen stories up."

"I'm not stupid." He hurried past Ben, into the bathroom, quickly shut the door, turned the lock.

The lock was just a formality, Ben could get in here any time he wanted. But it gave Mike a sense of privacy, however small and false. He quickly turned on the water and suddenly remembered something else. He went over to the linen closet, opened it, stooped over, and dug through the towels on the middle shelf. He found the pen he had hidden here—*When? How long have I been here? How many times have I gone through this?*—and the tiny vertical lines he had made on the wall to his left. Six of them. One mark for each shower. He drew a seventh line. But did one shower equal one day?

He moved the towels around until he found the tiny vertical lines on the right wall. These lines represented meals. There were thirteen. If he was eating three meals a day—and he couldn't say for sure that he was—then he had been here slightly more than four days.

The problem with this system for marking time was that he had no way of knowing what equaled what.

Mike suddenly remembered something else, dropped to his knees, and shoved his arm in between the wall and the hot water heater. He dug under the stacks of loose tiles until he found the screwdriver. He needed to sneak it into the bedroom, but every time he came out of the shower, Ben patted him down. He remembered this clearly, Ben's powerful hands moving over his body in a way that felt disgustingly intrusive, intimate. He grabbed a washcloth off an upper shelf, wrapped it around the screwdriver, and shoved it back farther into the closet, right behind the water heater.

He didn't know who had left the screwdriver or the pen in there, but was grateful for the oversight.

He showered in under sixty seconds. It cleared his head, more memories surfaced, and with each memory he reclaimed, his fear ebbed a little farther. He was alive. One way or another, he could get the fuck out of here.

With the shower still on, the water covered any noises he might make. He dressed quickly in clean clothes that had been folded on an upper shelf in the linen closet. Not *his* clothes. But his size. Shorts, T-shirt, but no socks. *You might hide something in them,* Ben had told him.

Yeah? Like what? Sand? Soap? A screwdriver?

He lowered the lid of the toilet, stepped up onto it, climbed onto the back of the toilet tank. He must have done this before, it made sense. But he had no memory of it. He peered out the small window, the tip of his nose pressed against the glass. He couldn't see much: a sprinkling of lights far out in the blackness and, closer in, a single spotlight that illuminated a beach. Ben was probably telling him the truth about being fifteen stories up. He craned his neck, peering upward. He saw the edge of an eave and what looked like metal bars climbing up the wall to his right.

Penthouse? Was he in a penthouse?

He stepped down again and dropped his head back, studying the ceiling. Panels, large, square panels, the kind that could be pushed up and slid to one side. If he could find something to stand on . . . The sink? Would that give him the height he needed? No, better yet, the shelves in the linen closet. If he could stand on the top shelf without the whole thing collapsing . . . yeah, it might work.

Just then, banging on the door. "Your five minutes are nearly up, kid!" Ben shouted.

"I'm done," Mike called back and turned off the shower. He rubbed his hair with a towel, picked up the electric shaver, opened the door so Ben could see he was about to shave. "Can I finish up?"

"Grow a beard," Ben replied, poking his head inside the bathroom.

"There's no toothbrush or toothpaste in here."

Ben rolled his eyes. "I'll get them. Your food's not getting any warmer."

He turned on the electric razor, rubbed a clear spot in the mirror, and saw that Ben was no longer in the doorway.

Now, he thought. *Fast.*

He turned, the razor still on, and hurried over to the linen closet, dug out the washcloth with the screwdriver inside, and poked his head through the doorway. Clear. The coast was clear. He dashed into the bedroom and looked around frantically for a place to hide the screwdriver.

Under the mattress. Quick, Jesus, quick.

He lifted the upper left corner of the mattress, tucked the screwdriver under it, and was sitting at the table near the window, eating his meal, when Ben returned with a tooth-brush and toothpaste.

"Oops, almost forgot," Ben said and motioned for him to stand. "Get up. You know the routine, kid."

He got up, spread his legs, extended his arms. As the pat down began, he said, "I think you enjoy this, Ben. I think there's a perv inside you."

Ben's hands went totally still, pasted to Mike's ribs. Then, suddenly, Ben squeezed hard, lifting Mike off his feet as though he weighed no more than a flower, and threw him up against the wall. He slammed into it, air rushed from his lungs, his knees buckled. Before he hit the floor, Ben grabbed him by the front of the shirt and pinned him to the wall with one hand and pressed the muzzle of a gun to his cheek with the other. The barrel sank so far into Mike's skin he felt its outline and weight against his upper molars.

"Listen real close, Mike Holcomb. I don't like being your fucking caretaker any more than you like being here. I hate kids. I especially hate teenagers. I'd love nothing better than to shoot your goddamn head off. If I did it now, right snug up against your cheekbone like this, the bullet would shatter the inside of your mouth—teeth, roof, and tear out part of your tongue, too. If you were really unfortunate, it would rip away pieces of your sinuses, your nose bone might collapse, and, depending on the angle of entry, it might take out your eye. But you'd probably live because the bullet would exit through your other cheek. So just think about that, Mike, before you piss me off again."

Tears rolled down his cheeks, his breath had stalled in his chest, the inside of his mouth had turned to dust, his eyeballs felt as if they had torn free of the tendons and muscles that rooted them in the sockets. Any second now, his bladder would surrender.

"Do we understand each other, kid?"

"Y-ye-yes," Mike whispered.

"Good." Ben's arm dropped to his side. He brushed at the front of Mike's T-shirt, then shoved him back down into the chair. "So eat your goddamn food."

Mike's hand shook as he dipped his spoon into the soup. He blinked back hot, burning tears. He felt scooped raw inside, as though the marrow in his bones had been vacuumed out, sucked clean. He thought of the screwdriver under the mattress and wondered how many people he would have to stab to escape this place.

3
Nora

*Using time as God-given, we have created
the laws of physics.*
—*Fred Alan Wolf, 1988*

Nora McKee watched the digital clock flip to the next minute: 2:19 A.M. But since they had gone back three hours when they had transitioned from Waverunner around 3:30 this morning, then the real time, her body time, was what? Six-thirty? Seven? She wasn't sure. She was never sure. It was a kind of jet lag.

Insomnia, that trickster, that little devil, danced around her. Every time she shut her eyes, she saw Kincaid at the window in their bedroom at Waverunner, a silhouette against the moonlight, Sunny beside him with her paws on the windowsill. It was one of those mental photos that would stick with her for months or years, she thought, its clarity faithful to the most minute detail. Her head was filled with such photos.

She finally threw off the sheet and swung her legs over the side of the bed. She needed one of her soporifics. A glass of milk. A bite of cheese. And if those failed, then a melatonin or a glass of wine. Kincaid stirred as she stood, but he didn't wake up. Neither did Sunny, passed out on a rug at the foot of the bed.

Nora made her way up the hall, past the bedrooms where Curtis and Kat slept, where her brother and her closest friend slept, and into the living room. Tyler's medical kit was still on the coffee table, the bloody towels still pooled on the floor, the plastic tarp still covering the couch cushions. She left everything where it was. In the kitchen, drops of dry blood spotted the tile, and a half-eaten apple, an empty beer bottle, and a nearly empty bottle of ginger ale remained on the table. She didn't bother picking up any of it.

In her other life, when she had been married to Jake, she would not have been able to live so closely with five other people. She wasn't entirely convinced she could do it now. She had lived with these people for months, yet each couple had had a separate apartment. But the house was communal living, where six towels hung in the bathroom, other women's makeup found homes next to hers on the bathroom sink, where she never was sure who would be sitting across from her at breakfast.

Yet, much of the household stuff was strangely random, a reflection of their individual tastes that somehow accommodated the others, as if, at some level, they were of one mind, like a hive of bees. She hadn't bought the ginger ale, for instance, but a few sips had calmed her stomach after the transition. She had bought the mangos and most of the fresh fruit, and the others had feasted on it. Kat had bought the Dutch cheeses, Curtis had found the superb wine, Di had discovered a great fish market. Kincaid and Tyler, both of whom were terrific cooks, had bought the spices, the raw materials for delicious sauces, and had cooked the evening meals every day since they'd moved here. Somehow, it all worked.

Even so, she had to resist the urge to scoop up the dirty towels; to tear the tarp off the cushions; to toss out the ginger ale, the empty beer bottle, the browning apple. She had to remind herself that at some point there would be a collective hiccup called, *Let's clean the house* and within an hour, the rooms would be transformed.

In a way that she didn't understand yet, the chip unified them, as if they were members of a closely knit tribe that shared the same lineage, the same vision. In the beginning of their stay here, they had discussed all the retrievals they would do once they had retrieved Nora and Tyler's mother. But for months now, no one had even mentioned that possibility. It was as if, at some level, it had become obvious to all of them that retrieving thousands of the disappeared just wasn't realistic. Now, with Diana's pregnancy, it was out of the question.

But if retrievals would not be their future, then what was?

Could they, for instance, choose a spot in the past and then rid themselves of the chips and live out their natural lives? Just the thought of it, of not having the freedom to move around in time, left such a gaping void inside her that she knew it wouldn't work for any of them. As much as they talked about living *normal, ordinary* lives, they meant it in terms of *being chipped*. The bottom line was that she—all of them—were addicted to the freedom of moving around in time, to the adrenaline rush of it all, to the fact that they could do what others could not. There were other, less obvious benefits that she was discovering: she was healthier than she ever had been, her senses seemed much sharper, sex was beyond anything she had ever experienced before, and on some inexplicable level, the six of them—and Sunny—were *connected.*

She fixed herself a platter of snacks, poured a glass of milk, sat down at the table and ate, pondered, and ate some more. She wished she could wake Di so the two of them could whisper and commiserate, but the rejection of the chip had left her weak and exhausted.

Nora knew what that was like. Two weeks after they had settled into what was supposed to be their new life on Aruba, her body had rejected a chip. She hadn't shut her eyes when

she had been huddled over the toilet bowl and had seen the
bloated ticklike thing that had fallen into the water. It had
struggled for several ugly moments, its little legs moving,
scrambling, its body writhing as it tried to right itself. It was
one of the most singularly disgusting things she'd ever experienced. But her chip had been rejected because Curtis had
insisted they all inject themselves with the new, improved versions, so they would have the same advantages. She had
expected the rejection, been prepared for it. But Diana was
not. Diana was pregnant and that had changed everything.

Nora ran her hands over her face and tried to put herself
back in Waverunner earlier this evening, before she and Kincaid had gone to bed. Had she felt or seen or heard anything
out of the ordinary? Had she sensed anything that she had
dismissed as insignificant? Or had she seen anything unusual in the past few days? It seemed that she hadn't, that
she and Kincaid and the rest of them had established a routine, that they were drawing closer to their immediate goal—
their first retrieval.

Two days after they had moved into Waverunner, the
group had tried to transition back to 1695 to retrieve her
mother but had failed. They just couldn't get to where they
wanted to go. Curtis, as flummoxed as everyone else, had
speculated that the chip had blocked them because they
weren't ready. That was the first indication, at least for Nora,
that the chip was more than just an interface between man
and machine, more than a technological masterpiece that enabled time travel. She now wondered if, in fact, it might pos-
sess a kind of rudimentary intelligence. BIOchip, after all,
implied that it was composed of biological elements. But
quite frankly, it spooked her to think of it in this way. And
why would it block their access to Blue River in 1695 when,
in their practice sessions, they had been able to transition to
eras even more exotic?

Suddenly, without any conscious intent, without any of
the usual symptoms, she found herself back at Waverunner,

but mired in air that had the consistency of honey. She still held a slice of Gouda cheese in one hand and a cracker in the other, which she quickly popped into her mouth. She saw her earlier self sitting up in bed, Kincaid at the window, Sunny beside him.

She—*Nora now*—stood in the doorway, watching, waiting, an observer, a kind of voyeur. She immediately understood that she somehow had triggered a replay of the events that had happened earlier this evening. Curtis had alluded to this phenomenon, but she never had experienced it and had no idea what the rules were.

Since she went nowhere without her cell, her link to the larger world, she slipped it from her shorts and stepped back into the hallway, struggling to move in the unnaturally thick air. An ant struggling to move through a bowl of New England clam chowder would feel like she did, she thought. Given Sunny's position, she realized she had a few moments before the first tear gas canister would shoot through the bedroom window, so she called Curtis first. Perhaps she could prevent his injury.

Will it change something else? She didn't know.

It seemed to take forever for her thumb to exert sufficient pressure on the speed-dial button for Curtis's number. It was as if her fingers didn't really belong to her. And as she stepped farther back into the hallway, it took a lifetime, one foot and then the other, everything around her fuzzy, as though she were seeing it from behind a gigantic scrim.

Curtis answered on the first ring, his voice thick, slurred, unnatural. "Ryan, it's Nora. Get out of the apartment now. They've found us. I'm in a replay and if you don't leave immediately, you'll be injured. We meet at the house, three hours ago."

"We're gone."

She disconnected, called her brother's cell. As it rang, Sunny moved toward her, but because everything unrolled in such excruciating slow motion the dog looked as if she were suspended in the air, swimming through it, her long, graceful legs moving counterpoint to each other. Then she stopped and barked, each bark long, drawn out, reverberating against the thick air.

That's why she ran out of the bedroom in the original version of these events. She saw me in the replay.

"I'm awake," Tyler said sleepily. "What's up?"

"Get out, Tyler. They've found us. Go to our house three hours ago."

"Done." He disconnected.

A heartbeat later, the tear gas canister arced through the bedroom window, but even it moved in slow motion, turning end over end like an acrobat on a high wire who just couldn't get up to speed. Kincaid looked to be airborne now, legs spread out, one in front of him and the other in back, as if he were vaulting in slow motion over an impossibly high pole. He moved in the same languid way across the beds, one hand covering his mouth, his other sweeping their backpacks off the bureau.

Since Nora didn't know how she had transitioned into the replay, she didn't know how to get out of it, either. She just backed up against the living room wall, watching helplessly as the other Nora paced restlessly about, calling the others. *Who already know now.*

She squeezed her eyes shut and thought of their house in Santa Cruz, of that wonderful kitchen with the simple wooden table and the wooden chairs with the pumpkin-colored cushions, of how *normal* their lives might be there. She willed herself to that spot, that time a few minutes ago when she had left while the others slept, and drew the house around her, a target no different from that of another time.

Reach and release, that was how Curtis had taught them. So she reached and released, over and over again, and when she opened her eyes, she was no longer in their Waverunner living room. She wasn't in their home in Santa Cruz, either. She didn't know where the hell she was.

Around her, hills exploded with spring, thickets of trees scattered across them. The sky was a heartbreaking blue, so perfect that it looked as fragile as newly blown glass. She thought it might shatter if she breathed too hard, moved too suddenly. She turned slowly, aware of the soft grass beneath her bare feet, of the leaves that drifted through the air as the wind blew.

She completed her turn and saw the shapes of buildings against the hills and started walking toward them. Her overwhelming impression was that none of it was real. It could be some clever holograph created from her memories, like that holo-deck on the USS *Enterprise*. Any second now, Whoopi Goldberg would appear. But Nora didn't have any memory of a place like this. Was she dead? This suddenly seemed to be a viable possibility, that she had died during the transition to the replay. Or when she tried to transition from the replay back to Santa Cruz. Heart attack. Cerebral hemorrhage. Something quick, irrevocable, final. It had happened to some of the Travelers in SPOT.

And with her body dead, her soul had rallied on and on. But if she was dead, why could she feel the pleasant breeze? And why was the fecund sweetness of grass and greenery filling her senses? And if this was a holograph, wouldn't she be wearing something other than the clothes she had worn to bed?

In front of the buildings, at the base of a shallow hill, rose a monolithic, phallic object. Seven, maybe eight feet tall. As Nora neared it, she realized it was a giant quartz crystal the color of an anemic flamingo. Its erratic edges glinted in the sunlight and it drew her like iron to a magnet. When she reached it, she stood there staring at it, astonished that it was here, puzzled about how it had gotten here. Wherever *here* was.

Her gaze dropped to the concrete base in which it was embedded. Handprints decorated the base, with a name under each one. *Lea, Bob, Nancy*. Nora ran her hands over the giant crystal, then wrapped her arms around it and pressed her cheek against its cool, rough surface.

It seemed to pulsate with energy—not heat, but something less defined that she felt in her muscles and bones, the essence of her being. *Where am I?*

"Welcome to my world," said a voice behind her.

Nora leaped away from the crystal and saw a man seated on the other side of it, his legs in a lotus position, his feet bare. His loose, dark pants had that soft look of organic cotton. His celery green T-shirt bore a Chinese symbol on the front. The salt-and-pepper hair and beard, the glasses perched on the bridge of his nose, the steady intensity of his gaze— she had seen this guy somewhere before. She never forgot a face. But it took her a few moments to place it: a photo that either Curtis or Kat had shown her and the others during a training session.

"The crystal is from Brazil," he said. "If memory serves me, you're Nora McKee."

"And you're Russ Berlin," she blurted. "You were the physician at SPOT, the guy in charge of the chips, the doc who chipped all of the Travelers." She remembered that Curtis had said there had been rumors that Berlin and Mariah Jones, the chip's inventor, had been lovers. "You sabotaged the chips for Mariah."

He looked . . . what? Sad? Resigned? Filled with regret? Or merely amused? She didn't know. He leaned back on his hands and extended his legs, his bare toes curling, straightening.

"I made a choice. And it didn't have much to do with Mariah. Do you have any idea where you are?"

"No."

"Nellysford, Virginia, on the grounds of the Monroe Institute."

She'd been to Virginia once, but had never heard of Nellysford or the Monroe Institute. She didn't trust her legs to keep her upright and sank to the ground. She glanced at the digital watch that she wore around her neck, the faithful time and date keeper that once had belonged to Kat. The tiny biochip inside it provided a date and the local mean time, the readout unfailingly accurate regardless of what era she was in. The era was her own, but the year wasn't: April 16, 2006, 2:12 P.M. Nearly a year ago.

"Easter Sunday," Berlin said.

"What's the Monroe Institute?"

"This is where people are taught how to attain altered states of consciousness. It's famous because of Robert Monroe's books on out-of-body travel."

"How . . . how did I get here?"

"I'm not sure. If you learned to do something new with the chip, that might create the conditions that would attract you here. It's also possible that you're at home sleeping and are traveling out of body."

She pinched her arm, felt it. "I'm not dreaming."

"Then you must have learned something new with the chip."

"I did a replay. I don't know how I did it, but that's what it was."

He leaned forward, his face intense, serious. "Why?"

"Why should I tell you anything?"

"I'm just trying to help."

Nora laughed. "Right. You and Mariah threw our lives into chaos. Now you're sitting there like Buddha, offering to help me. Excuse me if I find that hard to believe, Dr. Berlin."

"Well, then allow me to prove my sincerity by offering a few facts that you probably don't know about the history of SPOT. In 1982, Joe Aiken and his old man attended a ten-day training session here at the institute. Aiken senior was getting ready to retire from his senate seat and young Joe was going to run for the seat. So the old man was passing on the torch. At the time, Aiken senior was the only senator who knew about SPOT. Ian Rodriguez, Mariah Jones, and I also attended that training session."

It was all news to Nora. Rodriguez had been SPOT's director, and Aiken senior had procured government funding for the time travel program. He had passed on long before Nora had been drawn into the picture; her only contact had been with Aiken junior. But it wasn't clear to her why any of these people would attend a training session at a place that taught people how to attain altered states of consciousness. "So?" she said.

"The other person who attended that training session was your mother."

Now she was sure this guy was full of shit. "My mother owned and ran a food-catering business in Boston with my dad. She was a lapsed Irish Catholic who lit candles on Sunday and prayed for the living and the dead. She wouldn't have any interest in a place like this."

"You were just a kid then," Berlin remarked. "How could you possibly have known what her deeper interests were?"

"Because my brother would have known it."

"At the time, your brother was a teenager with raging hormones. He had his own life."

She still thought he was full of shit, but he had her full attention now. "Go on."

"Joe's father had been working with Mariah since 1970, twelve years by the time we took the training here. Mariah was still the director then and Ian and Lydia Fenmore were Travelers."

Fenmore had long since been promoted to assistant director when SPOT had collapsed. "Was Lydia at the training session, too?"

"She was supposed to be, but couldn't make it."

"And why were you there?"

His cool demeanor now developed fissures. Emotion crept into his expression, his voice. "I was a resident in pediatric oncology in Baltimore and had just lost my son . . ." His voice faltered. ". . . to cancer. I was looking for answers. My search brought me here."

He paused, looked away, swallowed hard. Nora regretted asking.

"Anyway, young Joe Aiken was quite the dapper ladies' man back then, about a hundred pounds thinner and twenty-five years younger than the Aiken you so deftly deposited in the lobby of the FBI at the end of October 2006. Or will deposit there. That's still in my immediate future. Well, not really. It . . . hell, you know what I mean."

Yeah, she did.

"He and your mother were quite taken with each other."

This guy was beginning to piss her off. "My mother loved my father. She would never have gotten involved with the likes of someone like Joe Aiken." The obese, lying-sack-of-shit politician who had tried to recruit her for SPOT, who had double-crossed Curtis and Kat, and who had intended to use the time travel technology for his own corrupt agenda.

"We never know our parents," Berlin said quietly. "We like to think we do, but we don't. And your mother was searching for something and began to discover it here."

"Sure. In altered states. In out-of-body travel." She laughed. "I suppose she smoked crack cocaine, too."

He ignored her sarcasm. "By the end of our ten days here, I was involved with Mariah and had decided to go to work for SPOT, and your mother was involved with Joe. All of us had been chipped and had gotten a taste of what that meant. Mariah offered your mother a position with SPOT, but she didn't want to leave her family."

My mother, chipped? My mother, able to travel in time? My mother, a Traveler? One of the original Travelers? Nora couldn't wrap her mind around any of it. "You have *proof* of this? Proof that my mother was here? That any of this is true?"

"Yes, but we'll get to that. Mariah believed your mother had enormous potential as a Traveler. We all did. But since she didn't join SPOT, she presented quite a dilemma for

Mariah, Ian, and Joe senior. They couldn't afford to have an outsider knowing about the technology. However, your mother was their friend, their coconspirator, and Joe junior's lover. So they swore her to secrecy. Fortunately, her body rejected the chip before we left and her relationship with Joe ended not long afterward. But when Lydia Fenmore heard about all of this, she went ballistic. She was Mariah's golden girl and apparently felt threatened by Mariah's admiration for your mother. So she set in motion a series of events that led to your mother's arrest and disappearance a year later."

"Lydia had her arrested?" Nora balked. "But you, Ian, Mariah, Joe . . . all of you must have known about it. And you *allowed* it to happen?"

"We didn't *allow* anything." He sounded angry now. "None of us knew about it until after the fact, and by then, it was too late. Lydia refused to tell anyone where she had disappeared your mother. And that was that. At some level, I don't think Joe or Mariah ever quite forgave her for it."

"A fascinating story, Dr. Berlin. But where's your *proof*?"

With his ankles still crossed, he stood in a single fluid motion and held out his hand. "In the main building."

Nora refused to grasp his hand and hesitated about accompanying him anywhere. It would be easy to hate this man, Berlin. Easy to hate him for what he had done inadvertently to her life, for what he had just told her about her mother. But suppose he was telling the truth?

She stood and they headed up the hill toward the closest building. The stones along the path felt cool against her bare feet, the air sweet in her nostrils. Nora suddenly wished she had shoes and a change of clothes. But they seemed to be the only people around. It was Easter Sunday, after all, and apparently the employees weren't working.

"On one timeline, Jake and I are eating Easter dinner at my brother's house on Cape Cod."

"And I'm having Easter dinner with friends in Sarasota.

Those people continue to exist and thrive, Nora. And because they haven't yet experienced what we have, we're like future versions of our own selves."

"Are there ever bleed-throughs from us to them?"

"Yeah, I think there are."

Berlin opened the door and they stepped into a wide, friendly room on the ground floor of the two-story building. Couches, tables and chairs, a coffee bar, bookcases loaded with books, a TV, and a selection of DVDs. A laptop on one of the tables was open, booted up, already online. The large windows overlooked the spectacular countryside. Very Zen, she thought.

"This is where everyone gathers in the evening to relax and talk about their experiences," Berlin explained. "The whole place is wireless now. During the training in 1982, we didn't have laptops, computers, or the Internet. Your mother favored that red couch over there." He pointed at the couch under the window.

Nora had the sudden feeling that Berlin was lonely, that if she were so inclined, he would be delighted to give her the complete tour—of both past and present. "That's nice, but I'm not here for the tour, Dr. Berlin. And c'mon, was that red couch really red in 1982?"

"Actually, that's a new red couch."

"Well, *that's* encouraging."

He poked at his glasses, nudging them farther up on the bridge of his nose, and went straight over to the bookcase. He ran his finger along the spines of a dozen photo albums, selected one, brought it over to the couch, sat down.

This was starting to feel like a family trip down memory lane, Nora thought, but sat beside him as he opened the album. "These days, all the photos are digital. But back in 1982, we still used regular film cameras."

We. Did that mean he worked here? Lived here? What?

Berlin flipped through the pages and finally opened the

album up wide, revealing a heading—1982 TRAINING SES-
SIONS—and two pages of color photos. He peeled the plastic
away, removed six pictures, and handed them to her. A pall
of unreality seized her. It was her mother, all right, prettier
than Nora remembered, her black hair loose, tumbling to her
shoulders, her flawless skin the color of bone.

In one picture, she and a vastly younger, thinner Joe
Aiken, Jr., had their arms around each other and were clown-
ing for the camera. In another, her mother was the center of
a group photo with Ian Rodriguez, Mariah, Berlin, and both
Aikens. In yet another, the group had been photographed
outside, around the crystal where she and Berlin had first
spoken. All the pictures had a faded sepia look to them. She
felt they were genuine.

She didn't know just then how she felt—numb, shocked,
astounded, pissed off. "I owe you an apology," she said.

"You have every reason to be skeptical."

"May I have these pictures?"

"Absolutely. Tell me about your replay."

She hesitated. Even though Berlin seemed to have been
honest with her, she wasn't quite ready to trust him. Yet, as
the gatekeeper of the technology—that was how she thought
of him—he knew as much as Mariah Jones had about the
chip, about the entire time-travel program. She said as much,
identifying him as the gatekeeper, and then told him what
had happened, but omitted details about where they were living and who was injured. Berlin absorbed it all.

"Did you see your attackers?" he asked.

"No."

"Do you know a man named Wade?"

She shook her head.

Berlin went over to the laptop, tapped a couple of keys,
motioned her over. "Here he is. Have you ever seen him?"

He looked like a thug, she thought. But a slick, polished
thug in an expensive suit, with a pierced ear, and lots of gold
around his neck. "No, I've never seen this guy. Who is he?"

"A mercenary, chipped back in the 1990s, when Ian was SPOT's director. He's one of the men who does the very dirty work."

"Everything SPOT did seems pretty dirty to me."

"Some people who were arrested by Freeze and brought to our facility were considered unsuitable for a disappearance. So Wade took care of them. He would go into their cells at night and slit their throats. Or he would take them back to the big bang. Or if it was a woman and Wade liked what he saw, he would disappear her to the dawn of time, watch her freak out, rape her, and then who the hell knows. He may be the one in charge of the raid on your safe house."

"You *knew* this and *allowed* it to happen?"

"You keep using that word, *allowed,*" he shot back. "I didn't know about Wade until toward the end. I didn't know it until Mariah came to me in the final months and gave me all the evidence. That's why I agreed to help her, to sabotage SPOT's chips. The agency was totally out of control by then. No safeguards, no oversight, Ian and Lydia running the agency like dictators, people like Wade doing unspeakable things . . ." He was nearly shouting and suddenly caught himself, ran his hands over his face, swallowed. When he spoke again, his voice was nearly normal. "Morally, ethically, I knew that if I didn't get the hell out, I was as monstrous as they were."

Moments passed. Neither of them spoke. Nora took another look at Wade, memorizing his face. "Does he have the new version of the chip?"

"I don't think so. The chips we were using in the mid-nineties were good, but only lasted a few years. Wade got chipped every other year or so. I know because I chipped everyone. He didn't come in during that last year."

"What about the thousand new chips you and Mariah supposedly sold to Joe Aiken, Jr., and his buddy Senator Lazier for millions? He could be chipped with one of those?"

"That sale never happened. You and your people intervened before we could finalize it. As far as I know, those thousand chips and whatever Curtis took from Mariah's freezer are the sum total of what exists. Without the equipment I had at SPOT, I haven't been able to produce very many. It's possible, of course, that Senator Lazier got his hands on some of the new chips, maybe through Mariah, as a sweetener for the deal. But if so, there aren't many."

"Then that gives us an edge."

"Absolutely."

So the news wasn't all bad.

"You and I can keep in touch with text messages if we aren't more than a year apart. Does that interest you?"

"Yes. But how . . ."

"A different kind of chip and programming code. I'll show you. Let me have your cell for a second."

She handed him the cell. Berlin popped off the back and, from the pocket in his shirt, brought out a cellophane pack, opened it, turned it upside down over his hand. A fleck of metal fell into his palm and, with a pair of tweezers, he attached it to something in the back of the phone. He popped the cover back on and attached a gizmo to the place where the charger cord went, then connected the gizmo to a USB cord that he plugged into the laptop. As he worked, he said, "When your replay happened, it was so you could prevent an injury rather than see your attackers, right?" When she nodded, he added, "That's significant."

"Significant how? The whole thing happened spontaneously. It's not like I *chose* to do any of it."

"Which is what makes it even more intriguing. You see, the new chip has the capacity to learn, and in learning, it evolves. As it evolves, the probability fields available to it expand enormously."

"You're making the chip sound like an artificial intelligence."

He glanced up from the laptop screen and looked at her as though she were a naïve child. "That's exactly what it is,

Nora. Except that it's part of you. Of me. And it has an affinity for its own kind. That's how you ended up here. The chip
calculated the fields and selected this time and place because
you needed certain information."

Okay, he was spooking her. The BIO in the biochip now
took on a whole new meaning and she definitely didn't like it.

"You were a psychologist, right? In your life before?" he
asked. "A Jungian, if I remember."

"Uh, yeah."

"Then you're familiar with the term *synchronicity*. The
chip dives into what we think of as random chaos and taps
into the underlying order that every synchronicity always
highlights. No matter where you go, where you hide, other
Travelers eventually will find you. It could take days, weeks,
years. It all depends on *intention*. I figure that in the first
couple of months after SPOT's collapse, things were in such
disarray that there was no organized effort to locate your
group. That obviously has changed. And the more focused
your adversaries become on finding you, the easier it will
be."

"Then the same must be true for you, right?"

His eyes met hers and in them she read the strange twists
and turns that his life had taken since SPOT's collapse—not
the specifics, not the stops in this era or that town, but his
loneliness, his isolation. "Yes." His voice was so soft she had
to strain to hear it.

"So why are you here? In this place? Why not go way
back in time, where it will be more difficult for them to find
you?"

"I could ask you the same question."

"Because it's easier to live in the time you know." Because they could do their work more efficiently with the Internet, cell phones, WiFi. "Because this time is home."

"Exactly." He unplugged the gizmo from her phone and
passed it back to her. "I'm not as high a priority for them as
you and your group are. I'm hoping they think I'm dead.

And even if I *were* a priority, this place is safer than most because of the exploration of consciousness that goes on here. The accretion of positive energy helps to deflect Travelers whose intentions are suspect."

"So we should find an area that has the same kind of energy?"

"If possible. But there aren't many spots left like this." Then he grinned and stabbed his thumb over his shoulder. "There's a house up the road for sale."

Just then, a buzzer sounded somewhere in the building. Nora thought it was coming from upstairs but couldn't be sure. "Hello," called a female voice. "Russ? You here? I saw your car out front. Since you couldn't join us for Easter dinner, I've brought leftovers."

Shit, Berlin mouthed, then called back: "I'll be up in a second, Lea."

Lea. One of the names preserved in the cement foundation around the crystal. Nora scrambled to her feet, the photos clutched in one hand, her cell in the other. "What's your cell number?" she whispered.

"It's written on the back of one of the pictures. It only works for text messages."

Footfalls on the stairs, then Lea appeared, holding a glass dish of Easter leftovers, looking surprised and embarrassed. "Oh, Russ. I'm sorry. I didn't know you had company."

Nora was struck by her quick, engaging smile; animated eyes; and a kind of genuineness that she hadn't encountered in years. Her long, blond braid curved gracefully over one shoulder. She was shorter than both Nora and Berlin, yet her presence seemed to fill the room.

"You're not interrupting anything," Nora assured her and tugged at the sides of her shorts. "I, uh, ducked outside to pick up yesterday's mail and locked myself out. Pretty embarrassing, prancing around in my pajamas. Anyway, Russ had an extra key."

"She's visiting Pam," Berlin said quickly.

Nora had no idea who Pam was, but Lea obviously did. "How great. Pam can use the company right now. I can give you a lift back, Nora. It's on my way."

"No, thanks. I'm fine. It's actually a great day for walking. I mean, is this weather fantastic or what?"

Never mind that it was the middle of the afternoon on Easter, and that people at Pam's home were probably up at dawn and didn't go out in their pajamas. Lea was quite gracious about Nora's apparent eccentricity. "It's just wonderful," she agreed.

"Lea, it was terrific to meet you. But I'd best get going," Nora said, then gave Berlin a quick hug. "Thanks again for your help." In a whisper, she added: "I'll text you." With that, she smiled at Lea and headed out the door without looking back.

She moved swiftly down the path toward the giant crystal, ducked behind it, and transitioned from there. She emerged with shocking ease in her kitchen in Santa Cruz, the photos still in her hand. She glanced at the wall clock. She had been gone only twenty minutes in real time. She immediately noticed there was no blood on the tile floor and ran into the living room. No medical kit, no bloody towels, no plastic tarp on the couch. Curtis hadn't been injured. Had anything else changed?

She hurried through the hall, opening doors, counting bodies, making sure everyone was there, breathing. Yes, yes. All bodies accounted for, even Sunny. She stepped back into the living room and started turning over the pictures until she found the one with Berlin's info:

Janitorial & Handyman Services
Call Russ Child @ 434-361-5555

A janitor. The brilliant Dr. Russ Berlin was now a janitor in a place that taught people how to enter altered states of consciousness. Good God. Nora sent him a text message, just a simple thank-you. Before she reached the bedroom, her cell jingled with an incoming message dated April 16, 2006, eleven months in her past:

> My thanks to you. Just remembered. Somewhere in Blue River 1695 is a place for the disenfranchised. It's supposedly a legend, like Camelot, but most legends seem to have a basis in fact. Anyway, keep that in mind when you go back to retrieve your mom.
>
> I may be the gatekeeper of the technology, but you and your group are its explorers. Holler if you need help. RB

4
Leverage

*Time isn't a river flowing from past to future.
It's multidimensional, everywhere and
nowhere.*

—Mariah Jones, 1987

March 15, 2007, 5:35 A.M.

He stood inside the empty apartment, his Glock tucked
under his shirt, in the small of his back, his eyes slowly scanning the room. Shards of glass from the busted window still
littered the living room floor and glistened in the glare of the
overhead lights. A faint stink of tear gas lingered in the air, a
sickening sweet scent. That wouldn't last long, he thought,
what with the hot wind blowing through the broken window.

The whole operation had gone badly, hardly a surprise.
Since that night Wade and Ben had shown up in his living
room in Key Largo, Eric Holcomb had learned that Wade's
hubris knew no boundaries. He was right, always. His way or
the highway. He had insisted on using the tear gas canisters,
and now here they were, with three empty apartments and
Nora's group on the run again.

He moved forward, his shoes crunching over the broken
glass. This first-floor apartment was where Ryan Curtis and
Kat Sargent had been living, and it was obvious that they

had been in the process of moving out. Empty boxes were stacked on the couch, piles of books and clothing lay scattered around. He opened the fridge, helped himself to a bottle of water, then opened the freezer. Empty, except for ice cubes. Again, not a surprise. The syringes probably had been the first items they had moved.

As he stood there sipping water, he suddenly realized he had dual memories of what had happened in this apartment. How the hell could that be? Frowning, he set the bottle down on the counter and walked into the back bedroom and stopped in front of the window.

Lights from another apartment spilled out across the lush garden bursting with bloodred bougainvilleas. In one memory, he distinctly recalled coming in through this window with Wade, the two of them cornering Curtis. And Curtis, rather than transitioning, had demanded to know who was paying them. In that memory, Kat was shouting at Curtis to get away, Wade had lunged at Curtis with a knife, and the blade had cut into his upper arm. Then Kat had hurled herself at Curtis—and transitioned him.

In a second memory, Holcomb entered through the window alone after Wade had fired canisters into the apartment, but the place was as empty as a pillaged grave. He didn't understand how he could have two memories of the same event. Had both happened? Were both real?

The question seemed irrelevant. The only event that mattered was the second one, where Curtis had *not* been injured because the apartment was empty and the six members of Nora's group had escaped. He knew better than to mention the two sets of memories to Wade. He had no interest in anomalies. *Shit happens:* that was how he explained anything that didn't fit into his database of knowledge about the chip, transitioning, time travel, women, marriage, life in general. For a man who supposedly had been chipped for at least ten years—and thus able to travel anywhere in time he chose—Wade was shockingly free of curiosity.

You go back, do the job, look around, get a taste of what the era's like, then you go home. Keep it simple.

Holcomb wished, as he had many times in the past four months, that he never had agreed to be a part of this madness. Yes, the money he'd been paid was comforting and it was good to know he and Mike still had their refuge in Key Largo. But every day, Wade's reckless certainty, his military mentality, his rules and restrictions on Holcomb's life hammered home an indisputable fact: Wade, imbued with unimaginable power, was a sociopath.

He glanced back through the bedroom doorway, didn't see Wade lumbering in, and quickly punched out his son's cell number. Holcomb hadn't spoken to Mike in several weeks and hadn't seen him since Holcomb and Wade had left the U.S. in mid-January, following a lead that Wade supposedly had gotten on the group's whereabouts. Puerto Rico. Saba. Dominican Republic. St. Barts. And, finally, Aruba. At each port in their ridiculous journey, Holcomb and Mike had traded text messages and e-mails regularly and now and then, when Holcomb could get away from Wade, he and Mike had spoken by phone. Even though Wade had discouraged any communication, he'd been wise enough to back off on that score after Holcomb had made it clear that no one and nothing would keep him from his son. But all communication had stopped a week ago.

Why?

The number rang and rang at the other end. Even Mike's voice mail didn't kick in. Maybe the service was down. Or he was in a pocket of Palm Beach where cell reception was poor. He considered calling Mike's girlfriend, but Holcomb had met her only once and didn't have any idea what the hell he would say to her. *Hey, Ann, it's Eric. I'm out of town on business and Mike isn't answering his cell. Is he okay?* Yeah, that would go over in a big way. On a teenager's list of the gross and the disgusting, an overly protective father was second only to an overprotective mother.

As he turned away from the window, he realized the first memory, of Curtis being sliced, was fading, like a particularly vivid dream might do within a few minutes of awakening. Perhaps it hadn't been a memory at all, but some sort of anomaly caused by the chip.

Yet, suppose—just suppose—both events actually *had* taken place? Perhaps the first memory was what had happened initially and then one of the six had somehow managed to change it, creating a new version of the event. Was that possible? Had Wade ever mentioned anything like that?

Over the top, he thought. But once you had seen dinosaurs, he thought, anything was within the realm of possibility.

Holcomb searched the bedroom, jerking open every drawer in the bureau, the nightstand. Nothing but pens, paperback books, hair clips. He opened the closet doors and removed the hangers that still held clothes and checked every piece of clothing. He knew all about the kinds of things left behind in pockets.

Over that long weekend in January when he'd last seen his son, Holcomb had found a condom and the remnants of a joint in the back pocket of Mike's jeans. Personally, he was delighted that his son was using condoms and that his drug of choice wasn't cocaine, Ecstasy, heroin. Given what he was doing, what he was involved in, he hardly felt that he could call his son on either count. So he had said nothing. But the six Travelers weren't his son, so when he felt the shape of something in the pocket of one of the skirts Kat Sargent had left behind, he removed it.

It was a photo printed on regular paper, one of those hasty things you did when you wanted an image and who cared if it wasn't on shiny paper. It showed her and her cohorts with their arms linked, middle fingers standing at attention, and a sign that read: *Fuck you SPOT and all your minions.*

Holcomb laughed in spite of his frustration and slipped

the picture into his pocket. He was patting down one of the dresses when Wade hurried in.

"Yo, Mr. H. I think we're done here."

Hey, asshole, you're done; get lost. "Yo, Wade. The tear gas canisters were a big mistake. Nothing like warning the enemy."

"That was intentional. See, Mr. H, these people are like vampires. They're slippery, smart, and know things about time travel that we don't. But in the same way that vampires have to return to their coffins during the daylight, these people need a home base, a haven to which they can retreat in between transitions or when they're cornered or injured. Every Traveler has one."

"Ah, okay, I get it. Coffins in various times."

Wade rolled his eyes. "Mr. H, the vampire thing was an analogy."

Gee, really? "Their home could be anywhere, in any time."

"That's true. But for the last four months, their safe place has been Waverunner, in our time. And I think they're still on the island. This is the time they know best, where they feel most comfortable. They were in the process of moving out, probably rented or bought homes somewhere on the island. Makes sense. Three couples who presumably want what most couples want—to establish roots, start families, the whole nine yards."

"That's a big presumption. Not everyone in a relationship wants a family. Not everyone in a relationship wants the whole nine yards, Wade."

Wade's slow, sly smile reshaped his cruel mouth in such a way that it was easy for Holcomb to imagine him as some medieval inquisitor, relishing the agony he would bring down upon the sinner. He brought a plastic bag from his pack. "Take a look at this. I found it in the trash of Quinta twenty-four. The Walrave apartment."

A pharmacy bag from the Hilton. Inside was an opened

box for a pregnancy test. The spent tube indicated the user was pregnant. "So Diana Walrave is pregnant?" Holcomb asked.

"You got it. Now, if I were her—or the daddy to be—I'd be thinking about how time travel would affect my baby. I'd probably be inclined to stay where I am for the duration of the pregnancy. I wouldn't want to risk transitioning any- where. Even in SPOT, there were rules about pregnancy. If you and your partner were trying to get pregnant, neither of you could be chipped. Once the woman was pregnant, the man could be chipped again, but the woman had to remain unchipped until she was finished nursing."

Wade was a bottomless pit about this kind of historical trivia.

"That's going to make it easier for us. We secure their home base here on Aruba and at the same time flush out the others in 1695. The stun gun dislodges their chips and they're stuck back there. So we give them a choice: in return for their supply of the chips, we transition one of them back to our time and give them a chip so that person can return for the others."

"How magnanimous of us," Holcomb said.

"But of course we don't let the person go back for the others."

"I thought the point was to dislodge their chips so they'd be stuck permanently in the past."

"The point, Mr. H, has always been the chips. Unfortu- nately for us, when SPOT fell apart, our access to the chips ended. We have a couple dozen left from a batch that wasn't sabotaged by Mariah Jones and her buddy Berlin. The night everything went down, Mariah was going to sell a thousand chips to the government. New, vastly improved chips. But Curtis, Nora McKee, and the rest of them intervened, Sena- tor Aiken went to prison, Mariah and Lydia Fenmore disap- peared, and Berlin took off. We have every reason to believe that Curtis's group has those chips."

In other words, Holcomb thought, if they didn't get the chips, the technology would be lost to *them*, the government, who paid Wade a ridiculous amount of money for his mercenary work, and Wade would be out of a job. Yeah, things were starting to add up now. If Wade had told him all this in the beginning, Holcomb might not be here now.

No, that wasn't true. He would be here because of the money. The fifty grand Wade had left on Holcomb's coffee table that night in Key Largo, minus what he'd used to pay bills, was in an offshore account in the Bahamas, just like some of the two hundred grand he'd been paid when he had finished training. The rest of the money was hidden in the Key Largo house. "And you got this information how?"

Wade pointed his finger at Holcomb. "That, my friend, is our next stop."

They went outside, where the complex managers, a husband and wife, were arguing with the local cops, chattering away in Papiamento, the island dialect. They both gestured angrily toward the shattered windows. The woman, an attractive brunette, saw Holcomb and Wade and strode toward them quickly, everything about her body language suggesting that she was royally pissed.

"Excuse me, Mr. Wade. Unless new windows are installed, I have three apartments that can't be rented. That means a loss of revenue. Just who is paying for those windows?"

"You are, ma'am." Wade didn't skip a beat. "You were harboring terrorists and the broken windows are just part of the consequences."

"*Terrorists?* They were customers. People we had known for some time. Just because *you* say they are terrorists, doesn't mean they are."

Holcomb didn't like this. With flyers being posted around the island that identified Nora McKee and the others as fugitives, they depended on the local populace for leads to their location. But if word got around that the American feds were bastards, there would be no reports.

"How much do you figure new windows will cost?" Holcomb asked.

He felt Wade tense up.

"They have to be completely replaced," she said. "Four windows. It's going to cost at least five hundred a window."

Two grand. Holcomb slipped his wallet from his back pocket and counted out five hundred in cash. "This is all I have on me right now. But I'll be back later with the rest of it."

She looked shocked, then grateful, and finally smiled. "Thank you, Mr. Holcomb. Perhaps your companion"—she pinned Wade with her vivid blue eyes—"could take some public relations lessons from you."

Wade didn't bother hiding his disgust. He stalked off, headed for their rental car, his long strides eating up the pavement. "You'll have to excuse him, ma'am." Holcomb turned on every bit of charm he could dredge up. "He's had family problems lately and is taking it out on everyone around him."

"We've all got problems," she said, folding her arms at her waist. "This incident here is going to hurt our business. It'll be out on the Internet by tomorrow, if it isn't there already. I just don't understand how any of this happened. My husband and I have known Ryan Curtis as long as we've owned this place, since the late eighties. He and Kat have been coming here together for years and they're the kind of guests every proprietor hopes for. Their friends have been equally ideal. I can't believe they're terrorists."

They aren't. They're time travelers. "When did they give their notice that they were moving out?"

"Two weeks ago, just like I told Mr. Wade."

"Did they give any indication where they were going?"

"Back to the States."

Sure. Spread the cover-up story, the lie, and it covered your tracks. Hardly original. Granted, he was no expert on this stuff. But when Mariah Jones had transitioned Curtis's partner to parts unknown and Curtis had gone rogue to find her, Aruba was the place he'd looked. Their haven. Where they'd been coming for years.

"Thank you very much for your help. I apologize about the windows."

When he got into the SUV idling at the entrance to the parking lot, Wade hit the accelerator, the car lurched forward, and he swerved onto the highway. "That was fuckin' idiotic, Mr. H."

"You want to find these people, Wade? Then you'd better act in a way that makes the locals think we're nice guys. Otherwise, watch how fast the locals clam up."

"You're paying for her goddamn windows. That makes *you* look weak. No one likes *weak*, Mr. H."

"And everyone *loves* a bully?" Holcomb laughed. "Jesus, you don't get it, do you? You really don't *get* it. The owners of Waverunner have been here since the late eighties. They probably know everyone on this island who is anyone and the word has gone out that you're a bully asshole. You think that's the way to find these people? Okay, we'll try it your way and we'll still be here five years from now, hoping to get our hands on those chips."

And Wade, who just had to get in the last word, spat, "You don't have any idea what you're talking about."

"You've got all the charm of a cockroach."

They drove in silence the rest of the way to the Hilton, Wade racing down the highway and careening into the parking lot so fast that he nearly struck a man and a woman who had just stepped off the median. They leaped back and Holcomb snapped, "Christ, you nearly hit them."

"But I didn't," Wade barked and swung into a parking space.

He leaped out of the car, slung a small duffel bag over his shoulder, and headed inside before Holcomb had even opened his door. Yeah, this was going to be a barrel of laughs, Holcomb thought, and hurried on into the massive lobby.

Despite the fact that it was almost six a.m., the casino off to his left was still filled with people. Slot machines rang, clouds of smoke rolled out the door. Wade, looking impatient, waited in front of an open elevator on the far side of the lobby. "Walk any slower and the sun will be rising," he grumbled.

Just as they got in, a woman in black pants and a T-shirt with NAMASTE written across the front ran into the elevator. "Thanks for holding it," she said breathlessly, flipping her braid over her shoulder. "I really appreciate it. The other elevators are so incredibly slow."

"Uh, this elevator only goes to the penthouse, ma'am." Wade gestured toward the panel where the floor numbers usually were. "That's why there're no buttons."

"Oh." She looked surprised. "A private elevator just for the penthouse? For just *one* penthouse?"

"Just one." Wade sounded annoyed now. "You'll have to use another elevator."

"How do you get up there without any floor numbers?" she persisted.

"A card, ma'am, a card. If you don't mind . . ."

She smiled graciously, patting the air with her hands. "You, my little friend, should not be so agitated at this hour of the morning. I think yoga would do you good." She had been backing up as she spoke and now she winked and stepped out. "Ta-ta," she added with a small, taunting wave.

"Fuckin' fruitcake," Wade said as the doors whispered shut. He stuck his card in the slot.

"Takes one to know one."

"Go fuck yourself, Mr. H."

The tension between them thickened as the elevator ascended, its whispers slick, almost lascivious. Wade flicked his hand against the card, as if force would make the elevator move faster.

At some level, Holcomb must have been expecting what happened next, because when he caught movement in his peripheral vision, he leaped to the side, and Wade, who had lunged for him, crashed into the elevator wall. Holcomb slammed his fist against the STOP button, and the abrupt cessation of movement threw Wade back, causing his stun gun to skitter across the floor. Holcomb swept it up and zapped Wade in the neck.

He felt a grim satisfaction as the man's knees buckled and he dropped to the floor, drooling, writhing like an injured snake. Holcomb quickly patted him down, removed his nine millimeter and a knife, and dropped them in his duffel bag. Wade's nose started to bleed; his body was rejecting his chip. The blood flowed faster and faster and Holcomb, afraid he might drown in it, rolled Wade onto his side. Wade, body still twitching, drew his legs up against his chest.

"Let's get a couple of things straight, Wade." Crouched next to his body, Holcomb spoke softly. Blood pooled beneath Wade's cheek, a real mess here on the elevator floor. "Don't try to fuck me over like that again. I've played by all your bullshit rules. And since your body is rejecting the chip, I could just grab your shoulder and disappear your miserable ass to some brutal point in time where you would last about sixty seconds. And if I'm figuring this right, you've got no chips left. So, pal, since I've still got a chip, I'm your last best hope. And we'll talk about that once we're in the penthouse. Got it?"

Wade continued to twitch and bleed. Holcomb pulled a towel from the duffel and used it to clean up the blood on Wade's face, on the elevator floor, and found the spent chip. It looked like a deflated tick.

The towel soaked through with blood and Holcomb stuffed it back into the duffel with the flattened chip. He went through Wade's pack and removed another gun—a second nine millimeter—and tucked it into the back of his jeans. He also removed a card with the Hilton logo on it from his shirt pocket and guessed it would open the door to the penthouse.

Wade started coming around, groaning dramatically, trying to turn over. He finally managed to roll onto his knees, but remained huddled over, forehead touching the floor like a Muslim at prayer. His splayed fingers twitched, tightened, curled, then flattened out completely, and he pushed himself up. His eyes narrowed, blinked, and he ran the back of his hand across his nose. He was sweating so profusely that his face glistened in the dim elevator light.

"You fuck," he said. "You stupid fuck. Now you're going back alone."

Good. He could handle *alone.* He could handle anything as long as this moron wasn't part of the journey. "So I'm right. There aren't any more chips."

"Bullshit. It's just . . . too risky to chip myself sooner than seventy-two hours after a rejection."

Uh-huh. Holcomb hadn't heard that rule before. He stood and disengaged the STOP button. He caught sight of himself in the mirror on the back wall, a disheveled, slender, tall man with thick, khaki-colored hair fading at the temples, who might be a banker, a CEO, a dot-com millionaire—or just a tourist who had slept in his clothes. Holcomb ran his fingers through his hair, straightened his casual island shirt, and was suddenly grateful that he had continued to pay for his gym membership. Wade was a strong bastard, but Holcomb was stronger.

The elevator halted, but the doors remained closed. Holcomb slipped the Hilton card into the slot and the elevator doors opened into a magnificent sunlit suite—where good ole Ben stood at attention, decked out completely in white, like a guru who had found nirvana.

"Mr. H," he said, with a wicked grin that shrank in small, barely perceptible increments as his eyes fixed on the weapon that Holcomb held.

"Mr. Ben," Holcomb replied, and suddenly felt as if he were in an episode of *Sesame Street.* "Long time no see."

"He's chipped, I'm not," Wade said quickly, as he got to his feet. "Boss doesn't need to know that."

Ben nodded and they all went inside. Holcomb suddenly understood that his hunch about his having the last chip was correct. These bastards were desperate, limping along like cripples. Yes, they still had cash and clout and the capacity for creating chaos. But they didn't have chips. And without chips, they didn't have much of anything at all. He slipped the gun under his shirt, where he could reach it easily.

Ben led them into a spacious living room with a wall of glass that overlooked the Caribbean. The day was dawning clear, brilliant, and all that Caribbean blue looked close enough to touch. Way out in the distance, Holcomb saw the unfurled, splendid sails of the early morning windsurfers who were drawn to Aruba by the constant trade winds.

They sat at a carefully laid table, where everything matched. Napkins with plates, plates with silverware, silverware with the island motif of easy living, happy living. As it said on the local license plates: ARUBA, ONE HAPPY ISLAND. Yes, indeed.

The man who emerged five minutes later from one of the back rooms looked like every pundit who had paraded across the TV screen in Holcomb's old life. Pale face. Full mouth. Hair cut to perfection. His casual clothes fit him well, tailored to the specifications of his waist, chest, the length of his legs. He smiled on cue, as though his consultants were in another room, prompting him through a hidden mike. It was enough to make Holcomb gag.

"Wade, good to see you," the man said, his hand outstretched.

And good ole Wade shook his hand, then made his introductions. "Senator, this is Eric Holcomb. Mr. H, Rick Lazier."

Of course. No wonder the guy looked familiar. Lazier, a senator from the Midwest, was one of CNN's favored guests. Chairman of the Senate Intelligence Committee, he was the golden boy of the Internet political blogs, of the Sunday talk shows, a magnet for fund-raisers, and a possible contender for a presidential run in 2012. Those on the left talked about him as the next JFK; those on the right called him the next great communicator, a Ronald Reagan minus the movie shit. In Holcomb's book, anyone who appealed to both the left and the right was a dangerous illusion. Today's America had no room for a middle path.

"Please, make yourselves comfortable. Breakfast is piping hot." Lazier's gesture included the serving tray on wheels, the perfectly set table. They all sat down, even Ben. "I trust your accommodations are comfortable, Mr. Holcomb?"

His accommodations, the little he'd seen of them, were just fine, thanks. A suite down the road at the Radisson. Carefully wrapped chocolates left on his pillow in the evening, like treats from the Easter bunny. A bar stocked with Aruba's finest liquors. "They're great, thanks."

Lazier, with his elbows propped on the edge of the table, pressed his fingertips together, the fingers splaying so that they formed a kind of teepee. Then he pulled the serving tray closer, passed out the platters covered with metal tops, and got up to serve coffee. Quite the gracious host, Holcomb thought, and removed the lid covering his platter. Eggs, strips of bacon, slices of fresh fruit and cheese, flaky biscuits with steam still rising from them. Holcomb was certain the coffee had come from Venezuela, just fifteen miles south.

When Lazier sat down again, he regarded Wade with an expression that Holcomb couldn't read. "So, they got away."

"Yes, sir," Wade replied. "But they're somewhere on the island. In *this* time. We have a lead."

We do? Holcomb leaned forward with great interest as Wade brought out his PDA.

"In the last month," Wade said, "there have been thirty-five home or condo sales on the island. Of these, twenty-two have been for half a million and above. Condos on the beach, mansions in secluded parts of the island, time-shares. I've discarded those. That leaves thirteen properties."

"Why discard the others?" Lazier asked.

"Because our little group of Travelers wants to blend in, using the local populace as their camouflage. Of the thirteen, four sales are particularly interesting. Modest homes in modest neighborhoods in and around Oranjestad."

"If I were in this group," Holcomb said, stabbing at his eggs, "I wouldn't stick around Oranjestad. I'd go inland, to one of the other cities. And I would rent, rather than sink my money into property."

"They'd buy and stay around Oranjestad," Wade snapped. "It's where everything is happening. It's where there are services, supplies, doctors—"

"C'mon," Holcomb interrupted. "They can bop around through time for services, supplies, and doctors. They're six Americans who are passing themselves off as ex-pats. They're elsewhere."

"There're only two other towns of any significant size," Ben said. "San Nicolas to the south, near the Valero oil refinery, and Santa Cruz, about thirty minutes inland."

"What do we have for sales or rentals in those places, Wade?" asked Lazier, and snapped a strip of bacon in two.

Wade looked irritated, but fiddled some more with his PDA, and after several long moments, he said, "Ten sales, eight long-term rentals."

"Okay." Lazier sat forward, hands folded around his coffee cup. "We have three couples. So we're looking for three small houses, perhaps in the same general area, purchased around the same time. Or perhaps one house large enough to accommodate six people. Do we have anything like that?"

More scrolling through the listings, then Wade said, "February twenty-sixth and seventh, three homes sold in San Nicolas. The houses are within a couple of miles of each other. On March first, two homes sold in Santa Cruz, and they're within a few miles of each other. But proximity doesn't mean shit in those towns, Senator. They're small to begin with."

"And for rentals?" Lazier asked impatiently.

Wade spat out the figures.

Lazier nodded, apparently liking what he heard. "Now our list is narrowed considerably."

"Who were the buyers and renters? That information should be there," Holcomb said, breaking open one of the biscuits. Real estate, after all, had been his expertise. And how different could real estate be here in Aruba? There would be a paper trail of information, and he was certain the entire paper trail was on Wade's PDA. He raised his eyes from the biscuit to Wade.

The other man sat there, motionless, the PDA clutched in his hand, eyes pinned to Holcomb, anger radiating from him like a foul odor. Once or twice in his other life, a judge had regarded Holcomb the way that Wade was doing now and he had known right then that he had lost. The difference this time was that Holcomb knew that as the only person in the room who was chipped, he had the upper hand. He had what everyone coveted. So he met Wade's piercing gaze and permitted himself a small, gloating smile.

"There's nothing in the names," Wade snapped. "They're all corporate and bogus."

"For Chrissakes," Lazier hissed, then snatched the PDA out of Wade's hand. "I don't care what the two of you do to each other when you're out of my suite. But in here, you will attempt civility." Then he dropped his eyes to the screen, his thumb and forefinger tapping, tapping. "March first. One home in Santa Cruz was sold to a corporate entity registered in France. The other home was rented to a corporate entity in the Netherlands." The senator raised his eyes from the screen. "I'd say that's where you people start. With the rentals. And at the same time, we hit them in 1695. Wade, you and Eric cover 1695 and Ben, you and your people find their place in Santa Cruz."

"There's a, uh, problem," Wade said. "My body rejected my chip. Mr. H can transition me. But like you've said yourself, sir, in a distant era, it's best to be self-reliant. And frankly, since none of the six have ever seen Mr. H, I think he should cover 1695."

Interesting, Holcomb thought, that Wade didn't tell the senator *how* his chip had been rejected. He didn't want to look incompetent. And Holcomb didn't correct Wade about how Curtis had seen them in at least one version of events. Did Curtis have a dual set of memories? Did Wade?

"Did they train you well enough for that, Eric?" the senator asked. "A solo journey to a dismal past?"

Holcomb thought of the many weeks he had studied the era, memorizing the minutia, the nuances, of daily life in Blue River circa 1695. "Yes, they did a fine job. I'm completely indoctrinated."

Lazier smiled and sipped at his coffee. "Excellent. But just to guarantee cooperation, I've taken certain precautions." His eyes slipped toward Ben, who got up from the table and went down the hall.

Wade frowned and squirmed in his seat, picking at the food left on his plate. He obviously hadn't been clued in about what the guarantee involved, and didn't like it. Throughout Holcomb's training, he had gotten the impression that Wade and Ben were connected at the hip. What one knew, the other knew. But Wade could be a good actor when it suited him, and Holcomb immediately wondered if he had been set up in some way, if this was a different take on the good cop/bad cop routine, with Lazier as the judge.

And then Ben returned with one arm slung around Mike's shoulders, and the other pressing a gun into his ribs. Shock whipped through Holcomb's body, rendering him mute. *Mike, here.* No wonder he hadn't answered his cell.

"Dad," Mike whispered, his eyes brimming with tears.

Holcomb shot to his feet, his chair crashing to the floor. "What the *fuck* are you doing?!" he shouted at Lazier.

"Sit down, Mr. Holcomb." A smirk reshaped Lazier's mouth. "And let's discuss this without shouting, shall we?"

"Don't patronize me, you fuck. You've kidnapped my son and—"

"Sit down, Mr. H," Ben snapped, tightening his arm around Mike's throat.

Holcomb grabbed his chair, jerked it upright, sank into it. His mind raced. The weight of the weapon tucked into the small of his back suddenly felt like a bag of concrete. The muscles in his hand tightened, screaming to reach for it, but Holcomb knew that if he did, Mike would be dead before he ever fired a shot.

"Very wise, Eric, not going for the gun," Lazier said. "Wade, relieve him of the weapon and be sure to remove the weapons in his duffel bag." Then, to Holcomb: "There're security cameras in the penthouse elevator and the moment that button for the penthouse is punched, they come on. So I know why Wade's body rejected his chip. I know that you have two guns, a knife, and the stun gun." Now he sat forward, hands folded together almost demurely, displaying perfectly clipped nails, a small, satisfied smile on his face. His fingertips touched the underside of his chin. "Your son is our insurance policy that you do what we hired you to do. You've been paid a great deal of money already—about a quarter of a million taxpayer dollars, Mr. Holcomb. Your son's presence here will ensure a return on that investment."

While Wade moved in to get the weapons, Holcomb looked away from Lazier, at Mike. "Have they hurt you? Molested you?"

"*Molested?*" Lazier laughed. "Good God, Eric. We're not sexual perverts."

"I'm asking my son," Holcomb snapped.

"No," Mike said softly. "But they keep me drugged and tied up. Dad, what's going on? Why's this happening?"

"Are they feeding you?"

"Yes."

"How long have you been here?"

"I . . . don't know," Mike admitted.

"How long?" Holcomb snapped, looking at Lazier.

"About a week," Lazier said. "And the more cooperative Mike is, the more privileges he gets."

A pulse hammered at Holcomb's temple; his blood pressure soared. He struggled to calm down so that he could think. "And I'm supposed to believe, Senator, that if I bring back the Travelers or the chips or whatever the hell it is you want, you'll release Mike and that'll be that?"

"You have my word, Eric."

"Your word's not good enough. I need some guarantees, too."

"You're not exactly in a position to ask for guarantees," Lazier said, with that small smile widening, pulling away from his teeth in a kind of grimace.

"Actually, *Rick,* I am. I'm chipped and you're not, Ben's not, Wade's not. I've got the only chip. That makes me your last best hope for putting SPOT back together again."

Lazier's smile started shrinking and somewhere in the darkness of his eyes, Holcomb saw wheels turning, plans entertained and discarded. Then Lazier gestured at the seat that Ben had vacated. "Sit down, Mike."

Ben pushed him none too gently toward the chair and Mike collapsed into it, fighting to hide how terrified he was. Ben then took up his position behind Mike's chair, and Wade now stood behind Holcomb and pressed something cold and hard against the side of his neck.

"Here's the deal, Eric. Wade is now holding a stun gun against your neck. If I tell him to activate it, your body rejects the last chip, Ben shoots your son, and since I wouldn't need you anymore, Wade shoots you. Then I proceed with plan B and find the Travelers here on Aruba. So my guarantee is simple. You do the job for us and get your son back. What the two of you do afterward is your own business."

"You won't find them here in Aruba. As soon as Wade decided to shoot tear gas canisters into their apartments, they transitioned. And since I'm the only person here who is chipped, I'm the only one who can go back and find them. You play the game my way or I don't play."

Silence.

Lazier just glared at him, then said, "Shoot the kid, Ben."

"Then you'll lose your time travel program completely" Holcomb said quickly. "Because I won't cooperate. So you might as well shoot both of us."

"Sir?" Ben asked, pressing the gun hard into the base of Mike's skull.

Mike's eyes were squeezed shut.

Lazier looked very unhappy. That was good. "And your conditions are, Mr. Holcomb?"

"Let Mike go. I'll do what you want me to do."

"Nope."

"Don't restrain or drug him."

"All right, we can live with that," Lazier said.

"And I need to know how reliable your information is that the group is going to transition to 1695."

"It's logical," Lazier said. "The disappearance of Nora McKee's mother in 1983 was the defining event of Nora's life. Once she realized what SPOT was about, retrieving her mother was her goal. And I know that much for a fact."

"But it's not necessarily the goal of everyone else in the group." *Keep the dialogue going.*

Lazier leaned forward, arms folded at the edge of the table. "These six people are no longer just individuals who are chipped. They're a collective, a tribe, unified by their situation and their *intentions*. They work for the good of the group, Eric. The goal of one becomes the goal of the tribe."

"Like vampires, Mr. H," Wade added. "Just like I told you."

"We know the date to which Nora's mother was disappeared," Lazier continued. "Wade has provided you with photos of her. Finding her won't be difficult. She'll be there. And so will McKee and Kincaid and perhaps some of the others as well." He slapped a bankbook down on the table. "And just to show you that we're sincere, the additional three quarters of a million is already in an offshore account in your name." He pushed the bankbook toward Holcomb.

Holcomb's hands were none too steady as he picked it up, paged through it. Legit, as far as he could tell. He turned it over and over again, his mind racing. Could he grab Mike and transition? His eyes met his son's.

"Dad, no, please, don't do it," Mike hissed. *"Fuck them."* He looked around wildly and grabbed Holcomb's hands. *"Fuck all of them, don't do it."*

And in the brief instant that his son's hands were clasping Holcomb's, he *reached* for his safe spot in the past, *reached* and *reached*. He felt the chip straining to do what it was designed for, felt his grasp on his son's fingers tightening, heard the hard, steady hammering of his heart. But nothing happened. And then Ben jerked Mike's chair back, breaking their connection.

"No touching," he barked.

Holcomb suspected that the room was protected some how, that no one could transition *from* or *to* this place. But how? How did they do that? What could possibly block the power of the chip?

Don't do it, Mike mouthed.

"So, do we have a deal, Eric?" Lazier asked.

Holcomb slipped the bankbook in his pocket. "Yes. As long as you understand one thing, *Rick*. Rick Lazier, senator from Idaho, right? Or is it Iowa? I always got stumped with the state." *Remember the name, Mike.* "So know this, Rick. If you mistreat my son, if you harm him in any way, I will find your sorry ass wherever it is and kill you."

Lazier shook his finger at Holcomb and cocked his head

in a way that made it obvious he considered the threat a joke. "Now, now, Eric. You're talking like a terrorist. We have a business deal that's insured. Nothing more, nothing less." Then he pressed his perfectly manicured hands to the table-top and pushed himself to his feet. "Now, if you'll excuse me, I have other business to attend to."

With that, Ben told Mike to get up, and as he did, Mike's eyes caught Holcomb's. *I don't know what's going on, but make it fast, Dad. Do what you have to do and get me outta here.*

Then Ben and Mike were gone and Lazier was already on his cell phone, his back to them, on to the next deal, the next maneuver. Wade jammed the butt of his weapon against the base of Holcomb's skull. "We've been dismissed. Grab your duffel and let's go."

When they were in the elevator, on their way down, Wade suddenly struck Holcomb across the face with the back of his hand, then kneed him in the balls. It happened so fast, so unexpectedly, that Holcomb didn't have a chance to protect himself. He dropped to his knees on the elevator floor, his balls on fire, a soft, horrible groan issuing from his mouth.

He knew he still had the strength to throw his arms round Wade's legs, to transition. But he sensed that whatever had blocked him in the penthouse from transitioning was still in effect. And so he endured Wade's tirade, his threats, his ob-scenities, endured until Wade drew his leg back to kick Hol-comb in the ribs again. Then he reared up, grabbed on to Wade's leg, and jerked him down to the floor with such force that the elevator shook. Wade's head slammed against the floor, and his stun gun and weapon spun away from him.

Wade passed out, and in those seconds of unconsciousness, Holcomb pushed Wade's hands beneath his body, straddled him, and jammed the butt of the nine millimeter under Wade's jaw. When Wade's eyes fluttered open, his comprehension was immediate. He knew the score. Holcomb leaned in so close to his face that he felt as if he were sinking into his skin, his eyes, his fetid, rotting soul. "Never fuck with my kid."

"I . . . I didn't know about it. I swear. Lazier . . . did this on his own."

"We've got new rules now, Wade." Holcomb got to his feet, the gun pointed at Wade's chest. "Get up."

Wade got shakily to his feet. Holcomb patted him down and found his car keys. He took his pack and slung it over his own shoulder.

"Move back until you're against the wall. Lock your hands on top of your head and turn around."

"Listen, man, you don't need to shoot me. You're—"

"Do it."

He did it.

Holcomb leaned close to him and whispered, "Here's the deal. I'll be back with what you need. But if any of you double-cross me, if you hurt my son, if you don't uphold your end of the bargain, I'll come after the bunch of you. And I'll start with you."

Seconds later, the elevator stopped, the doors opened. Holcomb punched the twelfth floor, stepped out of the elevator, and the doors closed, with Wade still kneeling inside it. For about two seconds, he considered racing up the stairs to the penthouse, bursting inside, and shooting everyone who stood between him and Mike. But he knew that Mike would be dead before he reached him. So he spun around and ran through the lobby, past the early birds on their way to the beach, meetings, breakfast. He didn't stop running until he reached the SUV. Then he threw himself inside and headed toward the Radisson, through the bright, early morning light.

Did they train you well enough for that, Eric? A solo journey to a dismal past?

He didn't know. The only thing that mattered was getting there and back with what they wanted so that he could take his son so far away from here that neither of them would be found again.

5
The Transition

*To do the work for which it was designed,
the biochip must become a part of you, like
an organ, a limb. As intimate to you as your
own skin.*

—*Mariah Jones, 1989*

During the night, something had changed. Kincaid couldn't say exactly what was different, but sensed it in his bones. Yet, he didn't feel threatened by it. As he puzzled over it, he suddenly realized that he had two sets of memories, one in which Curtis had been injured and Walrave had stitched him up, and the other in which Curtis had *not* been injured. Since there was nothing in the house that indicated an injury, at least not that he saw in his quick swing through the rooms, they appeared to be in the timeline connected to the second scenario.

Had Curtis done a replay to prevent his own injury? Did that mean Curtis and Kat would be able to make this transition with him and Nora?

Kincaid let Sunny outside, then went into the kitchen and started the coffee. He cut up fresh fruit, put out the cereal, yogurt, milk, fresh rolls, butter, so that everything would be ready when Nora got up. They both achieved transitions more easily on full stomachs. Something about blood sugar levels. He filled a mug with coffee and went into the work-shop off the kitchen.

Once upon a time, it had been a part of the garage, but the couple who owned the place had erected a wall in the middle of it, extended the AC ducts, put in vents, and created a workshop. It was here he had been experimenting with the recipe for the biochips; building a new, improved hybrid car; tinkering to his heart's content. The problem with the tinker-ing, though, was that in the absence of all the equipment he'd had at his disposal in Blue River, it was the equivalent of a caveman rubbing sticks together to create fire.

But he wasn't here now to tinker. Kincaid grabbed on to the corner of the workbench, pulled it away from the wall. He dropped to his knees in front of the exposed wall, pressed his fingertips against it, and moved his hands to the left, slid-ing open a wall panel and exposing a spacious storage area where they kept their packs and supplies. His pack and Nora's had been in here for weeks now, equipped with every-thing they would need for their journey except the era cloth-ing. His were in a closet on the other side of the garage, hers in their bedroom closet. They would put them on before they transitioned. The clothing had been made by a seamstress in the Dominican Republic, according to the specifications Kincaid and Nora had given her.

They had agreed on the most basic of basics to take with them: antibiotics, essential toiletries, flashlights, extra biochips, a weapon each and extra clips, cell phones, in the event they were separated upon returning, one set apiece of era cloth-ing. Even though Curtis had cautioned against taking their own clothes, Kincaid and Nora had packed a pair of jeans, a couple of pairs of wool socks, and a sweatshirt each. But they had argued about everything else. And in the end, their selections reflected their individuality. Kincaid needed gad-gets; Nora wanted certain foods. He was an information junkie; she was more tactile.

Initially, he had intended to take his laptop, an ultrathin

notebook that weighed less than three pounds. But Nora had reminded him of how cumbersome their laptops had been in 1968, so he had settled on his PDA, modified to a one-gig memory, large enough to hold just about anything he could possibly need on this transition. He also had chosen: an iPod with five hundred songs on it, a travel-size first-aid kit; a digital camera; a small, lightweight pot to cook in; several nylon tarps; and some Orikasa camp ware—flat sheets of food-grade polypropylene that weighed almost nothing and could be folded into shape.

Nora's pack held freeze-dried food for emergencies, extra batteries for the flashlights, her Pocket PC, water, several photos of her mother with her and Tyler, a reading light, a book, other female stuff. Their impulse, of course, was to pack everything they could think of from their own time that might prove useful more than three centuries back. But the reality was that they could comfortably carry between twenty and twenty-five pounds apiece, and even those parameters were pushing it. A pack that weighed between twelve or fifteen pounds was more realistic.

Since backpacks didn't exist in 1695, they had been forced to improvise. Their bags were nylon covered in lightweight fabric; had multiple zippered inner compartments, like their clothes; and were designed based on drawings from historical documents of the sort of bags that were used in 1695. But the bottom line was that no one really knew what a bag had looked like in that time, that era, that town, that outpost of utter darkness, ignorance, and brutality. History that far back, at least where the colonies were concerned, was founded mostly on speculation. So they had relied on their research—through the Internet's archives, costume stores, and various university history departments.

"Hey, Kincaid."

He glanced around. Nora stood in the doorway, the light framing her tall, slender body. Her breasts pressed against her white tank top; her black hair, still damp from the

shower, was combed back from her face; and her gym shorts
rode high on her long legs. Months ago, she had started running with him, usually on the beach, and her thighs and
calves were now taut, muscular. She clutched a coffee mug
in one hand and held a biscuit in the other. Just the sight of
her stirred something so visceral in Kincaid, something so
inexplicable, that he wanted to rush over to her, gather her in
his arms, and consume her whole.

"Hey, yourself, McKee. How'd you sleep? I heard you get
up a couple of times."

"I've had better nights. You?"

"Okay."

"Let's have breakfast and then fuss with all that stuff."

"What time do you want to leave?" Like they were going
on vacation.

"When we're ready," she said, then turned and went back
into the kitchen.

When we're ready: it had a Zen simplicity that appealed
to him. But then, when you could move through time with
the ease of a knife cutting through butter, the Zen of the moment had a whole new meaning.

He joined her in the kitchen, where she nibbled at fruit,
poured milk onto her cereal. "Alex, remember that book we
both loved, *The Man Who Turned into Himself*?"

As a former librarian at Blue River College, he not only
remembered the book, but had ordered two dozen copies for
the library. The story about dual realities: he knew where
this conversation was headed. "Sure. Why?"

"What's your memory of last night's events?"

He speared a slice of juicy mango, all smooth and plump
and gold. He had read somewhere that mangos were the perfect food, that you could subsist on them for years. He
popped the slice into his mouth, the taste so satisfying and
obscenely sweet that he could endure anything. Even Nora's
question about memory. "I've got two sets of memories," he
began and explained the truth as he saw it. She listened with-

out interrupting and the fact that her smile grew was a positive sign.

"I inadvertently ended up in a replay, Alex, and somehow prevented Ryan from being hurt."

Riddle solved. But he had a million questions about how she'd done it, what had happened. She said she didn't know *how*, but her description of what had happened was so vivid that he could imagine it.

"That means Ryan and Kat may want to join us in this transition," she went on. "How do you feel about that?"

"I don't want them there."

"Me neither." She sat forward, her dark eyes intense, focused, pinning him like a butterfly to a slide. "This is *our* transition."

"Hey, I'm grateful for their training and expertise and all that," he said, referring to Curtis and Kat. "But let's not forget how well we did in 1968 without any training. Without them. Without any idea of what was actually happening."

"You don't have to convince me." She pushed away from the table. "I need to get dressed. Be right back."

"Wait a sec, McKee. Hold on."

"What?" she asked impatiently.

"Do you think the others have two sets of memories?"

"Probably. But so what? They'll figure it out. Just like we have."

She strode off and he mopped up his plate with the last of his biscuit and returned to the garage. Sunny trotted in, Frisbee trapped between her teeth, tail wagging. Ever hopeful, this dog. She knew something was up and was asking that she be included, please. Hello?

Kincaid wanted Sunny's company on this trip. She could smell and sense what they could not and had been bouncing around in time longer than any of them. If only she could talk. If only she could tell him what it had been like when Mariah Jones had first chipped her back in the seventies, how she had escaped the lab, and what she had done in the years until

Nora had found her in the woods outside Northampton, in 2006. If only. But in all his research, he hadn't found a single reference to golden retrievers in 1695 and thought her presence might draw too much attention to them. "You're going to sit this one out, girl, but we'll be back before you know it."

The Frisbee dropped from her mouth, and she cocked her head to the side and began to howl, the single most pitiful and mournful sound he'd ever heard. It went on for so long that he finally pressed his hands to his ears and muttered, "Okay, Christ, I get it." But what did he really get? That the dog understood what he was saying? That the dog wasn't really a dog at all, but a human consciousness trapped in a dog's body? "Have a treat." He tossed her a treat from a bag of canine goodies on the workbench, and Sunny became just a dog then, hurrying off with the doggy treasure clenched between her teeth.

Kincaid went over to the closet, removed each item of clothing from its hanger: a linen shirt, wool breeches fastened with a hook and eye, stockings made of tailored cloth, boots. He hated the clothes. They were uncomfortable, restrictive, and despite the cool air that was pouring through the AC vents, they were hot. He pitied the men of the seventeenth century.

As he worked the boots onto his feet, Nora hurried in, her skirts rustling, and snickered. "You look like a Pilgrim in drag."

She said this as she stood there in a long skirt stitched at the waist to a bodice that flattened her breasts into nonexistence. The women in the seventeenth century had it worse than the men, he thought. "You should talk. You look like you walked out of *The Handmaid's Tale.*"

He stood, his toes screaming inside the boots, and brought out their wool cloaks. He flung his around his shoulders and suddenly wondered what he was supposed to do with his hair. He had let it grow these past few months, along with his beard and mustache, but his hair wasn't long enough to pull back into a ponytail and even if it was, what would he secure it with? Rubber bands didn't come into existence until 1845.

He pulled his hair back behind his ears and tugged a felt hat down low over his forehead. "How's this look?" he asked.

She cracked up. "Ridiculous. I think I prefer clothes from the sixties."

"Where's your coif?"

She wrinkled her nose with distaste and opened her hand, revealing the white linen cap that would cover her hair. It was made to accommodate a hair bun, but Nora apparently wasn't going to put her hair in any bun. She stuffed the coif in an inner pocket of the cloak. "I don't think I can wear these clothes more than hour, Alex. They make me feel like I'm living under the Taliban."

"With any luck, we won't have to wear them long."

He crooked a finger at her and she came over and stood beside him, in front of the mirror. Even in clothes from another era, they looked good together, and in a crowd of seventeenth-century people, they could pass for a pair of commoners. Except that Nora, who stood six feet in her bare feet, probably was taller than most women in the seventeenth century. And if anyone from that era examined their clothes closely, the person would find items that hadn't been invented yet: buttons; zippers; Velcro that held inner pockets together.

"I think we're about ready," he announced.

"Let me send Tyler a text message."

"Why? He knows the particulars. He's not even awake yet."

"Just so he knows." She walked away from him, across the garage.

Kincaid frowned, finding it strange that she would do this. In fact, now that he thought about it, he wondered about Nora's replay, if something else had happened that she wasn't mentioning. He watched her in the mirror as she squatted down and pawed through her bag. "Something happened after we went to bed last night. Something other than the replay. What was it?" he asked.

"What?" She glanced up, stood, hoisted her bag with a kind of Mary Poppins determination. "What're you talking about?"

"I don't know. It happened to you, not me."

"What happened to me, Alex, was that I found out I'm going to be an aunt and did a replay, which I've never done before, and it altered Ryan's injury. That's why we're about to transition to 1695 before the others get up."

"Something other than that."

She rolled her eyes; sat beside him on the garage floor, her bag in her lap; and grasped his hand. "Please, let's go find my mother, okay?"

He noticed that she neither confirmed nor denied it. Kincaid took her hand and they were quiet for a moment, preparing themselves, getting into their *zone*. He felt his own rising anticipation and excitement, that quickening of his senses, that telling hunger for the *experience*, whatever it would be. Already his throat tightened, his heart drummed, and his body had slammed into the groove called addiction. *The state of being enslaved to a habit or practice or to something that is psychologically or physically habit forming, as narcotics, to such an extent that its cessation causes severe trauma.* That definition had come from Webster's and fit all of the Travelers. Time travel was their narcotic.

Finally, he murmured, "Blue River, Massachusetts. January sixth, 1695."

Suddenly, he heard Sunny barking on the other side of the door that led into the house, Sunny, who knew what they were doing, that they were about to transition without her. The door opened wide and Curtis stood there in his boxer shorts and a T-shirt, frowning with suspicion. Sunny shot past him, racing into the garage, and straight toward Nora. The dog leaped up, her paws struck Nora in the chest, and then the chip took all of them and everything vanished—the garage, Curtis, the safety of their own time.

Nora, Kincaid, and Sunny emerged in a blinding snowstorm, the wind howling, the light the color of old bread. The shock of it—the abrupt change from tropical heat to biting cold, from the garage of their place in Aruba to a complete whiteout in the middle of nowhere—brought Nora to her knees. She sank into the snow. Since she was still clutching Kincaid's hand, he went down with her.

In front of them, no more than a foot away, Sunny struggled to her feet, shaking the snow from her fur. She weaved toward them, licked their faces as if to apologize for shoving her way into the transition, then lifted her snout into the air and snapped at the falling snow.

Kincaid stumbled to his feet, pulled Nora up, and shouted over the roar of the wind. "Let's find shelter!"

Nora gestured wildly at Sunny, who was on the move and seemed to know where she was going. They lurched through the storm, she and Kincaid, their boots sinking into the snow, the stuff sticking to their lashes, their cloaks. Every time she thought she'd lost sight of Sunny, the dog raced back toward them, barking furiously, urging them to hurry.

Sunny led them into a dense thicket of pines where the trees grew so closely together they were forced to crawl beneath the branches. When they reached a small clearing, they crashed from exhaustion. Nora struggled to catch her breath, grateful that the surrounding trees formed an effective barrier against the worst of the wind and snow. But where were they?

In her research of weather in Blue River in the first three months of 1695, she'd found reference to only one blizzard. But that was in February. The storm had lasted three days and had delayed the beginning of the investigation into the witchcraft allegations because the magistrate from Boston hadn't been able to get to the town. Did that mean they had overshot their target and were in February 1695? Or that the facts she'd found were wrong?

She blew into her hands to warm them, then dug into her heavy clothing and brought out the digital watch piece. She rubbed the face of it with her thumb and felt a kind of sinking despair. "Alex, it's February ninth, 1695. Local mean time is three-fifty. You want to go back and try again?"

"How could we be so off target?" He raked his fingers through his snow-covered hair and stabbed a thumb toward Sunny. "She complicates things." He brought out his gloves and worked them onto his hands. Sunny moved closer to them, but didn't huddle for warmth. Her thick coat did that for her. "It means that your mother's been here for weeks already, Nora, that she's integrated into the life here."

Or she's dead, Nora thought but didn't say.

"I think our chances of finding her are better if we go back closer to the date she was disappeared," Kincaid said. "Let's return to our time first and drop off the d-o-g."

A plan, any plan, was preferable to staying here. They positioned themselves, touching each other and the dog to make sure they transitioned together, and Nora *reached* for Aruba, their home in Santa Cruz, the garage, *reached and released*. Nothing happened. Alarmed, she and Kincaid looked at each other.

"Maybe we should just reach for the day after she was disappeared, Nora, January seventh, and forget the detour."

And, again, they *reached* and *released*, the way Curtis and Kat had taught them, and again nothing happened. Nothing. Her alarm bit deeper. "Why isn't it working?"

"I don't know," he said. "Let's try another date, anything. January eighteenth, same year." But again, it didn't work.

"Jesus, Alex, are we *stuck* here?"

"Right now we are. Look, it's going to be dark soon. We

should set up some sort of shelter. We can try again in the morning. Maybe we just need to sleep on it. Or maybe we ended up in February because January is closed to us for some reason. I don't know. Let's look for a place to camp."

"To camp," she repeated. Hey, great. They had brought a PDA and an iPod, but no blankets; a digital camera, cell phones, flashlights, and extra biochips, but no tent. And they couldn't get home. Wonderful planning. "We really didn't think things through, Alex."

"Let's find a spot that isn't so open."

They started walking beneath the canopy of the trees, Sunny leading the way. Now and then the wind whistled under and between the trees, blowing snow that had begun to drift at the base of the trunks. The air smelled of dampness, pine, and elements so raw and alien that Nora felt as if they had landed in the middle of *Stranger in a Strange Land*.

They crossed a frozen river and followed it as it curved and widened. On her right, the trees thickened, dense shadows pooling beneath them. They finally stopped where fallen trees formed a barrier at their backs and the towering, leaning pines on either side of them provided shelter from the snow.

It was nearly dark now. They turned on their only solar-powered flashlight and one that was battery powered and pawed through the branches on the ground looking for wood that was dry enough for a fire. Slim pickings. But they dragged or carried what they found to a central spot not far from the banks of the river. While Kincaid arranged the wood, Nora and the dog navigated the shallow slope that ended at the edge of the frozen river. She slammed the heel of her boot against the ice, breaking it open. Sunny lapped at the cold, fresh water. Nora removed two empty plastic bottles from her pack, filled them to the brim. She tilted one to her mouth. It was the best water she had ever tasted.

The air was black as ink and the beam of the flashlight seemed no brighter than a firefly. She and the dog made their way back toward Kincaid, who had managed to get a fire started, but the flames were small, anemic looking, flickering and hissing as they met damp wood.

"Here, drink some." She passed him the bottle. "It'll boost your spirits."

"Thanks." He sipped, and his eyes widened. "Fantastic. Can you fan the fire for a minute? I know how to get this sucker going."

He pulled his pack closer, dug around inside, and brought out a small can of lighter fluid. "Not an item we agreed on. But, oh well." He popped off the top and squirted the stuff over the logs.

Flames burst from the pile of wood and burned hot, fast. Kincaid added dry twigs and a couple of smaller branches to the fire while Nora kept fanning the flames with her hands. As the wood began to burn in earnest, Kincaid reached into his pack again and brought out two nylon tarps and some cords. "More stuff we didn't agree on. Ultralight nylon tarps. One is eight by ten, the other six by nine. Total weight is just a shade over a pound. Not bad, huh?"

"Contraband. Thank God. How do we make a shelter with them?"

He gestured at the closest trees on either side of them. "We secure the largest one to the trees, pitch it low and tight, so we've got protection on three sides, and use the smaller one as the floor. I'll need a couple of those long branches we found and some rocks."

Within fifteen minutes, they had shelter—crude, snug, but effective and spacious enough for the three of them. It was close enough to the fire so they wouldn't freeze to death during the night. Their wool cloaks were large and heavy and they probably could use one of them to pad the tarp that served as the floor and the other for covering themselves, Nora thought.

They huddled in the mouth of the makeshift tent and Nora brought out some of her emergency food supplies. She hadn't taken a third mouth into account when she had packed, but there was enough to go around. She opened two vacuum-sealed packets of tuna fish, divided the fish three ways, and put a serving on each of the three Orikasa plates that Kincaid unfolded. She put some water and freeze-dried clam chowder in a very small pot and heated it over the fire, then used one of the plastic spoons to scoop the soup into a pair of Orikasa bowls. She polished off half of her bowl and gave the rest to Sunny. Hardly fine dining, but everything tasted indescribably good.

Afterward, they burned the wrappers in the fire and went down to the hole in the river again. They filled a lightweight canteen, rinsed the camp ware, then collected more wood, which they set by the fire so the heat would dry the damper branches. By six p.m. they were done and she immediately wondered what time the sun would rise. Five? Six?

Not soon enough. The darkness loomed around her, around them, and pressed up against their fire as though it intended to swallow it. A kind of atavistic need for light and warmth rose up inside her, as if she were a cavewoman at the dawn of time who had just discovered that fire would light and heat her cave, cook her meat, and keep wild animals away.

Kincaid spread out the smaller tarp very close to the fire, so they could all sit on it, Sunny wedged between them for warmth. Their cloaks were large enough to cover most of the dog's back and although she stretched out, her ears twitched, listening, and now and then she raised her head, listening harder. Nora heard only the crackling of the fire and the wind whistling and shaking the trees.

They were both uncharacteristically silent and she sensed that Kincaid's restless mind was eating away at the problem with the chips, trying to solve it. In the early days of their relationship, before she had met Jake McKee, much less married him, she had been intimately familiar with Kincaid's silences. He was working on his hybrid car then, trying to solve some of the design and fuel issues. But she had taken his silences personally and had believed that she was somehow at fault.

"Ryan talks a lot about how the chip calculates thousands of probabilities to find the one that best suits a Traveler's purpose," Kincaid said finally. "And that sometimes when you don't make your target, you have to trust that the chip brought you to the right place and time."

He, like Berlin, made the chip sound as though it were a living thing, she thought. "And?"

"What do we know about Blue River in February 1695?"

"That it was a long and miserable month in which the hysteria around the alleged witches and their pending trial had reached a fever pitch. And there was a blizzard. As a result of the storm, the magistrate from Boston and his clerk couldn't make it to Blue River until later that month. That delayed the investigation into the witchcraft allegations against the three women."

"Do we have dates on all this?"

"Uh, yeah, on the PDA. Why?"

"I've got a theory." He sounded excited and quickly brought out his PDA and turned it on.

The weirdness of the whole thing—that they were sitting in a woods in the late seventeenth century poring over files on a PDA—made her laugh. Kincaid glanced over at her, and in the soft glow of the light from the PDA, she saw the mythic face of the man she had fallen in love with years ago, the first time she had set eyes on him in the Blue River College library. Now he grinned at her, acknowledging the weirdness of the situation, and that grin spoke to her. *Yeah, it's weird. But we'll figure it out. We always do.* Kincaid, her coconspirator.

"Listen to this, Nora." He began to read: "Magistrate Goodwin and his clerk were supposed to arrive in Blue River on February fifth, to begin their investigation. But four days earlier, Boston was hit by a blizzard and then the system moved south and east to Blue River. By the time the storm had moved on, the temperatures had plummeted and every town in the Massachusetts Bay Colony was cut off from its neighbors. Travel was impossible. Magistrate Goodwin didn't arrive in Blue River until February twelfth. The first hanging happened a week later, on the nineteenth." He paused and glanced up at her, grinning. "That explains it. Why the chip chose this probability. It's brilliant."

She obviously was missing something. "Explain, okay? I don't get it."

"*We're* the magistrate and the clerk. We've got *identities*. And as the law of the land, we'll have more access to what we need than we ever would have on our own."

It was brilliant, all right, and it spooked her. Once again, it hinted at the chip's underlying intelligence that Berlin had spoken of so eloquently. It also meant that by tomorrow morning, they would have two days to find her mother before the real magistrate and clerk arrived from Boston. She said as much and added, "You'll have to be Goodwin. I doubt there were any female magistrates or female clerks."

"You're not only my clerk, but my wife. You record what's said when I interview the witnesses. And Sunny goes where we go. Who's going to deny a magistrate and his clerk and wife their dog?"

Sunny suddenly growled, and at first, Nora thought it was because she understood they were talking about her. But when Sunny got up, body hunched, ready to spring, teeth bared, Nora realized she heard something threatening. She and Kincaid acted quickly—stashed away the PDA and camp ware, got their weapons out. Then they grabbed their bags, Kincaid snatched up the tarp they'd been sitting on, and they moved back into the makeshift tent with Sunny.

Moments later, she heard what the dog had heard, the pounding of hooves, echoing through the woods.

6
Berlin

Time is nature's way to keep everything from happening at once.
—*John Wheeler*

Nellysford, Virginia

On the morning of April 17, 2006, Russ Berlin was steeped in the smell of Pine-Sol and Clorox. The odor drifted upward with the spiral of steam that rose from the mop bucket. Back and forth the mop went, across the length of the common room, a rhythm so mindless that his thoughts were free to travel. But his thoughts, those bastards, stayed in the real world, tallying up his bills and checking them against the balance in his bank account.

Not a pretty picture. Contrary to what he had led Nora McKee to believe, he was not a rich man. He wouldn't even qualify as middle class. In fact, he was running on empty. He supplemented his janitorial salary by teaching private yoga classes, but he didn't make enough to save anything. Most of the money he had saved from his years with SPOT—blood money, that was how he thought of it—had paid for his bungalow a mile up the road, a used car, and had sustained him for his first six months here. He still had a CD for fifty grand in the Isles Bank on Cedar Key but didn't dare go anywhere near there yet. Even though SPOT had collapsed, their now abandoned facility was under investigation by the FBI and IRS. He suspected the accounts of every SPOT employee had been impounded.

Of course, he could resort to theft—bank theft in which he stole from one time and brought the money to his own time. The perfect crime. But it violated everything he believed in.

What had happened to the twenty mil that Senator Joe Aiken had paid for him and his wife to become the first time travel tourists? And to the five million that Mariah Jones had demanded from Senators Aiken and Lazier in return for a thousand syringes? And where had Mariah hidden those syringes?

She had disappeared in the chaos at the biker bar north of Cedar Key on the night SPOT had collapsed. He was fairly sure that she was dead, that she finally had reached the end of one of her timelines. Did that mean she had died on all her timelines? He didn't know, yet at some level, it wouldn't surprise him if she suddenly showed up. But unless she did, the location of those thousand syringes would remain a mystery.

And whenever he ran into *that* wall, he invariably felt an urge to see a movie, a real movie in a real theater, on the timeline of his birth. Every now and then, he transitioned to L.A. or Kansas City or Anchorage or Honolulu in late 2006 or early 2007, bought a newspaper, found a movie that sounded good, and headed to the nearest theater. His last excursion had been a month ago, when he went to Seattle in December 2006 to see *The Fountain*.

For ninety minutes, the hallucinogenic visuals had swallowed him and not once had he thought of SPOT, Mariah, the chips. But when he'd left the theater, he'd been so disoriented, so totally out of it, that he'd had to ease himself back into the world. Coffee at Starbucks. A stroll through a bookstore. At an Internet café, he had Googled himself, a reality check, and found only two references, on conspiracy sites, about his role in the collapse of SPOT. He practically had been erased from his own timeline. He hadn't gone to a movie since then.

His cell suddenly belted out a song from *Fame,* announcing the arrival of a text message. He set the mop in the bucket and stepped outside, where the air was clear, cool, fresh, and the cell reception better. He navigated to his message box and picked up the newest text message. It was from Nora McKee, dated March 15, 2007, at 8:37 A.M.:

> Doc, in about 5 minutes, Alex & I will transition to January 6, 1695, Blue River, to find my mother. Ryan, Kat, my brother, Tyler, and his wife, Diana, are living @ 174 6th Street, Santa Cruz, Aruba.
>
> The events at Waverunner that precipitated our flight—and my replay—happened around 3:30 AM on 3/15/07. Even though we supposedly can't transition to the future, 2007 isn't really that for you because your natal timeline is the same as mine. Besides, you went back to the spring of 2006 to hide. So, the way I see it, you shouldn't have any trouble coming forward to what is actually *your* timeline. What a joke, *me* explaining to *you* how it works.
>
> Perhaps if you transition to the time of the raid, you'll be able to see the people responsible and will recognize them. Then again, I can't blame you if you don't want to get involved. I'll be in touch.
>
> Nora

He read the text message several times, snapped the cell shut, pressed it to his forehead. He didn't want to get involved. Couldn't afford to get involved. *Been there, done that, no thanks.* And yet, by virtue of his relationship with Mariah, with SPOT, with the whole stinking mess of his life since that training course here at the institute in 1982, he was involved *already.* He was chipped. He was slowly creating

more chips. He was the gatekeeper. And if SPOT was struggling to resurrect itself, to enter its next incarnation—which
was what it sounded like—he couldn't allow that to happen.

Berlin walked quickly along the side of the building,
headed for the parking lot. His gut told him that Wade was
behind this. But Wade and who else? For the kind of raid
that Nora had described, a government agency would have to
be involved. Senator Rick Lazier? Possibly. But who was
pulling Lazier's strings? A foreign government? Someone
higher up in the U.S. government? How high?

What about Aiken junior? Had he even been convicted
yet? Or had he, like other cronies in the shadow government
that possessed the technology for so many years, already
been provided with a new identity and sent off somewhere to
live out the rest of his life?

And that was the true horror of it, that men vested with
such power, vast amounts of money, and unchecked freedom
had done pretty much what they wanted to do for thirty years
and gotten away with it. Just what had he thought he was
going to do here at the institute, as a janitor? Hide out indef-
initely? Mop floors and chase dust bunnies for the rest of his
life? Ever since he had fled here, he had known at some level
that he eventually would have to confront the consequences
of his participation in SPOT, a monster he had helped to
create and sustain.

He reached his old Subaru and ran his hands over the
hood, remembering the day he had bought it from a guy in
Batesville. Four years old, 63,000 miles on it, a dark blue,
with leather seats and a GPS, a roomy trunk and a speaker
system to die for. He slipped behind the wheel and adjusted
the small fox magnet on the dashboard, a tribute to Robert
Monroe's last wife, who had considered the fox her totem.
Now it was his lucky charm.

Berlin drove fast, up the hill and away from the institute,
the tires kicking up dust and pebbles. He passed the home of
a famous writer, a famous publisher, a famous literary agent,

a famous psychic spy, a famous astrologer. It seemed that everyone who lived on or near Roberts Mountain and the institute was renowned in his or her particular field. *Russ Berlin, time traveler, gatekeeper.* He said it aloud and exploded with laughter. It sounded ludicrous. But even more ridiculous was that it was true.

He knew that a certain legend had grown up around him since SPOT's collapse and that it wasn't particularly flattering. He was pegged as the man who had sided with Mariah by sabotaging the biochips—not to bring down the collapse of SPOT, but for profit. He didn't have any illusions about correcting the legend. Yet, in his basement was a floor freezer that held fifteen new biochips, nestled in their beds of cold blue luminous gel, inside syringes. He could make them, yes, but finding the ingredients had become an exercise in discretion and cost him more money than he made right now. And so the production had stopped.

But these biochips, he knew, were as pure and powerful as the ones that Ryan Curtis had taken from Mariah's freezer in 1968.

In 1968, on his natal timeline, Berlin was thirteen, a hormonal teen leading a mindless existence in Fairfax, Virginia, and time travel was as distant from his life as Earth was from Jupiter. As the only child of an attorney and a physician, he'd had more freedom than his friends yet was closer to his parents than any of his friends were to their parents. He led a life of privilege, but what was expected of him in return had been, at times, almost too much to bear. He had redefined type A behavior through his middle and high school years. His parents wanted him to attend Harvard or Yale; instead, he had won a full scholarship to Johns Hopkins for college, then went on to medical school, and had specialized in pediatric oncology.

In the last year of his residency, leukemia had killed his four-year-old son. For weeks and months afterward, Berlin sleepwalked through his daily life, struggling to hold on to his job, his marriage, his sanity. A few months into his new career specialty, he unraveled completely during a consultation about another boy with leukemia, acknowledged that he could no longer function, and quit his practice. He had sought answers in the unconventional, the unproven, the strange, the mysterious, and had ended up at the Monroe Institute. He had hung on to his marriage for a few months after that, but in the end, the chip had won. And now here he was, many years later.

Berlin drove through a tunnel of green, where the trees on either side of the road rallied with new growth, and turned in to his driveway half a mile later. His acre was heavily wooded and gave him enough privacy to come and go as he pleased. He pulled up under his favorite oak tree, got out of the car, and hurried along the stone walkway. He paused briefly in front of the small, ceramic Buddha, now surrounded by spring flowers, bowed his head slightly, and brought his palms together in an attitude of prayer. "Namaste, my little friend," he murmured, then continued on.

He owned the bungalow free and clear, fifteen hundred square feet with hardwood floors, a fantastic back porch that overlooked the woods, a sunroom filled with plants, two bedrooms, and a full basement. When he had bought it, the place had been a sorry sight, run down and neglected, the land overgrown. He was still restoring it, a work in progress, like his own life.

Berlin rarely locked the front door, but always locked the door to the basement. That was where he went first, down a flight of stairs to what looked like a game room—a TV, a pool table, bookcases, a guitar, two comfortable couches, even a fireplace. He pressed his fingertips to the fake panel wall on the far side of the room, slid it to the side, and entered his workshop, the place where he lived his real life.

Even the cool air here smelled different, rarified, of cinnamon and lime from unlit candles that Lea had given him. He swept past the floor freezer that held the last remnants of biogenetic material that he used in the chips, the fifteen chips that he had created and the half dozen he held in reserve. In the event of a power outage, a propane generator would kick in, keeping the inside of the freezer at exactly the right temperature to preserve the contents.

Berlin threw open the closet doors and grabbed his worn backpack from an upper shelf. He had used it on countless transitions with Mariah and, later on, by himself. It had multiple inner pockets, including one that was insulated and would hold dry ice and two extra syringes. He tossed it on the nearest chair and studied the wall shelves that held folded T-shirts and sweaters, shoes, yoga pants, jeans, shorts.

Aruba. What the hell did he know about Aruba? Hot. A tourist destination. Dutch origins.

Okay, jeans, T-shirt, Reeboks. The jeans would be too hot for Aruba, but they would add weight to his pack, just like the Reeboks. Best to wear both, leaving a weight allowance for other things. Besides, he learned early on that sandals could come off during transitions. Yoga pants: they were lightweight and would double as pajamas, just in case he had to stay a night. A change of clothes. Toiletries. And for cold weather?

Not this trip, he thought. If he interfered in Blue River 1695, it would be on a separate trip. This transition would be exploratory, nothing more. Besides, he could comfortably carry about twenty-five pounds in his pack. Thirty if he was in terrific shape—which he wasn't.

Money. Well, he was pretty short in that department. A hundred in twenties would have to do. Passport? He didn't have one.

Weapons: a stun gun and the Glock model 26, a palm-sized weapon that weighed 21.75 ounces. It had eleven rounds of 9-millimeter parabellum bullets and wasn't encumbered by any safety latches. The safety features were built in; the gun wouldn't fire unless you pulled the trigger. *Draw, aim, fire:* simple and clean.

Laptop: did he need it? He didn't know. But since wireless Internet was a plus and he vaguely recalled that the island of Aruba was well wired, he decided to bring his PDA. Cell: yes. It went into the pocket of his jeans. He set the pack on the scale. Once he added the dry ice and a couple of syringes, it would be at about ten pounds. Perfect for a quick trip.

Done? His gaze slowly scanned the closet. Nothing leaped out at him, nothing shouted, *Take me, you need me.*

Berlin shut the closet doors and hurried out into the game room, closing the panel behind him. As he went up the stairs and turned off the lights, his excitement deepened. Already, he could sense the chip gearing up, responding to his intentions, calculating probabilities, preparing itself—and him. It had taken him years to understand that the chip not only calculated probabilities but triggered the secretion of certain hormones and neurotransmitters that helped prepare the body for the transition.

During his last several years at SPOT, he often took blood samples from Travelers before and after they transitioned. He'd found that the most dramatic increase was in serotonin, a hormone produced in the pineal gland that controlled appetite, mood, memory and learning, body temperature, and muscle contractions, and regulates the endocrine system. It was also a neurotransmitter, a chemical that allows communication between nerve cells. Since Mariah initially had developed the chip to cure insomnia, and serotonin helped regulate sleep patterns, this made perfect sense to him.

And it was the effects of the serotonin he felt as he settled down next to the ceramic Buddha in the front yard, a pleasurable buzz; a flowing, Zen-like peace; a certainty that all was fine in his world. He had felt like this during one of his many transitions back to the point *before* his son was diagnosed, when he was sure he could change the outcome of his son's illness.

I could do it now. Change everything. Go back to before

he was diagnosed and . . . What? Bring him forward? Would he be able to do that? And if he could, what sort of timeline would he create? Would his son survive longer? Or would some terrible event end his life at the age of four, just as the leukemia had? Was your date of death written in your genes?

He didn't have answers to any of it.

Berlin shut his eyes, aware of the birdsongs that drifted through the pleasant spring air, the rustling of branches as the slight breeze skipped through the nearby trees. He adjusted his legs into a lotus position, rested his wrists against his thighs, palms turned upward, thumbs and forefingers touching, completing a circuit of energy, and altered his breathing. He was so deep inside himself that he didn't hear the car that turned into his driveway or the whisper of footsteps across the grass until it was too late.

"Russ?"

Lea Cuthoney stood there, yoga bag slung over her shoulder. She wore sandals, black yoga pants, and a pale blue shirt with NAMASTE written across it in deep green.

"Lea."

"Are we going to have a yoga class out here? That'd be fantastic. The weather's perfect."

Yoga class, yoga class. Christ. Her class was today, right now. He struggled to pull himself back from this blissful state he was in, so that he could speak, but all he could muster was, "Uh, well, sure. . ."

He pushed to his feet, swayed unsteadily, and nearly fell over. Lea caught his arm and he grabbed on to her shoulder and suddenly felt as if his head had been filled with Silly Putty. His vision glazed over, his ears popped, and then his yard, the Buddha, Lea's car, the sweet songs of the birds, the trees bursting with spring—all of it vanished.

His next breath tasted of everything alien to the hills around Nellysford: the tropics, salt, ocean, heat. It was dark, windy, and he was on his hands and knees, fingers sinking into warm sand, the inside of his mouth desert dry. Berlin rocked back onto his heels and glanced around quickly. He was in the midst of odd, crooked trees illuminated by a nearby sodium vapor light. Lea was a couple yards away, sprawled on her side, clutching her yoga bag to her body like a child with her teddy bear, her sandals gone. Her bare feet twitched.

"Christ," he hissed, then hurried toward her. Even if she was marginally conscious, he could transition her back to the moments before they had left. Then he wouldn't have to explain anything to her. But when he reached her, she already was completely conscious, raising her head.

"You okay?" he asked anxiously.

"I . . . I feel like I got hit by . . ." She looked around slowly, her expression shifting from surprise to shock to outright incredulity. She rubbed her hands against her thighs and dropped her head back, peering up at the crooked tree that sheltered them. "Ooookaaay." The word slid out with her breath, then her index finger popped up. "Divi-divi trees. They always lean in the direction the trade winds blow. Trade winds mean the Caribbean. Somewhere in the Caribbean. The ABC islands. Aruba, Bonaire, Curacao."

She turned her eyes on him and burst out laughing. It was the oddest reaction Berlin had ever seen to a transition. But then, Lea wasn't just his yoga student. She was a trainer at the institute who guided her charges through ten days of rigorous explorations into the unknown.

"So are we out of body? That's it, isn't it? We're at the institute practicing OBEs, and we agreed to meet somewhere while we're out. It's the only thing that makes sense." She paused, stared at him. When he didn't say anything, she rushed on. "Talk to me, Russ."

"I . . ." He didn't know where to start, what to say. *Eliminate the obvious.* But what was obvious? "We're not out of body. What was the date and time when you stopped at my place for your yoga class?"

"Around noon, April seventeenth, 2006, the day after Easter."

He slipped out his cell phone, glanced at the time. The chip embedded in it had done its job. It read: 5:37 A.M., March 15, 2007. "Take a look at this."

"Two thousand and *seven*?" Her smile faded like last summer's tan.

Fuck, oh fuck. What could he say to her? What could he tell her other than the truth? The truth wouldn't set either of them free, but she needed to hear it.

"I didn't mean to bring you here, Lea. I apologize. But I was about to transition when you showed up, and when you grabbed my arm to keep me from falling, it just . . . happened." Like she would understand any of that, he thought, and instantly regretted saying it.

"Transition. 2007. Aruba." She paused, frowning, then leaned toward him and whispered, *"Time travel?"*

He nodded. It shocked him that she didn't shoot to her feet and race off into the dark shrieking. Once again, he attributed this to her years at the institute dealing daily with issues that consensus reality considered to be weird, inexplicable, nonsensical. To her, time travel was probably just another level of high strangeness, the internal made manifest, perhaps the next step in her evolutionary path. And so he gave her the sixty-second summary: SPOT and its collapse, Mariah Jones, the biochip, disappearances, Travelers, Nora McKee and her group.

"The same Nora whom I met?" she asked.

"Yes."

She nodded, then glanced around quickly, patting the ground around her. "What happened to my sandals?"

"They're, uh, floating around in time somewhere."

"Floating around in . . ." She laughed. "Instead of space debris, we have time debris." She shook her head, unzipped her yoga bag, and brought out a pair of soft, black flats and slipped them onto her feet. "I'll take your word for it."

Then they were up, moving quickly through the trees, ducking to avoid the low-hanging branches. She fired questions at him, not about the history of SPOT—she didn't seem to have any problem accepting any of that—but about why he was here, now. He told her about Wade and the other mercenaries like him, and what had happened to Nora and her group, and then the trees ended and they stopped.

A delivery alley stood between them and a sprawling resort—the Hilton. It was lit up like some historic landmark. The parking lot looked full, but there weren't many people out and about, not at this hour. "Now what?" Lea asked.

"I don't know. The chip brought us to this location for a reason, though, so let's head toward the hotel."

"I look kind of conspicuous carrying a yoga bag."

"Stash it over there." He pointed at the trees to her right. "We can come back for it."

While she moved away from him to get rid of her yoga bag, he unzipped his pack and brought out the Glock. He hated everything about guns, but early on in his career with SPOT he had discovered that a weapon could tilt the odds in his favor. He tucked the gun under his shirt, and when Lea returned, they crossed the alley and started through the huge hotel parking lot.

"What prompted you to seek refuge at the institute?" Lea asked.

"I trained there in 1982—along with some of the people who became major players in SPOT."

"That doesn't answer my question."

He liked her bluntness. Even though she hadn't transitioned before, he supposed her work at the institute made her a kind of time traveler. He felt that he could speak to her as an equal. "The nature of the work done at the institute is positive. That energy helps to hide me."

"Energy." The word rolled off her tongue as though she was testing it. "You mean, like, power spots? Ley lines?"

"In a sense. But it's more grounded than that. Monroe developed his process through trial and error, mapping the geography of inner worlds, and then invited others to join him in that journey. That intent is positive and powerful, and I don't think it can be penetrated easily by people whose intentions are selfish, greedy, or evil."

"You're an idealist, Russ. Monroe never put a spiritual spin on his process, his teachings. What you get when you go through the program depends on what you're willing to experience, how far you're willing to venture into unexplored realms, and how much you're willing to unlearn and to release."

"Other people have put their experiences into spiritual contexts and that's what protects me."

"I doubt it," she said. "But I'm glad you think of it like that. Maybe your *belief* in that process is what protects you."

He looked at her in the odd brilliance of the sodium vapor lights—Lea, with her beautiful braid, her presence larger than the outdoors—and realized that *she* was his teacher right now, that *she* could probably call the shots better than he could. "Hey, am I going to be fired?" he asked.

And she laughed. "Only if you really piss—"

The shriek of tires eclipsed the rest of her sentence. A dark SUV swerved into the lot, engine roaring, and Berlin realized the driver didn't see them. He grabbed Lea's hand and leaped back onto the median. The SUV raced past them and veered into a parking space at the end of the row.

"Goddamn maniac," Berlin spat, then felt a slight vibration in his right ear and suddenly understood. "This way." They ducked back into the thick foliage and trees that filled the median.

"What?" Lea whispered.

"Just a hunch," he whispered back, and peered over a hedge of gardenias, watching the SUV.

Two men got out, lit by the yellowish glow of the parking lot lights. Berlin immediately recognized Wade's macho swagger, his thick neck, his buzz cut. A stud in his right ear glinted like a mirror reflecting sunlight. Diamond? Probably. He remembered Wade as a guy with a fondness for expensive things. Berlin had never seen the other man before: curly brown hair, a neatly cut beard, a trim six feet.

Everything about them screamed that they weren't getting along. The other man's body language signaled tenseness, contraction, a pulling into himself; Wade strode off ahead of him, swinging his arms with an apelike determination, as if he couldn't place distance between himself and his companion fast enough. His shirt flapped in the breeze and briefly flipped up in back, exposing a weapon.

Wade disappeared through the front door of the hotel and moments later, so did the other man. "Let me guess," Lea whispered. "Wade is macho man."

"Yes. I don't know who the other guy is."

"They didn't lock their car."

"I know." She was observant and had a finely honed penchant for details. He liked that. "Do me a favor. Wade has never seen you. Follow them into the hotel and find out what floor they go to. I'm going to search their car."

She hurried out from behind the bushes, then stopped, glanced back. "Just don't transition without me. I'd hate to get stuck in my own future."

"I'll be here."

As Lea hurried off, Berlin noted the time, just in case he had to return to this moment, and brought out his flashlight. It would be light in fifteen or twenty minutes and he wanted to be gone before then. He darted out of the foliage and made a beeline for the SUV, wondering if Wade and his companion were staying put for a while or were going into the casino for a last stab at the slots or the blackjack tables. Regardless, he had to assume they would return soon.

He opened the passenger door, slipped inside, quickly shut the door. He flipped the switch on the overhead light so it wouldn't come on again when he got out, then went to work. His search didn't take long. The rental papers were in the glove compartment: a three-day rental to Jeffrey Wade, whose local address was room 644 at the Radisson. Berlin filed that bit of information away for future reference.

The backseat held a few clothes, a bag of groceries. But under the front seat he found a small leather case that contained a laptop, one of the newest of the ultralight models, naturally. Only the best for Wade. Berlin turned it on and glanced back through the rear window. No sign of Lea or of Wade and his companion. Just a few more minutes, that was all he needed.

He got out his memory stick, slipped it into a USB port, and began clicking through files, e-mails, folders and subfolders, even the photos, scanning this and that, copying anything that looked promising. The complex picture that began to emerge troubled him, then angered him, then flat-out terrified him. He slapped the lid shut, put the laptop back into the case, zipped it shut. Why give the enemy an edge, any edge at all? He was taking this sucker with him and fuck Wade and Lazier and their schemes. And what had Lazier meant by the "extra insurance" mentioned in one of his e-mails that would make Eric Holcomb cooperate? And exactly who was this Holcomb? Why had they picked him to do their dirty work?

Well, part of that was easy. No one had seen him. He was new, fresh, an unknown entity.

He exited the SUV clutching the case, and there stood a hotel security guard. An armed guard. Tall. Surly. Not a local. And although he was smiling, the smile didn't reach his eyes.

Shit.

"Sir, is this your vehicle?"

"Yes. It's a rental. From Alamo. Why? Is there a problem?"

"You're staying here?"

"Room three fifty-six." How easily the lie rolled off his tongue.

"I'd like to see your license. And then the paperwork on the car."

"Certainly." Except that he didn't have a license. "It's in my wallet."

He tucked the computer under his arm, his mind racing, his mouth flashing dry, and reached into his back pocket for the stun gun. Then he transitioned back two minutes, creating a new timeline—small, yes, miniscule in the overall scheme of things, but new nonetheless. He emerged just behind the guard, zapped him with the stun gun, and caught him as he was falling.

Berlin set him carefully on the grass, where he writhed and drooled, twitched and trembled. He hated himself for resorting to this; the man was just doing his job. It was the equivalent of cheating. But he wasn't about to get arrested here.

He spun around and loped toward the hotel to get Lea, wanting only to beat feet before the guard came to and sounded the alarm. Lea appeared before he reached the doors, apparently realized something had happened, and broke into a run. As they raced back across the lot toward the field of trees, sirens shredded the air. Someone shouted, "There they go!"

"Shit," Berlin spat. "They must've had patrol cars on the grounds. Head for the trees."

"What happened?"

"I had to stun a guard." They ran across the road, ducked under the trees, and Lea swept up her yoga bag. As they moved more deeply into the shadows of the divi-divi trees, he said, "What'd you find out?"

"They're either staying in the penthouse or visiting someone who is. There's just one penthouse and the elevator they were on goes straight there. Wade and his pal wouldn't let me stay on the elevator."

Penthouse, private elevator, privacy. It sounded like Lazier, he thought. *Your tax dollars at work.*

The sirens closed in on them. Tires shrieked against pavement, blue lights flashed against the trees. They kept running. He couldn't transition yet. The precision required for a transition two minutes back was far more difficult than the transition that had brought him and Lea here. It had depleted him, left his energy scattered, and he desperately needed a few more minutes before he could even consider a transition.

He dropped into a crouch. Lea sank to her knees next to him. "Is there a problem?" she asked anxiously. "Can we get home?"

"I need a little more time. To recharge." Like an iPod or a cell phone. "It's been a while since I've done this." He talked fast, relating what had happened and what he had discovered on Wade's laptop. "They're out of biochips. Their plan is to force Nora and her group to turn over their supply."

"How?"

He quickly explained what he had pieced together from what he'd read. But at the back of his mind lingered that nagging question about the "insurance" Lazier mentioned to guarantee Holcomb's cooperation.

A kind of horror entered Lea's eyes and spread across her face, quickly, like a thick shadow cast as clouds race across the face of the moon. "Even if you go back to 1695, how can *you* stop this? You're just one guy."

"I'm the only one right now who *can* stop it. The technology is *my* responsibility. I know how to make the chips. I know more about them than anyone else on the planet. And I have enough chips to get everyone back."

"Do you have clothes for that era? Do you know how they talked back then? I mean, I know a little about history, and from what I recall about Salem—and that was only three years earlier—is that it was a small, closed society governed by superstition and hysteria. You're not going to be able to just stroll into town, Russ, without being noticed."

"I'll manage." After all, every town needed a doctor.

The sirens were nearly on top of them now, shrill, sharp, like the sound of fingernails drawn over a blackboard but amplified a thousand times. He gritted his teeth against it, pressed his fists to his thighs. Brakes screeched, doors clicked open, shouts rang out, dogs barked.

"Christ," he said. "They've brought out the dogs. C'mon."

They ran on through the trees, branches snapping back in their faces, clawing at their arms, snagging on their clothes. Berlin could hardly catch his breath, perspiration rolled down the sides of his face. He could see the end of the trees just ahead. Beyond that, what? Sidewalks? Open air? Neighborhoods? *Nowhere to hide, that's what.*

He ran faster, faster, Lea's hand clutched in his, and kept *reaching* for Nellysford, *reaching* and *releasing,* but nothing happened. He glanced back; a German shepherd tore away from the cops, leash slapping the ground as it closed in on them, its powerful jaws snapping at the air. It was perhaps eight yards behind them.

Then five yards.

Three.

Two.

"Do something!" Lea screamed.

The dog leaped.

Berlin's ears popped, the top of his head felt as though it were erupting, and then there was only the dog's howling, rising and falling in waves, echoing across time and space. They emerged in grass softer than silk near the Buddha in his front yard. His chest heaved, blood pounded in his ears, sweat sheathed his body. He could still hear the dog's fierce, frenetic barking and, certain that it had transitioned with them, rocked back fast onto his heels, prepared to defend himself.

But there was no dog, no darkness, no divi-divi trees, just Lea, sitting up now, both of them sucking in the sweetness of the Virginia mountain air.

7
Mike

*The newest version of the biochip is an
unexplored country.*

—Ryan Curtis

Aruba, 2007

Mike had a few privileges now—a TV, more privacy, no
restraints—and they hadn't drugged him since the day his
father had been here. He saw Ben only when he brought in
meals. A major plus.

The TV helped. He at least knew what day it was now—
March 17—and was fairly certain his father had been here
two days ago. But so what? He was still a prisoner. The door
to the room remained locked, there was no phone, and if he
shouted or pounded on the walls to attract attention, Ben
would gag him, restrain him, probably start drugging him
again.

He spent much of the day channel surfing, looking for international news. So far, he hadn't found anything about a
missing teenage boy from Palm Beach. Why not? *And how
the fuck did I get here, from point A to point B?* He had no
memory of that. None. His last memory of normal life was
the day his mother and stepfather had left for a cruise to the

South Pacific, and that was . . . when? What was the date? March seventh? Eighth? Ninth? He had said good-bye to them in the driveway as they were packing up the back of his stepfather's Hummer. They would be gone for three weeks. His mother wouldn't bother calling to check up on him, so no one but Ann knew that he was missing. Ann and the school.

But Ann might believe he was somewhere with his dad and the school didn't give a shit about anything except money. *Oh, Mike Holcomb is absent? He's probably traveling with his mother. Or visiting his father.*

Or perhaps Ben took care of the school angle. With a senator's resources, it wouldn't take much to tie up that kind of loose end. At what point would Ann begin to worry? When would she mention Mike's absence to her parents? To the cops?

Mike didn't know. He didn't know at which point anyone would be worried enough to contact the authorities. Then again, if the authorities were contacted, Lazier and his people might trace the report to Ann, which would jeopardize her.

Right now, he stood with his ear to the door, listening, straining to hear voices, movement, some sign of habitation. But there was only an eerie silence. He turned the knob, slowly, and pulled. Locked. What a surprise.

Mike hurried over to the long picture window and stood with his hands against the warm glass, peering down to the sunlit beach at the tiny women in colorful bikinis, even tinier children playing in the waves and sand. Dozens of colorful sails raced across the flat blue sea. Windsurfers.

From here, they resembled butterflies. Definitely an island in the Caribbean. Ann's father windsurfed, following the wind the way other men followed the stock market. "Blowing out of the east today. Twenty-five knots. I'll do the four-point-oh sail," he'd say. From him, Mike knew there were only a handful of prime windsurfing spots on the planet:

Maui, the Columbia River Gorge in Oregon, the island of Margarita, the Dominican Republic, Aruba. This place was not Hawaii or Oregon. The terrain was too flat and too arid. But it might be Margarita. Or the Dominican Republic. Or Aruba. All islands.

He backed away from the window, darted over to the bed, retrieved the screwdriver. A Phillips on one end, a flat head on the other. How convenient. He listened again at the door but heard nothing. Maybe, just maybe, they had left the penthouse. Maybe only he and Ben lived here and the senator had an adjoining suite or something. *Does it matter? Move fast. Now.*

The lock on this side of the door had been removed. But the handle was screwed in on both sides, so Mike started working fast with the Phillips. He felt like he was in the garage in the house in Key Largo working on his dad's Harley. An endless project, that Harley. During the years since his parents had gotten divorced, he and his father had worked on the bike, refurbishing it from the tires up. One of these days, it would be ready for the open road. He hoped the goddamn door didn't take as long to open as it was taking him and his dad to get the Harley in shape.

The first screw fell into the palm of his hand and he immediately went to work on the second one. In thirty seconds, it succumbed. He jerked on the handle, loosening it, but because its inner mechanism was connected to the handle on the other side, it was impossible to pull it out. Mike worked the flat edge between the door and the jamb and jiggled it back and forth, creating a deep groove in the wood. Pretty soon, he could dig the flat edge down into the wood and start working at the lock, trying to dig it out of the jamb.

Suddenly, the whole thing gave way and the door creaked open.

Mike stared into the large front room with the conference table where, two days ago, his father had sat. Where, two days ago, the senator and some asshole named Wade had talked about chips. Who was chipped and who was not. *Your son is our insurance policy that you do what we hired you to do,* Lazier had said to his father. Chips and 1695. But what did that mean? Who were the Travelers? What the hell had his father been hired to do?

His feet seemed to move of their own volition, taking him over to the table. He plucked an apple from a bowl of fruit and glanced toward the door to the right and then at the door directly in front of him.

An inner voice shouted at him to get out immediately. But leave and go where? To the police? He was an American in a foreign country who had no passport, ID, money, and didn't even know how he had gotten here. If he said he'd been kidnapped by a U.S. senator, no one would believe him. They would lock him up as a terrorist or something and fly him to some secret prison and that would be that.

He needed a phone. He needed to know what was going on, what it meant to be chipped or not chipped, why an American senator was involved in kidnapping, blackmail, and paying his father a fortune to do something.

To do what? What the hell is this really about?

He moved fast toward the door in front of him, senses alert, his body so tense that his muscles ached and cramped. Hand to the knob, he turned it. As the door opened, Mike sensed that he was about to uncover a secret so shocking that it would send him screaming back to the safety of his prison.

His heart slammed into overdrive, sweat erupted from his pores, and his body screamed to flee. But he moved slowly and cautiously into the second room, eyes pinned to the desk, where he saw a laptop, a few files, a stack of papers, and numerous cell phones. Each cell was a different model, color, shape, and all of them were plugged into a surge protector strip. Charging.

A dozen cells, he counted, all lined up like obedient soldiers. Mike grabbed the smallest one, checked for a signal, and quickly punched out a text message to Ann's cell:

Am being held in penthouse of a 15-story hotel probably on Aruba. Senator Rick Lazier involved. Weird shit. Can see windsurfers from window. No cops. Don't call my parents. Keep yr cell on. Luv, M

He pocketed the phone, opened the lid of the laptop. It was booted up already and connected to Wireless Aruba. The time and date appeared in the lower right-hand corner: 3/17/07, 2:19 P.M. He went into his Hotmail account, found a list of e-mails from Ann, clicked on the most recent one. He sent her the same message in an e-mail. Redundancy.

He clicked around quickly in the Word files, searching for anything that would tell him to take the laptop with him. And he found it, all right—files labeled *The Holcombs*, *Ann*, *Palm Beach Estate*, and a file with photos of the chip, how to store it, but no explanation of its function. When active, whatever that meant, it looked like a bloated tick or a pregnant spider; when spent, it resembled a deflated tick or a flattened spider. All equally hideous. He'd seen enough. He jerked the cord from the plug, slapped the lid shut, slipped the laptop inside its case, and slung the strap over his shoulder.

He swept up another cell from the lineup, yanked both cords out of the surge protector, then pulled open drawers and searched for money, a weapon, something other than the screwdriver that would give him an edge. In a bottom drawer of the desk, he found a money clip jammed with cash, along with a key chain with a remote control for a BMW. He jammed both in his pockets and ran over to the closet, hurled open the doors.

Shoes, he needed shoes. He grabbed a pair of expensive sandals, slipped them on, and tore into the front room, into the kitchen. He now knew what a chip looked like and if there were any in this penthouse, they would be in the freezer. But the freezer held only ice trays.

He raced for the front door, the laptop banging against his

right hip, the car keys clutched in his left hand, the screwdriver in his right. He dashed out of the room with his heart lodged in his throat, his chest on fire, and forced himself to move at a fast walk so that he wouldn't attract attention from the cleaning woman with her cart fifty feet ahead on the left. His eyes fastened on the EXIT sign at the end of the hall.

But just as he approached the bank of elevators, one of them opened and there stood Ben and the senator. Ben, decked out in a tank top and gym shorts, in all his body-building glory, rippling muscles damp with sweat. To his right stood Lazier, reading a newspaper. By the time Ben's eyes locked with Mike's, it was too late. The screwdriver had left Mike's hand.

The Phillips end sank into the soft tissue just under the senator's collarbone, and he shrieked like a stuck pig and lurched sideways, eyes wide with shock, blood already spreading across the front of his shirt, and slammed into Ben, knocking him down. Mike punched the DOWN button and tore up the hall, his long legs eating up the carpet, air exploding from his mouth. He paused long enough to break the glass case over the fire alarm, then jerked down on the old-fashioned lever.

An alarm screeched and pulsed, piercing his skull. Ceiling sprinklers whipped to life, twirling like ballerinas wired on speed, and spewed water everywhere. The lights in the hall went out, a safety light flashed on, and Mike burst through the EXIT door and flew down the stairs.

Before he had gone down five flights, hotel guests filled the stairwell, everyone fleeing the nonexistent fire. He was swept forward in this human tide and eventually the crowd spilled into the lobby, across the polished tile floors, and scrambled for the safety of the parking lot.

Mike raced outside, into the brutal heat, the relentless wind, his thumb pressing the alarm button on the key chain. He heard the Beemer's alarm off to his right and raced in that direction. Moments later, he was inside the car, his body sinking into the warm leather seat, his hands shaking so violently that he had trouble getting the key in the ignition.

And then he was pulling out onto the street as cop cars careened past him, sirens wailing, lights spinning. He had no idea where he was in relation to anything, so he hung a right and drove.

A fire engine roared past, then more cop cars. Blood pounded in his ears, adrenal gates slammed open, he jammed the accelerator to the floor. He passed hotels, gas stations, fields filled with misshapen trees. Then he hit a red light and braked, eyes darting from one road sign to the next. Every other car seemed to have a license plate that read: ARUBA: ONE HAPPY ISLAND.

How the fuck was he supposed to get off an island without a passport? Without any ID?

He would head inland. And then what? He didn't know, didn't have any idea. He opened the glove compartment and pulled out a car rental packet with an island map tucked inside. Okay, okay, he could read maps. He could do this, he had a great sense of direction. He flicked on the left blinker and when the light turned green, he hung a right and followed the signs for tourist attractions. A wild donkey farm, a butterfly paradise, towns with strange names.

And in his head, he saw the senator with the screwdriver sticking out of his upper chest, saw his father's face, pale and terrified, at the table in the penthouse. Sobs exploded from his mouth, tears flooded his eyes. He drove for miles through the hot light, hands clutching the steering wheel. Every few minutes, he anxiously checked the rearview mirror, the side mirror, making sure he wasn't being followed. He finally relaxed enough to take one hand off the wheel, to turn on the air conditioner, the radio. When his cell jingled, he swept it off the passenger seat, saw that he had a text message. *Don't read and drive, not here.*

Half a mile later, he pulled into a gas station and stopped at a pump. Killed the engine. Opened the text message.

From Ann. Images of her leaped into his head: Ann with her long legs, her preppy blond hair, a pale river that fell halfway down her back; Ann charming his father during that Thanksgiving weekend when all of this bullshit had started; Ann hooking a ten-pound fish when they had gone fishing in the Everglades. Ann, heiress to zero, the only genuine person he knew in the world of Palm Beach.

I knew it. I knew something was wrong. But this isn't just wrong, It's major. What do u want me 2 do?

He didn't know. He removed the laptop from the case and began clicking through the files in earnest now, hungry for information, insights, anything. He discovered photos of the Key Largo house, of his stepfather's estate; of himself, his dad, his mother, his stepfather; of himself and Ann at school, at a park, in his car embracing. He found files of his father's bank accounts, credit reports, mortgage payments, property tax payments, home owner's insurance payments, everything defaulted. And then in the next file, it had all been cancelled. His father's credit was stellar, he was an upstanding citizen, no problem, no problem at all.

Next file: an offshore account with a balance of $181,987,000.19, minus substantial amounts to Wade, Ben, and a list of other names, with his father's name down near the bottom, three payments for a total of one million. *For what?*

He clicked on a file called SPOT. As he read through it, fear turned his insides to a cold, sluggish mess, and then its tongue burrowed through him and he just sat there blinking hard, the inside of his mouth flashing dry. *Shit, shit, is this true? Some fucked-up secret government program that disappeared people into the past? Time travel?*

Mike turned off the laptop, slammed the lid shut, Ann's question bouncing around inside him. *What do u want me 2 do?*

Leave it to Ann to ask the only question that mattered. And he didn't have any answers. He didn't know what the hell she could do, a sixteen-year-old girl with no pull in any circles that might matter. He picked up his cell, thought a moment.

> Dunno. Just escaped hotel, stabbed a senator with a screwdriver, stole a car, headed inland. Def Aruba. It sounds nuts, but this involves some sort of gov't time travel program. My dad went back to 1695. Got a laptop, will get somewhere so I can send u files. Names to research: Alex Kincaid, Nora McKee. SPOT. Sen Rick Lazier. Let's keep it between us for now. Luv u, M

He slipped the cell in the pocket of his shorts, brought out the money clip, counted the bills. Nearly two thousand bucks. Fantastic. Enough to last until he could figure out what to do. He still wouldn't be able to buy a ticket off this island, not without a passport or some sort of ID, but he could survive with two grand. He *would* survive.

Mike got out of the car and went into the gas station. He felt exposed, conspicuous, obvious, his body stiff, aching. The inside of the building looked like any station in the Keys, with the usual gum and mints on a rack in front of the register, a wall of refrigerated items, and shelves of canned goods. He went for practical: bottled water, cans of ravioli and tuna fish, rolls, a can opener, soda, toothbrush and toothpaste, a small cooler and a bag of ice, fresh fruit. As an afterthought, he included a couple of T-shirts.

The cashier, a friendly guy with sagging jowls and hooded eyes, was perched on a stool, paging through an issue of *Playboy*. Behind him, a TV was on, tuned to CNN.

"You find everything, my friend?"

"Sure did," Mike replied and stared at the TV.

Wolf Blitzer was doing his usual shtick: the war on terror, D.C. politics, blah, blah, blah. But across the bottom of the screen were the words *Breaking News from Aruba,* and then, *Senator Rick Lazier's penthouse suite broken into, the senator assaulted, thief stole laptop, fire alarm set off . . .*

"We have breaking news from Aruba," Blitzer announced, and Mike dropped money on the counter.

The cashier handed him change and he rushed outside to the car. He drove in a kind of mindless state, passing small, impoverished villages, fields of nothingness, sun-parched tracts of land where only the weird trees grew, their twisted trunks and branches a strange testament to the twists and turns in his own life.

His cell jingled. An incoming text message. He ignored it and kept driving. Shadows now lengthened toward late afternoon and evening. He kept thinking about his dad, the years he'd spent in Key Largo living at the edge of an abyss, and trying to keep it from Mike. From everyone.

Mike found a shitty motel in Santa Cruz and checked in with cash, bought a two-day wireless card, and no one asked him for ID. The room had a tiny fridge, a dirty window, red curtains the consistency of gauze. He locked the door, put away the food, collapsed on the bed with his cell clutched in his hand, and shut his eyes. *Now what?*

He didn't know. He didn't know shit about anything.

His cell jingled again. He brought it up where he could see it. Another text message from Ann.

Am at yr place, let myself in w/key under doormat. Hate to admit it, but when I got yr first text, I thought you'd lost it. Now it's on CNN. They say the security cameras captured an image of the perp. Found intriguing info. Call me.

Mike set up the laptop, went online, and used the second phone to call Ann. She answered on the first ring, voice breathless, scared.

"A D.C. area code comes up," she said without preface. "Georgetown, I think. Are you okay?"

Okay in relation to what? Hysterical laughter bubbled up inside him. Yeah, you bet, he was okay, just fine, doing fucking great. Mike sat on the bed, the laptop resting on his thighs, the cell pressed to his ear. "I'm safe. But sooner or later they'll figure out which cells are missing from their arsenal. I'll get a prepaid cell or something. What'd you find out?"

She told him, delivering the information in a soft, measured voice. She was a geek who wrote code for Internet sites in her free time, so he knew that everything she said had been triple-checked, that it was more valid than he himself was at the moment. "Mike, you're so deep into shit you're not supposed to know about that our only recourse is to find the others."

"The Travelers?" he asked. "Is that what you're talking about?"

"Yes. It's like they're an urban legend or something."

"They exist," he said. "Look, I'm going to start sending you this stuff. Download everything onto my laptop there and take it with you when you go home. I don't know if it's safe for you to stay in the cottage for too long. When you get home, put all the files on memory sticks and hide the sticks."

"Okay, I'm walking into your bedroom. . . ."

As she got everything ready on her end, he started sending the files as attachments. "Are they coming through?"

"Yeah, they're coming. Are you sending them to my computer at home, too? Never mind. Of course you are. Mr. Redundancy, right?"

"Right." She knew him well. "Take my passport with you. It's in the top drawer of my dresser. I'll find a place where you can mail it to me."

"Should I show this stuff to my dad, Mike?"

"Not yet. Look, I don't want to stay on this cell. They may be triangulating the call or something. I . . . I love you, Ann."

Her voice sounded choked when she replied, "Please be careful. I've got a passport, you know. I can come down there and bring you yours."

"Not yet. We'll figure this out. I'm going to hang up, okay? We'll talk online. It's safer."

"Love you," she whispered, then disconnected.

A kind of despair seeped through him then. He went over to the window, eyes sweeping through the lot, through the late afternoon light. *Ditch the Beemer? Not yet. Better to switch the plates with another car out there. But wait until dark.*

Mike drew the curtains and backed away from the window, scared, uncertain, paranoid. He fell back onto the bed, into the faint scent of detergent, perfume, shampoo, the odors of whoever had slept here before him. He never had felt so alone.

PART TWO
AROUND THE BEND

*The great change in the river of time comes
when one rounds a particular bend to suddenly find the
river gone . . .*

—DAVID LOYE

8
The Village

Nature shows us only the tail of the lion. But I do not doubt that the lion belongs to it even though he cannot at once reveal himself because of his enormous size.

—Albert Einstein

The thundering hooves, the neighing, the bright torches that cast long, eerie shadows on the other side of the river, then a voice calling out, "Hello, this is James Cory of New York Food Supplies. We are bound for Blue River, but the storm has made travel impossible. Your fire looks inviting. May we join you?"

Nora was frantically patting the ground around the campfire searching for items from their own time. She found a flashlight, the empty lighter fluid can, a pack of matches, and stuffed everything into her bag. Sunny kept growling. Nora grabbed on to her collar and snapped on a leash, holding her back. A twenty-first-century leash, she thought, and hoped it would be invisible in the dark.

"Who the hell is James Cory?" Kincaid whispered. "Do we have anything on him?"

Nora scrolled urgently through her mental database of names from this time, but James and Cory were fairly common names in the colonies at the end of the seventeenth century. She came up pitifully short for specifics on a James Cory. "I can't think of anyone offhand. What should we do about the tarps?"

"Nothing. We brought them from Europe. Keep your gun handy. Come and warm yourselves," Kincaid called back to Cory. "I am Magistrate Alexander Goodwin from Boston, also bound for Blue River."

Nora slipped her weapon into an inner pocket in her cloak. Sunny had stopped growling and strained at the leash, and now sniffed wildly at the air. Nonetheless, Nora kept a tight grip on the leash with one hand, terrified that if the dog broke loose, one of these people would shoot her. If anyone asked about the leash, she would say that it, too, came from Europe. With her free hand, Nora added wood to the fire. On the far side of the river, the horses snorted and neighed.

"Our wagon is heavy," Cory called. "Is the river completely frozen?"

"Aye," Kincaid replied. "Except where it is shallow. Cross down that way." He pointed off to the left, well clear of where they had broken the ice to get drinking water.

Aye? If she had to speak in thee and thou and refer to the Almighty in every other sentence, then she was doomed. Done. Cooked.

Cory's group and its heavy, horse-drawn wagon came across the frozen river with all the subtlety of UFOs landing on the White House lawn.

The food supplier from New York was in the lead when they crossed, with the massive, cumbersome wagon behind him, and a man on either side of the wagon to keep it on the straight and narrow. They stopped well short of the fire and Cory dismounted, flicked his cloak back, and strode toward them, torch held high, his spine straight, his stance that of a warrior rather than a merchant.

"We are in your debt," Cory said.

He extended his hand and he and Kincaid shook. "This is my wife and clerk, Nora Goodwin," Kincaid said.

"A pleasure, ma'am." Cory's eyes darted from her and Kincaid to the dog, the tarp, the fire, a complete circuit that took in everything—every detail, every nuance.

"We do not have food that is hot," Nora said, then suddenly remembered a random fact that Kincaid had shared with her, that by 1688, coffee had replaced beer as the favorite breakfast beverage in New York. "But we have coffee." Never mind that it was Cuban coffee, a pound of Que Buen Café that had followed her from her Aruba life. "Unless you think it's too early."

"Coffee?" Cory held his hands up toward the fire, warming them. "That would be wonderful. It is never too early for coffee."

He was considerably shorter than she was, with collarlength hair that hung loose; a pouting mouth, and wide, beautiful eyes. In the light of the fire, he looked to be thirty-five, but she sensed that in full daylight, he would look ten years older.

Nora put their only pot on the fire, hoping the water inside would boil fast. "The dog. How beautiful she is," Cory remarked, crouching down. "Fur the color of fire. Extraordinary. I do not believe I have ever seen this kind of dog."

With good reason, Nora thought. The golden retriever wouldn't really make an impact until the nineteenth century in Scotland, as a retriever of waterfowl. "She is from Europe," Nora said, as though everything from Europe was somewhat mysterious, coveted, superior. "Her name is Sunny."

At the mention of her name, Sunny rolled onto her back and offered her belly for a scratch. Cory obliged her and Nora liked him for that. And she liked that his men were tending to the horses, sheltering them, feeding them, making sure they were taken care of before they tended to themselves.

"Your horses," Cory said, glancing around. "Where are they?"

"We were assaulted some time after the snow began to fall," Kincaid said. "It was nearly dark, we never saw the men closely. They forced us off our horses, then rode off into the storm with our horses and most of our supplies. We sought refuge here in the woods."

"You are not the first to be assaulted in these parts," Cory said. "There is something amiss in Blue River and with each journey we make here, the strangeness seems to widen."

"Do you think it is connected to witchcraft?" Nora asked.

He looked amused by her question. "I do not believe the witches are flying around through the darkness on brooms, ma'am, if that is what you mean. I am quite skeptical of the allegations against the four women in Blue River."

Four women? Historically, there were three women. She wondered what other inaccuracies they might discover.

"Then who might be behind these assaults?" Kincaid asked.

"The greedy or the desperate," Cory replied. "But some of the stories point to something monstrous, an invisible force or power that sweeps out of nowhere and overcomes anyone in the way."

It sounded like an urban legend to Nora, the seventeenth century's version of Bigfoot.

The water was boiling and Nora didn't dare use their Orisaka cups for the coffee. "Do you have something to drink from, Mr. Cory?" she asked.

"Certainly." He cupped his hands around his mouth and called, "Edward, Paul, could one of you bring something from which to drink? And fetch some food for breakfast. A very early breakfast. We should eat."

The other two men joined them at the fire and Cory made the introductions. Edward was his younger brother, several inches taller than Cory, broader through the shoulders. Paul Fry was black, sinewy, lean with muscle, and had the quietude of a man accustomed to observing. He produced three metal cups and Nora lined them up in front of her, placed a piece of cloth over the first cup, with a slight indentation in the middle, and spooned coffee into it. Then she poured the boiling water over it. Drip coffee, Cuban style. She repeated this for each cup, and when Cory asked why they weren't having coffee, too, Nora replied that their cups had been stolen.

Fry produced two more cups, a cooking pot, and proceeded to prepare breakfast. Edward Cory brought out some sort of flask and passed it around. Nora figured the customs in this era prohibited a woman from drinking, so she simply passed the flask on to Kincaid and sipped at her coffee.

"This coffee is excellent," Cory remarked.

Bet your ass. Eight bucks a pound at a local Aruban market. "I believe it comes from the Far East," Nora said.

"And your shelter?" Edward asked. "I have never seen anything like it. Is it also from the Far East?"

"We found it during our last trip to Europe," Kincaid said. "It is called nylon. Very effective against the wind."

And so it went, the Cory brothers observing, remarking, curious about everything, Nora or Kincaid spinning lies, speaking carefully without contractions. She had no idea if people in this time spoke without contractions, but so far she hadn't heard any of the men use them, so it apparently was a good thing to do. If anything, the men's speech seemed stilted with courtesy.

Fry remained silent, tending to the food in the pot, stirring, adding ingredients, stirring some more. "It smells delicious," Nora remarked. "What is it, Mr. Fry?"

He looked over at her, his large, dark eyes filled with such sadness that it tore at her.

"He cannot speak," Cory said. "His previous owner cut out his tongue because he refused to reveal where his wife and sons had gone."

Sweet Christ. "And he is now your slave?" Nora asked.

"Certainly not. He is a free man. Our partner. Our friend. And a magnificent cook."

Fry suddenly made some hand gestures and Cory read them, nodded. "He says you are taller than most men and wonders if this makes life difficult for you in any way."

His insight surprised her. Not once since the men had crossed the river had Nora stood upright; she had spent most of her time crouched in front of the fire. "My height is difficult for men who feel threatened by it," she replied.

Fry looked at her with astonishment, then threw his head back and laughed. He made some rapid hand signals and the Cory brothers smiled and nodded and sipped from the flask. Nora and Kincaid exchanged quick, surreptitious glances, clueless about the joke.

"Paul says you speak like his wife," Cory said finally. "She, too, is tall, white, and outspoken."

A black man's white wife. In this era. "His wife is in New York?"

"His wife is dead," Edward said, no longer laughing. "But Paul claims that he sees her, talks to her, that she lives on somewhere." He made a vague, rolling gesture with his hand. "That she is with us now. That she likes you."

Ghosts, spirits, the undead. Was she supposed to take this as a warning that she, too, might be killed for being a tall, white, and outspoken female?

Fry produced metal bowls and began dishing out the porridge. It steamed in the cold air, emitting a smell that made Nora's stomach growl. Yet, in the firelight, it looked like discolored southern grits. She dipped her spoon into the stuff— a metal spoon that Fry provided—and in that first taste identified kernels of corn, molasses, cheese, lumps of bread. She thought it might be the most singularly delicious food she ever had tasted. She liked that Fry dished out some of the porridge for Sunny, who lapped it up.

Afterward, everyone slept for a while, Cory and his men in the wagon, her, Kincaid, and Sunny under their tarp. When Nora woke, she was stiff and cold, and the men were up and moving about. The woods had lightened and their refuge grew in clarity. Pines, yes, and maples and oaks, but there were many trees in here that she didn't recognize, couldn't name. Had the nameless trees died off in the march of time toward the twenty-first century? The snow had drifted up so far against the trunks of the trees that sheltered them that it formed a barricade, a wall of white.

Her mouth tasted like the inside of a garbage disposal. She discreetly retrieved her toothbrush and toothpaste and a bottle of water, and she and Sunny made their way into the trees. The dog was on to a scent, but it seemed to Nora that Sunny was also giving her an excuse to run off into the woods and relieve her bladder. Her skeptical peers in the psychology department in her old life used to laugh at her for anthropomorphizing animals. But as she squatted in a woods more than three hundred years in the past, she had the last laugh. She knew she was right. Animals felt what humans did, just not in the same way. Sunny had shared her discomfort and given them both an excuse to get away from the others.

The wind whistled through the pines. She smelled the smoke of their fire in the air. Her urine steamed in the cold. Already, her body screamed to be free of the restrictive clothes she wore, but more than that, she wanted to get someplace warm. She and Sunny returned to the campfire, where Kincaid was making more coffee and asking how far it was to Blue River.

"With the snow, a journey of a few hours," Cory replied. "We can take you into town. You can sleep in the back of the wagon, if you are tired. I understand that the magistrate in Blue River who had the women put in the gaol died some time ago, some say because he was cursed by one of the accused. I presume you are going to be investigating this terrible business?"

Nora, now crouched next to the fire again, didn't recall this bit of background history. But it didn't surprise her that the death of the local magistrate was being blamed on a curse.

"We will conduct our own investigation," Kincaid said.

"We will speak to the women, to their accusers, to other people in town, and I will make my determination based on the evidence."

"Hysteria," Edward Cory remarked, as they began packing up. "I know three of the women well. They are good, compassionate people."

"Perhaps we should refrain from discussing this," James Cory said. "We are outsiders. The magistrate must conduct his investigation free of our opinions."

"I appreciate your opinions," Kincaid said.

Fry, who was cleaning up the dishes, made several rapid hand gestures and Cory nodded. "Paul says that Walter Chandler, the town reverend, was involved in the witchcraft trials in Salem. He and others, like Cotton Mather, were responsible for examining the accused men in Salem for the devil's marks and tested them for pain by running pins through the marks. Paul considers him to be a sadist."

A sadist with a fondness for young women. Very young women, Nora thought as she and Kincaid began packing up their belongings. In the life Nora had lived before Jake's arrest, the psychology courses she had taught at Blue River College included two advanced seminars on the witch trials in both Salem and Blue River. So she knew quite a bit about Cotton Mather and his father, Increase, who would one day become president of Harvard. Both of the Mathers were Puritan ministers who wrote extensively about witchcraft and were involved in the Salem trials. They, like Walter Chandler, a Bible-thumping Puritan of the worst kind, fueled the prevailing belief that the devil was alive and well and vigorously engaged in the corruption of souls and the destruction of the colonies.

After the debacle of Salem in 1692, Increase Mather apparently had an epiphany about some types of evidence used to accuse and convict witches. In 1693, he published *Cases of Conscience*, in which he expressed his concerns. But his son and Walter Chandler merely continued in the same vein.

In their worldview, proof of witchcraft included the usual signs: insensitivity to pain, devil's marks, a third teat through which the devil's animal minions nursed. *Indicia*—inferences—were also popular with Chandler and were usually sufficient to accuse someone of witchcraft. If a neighbor got sick after contact with the accused, if cows or other animals acted strangely when the individual was nearby, if Indians attacked with more frequency after the suspect moved to the town, if the town suffered famine, flood—it was all evidence. And *indicia* had been used to accuse the women in Blue River.

Dunking was another method that Chandler advocated. Tie up the accused and toss the person in the water. If the individual sank, he or she was innocent; if the person floated, then he or she had been rejected by nature and was in league with the devil. Chandler, like other witch-hunters, also relied on spectral evidence—where a witness claimed that an accused person's spirit or spectral shape suddenly appeared in a dream at the time the accused's physical body was at another location. Even though Increase Mather denounced this type of evidence after Salem, Nora knew that Chandler had continued to encourage it among witnesses in Blue River.

Historically, Chandler was infamous for his use of torture to extract confessions from the accused in Blue River. His favorite forms of torture were the use of thumbscrews and immersion of the hands and feet of the accused in boiling oil. He also seemed to relish the strappado, which consisted of a pulley and a rope. The hands of the accused were tied behind the person's back with rope, and then the device was attached to the rope and the person was pulled upward. Sometimes, weights were attached to the person's feet, which caused the shoulders to pop free of their sockets.

In her seminars, Nora had referred to Chandler as Blue River's grand inquisitor, a man who seemed to emulate Matthew Hopkins, a failed attorney and fellow Puritan who became one of the most brutal witch-hunters in England.

Between 1644 and 1646, Hopkins was supposedly responsible for the execution of more than two hundred witches, many of them tortured for their confessions. Chandler, though, never professed to be a professional witch-hunter. He simply masked his savage nature through a phony piety.

She always had taken her classes to the gaol—the old jail—now one of the town's several historical buildings. Behind it, the room where Chandler and his fellow sadists had conducted their tortures still stood, with the torture devices on grisly display. Back then, she never had imagined that she might one day see any of it as it actually had existed. But as they approached the edge of town in the back of the wagon, the snow still flying around them, it was one of the first buildings she recognized.

It stood somewhat isolated from the rest of the town, a wooden building with just two front windows and a brick chimney. Like many of the buildings from this era, the jail was covered with clapboards made of pine. Sixty years earlier, oak had been used extensively for the clapboards on buildings. But it tended to warp and pull free from whatever it was fastened to, so by 1695, oak was a rarity for clapboards.

Nora thought of the town as a thriving community of around eighty thousand people, including the college population. Now it had only several thousand people and consisted of a grid of a dozen streets, with the main commercial area stretching for maybe a mile along the center of town. General store. Apothecary. Church. Town hall. School. Gaol. Tavern. Inn. Slave quarters. Tailor, doctor, preacher, magistrate, chemist. All of it buried in snow.

Wherever she looked, smoke curled upward into the chilly, white morning air. The few people out and about were bundled up in cloaks and hats or huddled down in wagons that rolled from one end of the town to the other. The milky light slanted through the snow, transforming it into something magical, mythical. It also ate into her bones. The snow had been falling steadily since they had left the woods, and as it had melted, her wool cloak had absorbed the moisture, making it feel as if it weighed a hundred pounds. Kincaid looked to be as uncomfortable as she was, huddled in on himself, shuddering now and then. Sunny periodically shook the snow from her fur, but otherwise seemed more interested in the sights and smells.

The wagon pulled up to a grand, two-story building with a wide front porch now blanketed in snow. She recognized it as the Blue River Inn, another historic landmark in her own time. She and Kincaid, in the first incarnation of their relationship, had stayed at the completely refurbished inn one night, in a corner room on the first floor that supposedly had existed since the beginning.

She had lain awake most of that night, waiting for the departed and deceased from nearly three centuries of history to materialize. She had thought of Carl Jung in the castle he had built on the shores of Lake Zurich, watching a procession of monks in the mist and realizing they were ghosts. She had not seen any ghosts that night, but she had heard them, a weird rustling, laughter without a discernible source, the soft susurrus of murmuring voices.

Now here she was.

James Cory jumped down from the wagon, cloak flapping in the wind, shoulders hunched against the cold. He came around to the back, unhitched the door, and lowered it. "I will go inside with you. The proprietor is a friend."

"What about Sunny?" Nora asked.

"The magistrate's dog is welcome here, I am sure," Cory said.

"And where will you be staying, Mr. Cory?" Kincaid asked.

"Do not worry, my friend. We must unload the wagon at the general store. Then we will be in our rooms above the livery and at the tavern until the snow ends."

Nora and Sunny followed Kincaid and Cory into the building. Long before her eyes adjusted to the twilit room, the powerful smells nearly gagged her. Smoke, body odor, cooked meats, the faint stink of urine and spilled booze: it had all congealed in a single wave that crashed over her. Nora grappled blindly for something, anything, to hold on to, to steady herself, but grasped air and stumbled back. Suddenly, she felt a hand on her arm—Fry, it was Fry—and he took her bag in the other hand and led her over to a cane-back armchair. He made gestures intended to communicate something, but she didn't understand. He crouched in front of her and in the dust on the floor scribbled, *Stay here.*

A literate black man in 1695? That was about as rare as an honest politician in any time. But she was so grateful to be sitting that she merely nodded as he moved away. She glanced around for Sunny, realized the dog hadn't followed her into this room, and suddenly heard a man shouting, "Get that beast out of here!"

Nora stumbled to her feet. A short, plump man waddled quickly through the twilit room toward Sunny, swinging his cane like a farmer with a machete. Sunny, backed into a corner, bared her teeth, prepared to spring. Nora forgot where she was, how she was supposed to act. Red poured across her vision, her entire world shrank to the fat prick with the cane who intended to hit her dog.

And then she was running, screaming, waving her arms. But the prick was fixated on Sunny, his cane whistling through the air again and again. Seconds before she reached him, Fry slammed into the man, knocking him to the floor. He lost his grip on his cane and it rolled away from him, clattering. Nora swept it up and whirled around, only vaguely aware that everyone was staring, that the entire front room had gone still, silent.

The fat prick was pushing up to a sitting position, shaking his head as if to clear it, his wig askew, his pocked cheeks puffed out with anger and indignation. She swung the cane toward him, sank the end of it against his chest and leaned forward, so close to him that she inhaled the stink of his body. "Never go after that dog or any other animal in that way again. Do we understand each other?"

He tried to knock the cane away from his chest, but she pressed harder against it, forcing him back on his elbows, further humiliating him. He scrambled back on his butt until he was up against the wall and couldn't go any farther. Blood rushed up his neck and into his already ruddy cheeks. He blustered, "I am Reverend Walter Chandler and no wench speaks to me in that manner. Your slave . . . knocked . . . knocked me down and you . . . you are threatening me, and I will see to it that you are thrown into the gaol with the witches and . . ."

Once she heard his name, the rest of his tirade was swallowed up by the hammering of her own heart. *Chandler, fucker in the flesh.* Nora twisted the end of the cane, pinning him to the floor like a bug under glass, and whispered, "If people hear about your salacious interludes with some of the very young women in town, you will hang, Reverend." Then, more loudly, "Mr. Fry is a free man who was defending me." She dropped his cane, then turned away from him and went over to Sunny, still crouched in the corner, teeth bared.

But Chandler shouted, "I want this woman taken to the gaol and . . ."

"I am Magistrate Goodwin from Boston," Kincaid said loudly, and Nora turned around.

Kincaid strode over to Chandler, who peered up at him as if at a god, and got slowly to his feet. He started to speak, but Kincaid went on in the same loud, authoritative voice: "And the woman you referred to as a *wench*, sir, is my wife and clerk. And that dog that you intended to strike with your cane is *my* dog. If I were you, Reverend Chandler, I would apologize to the lady and be on your way."

"I . . . I will do no such thing. Women are not permitted to—"

"*Good day*," Kincaid snapped, then returned to Cory and the inn proprietor, both of them looking surprised—and amused.

Chandler, struggling to muster as much dignity as possible, headed for the door. But as he started past Nora and Sunny, the dog growled and Chandler cast a homicidal look their way. *You will pay for this*, those small, dark eyes seemed to promise.

Nora glared back at him. *And so will you.*

Then Chandler threw open the door, admitting a blast of cold air, and slammed it behind him.

9
Satan's Shadow

*Those who travel most easily in time are
prepared for the journey at every level.*
—Mariah Jones

Holcomb's eyes opened to the strange, gloomy shadows
that spilled down the colorless walls. An elephant-gray light
pressed up against the windows, revealing the snow that had
accumulated on the glass during the night. He shivered in
the endless, penetrating cold.

Trapped. Nothing had changed since he'd shut his eyes
last night. He was still trapped more than three centuries in the
past and couldn't get back to Mike. He had tried. And he
tried again now, *reaching* for Aruba, for his son, struggling to
draw the island's heat and wind around him, *reaching* for
the long, splendid beaches, the divi-divi trees, the paradoxi-
cal smells of desert and water.

He felt the chip straining like some worn-out plane trying
to reach takeoff speed, but nothing happened. He finally
threw off the heavy quilts, padded over to the chamber pot
on feet he couldn't feel, and relieved himself. Then he hurried into the front room and started a fire.

The water in the iron pot had frozen overnight, so he put

it over the flames and listened to the ice crackling and popping as it started to melt. He stood there rubbing his hands together, his mind a merciful blank.

By the time he had gone through his morning ablutions, such as they were in this miserable place, he had managed to shove the reality of his situation into the back of his mind and contain it. There, it would lie dormant until late tonight when it would rise, shrieking, from the ashes of his past, the detritus of his terrible choices.

He changed into clean clothes, pulled on his boots, swung his heavy cloak around his shoulders, and left his two rooms behind the apothecary. He trudged toward the tavern, moving up the middle of the road where the snow had been beaten down by horses and wagons. Huge drifts rose on either side of him, great white mythical beasts that appeared to be holding their collective breath. The snow kept falling and every so often a gust of wind hurled fistfuls of the stuff into his eyes. When he entered the tavern, he was so cold he thought his bones might shatter when he sat down.

He claimed his usual table, close to the fire, the absolute warmest spot in the room. He sat with his back to the window, to the blizzard, but the view from this side of the table depressed him nearly as much. A small, silent black kid turned the spits impaled with chickens, a pig. He probably had been here since two this morning; he looked lost, miserable, resigned to his fate. Beneath the roasting animals rested a skillet to catch the drippings. Even so, they often missed the skillet and caused the fire to hiss and sizzle and spit, and the smoke curled up into the kid's face, making his eyes water.

A skinny little cat skulked in the shadows under the empty tables, looking for stray bits of fallen food. It rubbed up against Holcomb's leg mewing pitifully. Definitely not Key Largo or Aruba in the twenty-first century. Yet, on the positive side, the aromas enticed him—warm bread, the sharp, tangy scent of that pie cooling next to the oven.

A serving woman brought him chicken and a stew made

of potatoes, beans, some sort of mystery meat, and freshly baked brown bread and drop cakes made with milk, eggs, and wheat flour. He asked her for an extra bowl for the cat and because she believed he was a VIP, she complied. Holcomb spooned some of the stew into the bowl and set it on the floor next to his chair. When the serving woman returned again, she had a thick ale, slices of cheese, and a dollop of butter, a real luxury. The food here was good, healthier than his diet at home, but every now and then he longed for a plump, greasy hamburger, fries loaded with trans fat. He was tempted to speak to the cooks, to coach them on how to make a burger, fries, a juicy egg sandwich. *Ever heard of Mickey D? Supersize me? Jesus God, give me grease.*

Since his arrival four weeks ago, his days began here at the crack of dawn and ended here after dark. Breakfast, like the other meals, had a certain routine. While he ate, he watched the cooks whipping up their mysterious meals of mush, conversed with the women who served the mush, and spent a lot of time drinking beer and bullshitting with the locals, founts of gossip and rumor. They believed that he was Ericson Ivers, a special emissary for the governor, William Stoughton, who had been in power since 1694. And because Stoughton had been chief justice at the Salem witch trials, people simply assumed that Holcomb was in Blue River to report on the accusations against the women charged with practicing witchcraft. He hadn't said anything to make them think otherwise.

The role provided an ideal cover, better than anything he could fabricate on his own. It also gave him carte blanche to visit the jail whenever he wanted and to speak to the townspeople about the accused. He had visited the jail and the accused only once, an experience so bleak and depressing that he hadn't gone back.

Sure enough, the owner of the general store and the jailer both stopped by his table before he was finished with breakfast. *Morning, Mr. Ivers. Any news about when a new magis-*

trate might arrive, sir? We are expecting a new shipment of supplies soon, sir. And behind them came the blacksmith, the owner of the inn, the teacher. Dawn was barely twenty minutes old and these people looked as if they'd been up for hours already. Four of the men were members of the town council, which was headed by Reverend Chandler, the tyrant who had been running Blue River for years. They all held the same opinion about the accused: guilty.

Holcomb was no expert on witchcraft in this era or any other. But he could recognize a pattern when he saw one, and the pattern here was obvious. Since the death of the town magistrate several months ago, Chandler and his council had become despots who ruled with impunity. Here in Blue River, at the tail end of the seventeenth century, a group of white men called the shots, using their interpretation of the Bible as the basis for their governance. It wasn't all that different from his own time.

Posted throughout town and inside most buildings, including the tavern, were Chandler's "Laws of Righteous Living." These "laws" were based on Chandler's interpretation of the Bible rather than on the Province Charter, which had been instituted in October 1691 and delineated the judicial and legislative systems of the colony. Holcomb could see the parchment from where he was sitting, nailed to a wooden post, written in fancy script:

1. *Thanksgiving day is the only day for feasting.*
2. *Breaking the Sabbath is punishable by lashes or punishment as deemed appropriate by the Town Council. No Man or Woman shall carry a burden on the Sabbath, shoot at wildfowl, fish, or bake on the Sabbath.*
3. *No Man or Woman shall condemn the Ministry or slander the Church or its Representatives.*
4. *No Man or Woman shall steal from another. Punishment is the stockades for a time deemed appropriate by the Council.*

5. Any Man or Woman accused of witchcraft shall be confined to the gaol and be examined for evidence of collusion with Satan. The examination shall be conducted by the Council and the Reverend. Only the Reverend, Council members, a magistrate and his clerk, an assistant, or a Representative of the governor shall be permitted inside the gaol.

6. Adultery, murder, and the practice of witchcraft are punishable by death.

7. Public drunkenness and slander are forbidden. Drinking on the Sabbath is forbidden. The Council will decide upon punishment.

8. Women shall be subservient to their Husbands, Father, Brothers, Uncles, and all other Men within their Families or face banishment from the community.

9. No Woman shall wear garments made with short sleeves or shorter in length than the ankle. No Woman shall wear lace. No Woman shall dress like a Man. No Man or Woman shall wear silver or gold.

10. Periwigs are forbidden, except when worn by the Council members.

11. Women shall tend to their homes and families and shall not be permitted to visit the gaol, attend school, or learn how to read or write.

12. In the absence of a magistrate, the law of the Council is supreme.

And on and on, a total of fifty laws on these postings throughout town and hundreds of others posted in the town hall and in the church. He just wanted to get the hell out of here.

Holcomb had targeted January 6, 1694, the same day that Nora McKee's mother supposedly had been disappeared to this black hole in history, but had overshot the target by two days. He had emerged behind the livery stable, wearing the only clothing he had that was specific to this era. No one had seen him. The first thing he'd done was find the general store and buy clothing with one of the gold coins that Wade had provided during his training. The coins were small—he had about a hundred of them—and so far he had spent only eight of them for his basic needs. As a result of the coins, most of the townspeople considered him to be a wealthy man and mistakenly equated wealth with clout, intelligence, wisdom. Word had gotten around that he was from Boston, which had started the rumor that he was acting as Stoughton's emissary.

Within two days of his arrival, he was practically crawling out of his skin and that had only gotten worse over time. He was worried sick about Mike and was desperate for information about him. He didn't think he could abide another second in this town, this era, among these close-minded, superstitious people. Despite his repeated attempts to transition, his chip seemed to be the equivalent of a flawed hard drive. It refused to boot up.

His life had revolved around one, horrifying thought: that he was trapped and couldn't get back to his son. He had struggled against a rising panic that Mike would be forever lost to him, that he would be killed or sold into some slavery market in Asia or shipped off to a secret prison in some far-flung corner of the world, never to be seen by anyone again. No telling what Lazier and his people might do.

Some nights he lay awake sorting through everything he had learned in his crash course with Wade about how the chip worked, searching for some stray fact that could get him home again. Other nights, he stared into the dark for hours, sifting through the terrible choices that had brought him to this point in time. He gained insight, but little else. And then there were the nights when waves of panic crashed over him and he paced and wept, paced and wept, and kept imagining that he heard Mike's voice, kept seeing his face during those terrible minutes in Lazier's hotel penthouse.

His only hope for getting out of here lay with Nora McKee and her group. They would be traveling with extra chips. Wade claimed that all Travelers carried extra chips. But so far, none of them had shown up, which brought Holcomb back full circle. How could Lazier say with any certainty that Nora and anyone in her group would transition to 1695? Just because her mother might have been dropped here?

It's logical, Lazier had said.

As though logic meant it was true.

He asked for another beer and a second bowl of the porridge and suddenly heard shouting in the main room.

"Get that beast out of here!"

He recognized Chandler's distinctive voice—quick, intense, fervent even when he mentioned the weather. For Chandler, all things were connected to God. Especially the weather.

This blizzard, for example, was punishment for the town's wanton ways, for the fact that the witches hadn't been hanged yet, for the corruption of women, God's way of saying He was really pissed off. In fact, Chandler's God was very Old Testament, the raging God of lightning bolts and Job, who reveled in the misfortunes of his followers, like a pig in shit.

Holcomb wondered what sort of "beast" had triggered Chandler's outburst. A cat? A hog? A chicken? A lamb or a goat? Unable to contain his curiosity, Holcomb pushed away from the table, swayed briefly, and realized that two beers for breakfast was two beers too many.

He made it to the doorway and stopped, gawking at the scene in the main room: Chandler on his ass, a dog with beautiful reddish gold fur cornered, teeth bared and ready to leap; a very tall woman whose face he couldn't see pinning Chandler to the floor with the tip of a cane; and a dozen bystanders who just stood there, aghast, but didn't seem to have any idea what to say, do, or how to act. It was as if he had stumbled into a theatrical rendition of a scene, but no one had given the actors any direction.

He experienced a weird buzzing in his left ear. He didn't have any idea what it meant, but it got louder as he stepped through the doorway and heard the reverend bellow, "I am Reverend Walter Chandler and no wench speaks to me in that manner. Your slave . . . knocked . . . knocked me down and you . . . you are threatening me, and I will see to it that you are thrown into the gaol with the witches and . . ."

The woman leaned down close to him and whispered something that Holcomb didn't hear. Then everything seemed to happen quickly, with another man stepping into the fray, announcing that he was the magistrate and the woman whom Chandler had called a wench was his wife. Chandler quickly fled through the front door of the inn.

Holcomb started to duck back into the tavern, where he could leave through its door and trot after Chandler to question him about what had happened. But something stopped him. *What?* His eyes swept through the room again. *The dog.* Mariah Jones supposedly had chipped a dog in her early animal experiments. The first and only dog. A golden retriever. And that dog, if Wade had been telling the truth, had been present during the final events in the biker bar that had rendered SPOT obsolete.

He looked more closely at the woman, at the man who called himself Magistrate Goodwin, and a wild, explosive surge of hope seized him. Nora McKee and Alex Kincaid. He hadn't recognized them in their era garb. They would get him home. They were his equivalent of the wizard in Oz. All he had to do was convince them that he was an ally. But suppose their chips were flawed, too? *You can get where you're going, but it's a one-way ticket.* Maybe all of them were stuck here. Forever.

His throat tightened and panic seized him in all its full-blown and hideous glory. Holcomb grabbed on to the doorjamb to keep himself from falling over and the vibration in his head increased in volume, intensity, frequency. He caught the look that Kincaid cast his way and suddenly wondered if the vibration was a kind of alert that another biochip was somewhere nearby. Perhaps it was Mariah's way of enabling Travelers in the same era to identify each other, an almost atavistic instinct that signaled "I'm like you," the equivalent of a cat or dog urinating to mark its territory.

Holcomb forced himself to move. He hurried over to his table and grabbed his cloak off the back of the chair, desperate to get out of here, into the cold, to clear his head. As he slipped outside, he saw Chandler just ahead, stumbling through the snow, his cloak flapping in the wind, snowflakes already gathering on his crooked wig. "Reverend," Holcomb called as he trotted to catch up with him. "I saw that spectacle in there."

"Ah, Mr. Ivers," the reverend said with a shake of his head. "What are we coming to when a woman is the magistrate's clerk and speaks to a man of God the way she did? And the free man . . . his behavior deserves at least thirty lashes. I am afraid that Satan's shadow falls ever more thickly across our town."

"Indeed." *Get him talking.* "And all in defense of a dog. Is it possible the animal is her familiar, sir?" *Why am I saying this kinda shit? What do I think I'm going to gain from collusion with this corrupt maniac?*

Chandler gave him a sly, knowing look. "I see that we think alike, sir. I hope that you will include this incident in your report to the governor."

The reverend's pocked face looked especially hideous in the snowy light— deep craters in his cheeks, eyes sunken to small, dark peas in their sockets, his prissy mouth twitching, twitching. "I fear that with the storm and all the snow we have had this winter, it will be spring before I can return to Boston with my report," Holcomb said. "And I am not so sure how effective this magistrate will be if his wife is consorting with Satan."

As soon as he uttered the words, he knew that if he thought about it long enough, he could rationalize what he was doing, could convince himself that he was pandering to Chandler so that he could manipulate him later on, use him, like any attorney worth his salt. But a wave of self-loathing crashed over him. He nearly gagged on it. *I'm just like him.*

No. No way. He wasn't anything like Chandler. He wasn't eaten up with this religious and superstitious bullshit, this pernicious need to control everything and everyone in his immediate environment. *Oh?* whispered the voice of his ex-wife. *Really? Then why have you attracted this, Eric? Why did you attract slime like Wade? Lazier? Chandler?*

And when Chandler looked at him, his eyes sly and scheming, the truth hit Holcomb. *We* are *the same, you and me. Separated by centuries, levels of education, background, but the same nonetheless, you slimy fucker.*

"Perhaps, Mr. Ivers, we can remedy the travesty. Would you care for a cup of hot tea?"

"That sounds most inviting, Reverend." *And you are going to . . . what? Just what the hell do you think you'll get from this? Information? Insight? A deal? Another Wade sort of deal?*

But Holcomb fell into step beside Chandler and two streets later, they entered the reverend's home, three simply furnished rooms with a fire in the fireplace and a wooden kitchen table with a basket of bread in the middle of it. "I will put on the water. Then we will go down into the cellar."

With a metal cup, Chandler scooped water from a basin and filled an iron pot that he placed over the fire. Holcomb's skin crawled. Was the water fresh? How long had it been sitting in the basin? Had the water been used for anything else, like washing? Even though Holcomb had been inoculated against a number of diseases when he had signed on to Wade's crusade, he came down with Montezuma's revenge a few days after his arrival, forcing him to seek help from the town physician. Dr. Webber had made Holcomb a sweet-tasting concoction that had cured him in a few hours. But he didn't relish a repeat.

Satisfied with his preparations, Chandler plucked a lantern off the shelf of a wooden cupboard, lit it with a stick from the fire, and gestured for Holcomb to follow him into another room, the bedroom. Like Holcomb's bedroom, it was basic. Quilts covered the straw bed, a chamber pot stood in a corner of the room, and a pitcher of water and a basin rested on a cupboard against the wall. In the sill of the very small window stood an unlit lantern.

Holcomb tried to ignore the dim stink of urine from the chamber pot. He didn't want to think about the disposal of body wastes in town. But suddenly, it was all that he could think about. Was everything dumped into the snow? Was feces buried? Did all this refuse seep into the ground, polluting the river after which the town was named? Did the drinking water come from Blue River?

Chandler swept a rug out of the way with the toe of his boot, revealing a crude trapdoor. He opened it, handed the lantern to Holcomb, and when he had gone down several steps on the ladder, Holcomb returned the lantern to him, knelt, and turned so he could climb down the ladder.

He had no great fondness for tight, dark, enclosed spaces. And right now, such spaces only reminded him of his own situation, trapped in the tight, dark, superstitions of the late seventeenth century.

And your mind, Eric? What kind of dark, enclosed space lurks inside it?

He gulped at the air. Moved. His right foot found the top step. The panic he somehow had managed to stifle in the tavern now shrieked and threw itself against a door in his mind and pounded its tight, powerful fists against it. He dropped his left foot to the top step. His hands turned slick with sweat, his muscles froze, and his body refused to descend any farther. *Shit, fuck.* "Uh, Reverend . . ." He rolled his lower lip against his teeth, unable to admit to Chandler that he was claustrophobic. He knew the reverend was the kind of man who would use it against him. *Just like I would do.*

Maybe it would be simpler to go to Nora and Kincaid, own up to why he was here, tell them what Wade and Lazier had hired him to do, then beg them for a chip so he could return to the twenty-first century to rescue his son.

But why should *they* help *him*? He had fired tear gas canisters into their apartments. And in one vaguely recalled version of events, he had enabled Wade to attack Curtis with a knife.

I'm not that man anymore.

He heard his ex laughing.

"Yes, Mr. Ivers?"

"Could you, uh, hold that lantern a little higher?"

"Of course."

But it seemed to take him a long time to do this and a different kind of panic welled inside Holcomb, the panic called *Holy shit I'm out of cigarettes and it's three o'clock in the morning.* Even though he hadn't smoked in years, that feeling was *right there*, in his face, and somehow analogous to not having sufficient light.

When he finally got down the ladder, he was a goddamn wreck, sweating, nervous, stomach twisted up in knots. The lantern created grotesque shadows against the walls, the low ceiling, the floor, out of which anything might emerge. He moved unsteadily away from the ladder, following Chandler to a wooden cupboard. The lantern hissed as Chandler set it down, the ambient light spilling over the sides, deepening the color of the wood.

Chandler opened one of the drawers and removed a box about two feet deep and half as wide. Beneath it was what looked like a bound book, smaller than the traditional Bibles found in every home. Holcomb wondered why Chandler hid the book down here and what kind of book it was.

The reverend removed the lid of the box. "These were found in the homes of the accused." He brought out six poppets, this era's version of voodoo dolls. Made of cloth, they were stuffed with hay or dry grass, had beans for eyes, human hair, and black cloth wrapped around their waists or shoulders, like sashes or cloaks. "This one"—he held up a doll with long black hair—"represents the woman whom Sarah Longwood cursed during an argument. She became ill and died four days later." He paused, his mouth twitching, and added, "That woman was my wife."

"I did not realize, Reverend. Please accept my condolences." Actually, he had heard the stories, the rumors, the gossip that the reverend's wife was prone to fits, that she frothed at the mouth, that she was cursed by one of the accused. Or had she cursed one of the accused? He wasn't sure anymore.

Chandler shrugged and set the poppet aside, dropping it quickly on the cupboard, as though the doll were hot. "This one"—he withdrew a poppet with white hair that resembled a wig—"was discovered in the possession of Catherine Griffin, who worked for Francis Travers, the gentleman who owns the general store . . ."

"Yes, I know Mr. Travers."

And yeah, Holcomb got it. Six poppets from the homes of the four women accused of practicing witchcraft. Maybe the poppets had been found where Chandler said they were, but he doubted it. He suspected that Chandler had planted them, and suddenly knew what Chandler was about to propose: that Holcomb should take one of these little voodoo shits and plant it in Nora McKee's room.

It wasn't so different, really, than the real estate deals that had unraveled Holcomb's life and branded him as an unethical prick in Dade legal circles. Free tickets to Fiji from a developer who hungered for zoning changes on a plum tract of farmland, an all-expenses-paid tour of the Galapagos to research man's impact on the environment from a group who didn't give a shit about the environment, and on and on. But there were levels to deceit. And even he couldn't justify *this* level, which would result in death by hanging.

So, hon, there's your bottom line. In his head, his ex laughed and laughed.

On the other hand, if Nora McKee's chip still worked,

then she probably would transition before she reached the jail. And if she couldn't transition, if her chip was as flawed as his own, then he would be able to bargain with Kincaid—her life in exchange for one of their extra biochips. No one would lose in that scenario. They would all get home. But that plan left a sour taste in his mouth.

"This is not enough to convict anyone, Reverend," Holcomb said.

"True." Chandler caressed the dark hair of the first poppet with his thumb. There was something obscene about it, about the care and obvious delight that he took in the caress. "But it's enough to accuse." He looked quickly at Holcomb, his weird, shifting eyes a blatant testament to his duplicity, greed, corruption.

Holcomb suddenly felt as if grease had been poured over his body, as if he were sleazy, gross, stinking of corruption.

"You are a witness to what happened at the tavern," Chandler rushed on in a quiet, quick voice, making his case. "And I will find spectral evidence and devil's marks upon her body. To rid Blue River of Satan's shadow, Mr. Ivers, we must be one step ahead of the devil." He pressed a poppet into Holcomb's hand and leaned toward him, the lantern's light throwing half of the reverend's face into shadow. His warm, fetid breath was the stink of hell itself, the hell of the senator's penthouse as he'd talked about "insurance," Mike seated across from him, Ben's gun jammed up against the base of his skull.

He didn't really remember what happened after that. He had a vague sense of physical speed, psychological haste, emotional darkness. And then he was outside, on his knees in the snow, slapping the white, wet stuff against his face, rubbing it frantically over his arms, his shirt, his cloak, struggling to rid himself of the stink of his own degradation.

10
Around Town

As the mind moves, so moves matter.
—*Dean Radin*

Kincaid and Nora followed the inn proprietor, Jacob Nash, up the cold, steep stairs to the second floor. He kept apologizing for Chandler's behavior, trying to explain. "His mind is not right, Magistrate. The evil in Blue River is poisoning his heart. Every animal he sees is a creature that Satan possesses."

"Our dog is not possessed by Satan or any other evil," Kincaid replied.

"Of course not, Magistrate. I did not mean to imply that he was."

"She," Nora said. "The dog is a she."

"Yes, ma'am," murmured Nash.

"And we appreciate your letting us keep her in the room," Kincaid added.

Nash favored his right knee and moved as though his bones were locked in a perpetual ache. His shoulders were hunched against the cold, against life, against the odds of surviving to the ripe old age of fifty. When he smiled, his rotting teeth screamed for a twenty-first-century dentist. Kincaid already hated this era.

"It is the least I can do, Magistrate. I am deeply grieved that James Cory witnessed what happened. He is a fine merchant, an honest, God-fearing man who done no one harm. Asks fair prices for what he sells. Makes that arduous trip from New York, bad weather or not, so that we here in Blue River have the food and supplies we need to survive the winter. Other merchants stopped making the trip soon after Sarah Longwood and Rebeka Short was accused. They was remembering Salem, three years past. It would be a dark day, indeed, if what Mr. Cory witnessed caused him to stop delivering to Blue River."

"Who was the first to be accused?" Kincaid asked, eager to hear history from anyone who was living it.

"Sarah. In October last, Reverend Chandler found a poppet in her bedroom and she cursed him and the magistrate. Then she cursed the reverend's wife, and not long after, the reverend's wife and the magistrate come down with a sickness and died. Then Indians attacked us, a herd of cows died . . ." He shook his head as if to say it was all mysterious and tragic. "One misfortune after another, sir."

"Tell us, Mr. Nash," said Nora. "Do you think these Indians have been attacking travelers outside of Blue River?"

"Perhaps. Or it may be the witches, Mrs. Goodwin. They are said to be capable of traveling in unusual ways. Or perhaps the witches seize others to do their bidding."

Yeah, right, Kincaid thought.

Nash was winded when they reached the top of the stairs and moved even more slowly toward the end of the dank, cold corridor. It was lit sporadically by torches where, in Kincaid's time, there were electric lights, Kincaid thought. When Nash stopped in front of a heavy wooden door, Kincaid, Nora, and Sunny stood behind him, watching as he unlocked it with a large key and pushed it open with the toe of his boot.

The room was spacious, with a large window that over-looked the street. Snow hissed against the glass. A fire already burned brightly in the fireplace, taking the chill off the air. Wood was stacked to one side, enough of it to get them through the next day. A lumpy straw bed covered in quilts was positioned close to the fireplace. The chamber pot in the far corner of the room reminded Kincaid of a toddler's training potty minus the seat. On a cabinet stood a pitcher of water, a basin for washing, folded cloths that he guessed were this era's version of towels, and a lit lantern. Sunny went right over to the fireplace and curled up on the thick rug in front of it.

"Do you find the room wanting, Magistrate?" asked Nash.

"It is very comfortable. Thank you." Kincaid didn't know whether tipping was normal in this era, but because they were getting the room for free, because Nash believed Kincaid was the magistrate, he handed the proprietor a gold coin. "We appreciate your hospitality, Mr. Nash."

His eyes nearly popped from their sockets. "Thank *you*, sir." He backed out of the room, pudgy fingers tightening over the coin, grin frozen in a rictus of delight, and shut the door.

Silence, settling through the room like a dream. Then the snow whispered against the glass again, addressing the tension between him and Nora. Her defense of Sunny had called unwanted attention to them, to their arrival in town, and the longer the issue remained unspoken, the larger it seemed. But Kincaid thought this issue had been dealt with way back when Sunny had become their companion, their eyes and ears through the unexplored continent of time travel.

"You did the right thing," he said, his voice soft, guarded as he tossed his bag on the bed.

"I put us at risk." She sank to the foot of the bed, set her bag on the floor at her feet, ran her hands over her face. "But Chandler's nuts."

"Yeah, he is." Kincaid crouched in front of the fireplace,

added more logs to the fire, and combed his fingers through Sunny's thick fur. "And if you hadn't intervened and he had struck Sunny with the cane, I would have broken his fucking neck."

Sunny raised her head at the mention of her name, licked the back of Kincaid's hand, and rolled onto her back.

"He's more despicable in person than he is in history."

He couldn't argue with that. "What would you like most to do with your mom when we retrieve her?"

She didn't hesitate. "Have a picnic. We were always going to drive up into the Berkshires for a picnic, but she and my dad were so busy, we never got around to it." She flopped back onto the straw bed, arm covering her eyes, hair a black river against the quilts. "Jesus, Kincaid. This whole thing suddenly seems impossible."

He dropped onto the bed, supported his head with one hand, and touched her arm with the other, moving it away from her eyes. "Nothing's impossible when we're a team. And right now, we're the law, you and me, and there isn't much he can do to us. So let's go over to the jail and pretend that we know what we're doing."

Sunny knew that word, *go,* and immediately heaved herself to her feet and, tail wagging, barked. Her eagerness to accompany them presented an immediate dilemma. Her presence anywhere in Blue River would draw attention. But they had made this journey together, the *tres amigos*, a time-traveling *Mod Squad,* and he understood enough about the chip to realize that there was a reason for this, that none of it was random. When the chip selected probabilities, it did so by factoring in the five Ws learned in elementary school: who, what, where, when, and why. Some doors were hurled open, others were slammed tight, sealed forever.

"Should she come?" Nora chewed nervously at the side of her thumbnail.

"Yes."

Firelight danced in Nora's eyes. "This is why I love you, Alex."

"Yeah? Why's that?"

"Because you're as nuts as I am."

Kincaid laughed. "Well, Nora, as my clerk, you need writing implements. Our first stop should be the general store."

She stabbed her thumb over her shoulder, indicating the parchment posted on the door. "I think number eleven forbids my writing anything."

He went over to the door and read through the "Laws of Righteous Living." "Fuck this shit." Kincaid yanked the poster off the back of the door.

"This is the era I used to teach and I don't recall ever hearing about anything like this. How many other details does history have wrong?"

"We're about to find out."

They freshened up, which in this time meant pouring gelid water into the basin and splashing it on their faces. They brushed their teeth, too, a real exercise in ingenuity—no sink, no running water. They had to rinse their mouths with water from the pitcher and spit into the chamber pot.

They removed their backup syringes from their packs. The cold weather had preserved them and now Kincaid hid them in the snow that had accumulated on the roof just outside their window. As long as the temperature stayed below freezing, the chips would remain in a dormant state.

Since Nash hadn't left the key to the room, they pocketed the smaller items from their own time and stashed the cookware in the straw of their bed. Everything else—extra clothes, shoes, their belongings—went into the cabinet.

In the lobby, Kincaid asked Nash if he had a wagon and horse to spare so that they could get to the gaol. Nash looked troubled by the request. His eyes darted nervously from Kincaid to Nora and then to the poster nailed on the wall. "Sir, the Laws of Righteous Living forbid women from visiting the gaol."

Yeah, the laws forbade women from doing just about anything. "And law five, Mr. Nash, permits the magistrate and his clerk to visit the gaol. Mrs. Goodwin is my clerk. And even if she were not my clerk, my position as magistrate supersedes any law that the reverend implements."

Nash smoothed his hands over his breeches, cleared his throat, gave a nod. "You are right, of course. I will have my wagon and horse brought out front."

"Thank you."

"You missed your calling, Kincaid," Nora whispered when Nash had left.

"As actor? CEO? Politician?"

"Bullshit artist," she said.

He grinned and tore one of Chandler's posters off the wall, balled it up, tossed it in the fireplace. "Whenever we see one of these, it comes down."

She whistled strains of the Beatles' "Revolution."

"Blue River needs a revolution. And as magistrate, I'm going to order that these posters be removed from every public place."

"Maybe we shouldn't interfere like this," she said. "You know, that *Star Trek* motto?"

"We're interfering just by being here."

The horse and open wagon drew up out front and they hurried outside, into the blowing snow. The driver helped Nora into the wagon, Kincaid lifted Sunny in, then climbed into the front with the driver. Kincaid asked the man to stop first at the general store.

The driver coaxed the horse forward, through the whistling wind, the blowing snow. Kincaid drew his cloak more tightly around him, trying to keep the snow from melting down the back of his neck. But it caught on his lashes, his brows, and dusted his hair. By the time the wagon drew up in front of the general store, he felt like a figure in a snow globe.

"Magistrate, the snow has such fierceness that I will wait in the livery," the driver said. "It has a fire."

"We will meet you there shortly," Kincaid replied, then helped Nora out of the back. Sunny, apparently believing she was going to be left behind, jumped out on her own and skidded through snowdrifts in front of the store. When Nora told her to stay just outside the door, she looked at them with those liquid amber eyes and barked as if to say, *Hey, this is unfair.* But she sat down, resigned to the wait.

The inside of the store was a far cry from the Whole Foods that would stand here in their own time. Yet, it carried a shocking array of goods. On their left were the foods: everything from baked breads, cheeses, and butter to fish straight from the river, flanks of beef hanging from heavy hooks, whole chickens—both plucked and unplucked—hanging by their bound feet, a slab of what looked like pork, potatoes, flour and sugar, cornmeal, cider. No fruits and vegetables, but plenty of honey, raisins, vinegar, and dried herbs.

In front of them and to the right was everything else, items arranged on tiny shelves in the long, narrow aisles: all sorts of tools, door knockers, both pewter and wooden plates and bowls, wash basins and soaps, candles, glass bottles, clothing and straw baskets, tobacco and pipes, a variety of guns, axes and hatchets, pottery, powders, linens.

They each picked out a change of clothes. Kincaid also selected a hat, two knives, a pistol, and Nora found a pair of boots. They got a slice of fresh beef for Sunny, which the butcher wrapped in a clean cloth, and some fresh rolls. They put all these items in a straw basket they'd picked up from one of the stacks at the front of the store.

They made their way to the very back, where they found parchment, quills made of goose feathers, tiny glass bottles of ink, and books, mostly Bibles, but also religious material by Cotton and Increase Mather. Nora picked up several quills, examined them, frowned.

"What do we know about quills?" Nora whispered.

"That they don't last long. Grab three or four." He knew that goose feathers were the most common quills and that the strongest were taken from live birds in the spring. The five outer left wing feathers were preferred because they curved outward and away from the hand when used by a right-handed person. "We can always come back for more."

"And ink? Will one bottle be enough?"

"Beats me."

"What's this stuff made from anyway?" She held the jar up to the light. "It looks like juice."

"Probably blackberry juice."

"Mixed with something to thicken it, though. Salt? Some sort of plant resin?"

"That sounds right."

She looked over at him. "You think they'll notice if I use my own pen?"

"Yes."

She put the bottle of ink and quills into the basket. "It's going to take hours to write a single word with this stuff."

"Time is one thing we've got plenty of."

She snickered and then he started laughing and they moved quickly up the aisle, struggling to muffle their laughter. Kincaid glanced around surreptitiously, but no one paid any attention to them. At the front of the store, Kincaid spotted two of Chandler's posters—one nailed to a shelf filled with tools, the other nailed to the opposite wall. He tore them down and handed them to this era's version of a cashier, the man who tallied their goods.

"I am Magistrate Goodwin, from Boston, sir, and these posters are no longer allowed."

The man's thin face seemed to constrict, the features narrowing, the skin growing tighter, showing the contours of bone. He wiggled his hawk nose, like Samantha in *Bewitched,* and peered out at Kincaid from under brows so thick they looked like awnings for his wide, brown eyes. His mustache drooped dramatically at either side; it seemed to weight the skin around his mouth, dragging it into a perpetual scowl. He combed his fingers back through his thick, dark hair, which appeared to have been cut with a bowl over his skull. "These laws are the Lord's."

"These laws bear the signature of Reverend Chandler, and as far as I know, he is not God. Your name, sir?"

He drew himself up a little taller. "Francis Travers, proprietor of this store."

"And a member of the Council," Kincaid added.

"Which doth make me proud."

Kincaid leaned forward, his face so close to the other man's that Travers leaned back slightly. "Then let us understand each other, Mr. Travers. Life in the colony is based upon legislative law, not Biblical interpretation, and certainly not upon the whims of Reverend Chandler. These posters will be removed."

Travers glared at him, then plucked items from the straw basket, tallied. "And the basket, sir?" His mouth pursed. "Shall I include it?"

"Include it." Then he added, "Even if it is considered blasphemy by order of the reverend."

Travers had no snappy response to that.

The sum was a pittance. Kincaid handed him a gold coin and Travers pocketed it. "I trust, magistrate, that *legislative* law has provisions for the punishment of witches?"

Go fuck yourself. "Legislative law hears the evidence first. How do I get to the livery, sir?"

Travers gave them directions. As they left, Kincaid felt Travers's eyes against his back, burning holes through skin, muscle, bone. Sunny leaped up when she saw them and they headed down an alley, toward the livery. Kincaid's anger over this religious issue disturbed him and he wondered if, in the future, they should implement a rule to keep their interference with a culture to a minimum. The prime directive on *Star Trek,* just as Nora had said. But until then, he intended to act his role as magistrate to the absolute hilt.

They rounded the corner of the building and the wind slammed into them, forcing them to move forward at a tilt, their heads bowed until they reached the stable. Inside, their driver and another man, perhaps the blacksmith, were warming themselves at the fireplace, and Sunny headed right toward them and plopped down at their feet. Both men laughed and leaned over to pat her.

They offered Kincaid and Nora hot cider, which they gratefully accepted, and Nora unwrapped the beef and set it on the floor in front of Sunny. She gobbled it up as readily as she did the attention from the two men. Kincaid noticed that even here the Laws of Righteous Living were posted. "Were these laws posted when the former magistrate was alive?"

"Indeed, Magistrate," replied the driver.

"And that magistrate followed them?"

The blacksmith blew into his hands, then rubbed them against his dirty breeches. "The former magistrate worked closely with the reverend."

"And you believe these laws are just?" Kincaid asked.

The two men glanced at each other as if they didn't understand the question, then looked at Kincaid. The driver said, "The reverend tends to our souls and the Council helps keep Blue River safe from evil. And so we follow these laws as closely as we are able." He leaned toward Kincaid, and when he spoke again, his voice was softer, almost a whisper, as if he didn't want God or Satan to overhear him. "But there are women in town who read and write, men and women who commit adultery, who do not adhere to the Sabbath, who break all of those laws. Perhaps the laws are intended to make Reverend Chandler feel good, sir." He and the other man chuckled, a private joke.

Nora touched Kincaid's arm. "The revolution won't start here," she said softly, then raised her voice. "We should move on to the gaol."

In Kincaid and Nora's time, the jail was a historic building, a lonely testament to the darkest period of the town's

history. The only original parts of the structure that remained
were the stone floor and the torture room in the back.
Tourists were still allowed to explore the jailer's room,
where the fireplace and brick oven were located, and the cell
block. But the rear room, the torture chamber, was no longer
accessible to the general public. It was preserved behind
glass, where the temperature was regulated for preservation
of the artifacts. Some of the original torture tools were laid
out on the wooden table, neatly labeled, with a brief explanation about how each one had been used.

The first and only time Kincaid had visited the jail, he'd
been with Nora, who was allowed into the inner sanctum because she taught seminars on this particular period in Blue
River's history. During those first few minutes inside the
room, Kincaid had wandered around in a kind of horrified
awe. He had touched the well-worn Bible from which Chandler supposedly had read during the torture sessions, to convince the accused to confess. He had held the thumbscrews,
stared into the pot that had been filled with boiling oil, examined the strappado, the rack, the gallows, the long pins
used to test the devil's marks. A crippling miasma had seized
him and he had stumbled out of the torture chamber, into the
bright, warm sun of a Blue River summer, and vomited on
the sidewalk.

When they approached the gaol now, he felt that same
creeping strangeness that had preceded the deeper horror
that had suffused him that day. He suddenly wondered if, in
some way he didn't understand yet, those images had been
memories from this transition.

A tall, muscular man rose from his chair near the fireplace when the door swung open and Kincaid entered, Nora
and Sunny right behind him. He didn't give the man a
chance to react. Kincaid strode forward, smiling pleasantly,
making it clear he was in charge. "Good day, sir. I am Magistrate Goodwin and this is my wife and clerk, Nora Goodwin, and my dog, Sunny."

The gaoler, the jailer, looked like one of those male models on the cover of a romance novel. Long hair, roguish features, broad shoulders beneath his linen shirt, muscular thighs pressing against the tight breeches. A beard. Mustache. But he clutched a pistol in his right hand.

"Magistrate," he breathed. "I heard you arrived. I am Paul Davies." His eyes flickered toward Nora, the dog. "You would like to speak to the witches?"

"To the *accused*, Mr. Davies. We have not yet determined that they are witches. We will require a table and two chairs, a basin of water, and enough bowls of porridge to feed ourselves and all of the accused."

Kincaid gestured, Davies frowned, Sunny pawed at the floor, and Nora said nothing.

"As you wish, sir. But the witches are fed only in the evening and women are not allowed in—"

"A magistrate's clerk is allowed. Rule five." He pointed at the goddamn poster nailed to the wall and barely resisted the urge to yank it down. "Those posters are now forbidden. Please remove that one, Mr. Davies."

"I . . . that is . . . the reverend . . ."

For Chrissakes. "Remove it. And tell me where I can find the things we need. And the accused will be fed *now*."

Minutes later, Davies led them through a heavy wooden door to the cell block. The stink was overwhelming—of filth and body odor, of despair and hopelessness. The only light came from the torch that Davies held, a torch placed farther down the corridor, and the tallow candles that Kincaid and Nora clutched in their hands. It wasn't enough light to chase away the rats that he heard scurrying through the shadows, to block awareness of the stink that suffused the air.

Davies had set up a table and two chairs outside one of the cells. And as Kincaid had requested, it held bowls of steaming porridge, a basin of water. Davies also had provided a basket of fresh bread.

Kincaid pulled out a chair, sat down, and Nora settled

across from him with the apparent ease of someone who had been doing this long enough to know the routine. Sunny paced the length of the first cell, her nose working the air. "And this corridor, Mr. Davies. Where does it lead?"

He suspected it led to the torture chamber, but Davies replied, "It is where the reverend and the council extract confessions."

Oh yeah, the nuances of language, Kincaid thought, then made a dismissive gesture with his hand. "And here, who is accused?"

"Sarah Longwood, Magistrate. During October last, she—"

"I am familiar with the events. Leave us. If we need you, we will call."

"But I am not allowed to—"

"*Leave us,*" Kincaid snapped.

He did.

Rustling in the cell. Nora brought out her parchment, one of the quills, the container of ink. Kincaid said, "Sarah Longwood, I am Magistrate Goodwin, this is my wife and clerk, Nora Goodwin, and we are here to record your testimony concerning the events that brought you here."

Minutes ticked by. Sunny whined and stuck her snout through the bars. Eventually, an emaciated, half-naked young woman with long, matted hair approached the front of the cell. He could hardly see her face through the filth smeared across it. From history, he knew she was eighteen or nineteen, but it was impossible to peg her age. Her gnarled, skinny fingers clutched the bars. "Please," she whispered. "I have done nothing. I have . . ."

"Just explain what happened," Kincaid said.

He could smell her—the unwashed clothes, the sweat, the earth caked to her bare feet and jammed up under her dirty nails, her fetid breath. In small, labored spurts, her story tumbled out, close to what Jacob Nash had told them. The poppet. Her cursing of the reverend and the magistrate. The death of the reverend's wife and of the magistrate.

"But the reverend hid a poppet in my room. And he . . . he . . . told me that if I . . . if I would . . . fornicate with him, he . . . he would not accuse me of . . . of witchcraft. And this, I swear, is my solemn truth, Magistrate."

"Has he tried to make you confess?" Nora asked.

Kincaid could tell that Nora struggled to keep her anger under wraps. Sarah's eyes filled with tears and she nodded and gripped the bars more tightly. Nora passed her a bowl of porridge, a spoon, some bread.

"Please, have something to eat," Nora said.

"Thank you," the girl murmured. "Bless you for your kindness."

Kincaid dipped a spoon into his own bowl of porridge. Either the taste was extraordinary or he was so hungry that even dog shit would be a feast. Sarah slurped at the porridge, scraping her spoon against the sides of the bowl, and then her fingers tore at the bread. He wasn't sure where to go from here, didn't know what questions to ask her. He just wanted to shout for Davies, knock him out, grab his keys, and free her. So he shoveled porridge into his mouth and fought to channel the rising tide of his horror.

"Sarah, did anyone new come into town during the summer or autumn?" Nora asked. "Did any new women arrive?"

"Many women arrived in the fall. With their families. People from the inland areas seeking the fresh fish from our seas, the fertile lands near our river, our growing community."

"A woman alone," Nora said.

"Catherine. She came in late summer, and Mr. Francis Travers, he took pity on her and offered her a job and . . . and . . . she was accused after the day of thanks, when the Indians attacked."

She spoke with a soft rasp, as though she had hairballs stuck in her throat. Kincaid kept staring at her gnarled fingers, the knuckles pale, scraped, bruised, damaged.

"I . . . I am not sure why she was accused. I believe it had something to do with Mr. Travers. Goods stolen from his store. Or goods found in her possession. She . . . she was next to me for many days, many weeks. She was good to me. She told me of a place where people like us are welcome. She called us the 'disenfranchised.' I believe the word means outcast. When I had the fever, she bargained with the monster Davies and got me cool cloths, herbs, extra servings of soup and porridge. And then . . . then one night the . . . the devil's minions came for her . . . and she fought. And ran free."

"What was her full name?" Nora pressed on. "Do you know?"

Sarah spooned more porridge into her mouth, then passed the empty bowl through the bars. "Catherine Griffin."

Kincaid squeezed his eyes shut, heard Nora suck in her breath. Catherine Walrave's maiden name was *Griffin*.

Nora's voice sounded choked when she spoke again. "How . . . how did she escape?"

Sarah leaned closer to the bars and whispered, "The monster Davies went in with fresh hay. He told her to go to the back of the cell, but she . . . she had a stone that she dug from the wall and . . . hit him with it. And then she ran. She ran promising that she would be back for us. For me. For Rebeka Short. For Lucia Gray."

"You saw this happen?" Nora asked.

"Yes. With my own eyes."

"Do you have any idea where she went?" Kincaid asked.

"To the place for the disenfranchised, Magistrate. I am sure of it."

"Who first accused you?" he asked. "Was it the reverend himself? Because he found the poppet?"

Her eyes flickered to the right and she whispered again. "Lucia Gray. She did not know what she was doing. I . . . I believe I was named during her confession."

Kincaid now saw the scars on the backs of her hands, on her thumbs, on her legs. "Is the doctor permitted to treat you?" Kincaid asked.

"I heard that the doctor left October last."

"So the town has no doctor at all?" Nora asked.

"I believe there is a new doctor, but it does not matter. No doctor is permitted to tend to the accused."

The door at the end of the hall slammed open and Chandler rushed in like a foul wind, cane tapping the stone floor, voice booming through the cell block. Behind him was Davies, gripping a torch. "This is not permitted!" Chandler shouted. "You must . . ."

Sunny leaped up, fur rising along her back, her growl low and feral, and bared teeth, causing Chandler to stop.

"Restrain that beast," he demanded. "Or Mr. Davies will shoot it."

Kincaid reached into the basket of goods they had bought at the general store, pushed his chair back, and stood, his new pistol aimed at Chandler. "You will not threaten a representative of the law, Reverend Chandler." His eyes darted to Davies. "And you, sir, will not show your weapon. Are we clear, gentlemen?"

Davies looked nervous and uneasy; Chandler merely looked defiant and waved his cane around. Sunny's growls deepened. "Women are not allowed in—"

"I am tired of you telling us what women can and cannot do," Kincaid snapped. "What men can and cannot do. The gaol is not your jurisdiction. It is *mine*, as magistrate. As of this moment, *you* are not allowed inside the gaol, Reverend Chandler. And you and your council will remove all the posters you have put up around town. Your Laws for Righteous Living belong in the church, not in public places. Furthermore, Mr. Davies, the accused—all of them—will be fed three times a day, every area will be cleaned *today*, and fresh hay and bedding will be brought in. You will provide these women with pallets on which to sleep, quilts to warm themselves. The accused are to have clean clothing and they will have the means to bathe—in private. The town doctor will be brought in to treat their injuries and . . ."

"No, no," Chandler stammered. "This is . . . you cannot . . . the accused have no rights to the physician, to—"

"Silence!" Kincaid slammed his fist against the table. "You are banished from the gaol. Leave."

Rage, shock, hatred: all of these emotions seized Chandler's face simultaneously and threw his features into chaos. His mouth twitched and pursed. A tic kicked under his right eye. A vein hammered and pulsed at his temple. The tendons in his neck looked like they might pop through the skin. Red spots now mottled his cheeks. Kincaid wondered if the bastard was about to have a stroke.

Before he could protest, Kincaid said, "Mr. Davies, escort the reverend out of the gaol, please. And he and members of the town council are not permitted to enter here unless I am present or my clerk is present."

Davies stammered, "I . . . this . . ." He looked nervously at Chandler, who just stood there in disbelief, the muscles ticcing, the veins throbbing, a man on the verge of sudden death. "Yes, of course, Magistrate."

Davies touched Chandler's arm, but the reverend jerked it free, shot Kincaid a look that would wither apples on their branches, and spat, "You have not heard the last of this, Magistrate. I will file a complaint with the governor's emissary."

Yeah, yeah, whatever. "Do what you must, Reverend Chandler. As will I. And Mr. Davies, we will be back this afternoon to complete our gathering of testimony. Please have the areas cleaned before then and be sure that you have arranged for the doctor to visit."

Davies nodded, but he didn't look too happy about any of it. He escorted Chandler out of the cell block, and seconds after the heavy wooden door thudded shut, Sarah Longwood and the other women applauded.

11
Mariah

*People like us, who believe in physics, know
that the distinction between past, present, and
future is only a stubbornly persistent illusion.*
—Albert Einstein

Nellysford, Virginia, April 24, 2006

Berlin pushed his cart down the hallway toward the laundry room. A new group would be arriving at the institute tomorrow morning and it was up to him to make sure that every room was clean, that the bathrooms were equipped with soap, shampoo, and other essentials, and that the audio equipment in each CHEC unit in the rooms was working.

CHEC stood for Controlled Holistic Environment Chamber. It was a bed, yes, but looked more like a train berth. Curtains could be lowered around it on all sides to block out the light and each CHEC unit had a set of headphones through which the trainer guided you to altered states of consciousness. Berlin had been through a number of the institute's courses over the years, but wanted to take the program where you learned to help the recently departed get to where they needed to be. He didn't have enough money now to even entertain the idea.

The closest he'd gotten was one weekend in between

training sessions several months ago, when Lea had offered to act as his facilitator. He had settled down in one of the CHEC units, donned the headphones, and with Lea guiding him had quickly moved through the various levels of consciousness that Monroe had mapped. First, there was Focus 10, the state of mind awake/body asleep. From there, he had spontaneously launched to another level, Focus 15, a state of "no time." He had ended up in Focus 21, the bridge to other energy systems, a place beyond the physical time-space reality, and found himself playing softball with a teenage boy he recognized as his son. Even though a part of him knew that Ricky had died years ago, he had allowed himself to be swept up in this alternate version of his son's life.

When the session had ended, Berlin had been so overcome emotionally that he had fled the CHEC unit, the building, the grounds. He finally had understood that even though Ricky had died on *his* timeline, he had survived on another and gone on to live a full life. It didn't mitigate his grief, but it made him less bitter.

In the laundry room, he unloaded his cart and deposited dirty linens into the industrial-size washer. It had been a week since he and Lea had gone to Aruba, seven days during which he had tried to forget what had happened, what he had learned, what he knew he was supposed to do. He had seen Lea only once since the trip, for a private yoga class outdoors. Neither of them had mentioned Aruba. They acted as if it never had happened.

Yet, he had gotten a substantial raise, mysteriously included in his last paycheck several days after they returned from Aruba. With this money, he had been able to produce five more biochips, created in an intense period of twenty-four hours, the most chips he'd created here in such a short span of time. But while he had tinkered in his cellar, he had felt an increasing pressure to act, decide, move, transition.

But here he was, piddling around with dirty laundry while the universe collapsed around him. It was all wrong. Yet, he felt paralyzed, skeptical, ridiculous in his belief that he alone could stop Wade and Lazier and the evil they had set in motion. Delusional: that was what he had become. Yes, his knowledge gave him an edge, but he would need help. A lot of it.

Even he wasn't sure about the full parameters of these new chips. The transitions he had done since he'd gotten the newer version had been smooth, except for the glitch in Aruba, where he'd had to recharge before he could transition himself and Lea back to the institute. But the Aruba trip had been exploratory and the other transitions had been for his own amusement. He never had attempted a retrieval.

It was entirely possible that retrievals had their own parameters and rules. But why? Why would a retrieval be different from any other transition? The only answer that made sense was the simplest: SPOT's records provided dates and locations to which individuals had been disappeared, but not the *exact* local mean time. So, in order to find and retrieve someone, you had to immerse yourself in the era, society, culture, town, whatever. *Immersion* was how retrievals differed.

Was a retrieval even necessary? It would be easier to go back to the day before Catherine Walrave's arrest, warn her, and prevent it from happening. Easier, yes, but it would change too much on *this* timeline. If Catherine weren't arrested, then Nora McKee would be an entirely different sort of person and might not react as she had when her husband was arrested twenty-three years later. If she reacted differently, then SPOT might not collapse.

It wouldn't work for all the same reasons it wouldn't work with his son. On *his* timeline, Ricky's death had launched Berlin's search for unconventional answers and ultimately had set his course with SPOT.

If A doesn't happen, how will Z be different? Or will Z happen at all? This seemed to be the essential conundrum of his life—and of the biochip. Every time he came up against it, he developed a massive headache and the scar that crossed the heel of his left hand began to ache, as if in sympathy. The scar was recent, from an injury sustained since he'd been working here. He had been changing a lightbulb, had slipped and fallen on the damn thing, slicing open a six-inch area of flesh that had required twenty stitches. Which he had stitched himself. Yeah, that was fun.

He parked the laundry basket against the wall and went downstairs to the room where people gathered in the evenings. He stood for a moment over his laptop, temples and hand throbbing.

Right now, in the last days of April 2006, Mariah was still alive, plotting her strategy for the destruction of SPOT, creating the new chips. And he, the Russ Berlin on Cedar Key, was already sabotaging the biochips and he and Mariah were creating new chips. Jake McKee was under surveillance. And Ian Rodriguez and Lydia Fenmore were ruling SPOT like royalty. Wade was running wild. The seeds for SPOT's destruction were being sown.

Berlin went into one of his webmail addresses, thought a moment, typed:

To: peoplesfriend@yahoo.com
Re: urgent question

Mariah, do these new chips come with a new set of rules and parameters? If so, how would they impact a retrieval?
RB

In the past, she usually answered his e-mails within a day or two. But whenever he included the word *urgent* in the subject line, she answered in minutes. He sat there, drumming his fingers against the desk, clicking the inbox impatiently. Twenty minutes went by. He went over to the fridge to fix himself a veggie wrap, and by the time he returned to the laptop, she had replied:

To: rberl@hotmail.com
Re: retrievals?!

And who, exactly, are we retrieving? You at home or work?
M

He had to be careful here. He never had been certain about what Mariah really knew about the future—how much of what she said was true and how much was bullshit. Did she, in April 2006, already know that SPOT would collapse in six months? That she would either vanish or die?

To: peoplesfriend@yahoo.com
Re: reprieve

Needed a break. Am at Monroe Institute, getting ready to go through a program. In case you've forgotten, the zip is 22958.
My time now: 8:36 AM EST.
Meet you by the crystal at 8 AM.

Every Traveler had techniques, methods, rituals that helped him or her target an area or era precisely. But Mariah was the only person Berlin knew who used zip codes to target her location in the contemporary world. When she went too far back for zip codes, she used latitude and longitude coordinates. Lacking that, she followed her instincts and let the chip do what it was designed to do. He closed down the laptop, slipped it into his pack, checked the time on his cell, and walked down to the crystal, where Nora McKee first appeared.

He settled on the soft grass, his back against the crystal, and targeted this area roughly thirty minutes ago. It happened effortlessly—no painful physical symptoms, no nausea. He checked the time on his cell, where the biochip faithfully reacted to the transition. 7:58.

It astonished him that he was excited about seeing Mariah. Their history had spanned twenty-four years—from lovers to friends to employer/employee to coconspirators.

He wasn't sure what he felt for her now. An elemental lust? Certainly—that never changed. But beyond that, he didn't have a clue.

Mariah emerged moments later, three hundred yards down the slope, a slender, dark shape against all the green. He waved and she waved back and strode toward him in her tight jeans, halter top, bare feet, her hair long, wild, in dreadlocks. The sun was behind her, making her dark chocolate skin seem to radiate light and energy. She looked utterly mythic, as if she had climbed down from Olympus just to sit with him by the Brazilian crystal.

As always, she appeared to be in her forties, which she probably was not. The truth, though, was that Berlin didn't have any idea how old she was. He tried not to think about that because it opened up so many unanswerable questions about the chip's impact on aging.

"Great spot for a reprieve, Berlin."

"Familiar," he said.

Mariah nodded, the light caressing the smoothness of her throat and neck. In a quick, fluid motion, she settled beside him on the grass, dropped her beaded bag on the ground beside her, and wrapped her arms around her legs, nodding her approval. "Interesting place for a vacation. Are you trying to recapture something by coming here?"

"Nope. Just doing another program," he lied. "This time, I'm going to explore Focus 27, how to help the recently departed get to where they're supposed to go."

"Who's going to help *you* get to where you're supposed to be?"

"You," he said. "Tell me about the specs on the new chips."

Her dark eyes held his for a long, uncomfortable moment. Then she turned her head to gaze out across the rolling hills again. She tightened her arms around her legs, pulling them closer to her chest. "We can go anywhere."

But *anywhere* would drive her crazy, he thought. It didn't show yet, not in late April 2006, not in an obvious, definable way, yet it skulked beneath the surface of who she was. Sometimes he glimpsed it in the preternatural brightness of her eyes, in a weird hand gesture, in an idea. In six months, she would be flat-out nuts, riding his ass like a banshee, sending threatening e-mails to the people in charge, transitioning the accused SPOT brought in, interfering and screwing up.

And yet, her craziness would work. It would bring down SPOT.

"We can stop time for brief intervals," Mariah went on.

Like Kincaid had done on Cape Cod, he thought. Like Mariah herself would do when, six months down the road, she would snatch Ryan Curtis and Jake McKee and transition them to the sixties. He didn't say any of this, though, because she was only in April 2006 and might not know what lay ahead. What he really wanted to ask her was where she was living right now, what she had been doing since she had disappeared in the early 1990s. But he didn't. He never had. At some level, he supposed he didn't really want to know.

"What about the rules for retrievals?" he asked.

"If we know the exact time, date, and place to which someone was disappeared, then it's easy. You go in, grab the person, get out. Unfortunately, the records I've been able to get my hands on aren't complete. Local mean times are hardly ever included. In some disappearances, the location in a particular era isn't included, either. And really, I'm sure some of these jerks lie about where they take the accused. So you have to immerse yourself in the era and hope you find the person. But once you immerse yourself, you can't get home until you've accomplished what you went there to do."

"You're *stuck* there?"

"Yes, unless you can convince yourself that the reason you're there isn't the *real* reason. Remember, Russ, that the chip responds to our deepest and most genuine intentions. This is especially true with the new chip. It's difficult to trick your own unconscious."

"So who did you try to retrieve? Where did *you* get stuck?"

"I tried to retrieve Catherine Walrave."

Of all the names she might have mentioned, this one shocked him the most. And, considering his own recent musings, it struck him as synchronous. "Why her?"

"I've always felt I owed her that much because of Lydia's actions. I got to January 1695 easily enough, but was promptly arrested as a fugitive slave. Black women in that era are pretty much condemned from the moment they take their first breath. The town's inquisitor, a short, fat, sadistic fuck named Chandler, tortured me, trying to get me to confess. During one especially bad session, I . . . I transitioned spontaneously and suddenly was home again."

"So the torture . . . changed your deepest intentions."

She laughed, but it was a harsh, bitter sound. "Yeah, you might say that."

"Were the other accused women in the jail by then?"

Mariah nodded. "The young woman in the cell next to mine, Sarah Longwood, told me that she had been accused of witchcraft when Chandler found poppets in her kitchen cupboard. She claims he put them there to get even with her father for spreading rumors that Chandler liked to have sex with young girls. I also heard that he accused her because she wouldn't have sex with him. So who knows what the real truth is?"

"Jesus," Berlin whispered.

"Historically, Chandler left Blue River in the summer of 1695, months after the three women he accused—including Sarah Longwood—were hanged. But here's the odd thing. A couple of months after I transitioned back from 1695, I was in a library in Boston that has one of the largest archives about the witch trials in Salem and Blue River. And in those archives, it stated that there were *four* women accused of witchcraft, that one of them escaped weeks before the trials began, and that Chandler fled. So, given what I know about how this whole process works, it seems that someone has gone back—or is going back—and as a result, events are changing."

"What other changes have you discovered?"

"That Sarah Longwood survived and went on to become one of the most outspoken critics of Increase and Cotton Mather. You know who they were?"

"Father and son, Puritan ministers whose writings were largely responsible for the beliefs in witchcraft and what types of evidence could be used to accuse someone of witchcraft—and to convict them. Did Sarah stay in Blue River?"

"No, she moved on to New York and gained some renown as a writer. She wrote a number of books about her experiences during the time she was imprisoned." Mariah reached into her beaded bag and brought out a small pamphlet. "This was her last published work."

Berlin stared at the pamphlet, entitled *What I Know to Be True,* everything handwritten in ink on a type of parchment. "You stole this from the library archives?"

Mariah rolled her eyes. "Oh, please. I bought it in a Boston market in 1716. Go ahead. Open it. Take a look at the last page."

As Berlin turned the fragile pages and marveled at the precise, beautiful script, he knew it was the genuine McCoy. Then he read through the last page of the pamphlet.

The syntax was weird, but the gist of what Sarah Longwood had written came through loud and clear. In January 1695, while in the Blue River gaol, she had shared an unusual friendship with a Negro woman in the cell next to hers who had been jailed as a fugitive slave. *She suffered gravely. Dunking, the piercing of devil's marks with needles or pins, the thumbscrews, the strappado, the boiling oil. In the darkness of the gaol, her screams echoed. . . .*

Berlin swallowed hard and his eyes skipped to the next section. *And one night the reverend took me in as witness to the horrors. They raised her up in the strappado, and I heard her bones popping. As Chandler lowered her toward the boiling oil, her shrieks pounded the hot walls—and she vanished.*

Berlin raised his eyes from the page. He couldn't read shit like this. Mariah took his hand and laced her fingers through his. "I'll show you," she said softly, and suddenly they were *there*, in that torture room, looped inside a replay, everything occurring in a terrible slow motion. He was forced to watch Mariah being tortured in front of an audience that included a young woman he took to be Sarah Longwood and two nameless men whose faces he would never forget.

He jerked his hand free of hers, but she grabbed his arm, the inside of his skull felt like it exploded, and suddenly they were in front of a roaring fire, he and Mariah, making love on soft quilts on the floor, winter whistling and raging outside. A part of him understood that Mariah had transitioned them to her haven in an undetermined time and place and that she was doing something at which she excelled: manipulating his emotions. But Berlin didn't care.

Since that first night they had spent together at the institute in 1982, he hungered for her body in the way that other people hungered for alcohol. Drugs. Power. She was his addiction, his nemesis, his escape, and the gauge by which every other woman in his life would be measured.

And when he awakened, he was in his own bed in Nellysford, it was nearly noon of the same day in April when they met at the crystal, and the smell of Mariah was everywhere. Clutched in his hand was an object with a piece of paper wrapped around it, held in place with a rubber band. Berlin sat up, rolled the rubber band off, and the paper popped free, revealing a dark green stone. It was about the size of his thumbnail, striated with black and silver, and as rough and uneven as a volcanic rock. But Berlin had never seen anything like this. It shimmered like aluminum foil, and when he held it up to the light, it became as transparent as glass.

Berlin set it on the mattress and smoothed open the piece

of paper, a note from Mariah: *Go back, make the changes, save Catherine and Sarah. You're the only one who can do it right. The stone amplifies the chip and vice versa. It was given to me by a rancher in Roswell, New Mexico, in 1947. But don't take my word for its origins. Experiment with it. Love, M*

Roswell. Right. Why was everything Mariah said couched in such unmitigated bullshit? A Roswell rancher in 1947 would have to be, by implication, Mack Brazel, who one day in July 1947 found metal debris scattered across his ranch after a violent thunderstorm the night before. He also found a shallow trench several hundred feet long that had been gouged into the land. He eventually dragged a large piece of the debris back to a shed and the rest, as they said, was history. The government impounded the debris, sealed off a section of his ranch, and the Roswell UFO legend was born.

Regardless of its origins, it was a beautiful stone and he picked it up again, rolling it around in his palm, admiring it. He became aware of a slight heat against the skin of his hand and realized the stone was warming up. Then it began to hum, like a tuning fork, and he could feel the vibration inside his skull, as though the chip was responding to it. *Like they're talking to each other.*

Intrigued, he swung his legs over the edge of the mattress, pressed the stone between both hands, and the humming grew louder, more intense, almost painful. And when he opened his hands, the stone glowed with a white light so intense and brilliant that he had to look away. Startled, Berlin wrenched back, but didn't drop the stone, and seconds later, its light abruptly went out.

His palms tingled; that was all.

When he set the stone down again, he realized that the scar on the heel of his left hand was fading, nearly gone.

"Sweet Christ," he whispered. *A stone that heals.* Would it cure leukemia?

No, don't go there. You can't change it.
But if he could . . .

Berlin moved quickly around the room looking for something to put the stone in—a velvet bag, a box, anything. He finally found the perfect holder, a key chain with a globe on one end, the continents and oceans rendered in miniature. He popped open the globe at the equator and carefully set the stone inside. He stared at it a moment longer, awed and mystified, then snapped the globe shut and set it on his dresser to take with him when he transitioned to 1695.

12
In the Dark

So here's the deal. We don't make deals.
—Nora McKee

Aruba, March 2007

Mike Holcomb woke suddenly, in the dark, starving. For a moment, he thought he was in the hotel room, bound and blindfolded, but then he moved his legs and his arms and rolled over and turned on the lamp and sat up.

No longer imprisoned. Except in a prison of his own making.

He turned on the TV, tuned in to CNN. While he watched the news, he ate cold ravioli from a can, slices of fresh mango, a banana, and paced back and forth in front of the slightly open curtains, checking the parking lot in front of the hotel. In the sodium vapor glow of the lights, he could see the lot was full now. That would make his job easier.

Mike checked his e-mail and found three new ones from Ann. In the first, she informed him that she was *reading* the files he had sent her, in the second she was *trying to wrap her mind* around all this, and in the last, she would *get back to him.* Yeah, great. She was having an intellectual argument and debate with herself and he was sitting down here on an island in the Caribbean without a passport or means to get home.

On CNN, it didn't take long for the Aruba story to come up, the next installment in the "investigation," complete with a video that clearly showed Mike's face. But the images the hotel had released to CNN had been digitally manipulated so that it looked as if he were breaking into the senator's penthouse. Mike wondered how much that had cost the senator.

"And in a second but apparently unrelated story from Aruba, local police closed in on a group of terrorists who were staying at an apartment complex near a beach popular with windsurfers. The raid took place early this morning . . ."

Terrorists? In Aruba? The only terrorists here were Lazier and his group, Mike thought, and turned up the volume.

The camera had cut to an attractive blond woman standing outside an apartment with a broken front window. Just above her head was a glowing neon sign that read WAVERUNNER. "I don't care what the police say. These people are not terrorists. I have known Ryan Curtis since the late 1980s . . ."

Mike heard nothing beyond the man's name. *Ryan Curtis.* In one of the files on the senator's laptop, he had seen that name, *Curtis,* the rogue Traveler from SPOT who had vanished last fall along with his partner.

Waverunner.

He rushed over to the laptop, Googled *waverunner +aruba,* and found the apartment website, with the address. He located it on a tourist map of Aruba and realized it lay toward the northern end of the island, just about a mile from the hotel where he had been imprisoned.

Curtis, here, in Aruba. How can I find him?

He probably had transitioned as soon as his apartment had been attacked. But transitioned to where?

Time to leave, he thought, and quickly packed his belongings, left the room key on the dresser, and hastened outside. He put his things in the backseat of the Beemer, then retrieved a screwdriver from the glove compartment and walked quickly to the back of the lot. He targeted an old, neglected Toyota, removed the license plate, and loped back to the Beemer. He exchanged the license plates and returned to the Toyota to put on the Beemer's plate. A few minutes later, he backed out of the lot and turned out onto the highway and just drove, the warm salt air blowing through the car.

His thoughts circled the inevitable: It wouldn't be long before his photo would make it to Google News, if it wasn't there already, and be plastered all over the island. Like a vampire, he would have to remain hidden during the day, do whatever he needed to do at night, and disguise himself in some way.

Cut his hair, grow a beard, wear glasses. That was about the extent of what he could do, so he would start there.

In Oranjestad, the island's largest town, the streets bustled with tourists. Mike guessed that many of them had come from the cruise ship that was in port. He found a parking spot and walked quickly up the block to a general store and ducked inside.

The place looked like it stocked everything from household items to clothing and food to tourist trinkets. He sped up and down the aisles selecting items that he added to his basket. Scissors, a pair of glasses with nonprescription lenses, two changes of clothes, toiletries, a towel and soap, silverware that included a long knife, some bottled water, more food. He found an electronics section and selected a one-gig memory stick, an inexpensive digital camera, a prepaid cell phone.

He felt distinctly uneasy as he got into line at the cash register and kept his head bowed so that the security cameras in the four corners of the store wouldn't get a good view of his face. He pretended to be reading the directions on the back of the prepaid cell phone and kept willing the line to hurry up.

By the time it was his turn, his anxiety had reached epidemic proportions. The stink of his own fear rolled off him in waves. His hands refused to cooperate and trembled slightly as he set his items on the counter. But this was Aruba, One Happy Island, and the clerk was chatting on her Bluetooth as she scanned his purchases and never even looked at him.

He was so grateful to get out of the store that when he finally reached the car, he spent several minutes inside with his eyes shut and his head resting against the seat. *This, too, shall pass,* his mother used to say during the divorce. He hoped to hell it was true.

A sharp rap on the window snapped his head upward. A cop stood there, his uniform tight, just like his face, and motioned for Mike to get moving. He pulled out of the space, eager to put as much distance as possible between himself and the cop, and headed southeast toward San Nicholas. At some point, the traffic dwindled to nothing and he turned off the road, into a field of the misshapen trees that covered the island.

He switched on the inside light, turned around, and dug through the bags of what he'd bought until he found the bag he needed. He set it down in the passenger seat, then turned the rearview mirror so he could see himself. His hair fell to just below his ears and now looked wild, windblown. Mike took a piece on the right between his fingers and pulled it out a little from his head and snipped. And kept pulling and snipping. When he got to the back, he gathered the remaining hair between his forefinger and thumb and cut it off. He glanced in the mirror again. A long piece of hair remained on the left side of his head, making him look sort of Goth. He cut that piece, too.

Hair covered the seat, his clothes, and he got out of the car and ran his fingers through his now very short hair and brushed it off his clothes and the seat. He also changed into a new pair of shorts and a T-shirt and slipped on his bogus glasses. He pulled his new cap down low over his forehead and studied himself in the mirror.

It changed his appearance, all right, and maybe, just maybe, it would spell the difference between being captured and remaining free. Whatever. He had done the best he could with what he had.

He pulled back onto the road and turned toward Santa Cruz, the largest town inland, which wasn't saying much. The entire island of Aruba covered fewer square miles than the Florida Keys. He finally found a small motel with a vacancy sign and went inside.

The place wasn't quite as decrepit as it looked from the outside. The spacious lobby smelled of fresh flowers, an episode of *Six Feet Under* played on the large plasma TV, and the clerk, a guy who didn't look much older than Mike, asked for his passport.

Panic. *I don't have a goddamn passport.* "Look, man, I had a major blowout with my parents tonight, okay? I think I left my passport back at their hotel. I'll have to get it tomorrow."

"Legally, I have to . . ."

Mike set five twenties on the counter. "Tomorrow. I'll get it then. I just . . . can't go back there tonight."

The kid eyed the twenties.

Mike's heart throbbed in his throat. He added another fifty. "That leaves me just enough to pay for the room."

"Shit," the kid murmured.

"They brought me down here for a family vacation and all they do is get drunk and beat up on me."

The kid swept the bills off the counter, and they disappeared into his shirt pocket. "Yeah, go ahead, man." He slapped down the key. "It's not like we're flooded with business."

"Thanks."

The kid made a dismissive motion with his hand and Mike swept up the key and hurried off in search of his room.

The room was okay—smaller than the first room, with an odd little fridge, which he jammed quickly with his food supplies. In ten minutes, he was online, and there were four more e-mails from Ann.

In the several hours since they had communicated last, she had decided that he was injured, had been recaptured, or was dead. But she also had set up a Gmail account where they could IM each other. She was using the encryption software developed by one of their classmates, so she felt the account was pretty secure.

Mike clicked on her last e-mail, pressed REPLY, and typed:

Still alive, kicking, and in a new motel. What's up?
   Mike, this gov't program has been disappearing people for more than 30 yrs. I think I found a website where the rogues gather: <u>www.disappeared.com</u>. Click it and you'll see what I mean. Maybe u should lv them a message. & I have more to tell u, but check the site first.
   OK. Be right back.

He clicked on the URL she'd given him and scanned some of the hundreds of entries on the message board. *Hi, my husband was arrested in 1979 for . . . Please help me. my daughter was taken away in 1983. . . . My grandfather was . . . My sister was . . . My closest friend . . . My fiancée . . .*

The postings came from all over the United States and from other countries as well. The disappearances seemed to go back to at least the early seventies and continued up until late 2006. The more he read, the more suspicious he got. It seemed possible that the entire site was a sham, a trap, a way to tag people as suspects—of some crime or another—just because they were pissed off at the government. Or, more specifically, pissed off at Freeze, the government agency that seemed to have made the most arrests.

But suppose the site was genuine? Suppose the Travelers ran it? He finally clicked on the CONTACT link and wrote:

My father was hired by a thug named Wade, who works for
Senator Lazier, to transition back to 1695 & cause Nora and
Alex to reject their chips so he can negotiate to get *their*
chips. Lazier and his people are out of chips. They don't
know how to make them. They took me as a hostage, as
"insurance" that my father would carry out their assignment. I
escaped. CNN has the lying video. I have all their files, enough
info to prosecute the whole stinking lot of them.
Please reply to AM@gmail.com.

He hesitated, then pressed SEND, and returned to Ann.

She told him that during the hours he had been silent, she
had driven by his mom's place in Palm Beach and had seen
half a dozen cop cars in the driveway. The entire estate had
been cordoned off. Afraid they would come for her next, she
had fled and was now waiting for her flight. He noticed she
didn't mention the airport from which she was flying or her
destination, clear signs that she believed her e-mail might be
tagged despite the encrypted software.

Any government person reading the e-mail would immediately think she was flying out of Miami, because that was
the closest international airport. He was pretty sure she had
flown a puddle jumper from Key West to Orlando and was
leaving from there. He also felt fairly certain that she would
fly to Aruba via Venezuela, the closest country. It was what
he would do.

Using his prepaid cell, he called her cell and she answered
on the first ring, her voice soft, hushed. In the background,
he could hear a voice on a PA speaker.

"I really wish you would rethink this," he said without
preface.

"Too late. I made my choices."

"Jesus, Ann," he whispered. "Your old man probably no-
tified the cops already that you're a fugitive or something."

"I left him and Mom a note, told them that I had to do
this, that you're in trouble, that I'd call."

"Your parents are really going to love me now."

She pretended not to hear that. "Got your passport and money. I'll call you at this number as soon as I land. The island's so small it shouldn't take you more than thirty minutes to get to the airport. Unless you don't have a car."

"I have a car."

"And I have more information. A lot of it. See you tomorrow, Mike. Keep the cell on. Love you."

Before he could tell her to please not do this, to please not take this risk, the line went dead.

He went back online and found a new message in the Gmail account:

Your encrypted software is sophisticated. It got my attention. If u have Lazier's files, u may be Lazier. Then again, u may be telling the truth. So tell me this. Who is Wade's right-hand person? What does he look like? What does Wade look like? Send e to KFC@earthlink.net.

Mike thought about it, about the questions this person asked, the verification he or she requested. And what the hell did KFC stand for? Kentucky Fried Chicken? And why ask him about Wade and his right hand? If the person who sent the message was part of Lazier's group, he or she would know the answers. So he wrote:

Anyone in Lazier's group would know the answers to your questions. It doesn't prove shit. These bastards blindfolded me, tied my legs to bedposts, handcuffed me, drugged me. & after my dad and Wade attacked you people at the Waverunner, they came to Lazier's penthouse, where I was dragged out like dessert. & you know what? Go fuck yourself.

He returned to Gmail's IM, but Ann was no longer there. He went on the Orlando airport site and searched for this evening's flights to Caracas and then searched flights from there to Aruba and decided she would be getting in somewhere between noon and three p.m. tomorrow. He sent her a text to contact him as soon as she could, then returned to the inbox. The newest message:

OK. Send me a file. Let's see if u've got what u say u've got.

Pissed off now, Mike wrote:

You tell *me* something they couldn't possibly know.

And he waited through a container of yogurt, devouring it like some starving soul in Africa.

Not possible. If u're who u say u are, u know only what they know. So we're going to have to trust each other. Wild Donkey Farm tomorrow, nine AM. I'll know u from the CNN video.

No, you won't. Cut my hair, am wearing glasses, look like a nerd. Why should he let this idiot set the terms? He wrote:

Lighthouse. 9 AM. You won't recognize me. Call me when you arrive.
Cell #: 297-647-9877.

A response came back moments later, confirming the time and place and a return cell number.

Mike flopped back on the bed and waited for the pounding pressure in his head to stop, waited for insights, illumination, a feeling that would tell him he was headed in the right direction. But all he felt, the only insight he gained, was that he was still shockingly alone, that his cash was down by several hundred bucks, and that tomorrow he'd better ditch the Beemer and find another set of wheels.

He rolled onto his side, brought his fisted hands to his forehead, and struggled not to let his terror overpower him.

13
The Between

You exist in many times and places at once.
—*Jane Roberts*

When they stepped outside the miserable jail, Nora experienced an overwhelming need to see the ocean, to know that it existed, to touch the water that would touch the shores of her own time more than three hundred years from now. She desperately needed to connect with something familiar that would rid her of the vivid images of her mother imprisoned in that jail, in the stink of it, the despair, the silence punctuated by the awful, scurrying sounds of rats, the darkness relieved only by the flickering light of the torches.

She knuckled her eyes, breathed in the cold, clean air. The wind had tapered off, and although it was still snowing, it didn't seem to be coming down as furiously as before. She dropped her head back, taking in the swollen, lead-colored sky, and realized several hours had passed. *Hours.* But her mother had endured *weeks* in that place and Sarah Longwood had been confined there for *months,* both of them tortured by Chandler, Davies, maybe the entire town council.

Nothing would please her more than to transition the lot of them back to the Big Bang.

"Don't," Kincaid said gently.

"We're powerless here."

"No, we're not." He removed the hat he'd bought from the basket she held, tugged it on. "Not as long as they believe we represent the law."

"Chandler isn't going to surrender his power, Alex."

"We're here to find your mother. That's the first thing. Whatever else we do in the process will help the consciousness in this era evolve."

"*Evolve?*" Nora nearly gagged on the word. "C'mon. What we've seen here on a small scale is the same psychological component that results in our becoming the biggest war machine on the planet. It's what will make us one of the few countries in the industrialized world that still has a death penalty. It's why we become a nation of people who are suspicious of anyone who isn't like us, why we blindly accept whatever the government tells us, why we have agencies like Freeze, like SPOT."

"I get the point."

"No, I don't think you do." She stopped. He stopped. Sunny stopped. They were in an alley between two buildings, alone except for Sunny. "In the Jungian scheme of things, Christ, as a symbol of the self, is incomplete because in Christianity Christ is viewed as the ultimate goodness. There's no room for a shadow, for evil, for the dark side. So, in the Jungian sense, the self's need for completion forces it to find that shadow elsewhere. So whatever or whoever is different from the established norm becomes the shadow. Witches. Blacks. Muslims. Gays. Democrats. Republicans. Environmentalists. The Commies."

"In other words, we're fighting the collective cultural soup. What my mother used to call dancing with snakes."

"Yeah, pretty much."

Kincaid drew his cloak more tightly around him, mulling

it over. "Well, you and Jung are probably right. But change starts with just one person."

"That's naïve, Alex."

His features suddenly hardened. "Is it? Are those women back there the same people they were before we walked into that cell block? Why do you think they applauded? It wasn't because of my oratory talents. Every time *our* beliefs come up against the beliefs *here*, something shifts, seeds are planted. That's how revolution begins. Maybe we're creating a new timeline. Maybe because of our interference, there'll be a timeline where war, poverty, and hunger don't exist. Where the oil greed never happened. Where the biochip never fell into the wrong hands."

His idealism always astonished her. Ultimately it had helped to bring down SPOT, given them access to the biochips, and totally changed their lives. But she didn't share it. She had once, when she was much younger, in college. In the years since, though, it had been replaced by rebellion against authority, whatever the authority might be, and its intrusion into her private life.

In the days when commercial air travel was still part of her experience, she had resented the long, tedious security lines, the removal of her shoes, her jacket, the hacks at the X-ray machines, the endless requests for her license, her boarding pass. She hated being herded.

Now it was even worse, what with the sealed Baggies for your makeup and personal effects, no bottled water until you had cleared security, young mothers with nursing infants looked upon with suspicion, elderly in wheelchairs searched and humiliated. She had read that the next tech wonder for security would be cameras the size of a fingernail embedded in the back of every seat on commercial airliners. Blink too fast, scratch your head the wrong way, lick your lips too many times, twitch too much and you might find yourself at Gitmo.

That kind of authority, which seemed to be bringing

democracy to its knees. But here, democracy hadn't even
been born yet.

Nora wrapped her arms around Kincaid, hugging him
close, grateful that time and circumstances had reunited
them. His cold cheek pressed against hers, his arms encircled her waist, their bodies pressed seamlessly together, as if
to acknowledge the differences that drew them to each other.
They balanced each other, she and Kincaid, following immutable laws of attraction. Yet, their relationship and their
chemistry were quantum quirks, the stuff that occurred at
molecular levels, impossible to prove absolutely unless you
opened your heart.

"You always smell so good," he whispered, his breath
warming the curve of her neck.

"We should find a bed," she whispered back.

And suddenly, the smell of his skin and hair rushed into
her, through her, and she hungered for his hands, his mouth,
his body, her lust so overpowering that she knew the chip had
kick-started their libidos. These feelings were part of what
made time travel addictive. He tried to slide his hands up inside her voluminous skirt, but there was so much fabric that
he gave up and slipped his hands up over her breasts. He
kissed her and she lost herself in the shape and texture of his
mouth and tongue, the warmth of his breath, the feel of the
skin on the back of his neck, with its intimate creases marking the passage of time. Despite her absurd clothes, she felt
him growing hard.

Shouts echoed through the alley and she and Kincaid
quickly broke apart, like teenagers caught having sex in the
back of a car. A wagon blocked the mouth of the alley, with
James Cory and Paul Fry on the wooden bench, Fry holding
the horse's reins and Cory shouting and motioning them to
come over.

"Shit," Kincaid murmured. "Were we doing anything in-
decent?"

"Breaking law forty-two: no public displays of affection."

They ran toward the wagon, Sunny in the lead. The wagon was too high for her to jump into, so Kincaid lifted her in and Nora scrambled into the back on her own. Odd behavior for a woman in this era, she thought, but she had broken that ceiling during her first five minutes here.

"Are you bound for the inn?" Cory asked.

"And something to eat," Kincaid said. "Will you join us?"

"Certainly."

"Mr. Cory, could you take a detour first?" Nora asked. "To the ocean?"

He turned on the bench, smiling slightly, regarding her with an open curiosity. "Of course. But there is not much to see, Mrs. Goodwin. No one ventures out in this weather."

"That's okay."

"Okay?" Snow caught on his lashes as he frowned. "I am not familiar with that term."

"It, uh, means I understand," she said.

Fry turned the horse into a gentle turn and they headed away from the main street. They passed woods, several rows of small buildings that she guessed were homes, smoke spiraling upward from the chimneys. Now more woods, where the snow was deeper and less traveled, an area that, in her time, would become Blue River's chichi downtown.

Nora sat up a little straighter, struggling to orient herself, to juxtapose her memory of twenty-first-century Blue River over the reality of Blue River in 1695. Impossible. She had no landmarks out here, nothing that looked even remotely familiar. But when the dunes came into view, landmarks no longer mattered. The wind had blown the sand into intricately sculpted works of art, rolling beige shapes broken up here and there by vegetation that had adapted to the brutal combination of winter and salt.

Once the wagon stopped, she climbed out and ran over to the snow-dusted dunes, down their slopes. Her boots kicked up sand and snow, while the wind whipped the water and hurled it into her face. She tasted the salt on her lips, felt it against her cheeks, her forehead, and that same sensual feeling swept over her that she'd experienced in the alley with Kincaid minutes ago. She stood at the water's edge, wind gusting off the water, burning her eyes, blowing her hair into a wild tangle, puffing her cloak out like a sail, waves breaking over the tips of her boots.

Nora sank to her knees and dug her fingers through the snow, into the cold sand beneath it, then let it trickle through her fingers. It felt cold against her skin, alien and yet familiar. In some buried pocket here on this beach, the sand from her own time existed already. In her mind's eye, she could see the lighthouse that would rise here one day, white as bone, majestic, a lonely testament to history.

More waves crashed against the beach and the water felt shockingly cold against her hands and forearms. It was so clear, unpolluted, so heartbreakingly blue that she cupped her hands into it. Behind her, she heard Sunny's shrill, almost piercing howl, then felt a crushing pressure in her skull . . . and emerged in the living room of her new home in Aruba, on her knees, with her cupped hands still holding the saltwater of an ocean more than three centuries in the past. Air exploded from her lungs, her hands dropped to her thighs. The water splashed against the tiled floor and beaded. Lights from the window glinted against the beads.

Something shattered behind her, and when she glanced back, there stood Curtis in shorts and a T-shirt, spaghetti and red sauce and bits of his plate strewn around him. "Nora," he gasped. "What . . ."

She sank back against her heels, her skirt billowing out around her like dark wings. "We need help," she blurted. "Got there February ninth, 1695. We're now at Feb ten. Staying at the Blue River Inn. They think Alex is Magistrate Goodwin from Boston and I . . ."

"Shit. Shit," Curtis lurched toward her like a drunk, weaving, his motions jerky, surreal.

Then she could see him *and* the beach three centuries in

the past, smelled spaghetti *and* salt air, felt the sand *and* the floor against her knees. *Bifurcation.* She couldn't seem to stabilize her presence in either time and suddenly imagined living the rest of her life like this, flickering between two times, ghostly, surreal, trapped in the between.

Curtis threw his arms around her and she stabilized, her breath coming in great, heaving gulps, as though her lungs had ceased to function during the seconds or minutes she had been flickering. "Grip my hand," Curtis told her. "The sensation will pass."

He didn't get it. This wasn't just a *sensation.* It was *real,* and she was afraid that any second now, she would be back on that windswept beach with everything she needed to tell him unsaid. "April 2006. Nellysford, Virginia. Near the Monroe Institute. There's a house for sale. Ask for Lea at the institute. Tell her you're a friend of Nora's. Or of Berlin's. He's hiding out there. I met him."

"Berlin?" Curtis exclaimed. "Dr. Berlin from SPOT? But how . . . ?"

Nora clutched his hand more tightly, struggling to hold on to this time, these moments, and kept talking. "I need information on Reverend Chandler, a merchant named James Cory, and the accused women, what happened to them. Sarah Longwood, Rebeka Short, Lucia Gray. My mother was imprisoned there. Catherine Griffin, her maiden name. She escaped to a place that welcomes the disenfranchised. That's how it's described. I need info on that place. And we need your help, all of you. We can't seem to transition back. Alex thinks we won't be able to until we've found my mother. We're at the Blue River Inn and . . ."

"Slow down, Nora, slow down. It's okay. You're stabilizing."

But she saw the lie in his eyes, in the tightness of his mouth. He was afraid, she knew, that if he released her, she would transition spontaneously, a boomerang through time. He shouted for the others.

Tyler loped into the room first, wearing boxer shorts and a T-shirt, his expression betraying everything that he felt, making it clear that he realized what was happening. "What do you need, Nora?" he asked urgently.

Panic. What did she need? More people, weapons, information—more, more, more. "Glow sticks. A stun gun. A map of how the area looked in 1695. More chips. More ammo."

The others were in the room now and they all took off in opposite directions as she raced on, trying to jam as much information as possible into whatever time she had left. Kat returned with a small, bulging, black velvet shoulder bag that she tied around Nora's wrist and tightened. "Hold on, Nora, hold on. Tyler's downloading information onto his PDA."

Hold on, hold on. . . . Her head spun; she felt nauseated; the smell of the ocean suffused her senses; the cold wind bit at her back. Suddenly, she and Curtis were both on the beach, sprawled in the sand, his arms still wrapped around her.

Sunny ran toward them, barking frantically. Curtis rolled away from Nora and stumbled to his feet—his bare feet. He was wearing just shorts and T-shirt—shivering from the cold. His teeth chattered, snow caught in his hair, his beard. "Jesus God, what's going on? This . . . this . . . has n-never ha-happened b-before." He danced around, trying to warm himself. Then Sunny and Kincaid reached them.

Kincaid threw his cloak around Curtis's shoulders, Sunny leaped up at him, barking, knocking him back, and Curtis and the dog crashed to the sand—and transitioned. Only the cloak remained, a rippling dark stain against the sand.

Nora stood there in mute shock, understanding at some level that Sunny had helped Curtis transition home. Kincaid whipped the cloak off the sand, drew it around himself, grasped her hand and tried to pull her up. But her knees refused to unlock. Kincaid dropped into a crouch, still clutching her hand. "What the fuck just happened, Nora?"

"I transitioned spontaneously and then . . . couldn't hold it. I . . . was in both places at once. Ryan was trying to hold me there. I . . . how're we going to explain Sunny's disappearance?"

"I don't know."

"What did you see?"

"We couldn't see you after you went over the dunes. But Sunny immediately sensed that something had gone wrong. She leaped out of the wagon and took off down the beach. I ran after her. What's that?" He gestured at the bag snapped to her wrist.

"Supplies."

"Hide it. Here they come."

Cory and Fry trotted up the beach, cloaks billowing in the wind. Nora untied the bag from her wrist and stuffed it into an inner pocket in the cloak. She and Kincaid stood, her knees popping, her joints creaking, her face now like ice. They needed an explanation for Sunny's absence. "She ran off" sounded lame, but she couldn't think of anything else.

"You are uninjured," Cory observed. "A relief. The dog behaved so strangely that we thought the worst."

"I tripped in the sand. Just clumsy."

Fry looked concerned, perhaps even suspicious, but made a hand gesture indicating that he was pleased she was unharmed.

"Where is Sunny?" Cory asked, looking around.

"Chasing something on the beach," Kincaid replied.

"We can wait for her in the wagon," Cory offered.

Wait how long? Nora didn't know whether the dog could transition back any more easily than she or Curtis or any of them. And could she target this precise moment in time?

As they stumbled up the beach after Cory and Fry, Kincaid leaned close to her. "Sunny's been doing this longer than any of us. Don't worry about her."

When they came over the dunes, Sunny appeared, trotting along, head held high, tail wagging. She wore a bright red kerchief around her neck now and held something in her mouth. For a moment or two, Nora actually believed that she *had* run after something on the beach, had caught it and was now bringing it back to them. Retrieving, that's what these dogs did. Except that she hadn't been wearing a red kerchief earlier.

Nora finally reached her and Sunny dropped a PDA in the snow-covered sand, and sat back, as if expecting a treat. She scooped the PDA out of the snow and sand, hid it in her cloak, and hugged the dog. "Good girl," she whispered.

Sunny barked and licked Nora, her breath smelling faintly of tuna fish. She had stayed in Aruba long enough to get fed, for Tyler to finish downloading information onto the PDA, and to have a red kerchief tied around her neck. Nora didn't have a chance to examine the kerchief until they were back in the wagon. Pinned to the inside of it was a note from Tyler:

> PDA powered up, should last 5 hrs. Local police have distributed our photos. We have to get out of here. Kat left for Nellysford to find the house you mentioned. We'll take as much stuff as we can. Look for us there after April 15, 2006, unless we get to you first.

Nora folded the note and slipped it down inside her boot. She was anxious to see what was on the PDA, but didn't dare bring it out now, while they were in the back of the wagon. Cory and Fry were undoubtedly already suspicious about their behaviors and actions. She didn't want to alienate them. These two men were probably their only allies in Blue River.

When they arrived at the inn, Nora left Sunny with the men and excused herself, saying she would be down shortly. She hurried up the stairs to the room, her cloak now so ridiculously heavy with contraband that it was a relief to remove it. She set the basket with their purchases on the bed, sat down, and took out Tyler's PDA, her own cell and PDA, and the black velvet bag that had been tied to her wrist. She eagerly opened the bag and gently emptied its contents onto the lumpy bed: glow sticks, two stun guns, a pair of hand-cuffs, an extra clip for their weapons, packs of matches, and a large packet of firecrackers.

Firecrackers?

Whatever. She retrieved her bag from the cabinet and zipped the new items into an inner pocket. Her cell jingled and she realized that somewhere on their trip to the jail and here, it had gotten turned on. During the moments she had been in Aruba, a new message had arrived. She clicked it.

April 28, 2006
    Am on my way to Blue River 1695. Saw Mariah. She went back to retrieve your mother, got arrested, & tortured by Rev. Chandler. Avoid him. See u there.
                              RB

Where? What month had he targeted? And why had Mariah tried to retrieve her mother? Out of guilt?

She checked to see if any more messages had come through during the brief time she'd been in Aruba. But there was nothing.

Nora slipped the cell into her bag, turned on the PDA. Six files. She started clicking through them, Tyler's roundup of historical info. She discovered that the colony was renamed the Province of Massachusetts Bay when a new charter was signed in October 1691 by King William and Queen Mary. Enacted seven months later, it basically stripped the colony of its independence. The governor was now appointed by the king, rather than elected, and his powers were greatly ex-panded. He, like the king, could veto acts of the General Court, was in charge of the militia and all its officers, and had the right to summon, adjourn, and delay the General Court.

Tyler had added an explanatory note about the General

Court, saying that it was basically in charge of all legislative activities in the province. It could pass laws, establish fines and punishments, levy taxes, but only with the approval of the governor. In other words, she thought, Reverend Chandler and his town council functioned as the General Court in Blue River.

The new charter absorbed Plymouth Colony, Martha's Vineyard and Nantucket, Maine, and portions of Nova Scotia. Within Massachusetts, half a dozen cities were listed on the map: Boston and Salem, Medford, Plymouth, Blue River, and Great Blue Hill—a place she'd never heard of.

Nora closed this file and went on to the next, Tyler's summary of information:

Nora, in a nutshell, here's what I was able to find. And to do this, I had to ask Curtis to show me how to slow down time. No telling how long it would have taken otherwise.

James Cory, his brother Edward, and a mute freeman, Paul Fry, owned New York Food Supplies. They claimed to be from NY but actually hailed from the town of Mystic Harbor. The town, if it ever existed, has been lost in time. I found only two references to this place, one from the U of Mass, the other from the historical archives at Boston Public Lib, that say it was an urban legend that existed among fugitive slaves and other disenfranchised people. It was supposed to be a safe refuge for those who were "victims of tyranny." The name Mystic Harbor meant secret (Mystic) refuge (Harbor). If you could find your way there, you were allowed to stay.

It was allegedly well hidden, on a hill between taller hills, with a nearby body of water (lake or river) that provided plenty of freshwater and fish. Its valley was fertile enough to grow all the other food the town needed. Freedom was the key to this Shangri-la—religious freedom, freedom from the crown, from intolerance against blacks, witches, whatever. The only reason history has any reference to this place at all is that James Cory, on his deathbed in Boston, claimed it was his only true home, and Sarah Longwood, who was with him when he died, wrote about it.

Even though we both know that Sarah Longwood was hanged along with Lucia Gray and Rebeka Short, it looks as if history has changed now. There were two other women who were accused—a white and a black. Sarah claims she witnessed the torture of the black woman, who vanished in thin air while on the strappado. A black woman who "vanished." Sounds like Mariah Jones, doesn't it?

Sarah and the other two survived and claimed they escaped the Blue River gaol with the help of strangers with "wondrous powers." I found no ref to Mom—either as Catherine Walrave or as Catherine Griffin.

Historically, Chandler remains a sadistic prick, but here again, history diverges. We know that he was involved in the Salem witch trials and then moved to Blue River and was responsible for the evidence against the three women accused of witchcraft. In the version of history that I recall, he left BR after the accused were hanged and went on to live in Boston and write the kinds of books about the devil and religion that made the Mathers so famous. In Boston, he lives to a ripe old age. But in another version of events, he's known for his "Laws of Righteous Living," the body of rules he and his council created to govern BR like despots. His evidence against the accused was thwarted by Ericson Ivers, Governor Stoughton's emissary, who supposedly was in BR to report on the evidence against the accused. Stoughton had been involved in Salem and had an interest in the outcome at BR. There was some sort of revolt by people in BR and this version of history doesn't reveal what happened to Chandler. But the town was liberated from his tyranny.

The only other thing I found on Ivers was that Chandler filed an official complaint with him about Magistrate Goodwin and his wife. Chandler's laws

forbade female visitors to the jail and apparently
Goodwin violated that law by bringing his wife and
clerk into the gaol to record testimony. Chandler also
claims that Goodwin removed the "Laws of Righteous
Living" from all public places.

Will keep looking for anything useful and hope that
someone—Sunny?—can transition to get it to you. We
can transition to you, but obviously there are no guarantees about our accuracy. Oh—one other thing.
Someone who claims he was abducted by Lazier's
people has gotten in touch with us through our website. The kid is supposedly Lazier's insurance to make
sure his father will do what Lazier hired him to do—
go back, stun you and Alex, so your bodies will reject
the chips, and then you'll barter for your lives in return
for *our* chips. He allegedly escaped and is hiding out
somewhere here on the island. One of us will check it
out. But watch your back, just in case it's true.

If you finish before we get there, look for us at the
house here first, then in Nellysford. Luv, T

Nora clicked through the remaining files, where her brother
had downloaded actual historical documents that supplemented
what he'd told her in his letter. She read through them carefully and found an interesting bit of information. After Blue
River was liberated from the tyranny of Chandler and his
council, the residents voted on creating a local government
for the people and by the people.

They voted in a chief officer—like a mayor—and five
council members. They voted on laws to govern the town, on
trade agreements with neighboring towns, agreed to expand
the school, and voted to allow all children, regardless of
gender, to attend. But the most startling tenets in Blue
River's new government, at least to Nora, were the separa-
tion of church and state, that "no man shall own another,"
and the abolishment of any kind of death penalty.

In short, it seemed that Blue River would emerge from the

darkest period in its history to become a fledgling bastion of freedom more than ninety years before the Constitution was ratified.

Or, at any rate, that was what happened in *one* version of Blue River's history. The version she hoped that she and Kincaid could bring about.

14
In the Tavern

Evil has a head start.
—*Lyall Watson*

Holcomb arrived at the tavern at two that afternoon, still disturbed by his earlier encounter with Chandler and by what it had revealed about himself. The poppet in the pocket of his breeches seemed to move, its little bean eyes pressing against his thigh. He should burn the goddamn thing, he thought.

He took his usual table close to the fireplace, where the black kid continued to turn the spits. The scrawny cat Holcomb had fed at breakfast this morning was curled up next to the kid. Now and then, the kid would let go of the spit to run his fingers through the cat's fur, and she'd stretch languidly, eyes opening sleepily, then curl up again. Two men at a table on the other side of the room hovered over their Bibles, apparently debating the finer points of scripture. Other than that, Holcomb had the room to himself.

A serving woman brought him a platter of chicken and some sort of corn mush, with slices of fresh brown bread and cheese. She offered him ale, but the two he'd had with breakfast had been enough. He asked for hot apple cider.

Halfway through his meal, Kincaid came into the tavern with two men, one of them black. He had to be a freeman, Holcomb figured, accompanying two white men into the tavern, something that simply wasn't done here by slaves or indentured servants. Kincaid looked uncomfortable in the era clothing, as though the breeches squeezed his balls and the boots pinched his toes. Holcomb sympathized.

They sat at the table to his right while the dog waited just outside the tavern doorway, a watchful sentry visible through the window. Where was Nora McKee?

With Kincaid only a few yards away from him, Holcomb expected his chip to start buzzing, humming, vibrating, as it had done before. But nothing happened. Did that mean Kincaid's chip had malfunctioned as well?

Shortly after Kincaid and his companions were served identical lunch platters, Holcomb got up from his table and approached Kincaid. "Good day, sir. I understand you are the new magistrate?"

As soon as Kincaid looked at him, Holcomb realized he was wearing contacts. It surprised him. Wade had led him to believe that Travelers never wore contacts because if they had to transition without warning, without time to remove them, the contacts could become fused to the eyeballs. Was this just more bullshit that Wade had fed him? Had Wade lied to him about *everything*? *Does it mean Mike is actually dead now?* He barely resisted the urge to grab Kincaid's arm and beg him for a chip.

"Yes, I'm Magistrate Goodwin. And you are . . . ?"

"Ericson Ivers. I am here to gather information for Governor Stoughton on the situation with the accused. May I join you and your guests?"

"Certainly." Kincaid gestured toward the other chair and introduced his two companions. "James Cory and Paul Fry."

"A pleasure," Cory said, but Fry just nodded.

Fry, the black man. The man's piercing eyes seemed to see right through Holcomb.

"Mr. Cory," Holcomb said. "Owner of New York Food Supplies. You are practically legendary in Blue River."

Cory laughed, his handsome face lighting up. "Infamous, perhaps."

"You were fortunate to arrive before this storm," Holcomb said.

"We were forced to seek sanctuary last night when the wind was especially strong. The magistrate and his wife had been stranded in the woods by thieves and thugs who accosted them and took their horses. They were kind enough to invite us to their fire."

Sure.

"I was not aware that the governor had sent an emissary," Kincaid remarked.

"And I was not informed that a new magistrate had been appointed," Holcomb replied. *And are we both bullshit artists or what?*

Kincaid's smile was quick, commiserating, charming. "It would seem, Mr. Ivers, that we have been left in the dark by our higher authorities."

"Indeed," Holcomb said. *It's called fucked over, pal.* "Have you had the opportunity yet to speak to the accused?"

Holcomb hated talking without contractions, in the stilted lexicon of the era. He had to think about what he was going to say before he said it. When he first had arrived here, he had said very little for fear of exposing himself as a phony. He had listened for *thee* and *thou* and *ye* and had heard his share. But he also had noticed that not everyone spoke that way. If anything, the daily speech here possessed an obvious courtesy, a deference to civilized manners. The only contractions he'd heard were in slurred speech from too many brews.

"We spent the morning talking with Sarah Longwood and

had hoped to return to the gaol later to speak to the others. But the day has gotten away from us. It will have to wait until tomorrow," Kincaid said.

"I would like to be present when you gather your testimony from the others, Magistrate. Unfortunately, I arrived after the former magistrate died, so I need firsthand information to take to the governor," said Holcomb.

"What do you know about the events that led to these women being confined to the gaol?" Kincaid asked.

Just the facts as history had written them and hearsay from his morning bullshit sessions. But when Holcomb started talking, he sounded like the attorney he was, presenting evidence about a case. "In late summer, Sarah Longwood was overheard cursing the magistrate and the reverend. The reverend's wife and the magistrate got sick not long afterward and died. Then there was an Indian attack on the town in which four people died. Then three cows died that belonged to Sarah Longwood's neighbor. The night that Sarah was taken to the gaol, a storage area in the general store caught fire and burned. The man who owns the store is on the town council. As you undoubtedly know, in the absence of a magistrate, the town council has absolute legal authority over Blue River."

Kincaid frowned. "Actually, they have no legal authority over Blue River. The king and governor are the ultimate authority, with the General Court beneath them, then the House of Representatives."

Uh-oh, fuckup. "What I meant was that since the magistrate's death, Reverend Chandler and the council have appointed themselves as the legal authority. And that is one area that concerns the governor."

"With good reason," Cory remarked.

"Then perhaps the first thing to address in your report is the way that the reverend and his council have abused their power," Kincaid said.

"I have done so already, sir," Holcomb replied.

"What do you know about Lucia Gray?" Kincaid asked.

"She is the youngest of the accused, just fifteen. In late summer, I think it was, she started having fits, tantrums, inexplicable rages in which she thrashed and spoke in a foreign tongue. One day in church, she had a fit and urinated on the altar. Lucia was the first to be accused and later claimed that Sarah's spectral form had come to her while Sarah was working on the farm with her mother."

"After Salem, spectral evidence was deemed inadmissible," Kincaid said. "Even Cotton Mather expressed doubt about it after the trials. Why would Reverend Chandler admit it as evidence for an accusation?"

It surprised Holcomb that Kincaid had done his homework. "Because he believes it to be valid proof of Satanic possession. Lucia named the other two women as well. Rebeka Short, a seventy-one-year-old grandmother, has lived in Blue River for half a century. Catherine Griffin worked at the general store and was arrested not long after I arrived. She escaped some time ago."

"Yes, I heard. Do you know how it happened?"

"I do not, Magistrate. I heard that the store's owner, Francis Travers, claims that he found several poppets in her work area and one of his employees saw her having a fit in the cellar. That alone was enough to have her accused."

"How convenient that Travers is a member of the council as well." Kincaid polished off the last of his corn mush. "I think I would like to speak to him about these poppets he found. The light will be gone in a few hours. . . ." He glanced at the window, apparently noticing, as Holcomb did, that darkness gathered in the glass. In February, with the inclement weather, night came early. "Perhaps you would like to join me when I speak to Mr. Travers."

"I would be delighted."

Over Kincaid's shoulder, Holcomb saw Nora coming through the tavern doorway; the dog remained where she was, but sat up now, attentive, watchful. Nora's cloak was draped casually around her shoulders, her boots clicked against the floor, and her skirt rustled as she moved into the room. He didn't need to plant a poppet in her room so that she could be accused of practicing witchcraft. She already looked suspicious, so different from other women in Blue River that it wouldn't be long before someone would accuse her of something.

Her height, for one thing, drew attention to her, six feet or more in the boots, which put her well beyond the height of most women in this era. Her eyes held a certain quality, too, broadcasting that she was not local and never would be. Then there was the way she held herself, with an awareness that she was equal to any man, an attitude as alien to the women in this era as their religious fervor was to her.

The men all stood as she approached the table. "Mr. Ivers, my wife and clerk, Nora Goodwin."

Holcomb wasn't sure what protocol required. A kiss on the hand? A handshake? He merely nodded. "A pleasure, Mrs. Goodwin."

"Likewise, Mr. Ivers."

She claimed the empty chair between Kincaid and Fry, flicked her cloak off her shoulders and onto the back of the chair, as though its weight annoyed her. The men sat down again. Holcomb thought she seemed nervous, uptight, but then again, why shouldn't she? She didn't fit in here and knew it.

"Mr. Ivers is here as an emissary of the governor," Kincaid explained. "He would like to sit in with us as we gather our testimony and has agreed to accompany us when we speak to Mr. Travers about what happened, exactly, with Catherine Griffin."

"What does the governor wish to know?" she asked, then thanked the server as she set down an identical platter of food. "What is his intent? Does he wish to be involved in these trials, as he was in Salem?"

She held Holcomb's gaze as she spoke and he resisted the

urge to look away. He sensed that if he did, she would *know* he was a fraud.

"I think he simply wants information," Holcomb said.

"And you, Mr. Ivers. What are *your* ideas on all this?" She spooned mush into her mouth but didn't look away from him.

"I am only an observer who reports to the governor," he replied.

"Then I see no harm in this," she said to Kincaid.

Chandler suddenly waddled into the tavern, breathless from exertion, his cane tapping the floor rhythmically, as if it were some sort of Morse code. His cloak was damp, his eyes wild, his wig gone, his own hair going every which way. With him were Travers, the portly owner of the general store, and Ezekial Rowe, the skinny town chemist, a Mutt and Jeff who looked as agitated as Chandler.

The dog, Holcomb noticed, watched them warily, sniffing at the air, as if reading their emotions through the odors they emitted. It edged past the doorway, into the tavern, and Holcomb had the distinct impression that the dog was eavesdropping. The creature spooked him.

"Mr. Ivers," Chandler huffed. "We, of the town council, are filing an official complaint with the governor's office concerning violations of the town laws by the magistrate and his wife." Chandler's small, dark eyes slipped to Kincaid, Nora, and then to Cory and Fry, as if they were implicated in these violations simply because they were sitting at the same table. Travers and Rowe nodded vigorously in agreement.

"And what violations are you addressing, Reverend?" *Oh, great asshole schmuck.* "Please elaborate," prompted Holcomb.

The kid who had been turning the spit now moved away from his post and crouched down next to the dog, petting her, combing his fingers through her golden reddish fur. The dog licked the kid's face, her tail wagged, but her gaze never left the table. And in front of them, Chandler leaned heavily on his cane.

"The magistrate defied God's laws by taking a woman with him into the gaol to hear the evidence. All over town, he has torn down the Laws of Righteous Living, he—"

"Excuse me, Reverend," Holcomb interrupted. "Where in scripture is it written that a woman cannot enter a gaol?"

Blink, blink went Chandler's eyes. "It . . . it . . . I . . ."

"Nowhere," Kincaid said, his eyes lingering on Chandler, then darting to Travers and Rowe. "The laws of the province are not based on scripture."

"According to the province charter," Nora said, "you are powerless, sir."

His face went blood red, his mouth twitched and pursed, and then he shouted, "Blasphemy! God's law is the only law!"

His cane whipped upward, and with the hooked end, he grabbed Nora by the neck and jerked her forward, forcing her to rise halfway out of her chair. She gasped, her eyes bulged in their sockets, and she grabbed on to the cane, struggling to jerk it away from Chandler before he tore off her head. The dog shot toward Chandler, slammed into his back, and he pitched forward, lost his grip on his cane, and slammed into the table, tipping it over. Food, cider, glasses, and utensils clattered and shattered against the floor.

Nora's chair slammed backward, all the men shot to their feet, and Kincaid hurled himself at Chandler, knocking him to the floor. The two men who had been reviewing scripture at another table scrambled out of the way and stared, aghast, as Kincaid and Chandler rolled across the tavern locked in a strange embrace.

Holcomb lurched toward them, grabbed Chandler by the back of his cloak, yanked him upward, and threw him against the wall.

"You stupid . . ." *Fuck*. ". . . man," he spat, wrenching back, breathing hard.

"You . . . you . . ." Chandler sputtered, his cheeks burning brightly, a white ball of spit gathered in the corner of his mouth.

"Shut up," Holcomb barked.

The dog was on the other side of the room now, panting but watchful, ready. Travers and Rowe looked paralyzed. Fry moved toward Nora, Cory toward Kincaid, the lines now drawn, the camouflage of courtesy torn away.

Chandler whipped around, his plump face ruddy with rage, and stabbed a chubby, dimpled finger toward the dog. *"That beast is dangerous and should be shot!"*

A crowd had gathered. People jammed the doorway, craning their necks to see what was going on. Nash, the inn proprietor, pushed his way through the swarm, bellowing, "Out of the way! Please get out of the way!" When he reached Kincaid and the others, he said, "Gentlemen, if you would take your disagreements outside. I have other guests."

"There are no disagreements, Mr. Nash." Cory spoke with the quiet authority of a god. "There is only heightened emotion."

Nash gestured wildly toward the mess. "Begging your pardon, Mr. Cory, but the evidence here says otherwise."

"Reverend Chandler started this dispute," Cory said. "And he assaulted Mrs. Goodwin. The dog was merely protecting her."

Nash glared at Chandler and shook a finger at him, like a schoolmarm scolding a naughty student. "You are not right in the mind, Walter." He leaned toward Chandler, his finger in the reverend's face now, his voice trembling with anger. "Did I not tell you there would be trouble if you continued your ways? Now look at what you have caused!"

"Fool!" Chandler cried. "You are like them, Jacob, all of them. Sinners, defilers, followers of—"

"Leave!" Nash roared as he flung his arm toward the door. "Leave my establishment. Now."

Chandler, a vein throbbing at his temple, his eyes narrowed to dark slits, didn't move. He tugged at his clothes, straightening them, struggling to regain his dignity. When he spoke, his teeth were gritted together, and his breath hissed through them. "This is not your concern, Francis." His cane lay on the other side of the room and, without it, he was forced to lean on a table.

"You heard the man," Cory said. "Leave the tavern, Mr. Chandler."

Maybe it was the "mister," instead of "reverend," that did it. Maybe it was just that Chandler finally had gone over the edge. His face turned bloodred so quickly that Holcomb thought he might be on the verge of a stroke. He bellowed, "It is *blasphemy* to speak to a man of God in this fashion! It is . . ."

Fry suddenly gripped Chandler's arm, spun him around as though he were a toy, and shoved him toward the door. Travers marched over to Chandler's cane, swept it up, and glared at the dog, the cane raised as if to strike.

The dog bared its teeth and Kincaid's arm snapped out, caught the cane, and jerked Travers toward him. "I have questions to ask you about Catherine Griffin, Mr. Travers. Do sit down." He whipped the cane out of Travers's hand and passed it to Cory, who thrust it at Chandler. Fry walked Chandler and Rowe out of the tavern, a hand on each man's arm.

Holcomb pulled over a chair from another table and Kincaid shoved Travers into it. "You ca-cannot do this," Travers sputtered, looking beseechingly at Cory. "Mr. Cory, how can you allow . . ."

"Let us understand each other," Cory said. "One merchant to another. I cannot continue to deliver food and supplies to Blue River if the law is not followed. And because I am Blue River's main supplier, this should give you pause, Mr. Travers. Magistrate Goodwin is here to do a job. The council should be supporting him in this effort."

Brilliant, Holcomb thought. A threat to cut off the food supply seized people's attention instantly.

"You . . . you would not do such a thing," Travers stammered, apparently seeing how quickly his own livelihood would dry up. If the general store had no supplies, it would have to shut down. And if the general store shut down, the town would die within weeks. Businesses would close; an exodus would ensue.

"Need I remind you, Mr. Travers, that this journey takes me two weeks? I could be delivering to towns much larger than Blue River that are closer to New York and be making twice or three times the profit," Cory countered.

This sobering assessment of the situation left Travers with a deepening frown that jutted down between his frightened eyes. He ran the back of his hand under his hawk nose, cleared his throat. "But . . . but without your supplies, we would have mostly local foods, Mr. Cory, and there is not enough of that to feed the entire town. You would not strand an entire town because of . . . of . . ."

"Yes, I would, Mr. Travers. And I suggest that you relay this information to the reverend and to the rest of the town council. And now, the magistrate and Mr. Ivers have questions about Catherine Griffin. And Mr. Nash"—he glanced over at the inn proprietor—"we will gladly clean up this mess."

"And pay for any damages," Kincaid added.

Nash looked placated. "Then please make yourselves comfortable at another table."

Misery lined Travers's face now—mouth plunging into a pout, jowls sagging, eyes hooded. He spat, "You have betrayed the council, Jacob."

"My allegiance is to my own conscience," Nash replied, then went over to Nora, who was rubbing the back of her neck. "I am sorry for his behavior, Mrs. Goodwin. May I get you something warm to drink?"

"You are not at fault, Mr. Nash. I appreciate your concern. I do not require anything else. Thank you."

Once they were all settled at the new table, Kincaid began his questioning about Catherine Griffin. Where were the poppets found? Who found them? Who saw her having a fit in the cellar? Was Chandler present at any time? Yes? Which time? When the poppets were discovered? They kept on like this for nearly half an hour, Kincaid bombarding Travers with questions, then Nora, then Holcomb questioning Travers until the man finally threw up his hands.

"Enough. Please. You confuse my memories with all these questions."

"Confuse your *memories*?" Holcomb leaned toward him. "But your *memories*, Mr. Travers, are what resulted in Catherine Griffin being accused. Your memories had better not be confused, or else you could be charged with false testimony."

"Me?" He looked shocked at the possibility. "But I . . . I did nothing. I did what Reverend Chandler requested. I . . ."

"And *what* did he request, Mr. Travers?" Nora asked. "What did Reverend Chandler want you to do?"

Flustered now, he looked at each of them, shook his head, then stared at his hands, fingers laced together on the tabletop. "I . . . no, that is not what I meant. You are twisting my words. You are . . ."

"Did he ask you to place the poppets in Catherine's work area?" Nora demanded. "Did he tell you to get one of your employees to testify about witnessing her supposed fit? Did he demand that you do the devil's work? Is that it, Mr. Travers?"

Silence.

Holcomb felt the shape of the poppet in his pocket. "I believe that Walter Chandler uses you and the rest of the council to stir up terror and superstition, Mr. Travers, because such an atmosphere makes it so much easier to manipulate the people in town." He brought out the poppet and set it in the middle of the table. "I believe he gave you a poppet just like this one to put in Catherine's work area. Or perhaps it was this very poppet."

Travers stared in horror at the grotesque little doll. His mouth moved, but no words came out.

"And the reason I say this," Holcomb went on, "is that the

reverend asked *me* to put this poppet among the magistrate's things."

Travers still didn't speak. But Kincaid cast a sharp glance Holcomb's way, eyes screaming, *When?*

Holcomb answered his question without making it seem that he was addressing Kincaid. "He did this shortly after the magistrate and his wife arrived, Mr. Travers, because he knew that a man of the law might discover the truth about how these women came to be accused of practicing witchcraft." *And I'm saying all this because I need your help, Kincaid, to rescue my son.*

Travers pushed away from the table and staggered to his feet. He looked terrified, eyes as huge as UFOs, mouth trembling. He raised his arm and pointed at Holcomb. "You . . . you are one of them. You have . . . a poppet, like the women did. You . . . you lie. . . . You twist my words. You . . ."

He whirled around and ran out of the tavern.

"I am sure we have not heard the last of this," Nora remarked.

Cory frowned and sat forward. "I do not mean to intrude, Magistrate. But I feel you and Mrs. Goodwin would be safer staying elsewhere. While I doubt that Mr. Nash would harm you, I cannot say that with any confidence about his friends on the council."

Fry, who had returned in the midst of all this, rapped his knuckles against the table and gestured rapidly with his hands. Cory nodded. For the first time, Holcomb realized that Fry was a mute.

"Paul suggests that you stay in the livery, with us," Cory said. "We have comfortable rooms and Sunny is most welcome."

"We do not wish to inconvenience you, Mr. Cory," Nora said.

Fry touched her arm and shook his head.

"It is not an inconvenience," Cory assured her.

Kincaid looked at Holcomb with renewed interest. "I deeply

appreciate your forthrightness about this matter. Would it be possible to obtain a written statement from you?"

"Yes. And I would greatly appreciate the same from you, Magistrate."

Kincaid nodded and looked at the window again. The glass was completely dark. Only the light from the fire chased away the deeper shadows. "I can have it for you first thing in the morning. Shall we meet here at seven?"

"Excellent," Holcomb replied.

They shook hands all around, and then Holcomb left the inn, his thoughts stumbling around like toddlers who hadn't quite mastered the art of walking.

The snow was little more than a dusting now, but the temperature had dropped to what felt like a single digit and the bitter cold bit into Holcomb's face and hands. He drew his cloak more tightly around him and hurried through the frigid darkness. He cut into an even darker alley and ducked into the rooms behind the apothecary.

Two rooms with a large fireplace, a brick oven, a few pots in which to cook, a straw bed made tolerable only because it was piled high with quilts. He added wood to the glowing embers left from the earlier fire, put a pot of water over the fire, then lit half a dozen candles to chase off the gloom. These candles were hardly the kind he was accustomed to in his own time. They were tallow candles, dipped in animal fat, cooled, and sometimes poured into molds. Their wicks were made from cotton. They smelled like shit, but when combined with the firelight created a pleasant atmosphere for reading or cooking.

He went into the next room and rifled through his things until he found the Baggie of coffee and a filter he had brought with him. He'd been saving it for a day like this one, when he desperately needed something that would connect him to his own time.

He pulled a chair up close to the fire, shrugged off his cloak, opened the Baggie, and inhaled deeply. Cuban: its aroma wasn't like that of coffee from any other country. The aroma filled him with such longing and nostalgia for home that he nearly wept. He desperately wanted to be in the Keys, with Mike, the two of them standing outside the Cuban bakery on U.S. 1, Holcomb sipping a *café con leche,* Mike gobbling down a warm guava and cheese pastry, the warm light rolling off them like honey.

And suddenly this cold, miserable room vanished and he was standing outside the sidewalk window of the Cuban bakery on U.S. 1 in Key Largo, standing there in his breeches, linen shirt, and boots, the warm sun pouring over him, just as he had imagined. A pretty Latina on the other side of the window eyed him with frank astonishment, as though she couldn't decide whether it was a joke or whether he was an escaped mental patient.

Behind him, a child laughed and shrieked, *"Mira, papi, mira el loco!"* Or: *Look, Daddy, look at the crazy man!*

He felt his mouth move, heard himself say, *"Un café con leche, por favor. Sin azucar. Mediano."*

The woman turned away, snickering, speaking rapidly to another woman behind the counter, and they both looked at him and laughed and then the other woman snapped her thumb and forefinger together and murmured, *"Carajo. Seguro que es un loco."* Or: *Fuck, a crazy for sure.*

The first woman slipped his coffee through the window and he dug out a bill from his breeches, slapped it down, and turned away, his cell phone ringing, buzzing, buzzing again. He walked fast toward the road, dug out his cell, his shock so extreme that he just stared at the phone, at the picture of Mike that was his screen saver. Then he brought the cell to his ear and heard his son saying, "Dad? Can you hear me? Dad? Is it really you?"

It's not happening. It can't be happening. It is *happening.* "Mike. Christ, where are you? Are you okay?" He moved fast toward the alley, headed for the area behind the bakery.

Where there were no cars, no background noises. "Mike? You still there?"

"Dad, I got out. Escaped. They're after me—looking for me, my face is on CNN. I'm at the Aruba lighthouse right now, and in a few minutes I'm s'posed to hook up with someone from the group of rogue Travelers and . . . and can you get here? To me?"

"I don't know. I'm not even sure how I got *here*," he replied, then explained where he was. "But look, these Travelers. There are six of them and a dog. Four of them are still in your time." He named them, gave Mike a brief history. "If you've still got Lazier's laptop, turn it over to them, but hold on to the memory sticks." *Our collateral.*

"Yeah, okay, I will." His voice dropped to an anxious whisper. "Try to get to me, Dad. Try right now. Try . . ."

And just that fast, Holcomb was back in his rooms behind the apothecary, more than three hundred years removed from his son, the cell still pressed to his ear, the cup of Cuban coffee he'd bought still in his hand, hot, steaming.

He sat heavily in the nearest chair, coffee spilling on his breeches, splashing onto the floor, his heart shredded into a million pieces. He raised the cup to his mouth and gulped at the coffee.

Real, that's real. That's Cuban coffee. I said no sugar but it's loaded. And if the coffee is real, then the phone call was real.

What was the date when he spoke to Mike?

Holcomb stared at the cell struggling to remember how to use it, how to navigate to the menu. Then his fingers remembered, and when he pressed RECEIVED CALLS, an unfamiliar cell number appeared in the window with the date and time. *March 23, 2007, 8:33 AM.* That meant that in real time, he had been gone for eight days.

Could he get back? Back to the moments before Mike called him? *Where's the lighthouse?*

Then he placed it, remembered where it was, remembered the day he and Wade had eaten lunch at the restaurant on the lighthouse cliff. He squeezed his eyes shut and reached—for Mike, the lighthouse, for March 23, 2007, 8:33 A.M.

And when he opened his eyes, he was still in a chair near the fire, more than three centuries in the past.

Stuck. Trapped.

Holcomb pressed his fists into his eyes and wept.

15
The Livery Stable
& After

*If you would be a real seeker after truth, it is
necessary that at least once in your life you
doubt, as far as possible, all things.*

—*Descartes*

The wagon clattered across hard-packed snow, through
the nearly empty street. The bitterly cold darkness wrapped
around Nora, chilling her to the bone. The breeze, blowing
out of the east, swelled with the scents of salt, water, the
wilderness of the open ocean. Nora felt that if she could follow these smells, she would awaken in her bed in Aruba. She
shut her eyes at one point, but those horrifying moments
trapped in the between came back to her and her eyes
snapped open again.

Perhaps that was what had happened to Mariah, neither
death nor life, but straddling times and worlds in the between. That place seemed symbolic of their predicament. Although they were still chipped, they couldn't transition at
will, yet it could happen precipitously, with the suddenness
of lightning.

A fog now rolled in, thickening in the spill of light from
the isolated lanterns that hung here and there along the road.
It swirled between the buildings, hugging the road like some

sort of insidious, alien life-form, and then drifted out to caress the wagon's wheels, to swallow up the horse's hooves, to transform the world into a place of mystery, weirdness, a Grimm's fairy tale.

Nora tightened her damp cloak around her, pulled her bag closer to her hip. She was glad to leave the inn. Even though Jacob Nash had asked them to reconsider and invited them to stay as long as they liked, Nora had the distinct impression that he was relieved to see them go. They had been nothing but trouble for him since their arrival this morning. Kincaid, diplomat that he was, made sure there were no hard feelings by paying him in gold coins for the damage in the tavern. And Nash, eager to clear the air—and his good name, Nora suspected—confided that he was no longer a member of the town council.

They weren't exactly following the *Star Trek* motto of noninterference here, she thought, but perhaps that was the intended nature of this particular trip. When she and Kincaid had gotten stuck in 1968, they had interfered quite a bit in certain events, but not in the way they had here. *Immersion* was how these journeys had differed. In 1968, they were accidental tourists; in 1695, they were steeped in the affairs of the culture and town, changing history by their interactions with the locals in ways that impacted their consciousness.

Kincaid was right. The women in the jail who had applauded his little speech had done so because they had never heard any man defend them as Kincaid had done. Chandler, Travers, skinny Rowe, the chemist, Nash—none of them had been challenged in exactly the way that she and Kincaid had challenged them. These experiences would be remembered and would change these people at fundamental levels.

Then there were the Cory brothers and Fry, witnesses to strange objects, events, explanations. From the information Tyler had provided on his PDA, she already knew these men would be changed.

Her head now ached with all the possibilities, and she sat

up straighter, watching the passing road. The horse snorted, broke into a fast trot, and Kincaid suddenly leaned forward. "Mr. Cory, do you know where the doctor lives?"

"Yes, sir. Just ahead."

"Could you stop there for a moment?"

"Certainly, Magistrate. Are you unwell?"

"No, no," Kincaid assured him. "I told Mr. Chandler that I wanted the doctor to examine the accused and I would like to make sure that he did what I requested."

Ha. Don't hold your breath, Nora thought. Tomorrow when they entered the jail again, she expected to find the same fetid conditions, the accused still waiting for the physician, and the jailer still conflicted about his loyalty to Chandler.

When the wagon stopped a few minutes later and Kincaid climbed down, Sunny sat up straight and whined. Nora whispered, "Relax. He'll be right back."

The fog tagged Kincaid's heels, as if playing hide-and-seek with him, then swallowed him completely, Jonah into the whale. Nora squinted, struggling to see him, but couldn't. In her old life in Blue River, the fog sometimes rolled through downtown and obscured everything in its path. Once, on campus, it had swirled around her ankles like spun sugar, looking good enough to eat. She had dipped her finger into it and come up with nothing. So to her, fog was the ultimate illusion, a magician's trick—*abracadabra presto.*

A few minutes later, Kincaid emerged from the fog as if from a dream, and when he climbed back into the wagon, she felt for his hand simply to know that he was real, solid, here. "He's not at home," Kincaid announced, and the wagon rolled on through an alley, toward the livery stable.

It was their second visit to the stable today, a large wooden building that loomed between the tiny schoolhouse on one side and a tailor's shop on the other. Fry jumped down from the wagon and pulled open the stable's massive wooden doors and Cory drove the wagon inside. The odors nearly overwhelmed Nora—of manure, horses, hay, sweat, hot metal from the blacksmith's area, heat from the massive fireplace, and burning oil from the numerous lanterns. She counted half a dozen men sitting around the fireplace, eating and drinking and laughing, and two more men came over to the wagon to greet Cory and Fry and to tend to the horse.

While Cory conferred with the men, they all got down from the wagon and Sunny sniffed the air, reading the panoply of smells. Fry motioned for them to follow him and led them through a doorway and into a narrow corridor that angled toward the front of the building. The horse and manure odor was fainter, but she could hear rats or mice scurrying around in the shadows.

They climbed stairs to the second floor, went through yet another door, and entered a large, comfortable room. The fireplace and half a dozen lanterns provided welcome warmth and sufficient light. The table and chairs, the thick cushions, the basket filled with bread, the pots simmering over the fire, the stack of books on a small wooden chest near the window—all of it spoke of home. On the right, Fry opened another door, where the bedroom was located, then gestured toward the door on the left that led downstairs to the street.

."But this is your home away from home, Mr. Fry. We cannot . . ."

He raised his hands, patting the air, and hurried over to the stack of books. He brought out parchment, a quill, an ink pot, and wrote, *Friends they are welcome. We have rooms downstairs.*

Then, as if he'd hoped for an opportunity to clarify his literacy, he added, *My wife taught me to read and write. For this she was accused. For this she was killed. For this my tongue was cut out.*

He gestured toward the pots simmering on the fire, at the basket of bread, and wrote, *Help selves.* Then he brought out a wooden bowl, scooped out chunks of hot chicken, blew on it, put it on the floor. He glanced at Sunny, and snapped his fingers, an invitation. The dog hurried to the bowl, tail wagging, and inhaled the food.

Cory joined them with steaming pewter mugs, and as soon as he handed one to Nora, she realized it was some sort of alcoholic drink. Since he had given it to her, she indulged. The ale was thick, spicy, and made her tongue tingle. The ale, combined with the warmth in the room, the thick cushion on which she sat, the murmur of the men's voices, relaxed her, took the edge off. Pretty soon, her body had molded itself to the cushion and she heard the soft hiss of snow against the glass, the crackle of logs in the fire, Sunny's sighs as she dreamed, every sound magnified, a punctuation point to this surreal journey.

Cory and Kincaid and Fry, through notes, were engaged in a lively philosophical discussion. Cory quoted Descartes, Kincaid quoted Aristotle, Fry quoted Galileo. Nora started to quote Kant, then realized that he wouldn't be alive for another . . . what? Three decades?

What about Newton? Could she quote Newton? Did she know enough about him to quote him? Newton was alive now, right? *Think, think.* Yeah, okay, she had it. Newton was born in the middle part of this century and would die in 1727. Once she had that bit of information, the rest of her limited knowledge about the man fell into place. "Mr. Cory, I am curious. Sir Isaac Newton theorizes that the motion of objects here and the motion of the stars are governed by the same laws. What do you think about this theory?"

Cory looked stunned. But Nora didn't know whether it was because she, a woman, had asked or whether he was just surprised to hear Newton's name in this room, now, in this company. He glanced at Fry, who went through the books on the small table and passed him two tomes. Cory held them as though they were sacred objects. Before he could speak, his brother, Edward, lumbered in, shaking his cloak free of snow, rubbing his hand through his hair.

"The cold is so extreme that ice is forming along the sand on the beach. And the fog continues to rise." Cory junior draped his cloak over the back of a chair and moved quickly to the fire, holding out his hands.

They all just stared at him. Nora actually had forgotten about him, almost forgotten that he even existed. Where had he been all this time? When no one spoke, Cory junior glanced back, at them, at the books that his brother held, and rolled his eyes.

"Ah, James. Not this again," he said, then turned back to the fire.

James Cory just smiled. "My brother thinks that I think too much."

"I do not think it; I *know* it." Edward helped himself to food from one of the pots on the fire, then filled a pewter pitcher with the ale and refilled their cups. He finally claimed one of the cushions, removed his boots, and rubbed his toes. "But I enjoy listening to what he has to say." He smiled.

James leaned forward, his thumbs caressing the cover of a book as if it were the skin of a woman he loved. It was then that Nora understood that *ideas* were what made James Cory tick. "Newton will change the world," he said as he held up Newton's opus *Philosophiae Naturalis Principia Mathematica.* "He describes a force that he calls *gravitas.* Have you heard of this?"

"Sheer brilliance," Kincaid gushed, then leaned forward to pull off his right boot. He raised it above his head and then let it go. "My boot falls because of this . . . this *gravitas.*"

"Yes!" James raised the Newton tome above his head, released it, and laughed with utter delight when it struck the floor. "*This* is God's law. Science."

"Walter Chandler would call that heresy," his brother remarked. "He was in the tavern earlier, maligning all of us."

"*He* is the heresy," James replied, and he, his brother, Kincaid, and Fry burst into laughter. "And what of Kepler's *Astronomia Nova*?" James went on. "Does it not describe the motions of the planets? And his *Epitome Astronomiae Copernicanae*? Also brilliant."

Nora realized they were all half drunk, and it struck her that she and Kincaid really were sitting here in 1695 drinking weird ale with men who were long dead in her time. And while they were discussing Newton and Kepler, she brought out her digital camera. Since she felt a little reckless, she didn't bother being sneaky about it. She got up, backed away from them, held the camera up, and snapped the picture. The photo was terrific. But when she looked up, the Cory brothers, Fry, Kincaid, even snoozing Sunny appeared to be frozen. A tall black woman stood in front of Nora, shaking her head.

"Excuse me. You've had too much to drink and this is totally fucked up." She snatched the camera out of Nora's hand. "If you show a digital camera to three men from the seventeenth century, and one of those men is James Cory, you'll be changing history in inconceivable ways. I can't allow it, Nora. In good conscience, I really can't."

"Mariah Jones." Nora stared at her, memorizing everything about her: the dreadlocks; the tight, muscular arms and legs; the undeniable beauty of her face, its perfect bone structure. She looked to be in her late forties, but that was impossible, wasn't it? "So you're like, what, the big brother of time travel?"

"James Cory has his destiny, just as you and Alex Kincaid have yours. Your destinies have intersected here, for particular reasons that are too convoluted and ridiculously complex to explain just now. To liberate this dreadful era of its witchhunters, Cory has to continue along the path he's on, with only minimal exposure to the techie wonders of your era. He—"

"How'd you find us?" Nora snapped.

"The chips have an affinity for each other. It takes practice to pick up on a specific signal, but all of us have the capacity to find others like ourselves."

"So this is, what, your specialty? Popping in and out of the time stream to stir up more chaos?"

"Some things just can't be permitted."

"Oh, I get it. This is just more of your usual manipulation."

"The ramifications of—"

"Spare me your bullshit, okay? Because of you, because of what you and fat Joe Aiken Senior proposed to my mother in 1983, because you chipped her, she ended up here, tortured by that scumbag Chandler. And because of all that, Kincaid and I are here. So if you're going to interfere, help us find my mother, so we can go home."

"You spoke to Russ Berlin," Mariah said, obviously surprised.

"Not by choice."

"And this happened where?"

"You act like God, so you figure it out," Nora snapped.

"The Monroe Institute, April 2006."

Nora said nothing.

Mariah just smiled, as if at something that had been revealed to her by Nora's silence. "I see," she said softly.

"No, I don't think you do, Mariah. You can't fuck with people's lives and then show up unannounced and act like God. So just bug the hell out and leave me alone."

She looked at Nora for what seemed a long time, but probably wasn't. "Look, you can go home any time you like. It's your need to find your mother that keeps you here. There are only a handful of immutable laws where the chip is concerned, and the one that applies to your situation now is that the chip takes its lead from your deepest intentions. Your intentions from the beginning have been focused on finding your mother."

"And the other immutables?"

"If you die on one timeline, you don't die on all timelines, but it certainly limits your options."

Nora blurted, "Is that what's happened to you?"

Her expression tightened. "Ask Ryan Curtis."

If I ever see him again, I intend to. "And the other immutable laws?"

"It's impossible to return to the exact date when someone was disappeared. You have to be conscious to transition. A stun gun will cause your body to reject a chip. The—"

"Tell me something I don't know. Like where my mother is."

"I don't know where she is. I'm not omnipotent."

"You seem to think you are."

Mariah leaned in close to her, eyes shining like dark, wet stones. "C'mon, Nora. Your old life with Jake wasn't that wonderful. And if it hadn't been for the chip, you and Kincaid might never have gotten back together. So in spite of the chaos of a fugitive's life, there are plenty of compensations. Heightened senses, heightened sexuality, the seduction of being able to move around through time with the ease of a bird through air."

She was right, of course, but Nora wasn't about to admit anything to this woman. "Show me how to freeze time, like you've done here."

"It's not frozen. We're just moving at a different speed than they are. Again, it's all connected to your intentions and needs."

"Why is it so important that James Cory not see the digital camera?"

"It's complicated."

"For Chrissake. You show up here, snatch my camera away, act like a benevolent dictator, screw up my life, Kincaid's life, and then you can't even tell me what the hell this is really about? Get lost, Mariah."

Mariah deleted the photo on the camera, removed the batteries, handed it back to Nora. "Okay, here's a piece of information for you, Nora. Senator Lazier is trying to resuscitate SPOT, which should be quite a feat since he has no access to chips and may not have more than a dozen, if that. Be that as it may, he gets five gold stars for trying. So he has enlisted the help of a desperate man to come back and strand you and Alex here. The idea, I believe, is that the man will then offer to transition one of you if you turn over your chips to Lazier. It also appears that Lazier has stooped to very heinous levels in this little scheme of his by abducting the man's son."

Was this what Tyler had referred to in his note on the PDA? "And . . . ? Is the man here yet?"

"I don't know."

"Then how do you know all the rest of it?"

Mariah rolled her eyes, as if to say that Nora was a silly young child asking stupid questions. "I just do."

"Where's his son being kept?"

"In Aruba."

"So go help him escape."

"He doesn't need my help. He's incredibly resourceful. If he makes it through the next few days, he'll be a wonderful addition to your group. The next generation of rogue Travelers."

Nora suddenly wondered if this, too, was a part of Mariah's plan, if even now she was manipulating the lot of them. "I'm somewhat confused on timing. You said you came from April 2006. So how do you know about the demise of SPOT? None of those events happen until late October 2006."

"I've been doing this a long time, Nora. And if you live long enough, you'll understand it." She gestured at Sunny. "I'm pleased that you're taking such good care of my dog. She may be smarter than all of us combined."

Mariah dropped the digital camera into Nora's bag, wagged her fingers at Nora. "Good luck," she murmured, and then she was gone and everything was as it had been before—the men talking, Sunny snoozing, the fire crackling—except that Nora was still seated on her cushion.

It took her a few moments to find her voice, to struggle through the effects of the ale she'd consumed, of what just had happened. She tried to remember exactly what Tyler had written on the PDA, then said to the elder Cory, "Mr. Cory, have you heard of Mystic Harbor?"

Emotions scrambled through his wide, beautiful eyes like spectators fleeing the scene of a disaster. He apparently realized that his expression betrayed him because he abruptly tried to mask his feelings, but it was too late and he knew it. Even his brother and Fry looked unsettled by her question. Since she still hadn't shown Kincaid the information on the PDA, he seemed puzzled.

"I have heard of this place," Cory finally said. "But I hear about many places in my travels. Why do you ask?"

Because on your deathbed you will claim that Mystic Harbor is your true home. "Is it a town in the province?"

"I do not know, Mrs. Goodwin."

"I have heard that it is well hidden . . ." *on a hill between taller hills, with a nearby body of water* . . . ". . . and that its valley is so fertile that the people who live there are able to grow much of what they need."

James Cory just stared at her, Fry nervously busied himself with straightening the books to his right, and Edward Cory gave a short, odd laugh, then said, "Paradise. May we all find such a place." He pressed his hands to his thighs and heaved himself to his feet. "It has been a long day, my friends. And if the snow has stopped tomorrow, James, perhaps we can leave?"

"Perhaps, yes. I would prefer slightly warmer temperatures, however."

Fry rapped his knuckles against the table and nodded in agreement.

Kincaid went downstairs with the men when they left. Nora was so whipped that it was an effort to keep her eyes open, to remove her boots, to rise from the cushion, to lift her bag. She weaved into the other room, grateful that the smaller fireplace there had warmed the air enough for her to move around in just her stocking feet.

Nora splashed water on her face, brushed her teeth with

water from the pitcher, and spat it into the chamber pot. It was a relief to remove the constricting clothes, which she folded and set on a chair, and to pull on clean wool socks and her jeans and a sweatshirt. Clothes from her own time comforted her. She dug out the extra syringes and, as before, hid them under the snow on the roof outside the window.

She wanted to wait up for Kincaid, to show him what was on the PDA, to tell him about Mariah, but as soon as her head touched the bed, she knew she wasn't going to be able to stay awake. So she set the PDA on the bedside table and then she was gone.

She woke at one point to the warmth of Kincaid next to her, his hands sliding up under her sweatshirt, his mouth against her neck, whispering sweet nothings. It was as if everything she had felt hours ago in the alley now rushed back and desire sprang from the center of her being. She rolled toward him, and his mouth found hers. They fumbled with zippers and clothes and made love, a quick, strange lovemaking that seemed to communicate all that she hadn't shared verbally, as if the chip enabled a kind of telepathy. Or perhaps she only imagined that she didn't speak. She didn't know. Didn't care.

Read Tyler's stuff. Mystic Harbor. I think it's real.

My mother's there. It's where she went.

And the Corey brothers and Fry know. I'm sure of it.

Mariah was here. Lazier wants our chips and took someone's kid hostage.

He was still inside her, moving as if against an impossible tide, but raised his head, whispered, "Nora, did you just say something?"

"Don't know," she murmured. "Telepathy?" She pressed her hands to the back of his head, drawing him down to her again, his mouth to hers, his chest to hers, his legs pressed against hers.

There was no discernible moment when it was over, when he rolled away from her or she from him. But when she woke again, it was dark, she was thirsty, she had a headache from the ale, and she was cold. The fire had burned down and Sunny was whining to go out. A quick glance at her digital watch told her it was nearly four in the morning.

"Can't you wait?" she whispered.

Sunny pawed the floor.

All right, so waiting till dawn was not an option. She rolled off the lumpy bed, pulled on her jeans, sweatshirt, and boots and fished out one of the glow sticks, her flashlight, her weapon. She grabbed her cloak off the chair in the front room, turned on her flashlight. She and Sunny went down the front stairs.

Outside, the air was cold enough to freeze the hairs inside her nose. She drew the cloak up so that she could cover half her face with it, and breathed into the heavy, stinky wool. The fog, thickening and still rising, reached her knees. Nora remained close to the building, huddled against it, and slapped the glow stick against her hand, so that it emitted a soft, green light. It created a weird effect in the fog, a ghost light. Fortunately, the street was deserted, with an isolated lantern lit here and there. Even if someone happened by, the light from the glow stick might be mistaken for a lantern and her jeans weren't visible.

Sunny sniffed around, did her business in the snow and covered it up, then sniffed some more and began to wander farther and farther from the stable, pursuing a scent. "Hey, Sunny," Nora hissed. "Get back here."

The dog ignored her and hurried on, intent on a singular mission. She vanished into the fog and Nora went after her, boots crunching over the snow, sinking into it, the cold biting at her and digging in like a hungry tick. Now and then, she glimpsed Sunny, moving faster now, around the corner of the building, into the alley, vanishing and reappearing again.

Sunny rounded the next building and disappeared. Nora broke into a run, and as she skidded around the corner of the schoolhouse, the wind caught her cloak and it slapped wildly against her body. Distantly, she heard the lonely howl of a wolf, echoing out through the terrible cold and darkness. The dog heard it too and froze, snout lifted into the air, tail twitching. Then she raced on and Nora stumbled after her.

Nora didn't recognize any of the buildings she passed. It was too dark, the landscape too unfamiliar. She knew that if she ended her pursuit right this second, Sunny would find her way back to the stable. But there would be no way for her to get inside and before anyone knew she was outside, she might freeze to death. The temperature, she guessed, was probably eight or nine degrees and she didn't know what kept Sunny moving without any kind of protection except her thick fur against the cold.

At the outer edge of town, Sunny finally slowed down, dropped to her belly, and crept forward across the snow, a canine commando, inching toward a flickering rectangle of light that spilled across the white. Nora had learned that when Sunny behaved like this, it behooved her to do the same. She hurried, hunkered over, toward the dog, knelt in the snow beside her, and set the glow stick on the ground.

"You wore me out," she whispered, and took hold of her collar. "You've got to stay. No more running." Sunny whined and licked Nora's hand. "Yeah, yeah, flattery."

Nora caught her breath, then raised up and peered through the window at an angle, so she wouldn't be seen by whoever was inside. But what she saw refused to connect to anything that she understood. Her brain, her consciousness, couldn't seem to interpret it, couldn't provide a platform for deciphering the images. It was as if she had flatlined and entered some other dimension altogether.

When the synapses in her brain fired again, the images flew at her, fast and furiously: a naked woman hanging upside down from the ceiling on some sort of pulley. Good

God, it was a strappado. And the woman was Sarah Long-wood.

Sarah's dangling, emaciated arms vanished to the elbows in an iron pot from which steam billowed. She shrieked through her gag, each muted scream causing her cadaverous body to heave so that her ribs protruded, so that the sharp blades of her hips pressed against the skin, threatening to pop through it. Walter Chandler, his face damp with sweat, cheeks ruddy with perverse excitement, shouted something and the jailer, Davies, yanked on the pulley, lifting her. Sarah's hands emerged from the pot, glistening wetly. *Hot oil*. Chandler had immersed Sarah Longwood's hands and forearms in hot oil.

She kept shrieking even when she was pulled up and fought the ropes and the pulleys, grappling wildly for something to grab. Chandler moved in closer to her, got right in her face, grabbed her by the hair, jerked her head upward, forcing her to look at him, and shouted, "What did you tell him, witch?"

Sarah had managed to work her gag loose and spat at him, then shrieked, "You are Satan, you . . . !"

Chandler wrenched back, gestured at Davies, and the jailer began to lower her toward the cauldron of hot oil again. She screamed and twisted and writhed and then went suddenly and completely still, silent. Chandler shouted, "Pull her up!" And Davies did so.

Chandler quickly untied her from the strappado and set her on the floor. He got down on his hands and knees next to her and brought his ear to her chest, right between her tiny breasts, listening for a heartbeat, some sign of life. Davies ran over and Chandler shouted, "Fetch the doctor! Quickly! Go, go!"

Nora doubled over, arms clutched to her waist, eyes squeezed shut. *Fetch the doctor.* And what would a doctor in this time do for burns, dislocated shoulders, and whatever other injures Chandler had inflicted on Sarah? Leeches, poultices, herbs. Sarah Longwood would die. *Because of me. Because I violated Chandler's stupid laws.* Her eyes opened, and she crouched and dug her weapon from her cloak.

She turned it over in her hands, debating whether she should fire it. She could aim for Chandler's knees, his leg, some spot that wouldn't kill him but would give her time to get into the jail and rescue Sarah. But the explosion from the gun might awaken the town and jeopardize both her and Sarah. Safer to create a diversion that would lure Chandler outside so that she could get inside, to Sarah.

She stood, pulled the flashlight from her cloak with one hand, still holding her weapon in the other, and peered through the window again. Chandler had turned Sarah over, pushed her legs apart, unfastened his breeches, and now was on his knees between her legs. *Jesus God.* He was going to rape her while she was unconscious.

Nora swung her flashlight and slammed it into the window, shattering the glass. Chandler lurched upward, eyes wide with astonishment, his sweaty face glistening in the firelight, and frantically tugged at his breeches, now puddled around his ankles. She quickly switched on the flashlight and shone it through the broken window, right into his face. His arms flew up to protect his eyes, and he stumbled back, tripped over his own breeches, and went down.

She swept up the glow stick from the snow, hid it under her cloak, and she and Sunny raced away from the window, through the fog, and tore up the alley between the jail and the next building. They paused at the corner of the building, Nora hunkering down close to the dog, breathing hard, the fog engulfing them, hiding them.

Heart hammering, Nora rose and peered around the edge of the building. Up the main road, lights from several lanterns lit up the fog like tiny suns. The sharp, cold wind whistled and whined and made the fog swirl and shift.

The door to the jail flew open and Chandler lumbered

out, just his chest, head, and lantern visible in the fog. He
waddled out as fast as his pudgy legs could carry him, the
fog closing up behind him. Sunny emitted a low, menacing
growl and Nora quickly ducked back behind the building
and crouched next to her. "Not yet," she whispered, an arm
around Sunny's neck. Motionless, hidden by the fog, Nora
willed Chandler to head away from her.

When she peered out again, Chandler and his ghostly
light were disappearing around the far corner of the jail. She
counted to five, then shot to her feet, and she and Sunny hastened toward the front door of the jail.

Inside, Nora listened hard. The firewood crackled and
hissed, while the wind whined through the chimney. She felt
certain that Davies hadn't returned yet with the doctor and
moved toward the heavy door that opened into the cell block.

Sunny led the way past the cells, where rats scurried
through the hay, where the accused slept—or pretended to
sleep for fear they would be next in Chandler's torture chamber. At the end of the cell block, the door to the torture room
stood open, the firelight illuminating the table of horrors
that, in Nora's time, would contain only a fraction of these
torture tools. The wind moaned through the broken window,
rattling the jagged vestiges with an unforgiving fierceness,
as if to knock them free. The air stank of burned flesh, hot
oil, filth, despair, as if the very gates of hell had been hurled
open.

The dog dashed past the table and whined, softly, almost
painfully, and when Nora reached her, Sunny was licking
Sarah's bruised and bloody face, her bruised feet, her naked
shoulders. She stopped short of touching her forearms and
hands. Nora knelt beside Sarah and shone the flashlight on her
injuries. She immediately wished that she hadn't. Her hands
and forearms were so badly burned that the skin was blister-
ing already. Pins stuck out of the birthmark on her hip. Festering sores covered her toes and the tops of her feet. Nora's
eyes flickered back to the burns.

Dear God, how can I help you? She didn't have any medical supplies with her to deal with burns. Sarah Longwood desperately needed a twenty-first-century trauma center, and even then, she might not make it. Nora knew that even if she could transition at will, she couldn't transition Sarah unless she was conscious. She might be able to carry her out of here and to the stable, though, just to get her away from Chandler.

Sunny suddenly growled, that low, threatening sound deep in her throat that meant someone was coming. Nora didn't want to use the gun and there wasn't any place in here to hide. She tightened her arm over Sunny's back and visualized how the air had looked in the moments before Mariah had appeared, visualized time freezing, stopping, going utterly and perfectly still.

The door banged open and Davies called, "Reverend, I have brought Dr. Webber."

Nora realized that the table momentarily hid her, Sunny, and Sarah, but that as soon as Davies and Webber came around the end of it, they would see them. She would have to shoot him. Shoot both of them. *Shit, c'mon, my need has never been greater. I don't want to shoot this bastard. I need to get Sarah out of here.*

She saw the jailer's legs now and the legs of the man with him, their breeches dirty, wet from the snow, the tips of their boots scuffed and worn. Sunny's body went tense, her fur went up, and then pressure escalated at the back of Nora's skull, whipped its way around her entire head—and the world went soft, blurry, soundless.

16
Flight

We know that the biochip is an interface
between technology and consciousness. But
we're still in the process of discovering exactly
what that means.

—Russ Berlin, M.D.

As soon as Russ Berlin entered the back room of the jail, the odors nearly overpowered him. Scorched—everything smelled scorched. And beneath this odor lurked others, of sweat, unwashed bodies, despair and hopelessness. He heard weeping from one of the cells, but it was too dark for Berlin to see who it was.

"Back here, Dr. Webber," the jailer said, urgently motioning him to follow.

They entered a small, stuffy room at the back of the jail lit by several lanterns and a fire. The ambient light spilled across a wooden table strewn with torture devices: thumbscrews, ropes and pulleys, weights, long pins, a branding iron, other devices for which he lacked names. Bile surged in his throat. He fought to swallow it back.

"Reverend," the jailer called. "I have brought Dr. Webber." Then, to Berlin, "I do not know where he went. But I am sure he will be back momentarily. She is over here."

Berlin followed Davies to the other side of the table.

There, lying on the floor near a small iron pot with steam rising from it, was an unconscious, naked woman with what looked like second- and third-degree burns from her fingertips to her forearms. Her shoulders appeared to be dislocated. Pins stuck out of a birthmark on her hip. Her feet and toes looked as if they'd been gnawed on by mice, rats, or worse.

This is what was done to Mariah. And you're the one who helped. I saw your face in the replay. His eyes snapped to the jailer. "Are you responsible for this, Mr. Davies?" Berlin demanded.

"No, sir. Reverend Chandler is responsible for confessions."

"This has nothing to do with a *confession*, Mr. Davies. This young woman has been *tortured*. Bring me a quilt and then go find the reverend."

"Is she dead, sir? Is the witch dead?" he asked anxiously. "The town cannot be robbed of a witch's death in this manner."

"*Find me a quilt*," Berlin snapped. "*Now*. Or she *will* die."

As Davies hurried off, Berlin caught a flash of movement in his peripheral vision. But when he turned his head in that direction, he saw only the flickering flames of the fire, fanned by the wind flowing through the broken window. Then he thought he felt something brush against his back and glanced around. Nothing. He was alone in this miserable hole. Spooked, yes, but alone.

He turned his attention to the young woman. Skin: pale, clammy. Lips and fingernails: faint bluish cast. Heartbeat: fast, thready. Breathing: shallow, ragged. She was already going into shock.

He eased the pins from her birthmark, one of them embedded four or five inches into the flesh, perhaps piercing muscle or bone. Impossible to tell. The bite marks on her feet, toes, ankles, even some higher up on her legs looked badly infected. On top of all this, she looked severely malnourished, dehydrated. If she was going to survive, she needed a miracle.

The stone.

Berlin shrugged off his cloak and covered her body with it except for her arms and hands. He was looking around frantically for something he could slide under her legs to elevate them when the jailer returned with the quilt.

"Leave us and find the reverend," Berlin said.

"I cannot leave you or anyone else alone for that long with the witches, Doctor. I am not allowed to do that."

"Then *I* will leave and she will die."

Now Davies looked genuinely perplexed and scared, his eyes darting from Berlin to the woman to Berlin again. He had the distinct impression that Davies wasn't as concerned about the young woman dying as he was about the residents of Blue River being denied the spectacle of her hanging and him being held accountable.

"I . . . I will find the reverend."

Thank God. As soon as the door closed, Berlin spread the quilt out on the other side of the torture table, where the floor was marginally cleaner, then ran back to the woman. He picked her up, shocked at how light she was, how thin, bony, frail, no more substantial than a shadow. Her long, greasy hair was matted and hung limply across his arm. He carried her quickly to the quilt, set her down gently, adjusted his cloak over her body, removed the key chain from his pocket. He popped open the miniature globe and removed the stone.

When he cupped it in his hands, the stone heated up and began to hum, the pitch intensifying, quickening, piercing his skull. Then the stone burst with that brilliant, powerful white light, like a sun going nova in a black sky. He couldn't look at it directly. Berlin moved the stone over and under and around her hands and fingers, never touching it to her skin, but making sure that the light spilled across every part of her that had been scalded and scorched by oil. He passed the

stone over both of her shoulders, then around her head and
neck and down the length of her body, each leg, each foot,
between the toes, where the bites were the most infected, and
back up again.

He found a rhythm to his movements, a smoothness,
sweeping up and down and around, again and again and
again. Color returned to her face. The blue cast to her lips
and nails started fading. The infected bites on her legs and
feet began to heal, and the redness and swelling in her hands
diminished. The charred, peeling skin between her fingers
flaked off. As he moved the lantern closer to her, he thought
he could see the formation of new, pink, healthy skin.

His mind raced, planning what he would have to do so
that the jailer and Chandler would think he had treated her
with whatever was available in this time. Bandages for her
hands, certainly. But did bandages exist yet? He didn't know.
Tough shit. He would use what he had and if anyone ques-
tioned him about it, he would say it was the newest thing out
of Europe. Who would challenge him? It wasn't like e-mail
or phones existed to check out his story.

As he brought the stone up toward her hands once more,
the light abruptly winked out. He returned it to the tiny
globe, pocketed it. Berlin examined her hands, checked between her fingers, felt for the dislocation in her shoulders,
looked for puncture wounds in the birthmark on her thigh.
Healing, every injury was now healing, as if the stone had
accelerated her body's immune system. He took her pulse,
listened to her breathing. Normal, all of it.

*Dear God. If it can do this for third-degree burns, it can
do this for leukemia. I can go back and use it on my son.*

Berlin brought bandages from his medical kit and wrapped
both of her hands. He found her clothes on a chair in the corner of the torture chamber, but they were so filthy, so putrid,
that he swept them up and dropped them into the pot of oil.

He would take her back to the village clinic, tell the jailer
that he would care for her there. He couldn't allow her to be

put back into the cell. He removed his cloak from her body and was wrapping her up in the quilt when the door slammed open and Chandler rushed in, leaning heavily on a cane, the jailer right behind him.

"Is she . . . alive?" Chandler asked, breathlessly.

Berlin forced himself to look at the sadistic little fuck who had tortured Mariah and now this young woman. Chandler's dark eyes widened in his pudgy cheeks and darted from Berlin's face to the woman rolled up in the quilt. Snow melted on Chandler's cloak, but his mottled face shone with sweat.

"Barely," Berlin spat. "Why did you send the jailer for me and then leave?"

"I . . . someone . . . broke the window." He gestured toward the small window, where jagged pieces of glass remained. "I gave chase. Will . . . she live?"

"If I take her to the clinic. Where I can treat her."

Chandler's cane whistled through the air and struck the table that held the torture devices. Everything shook. "I cannot allow that. She is a *witch*, sir. The witches stay here."

"You are not the jailer, Reverend Chandler. He is." Berlin gestured toward Davies. "Speak, sir."

"I . . . that is . . ." He looked genuinely terrified, eyes darting surreptitiously to Chandler, the young woman, Berlin. "But I am beholden to the town council and the reverend is a member of that council. I am not the final authority."

"*God* is the final authority." Chandler's voice boomed and echoed in the tight, hot room. "And God has told me that she is a witch. She has the devil's mark on her hip. She felt no pain when I tested the mark with pins, cannot recite the Lord's prayer, refused to confess when I used the strappado. She—"

"Silence!" Berlin shot to his feet and moved toward this fat, self-righteous prick.

The reverend stepped back, perhaps realizing for the first time that the village doctor, the *new* village doctor, here barely six weeks, might actually be a threat to him. Chandler's cane whipped up as if in defense, but the gesture lacked conviction. "I . . . I . . ."

Berlin shouted, "Let us put *you* on the strappado, Reverend, and as *your* shoulders are pulled apart, we will demand that *you* recite the Lord's prayer. We will stick pins in *your* hip, we will shove *your* hands and arms into boiling oil. And we will demand that *you* confess, that *you* name others."

"That . . . is *blasphemy*," Chandler stammered.

"*This* is blasphemy." Berlin gestured at the young woman. "And you are not the final judge of her guilt or innocence. The magistrate will decide that. If she dies here, now, from torture you have inflicted upon her, the people in this town will look upon *you* as a murderer." With that, Berlin returned to the young woman's side, lifted her gently, and started toward the door.

Chandler's cane whistled through the air and slammed against the door frame, blocking Berlin's way. "I cannot allow you to take her out of the gaol."

Think again, asshole. "I heard that the magistrate from Boston arrived yesterday. If you do not move aside, I will seek him out now and *he* will decide. His authority is greater than that of the town council."

"But *not* greater than God's," Chandler spat, his mouth pursing, his face anxious, damper and shinier with sweat.

"We are talking now about man's laws. Get out of my way."

The hatred in Chandler's eyes became a palpable thing, profoundly unsettling, ideas and possibilities spinning through them. Berlin believed that any second now, the reverend would swing his cane and smash in his skull. But Berlin didn't move. He understood that to show doubt or weakness in front of this bastard would bring injury or death.

Then, without warning, Chandler's eyes bulged in their sockets and he gasped and pitched forward, as if shoved from behind. Davies cried out and his knees buckled. They fell simultaneously, the jailer's knees smacking the floor, Chandler sprawling against the table, knocking the torture tools to the floor. As Davies struggled to rise, he fell forward and smacked his head against the floor and went still. Chandler, who had slid off the edge of the table, scrambled on his hands and knees trying to reach his fallen cane.

Berlin, too astonished to move, saw the cane skitter across the room, as if of its own volition, and suddenly the fabric along the right side of Chandler's breeches ripped and a piece was torn away. Chandler screeched that Satan was attacking him and rolled across the room, arms covering his head, legs kicking at his invisible assailant. Berlin lurched forward, toward the door, carrying the unconscious young woman in his arms, startled but not surprised when the door to the cell block slammed open. He caught movement in his peripheral vision again and suddenly understood that a Traveler was here and had slowed time, sped it up, stopped it— he didn't know how it worked and didn't care. He seized the opportunity for escape.

He raced outside, into the cold, the swirling fog, and set the young woman in the back of the jailer's wagon. The horses were now spooked, snorting and pawing the ground. He felt movement in the wagon as others scrambled inside, the ones he couldn't see or hear or touch. As he turned the horses toward his rooms two blocks west, a crushing pressure clamped around his forehead, raced around to the back of his skull and bit in even deeper. The top of his head felt as if it were being excised.

At some level, he understood what was happening. It was as if the energy field generated by the individual or individuals he couldn't see or touch was being hurled, like a net, over him, Sarah, the entire wagon, even the horses. But his understanding didn't diminish the physical agony. Berlin's hands flew to his head, seizing his skull, pressing against his temples, as if to contain or vanquish the pain, and the horses neighed and strained against the reins, trying to rear up, to free themselves.

Then, just as quickly as it had started, the excruciating pain ceased and the world around him moved in a surreal slow motion, as if the fabric of both space and time were being peeled away. Nora McKee sat next to him, clutching a glow stick. Despite the cold, her face shone with perspiration, and fatigue pinched the corners of her eyes. "You'd better hurry, Russ. I don't know how much longer I can hold this. My heart feels like it's about to explode out of my chest. I'm not quite sure how this works."

"*You* floored those dickheads?" He urged the horse forward.

"With a little help from my friend." She gestured behind her at the golden retriever stretched out alongside the young woman he'd placed in the wagon.

"Holy shit," he breathed. "Mariah's dog."

"She hasn't belonged to Mariah since 1976, and that was . . . well, more than three decades ago—or more than three centuries back—depending on where you want to count from. That makes her as miraculous as that little stone you used to heal Sarah's burns."

"*Sarah?* This is Sarah Longwood?" It meant he might be able to transition out of this era now. He said as much.

"According to Mariah we can transition whenever we want. The chip just takes its lead from our deepest intentions."

"*You* saw her?"

As Nora explained, the wagon crunched over the hard-packed snow. The cold numbed the tip of Berlin's nose and his bare hands and seeped through his clothes, into his bones. Around him, the world moved in that strange, languid slow motion. Nora was manipulating time, but it was costing her—he could see that in her face, her body language.

"Mariah just can't stop interfering. It's dangerous to believe everything she says, Nora."

"I don't believe *everything* she says, but I do believe what she says about the chip. Her advice worked for this time trick. Tell me about the stone."

"Mariah gave it to me. She claims it came from Roswell."

"Roswell," Nora repeated. "New Mexico and alien ships and all that shit?"

Berlin nodded and Nora laughed. But her laughter sounded false and he could see she was struggling to hold on to the time effect. He advised her not to try so hard. "It is what it is, okay? If it dissipates, it means we don't need it anymore. We've got another thirty or forty minutes of darkness, and with that and the fog, we'll be able to do what we need to do."

"And what do we need to do?" she asked.

"I need to get Sarah out of Blue River. You've got to find your mother. Then we can all go home." Was it really that simple? he wondered. If they did A, would they then be able to do B? Of course not.

Nothing in Mariah's world was as simple as ABCs.

"The people here think that Alex is the magistrate, that I'm his wife. Before tonight, before I . . . I saw what I saw, I thought we could free these women by Alex finding them not guilty. But the superstition here about the devil is a disease too far beyond anything that we can do. Life in Blue River is predicated on fear, terror, God—all the tools that governments use to control the populace. You *do* need to get her out of here. But where will you take her?"

"Remember the place I told you about in my text message? Where the disenfranchised are welcome? The Camelot of 1695? I think it's real. It's called Mystic Harbor," Berlin replied. He first had heard of it from a woman in Chandler's church, a reference in casual conversation. And then, later, he had heard it mentioned in the inn, the apothecary, like a rumor that had taken on a life of its own. It might just be one of this era's urban legends, but until he knew for sure, he would look for it as a refuge for Sarah.

Nora regarded him with a puzzled expression, then started

talking fast, describing everything that had happened since she had last seen him on the grounds of the Monroe Institute. Berlin reciprocated with a condensed version of his and Lea's experience in Aruba, and he suddenly knew that the desperate man Mariah had told Nora about was Eric Holcomb, whom he and Lea had seen last in Aruba, the man whom Lea had encountered with Wade in that elevator that went only to the penthouse. The "extra insurance" that Lazier had mentioned in an e-mail to Wade, the insurance that would force Holcomb to cooperate, had to be Holcomb's son, kidnapped and held captive by Lazier in his penthouse in Aruba. But he was sure that in his six weeks here, he had not met another Traveler until Nora, this evening.

"Who is this guy?" she asked. "Is Holcomb here? Can you describe him?"

"Not really. I only saw him from a distance. Lea got a much closer look at him. She was in the elevator with him and Wade."

"Why would they draw an outsider into this?"

"Because as far as they know, no one in your group has seen him."

"Do you think he's here already?"

"If my kid were being held hostage by Lazier, I'd be here. I'd be waiting for Nora McKee and Alex Kincaid, my stun gun handy."

"He may be as stuck here as we are," she said.

Yes, he might, Berlin thought, and that could change things considerably.

He pulled around to the back of his house and directed the horse into the two-stall stable. He handed the reins to Nora, jumped down, and tended to the horse, unhitching her from the wagon, leading her into the empty stall, feeding her, his mind jammed in fast-forward, a plan taking shape.

Sarah would need clothes and he would need supplies, more than he had in the house. That would mean a trip to the general store. Could Nora hold the time effect long enough for him to get away? Should she flee with him? What was the right thing to do here? He was clueless.

His arrival in Blue River in late November had coincided fortuitously with events. The previous doctor had left weeks earlier, not long after the former magistrate's death. Blue River, riddled with disease, superstition, and repressed sexuality, desperately needed a physician. So when Berlin had touted himself as a doctor from New York, the town had embraced him. Travers had rented him a small house, and Berlin had put out his shingle and proceeded to settle into life in this awful place.

To keep from drawing attention to himself, he hadn't asked about Sarah Longwood or any of the other women in the jail. Witches weren't seen by doctors. Only the jailer, the reverend, the magistrate, and members of the town council had access to them. Until today, he had never been inside the jail.

He knew that Catherine Walrave supposedly had been disappeared to Blue River on January 6, but as the weeks passed and he didn't see her in town, he began to question the accuracy of the date and suspected she was dead.

Now and then, when he was at the inn or the tavern, he asked about female newcomers. But with three thousand people in town and winter bearing down with such ferocity, people had more important things to worry about than who was new in Blue River. It wasn't as if there was a tourist board that kept track of these things.

As the village doctor, he'd been privy to the local stories and rumors. He had met all the major players in this warped little town, the movers and shakers, the pious, the terrified, the bullshit artists, the Mathers with their poisonous pens—even the governor's emissary, Ericson Ivers, who had sought treatment for a stomach ailment. He had bided his time, waiting for a sign. That sign had come tonight, when Davies had pounded on his door.

Now it was time to get the hell out of Dodge, but how and to where?

They got Sarah into the house. While Nora put wood on the fire and got food for herself and the dog, Berlin took Sarah into the back room, put her on his bed, covered her with a quilt. He checked her vitals. She definitely wasn't in shock; her color was excellent. So why was she still unconscious? Even though the stone appeared to have healed the worst of her injuries, it was so new to his experience that he had no idea how quickly she would regain consciousness.

Even if she was conscious now, he doubted if he would be able to transition her to his time. Mariah had remarked that with the new chip, they could "go anywhere," but that didn't necessarily pertain to transitioning someone forward from his or her natal time. Besides, he wasn't so sure he would do it even if he could. His century was so far removed from Sarah's reality that it would lend new meaning to "culture shock."

He returned to the front room, where Nora shoveled porridge into her mouth. "Holding the time effect consumes a lot of energy," she murmured in between bites. "I think if my stomach is full, I can hold it long enough for you to get out of town without being seen."

"I need to go to the general store."

"Sunny and I will go with you. We can be in and out in five minutes. In fifteen minutes, you can be on your way out of town."

"When this happened on Cape Cod, when Alex was doing it, how long did it last?" he asked, throwing his cloak around his shoulders again.

"Twenty or thirty minutes. But Alex didn't have any idea how he'd done it or how he'd controlled it. Once, he described it as comparable to a reflex."

A reflex. Yes, that made a kind of sense to him. A reflex was an involuntary response to a specific sensory stimulus. In Nora's case and in Kincaid's back on the cape, that stimulus was fear, the most fundamental of stimuli. And when that fear was connected to your own survival, the fight-or-flight response kicked in, which definitely would jump-start the chip.

"Would this time effect keep her unconscious?" he asked.

"I don't know, Russ. This is only my second experience with it. When it happened on the Cape, it enabled us to get away."

"What were you feeling in the moments before it happened?" he asked.

"Total panic. Sunny and I were hiding by the torture table. I didn't want to shoot Chandler or Davies or anyone else, but I sure as hell didn't want to be discovered, either. I didn't have any choice but to try to do the time thing."

The time thing. He smiled at that. Years ago, when he had gone to work for Mariah's organization, before it had morphed into SPOT, he had stopped wearing watches because the three watches he owned didn't work when he wore them. They ran too fast or too slow or didn't run at all. That was *his* time thing. He had taken his watches to a repair shop owned by a little Swiss guy who had tuned them up, put in new batteries, claimed they worked fine. But as soon as Berlin had put them on, they had gone haywire. Over the years, he had bought new watches, expensive suckers calibrated to atomic clocks and guaranteed to be immune to just about everything—including solar flares and a shift in the earth's axis. These watches malfunctioned, too, and he finally had given up trying to keep track of time. But suddenly, time was all he could think about. How much of it they had, how much of it they might need.

At the doorway, they paused and looked back at Sunny, who remained sitting by the fire, alert but obviously not willing to go anywhere. "C'mon, girl," Nora prodded. "A quick trip."

Sunny barked, but didn't budge.

"I think she wants to stay here," Berlin said. "Keep an eye on her, Sunny."

Two barks. Did that mean yes? "It seems like she understands everything we say," he remarked.

"Mariah chipped her in 1974, when she was two, which means she's over thirty. That's a long time among people, so it's not too surprising that she understands English. And that brings me to a question I figure only you or Mariah can answer. Does the chip slow down aging?"

"I think so. I don't know why or how much or what happens if the chip is suddenly dislodged. But Sunny and Mariah are proof that something's going on. How old do you think Mariah is?"

"I've only seen here once, tonight. She looked to be in her late forties."

"She's always looked that way. After I saw her at the institute—in April 2006—I started thinking a lot about her age, Nora, and piecing bits of information together. On our natal timeline, I think she was born somewhere between 1910 and 1920."

"*What?* That means she's . . ."

"Between eighty-four and ninety-four."

"Jesus, Russ. The implications . . ."

"Yeah, I know."

"How old are you?" Nora asked. "What year were you born?"

"How old do you think I am?"

"You look to be in your early forties."

"I'm fifty-nine," he said.

They stared at each other for a long moment, then Berlin shook his head. He couldn't deal with the age issue right now. Maybe he never would answer that particular question to his own satisfaction.

They headed outside again, where the fog didn't seem to be moving and the wind didn't touch them. The early morning noises he heard—the clatter of wagons, the neighing of horses—sounded long and drawn out, almost like echoes. He knew from the security videos he had watched from the incident on Cape Cod last October, when Nora and her group had escaped because of the time effect, that they were moving very quickly relative to the speed of everyone around them. Like hummingbirds, he thought. If other people saw them at all, it was as brief flashes of movement in their peripheral vision, like what had happened to him inside the torture room, when he couldn't see Nora and Sunny, but had perceived movement, felt something brush up against him.

The sky was lightening and several horse-drawn wagons went past, en route to the general store or the apothecary or the tailor or to gather firewood in the forest on the other side of the river. Not everyone, he thought, was swept up in the superstitious nonsense about witches. Some people simply went about their daily lives. Unfortunately, that group comprised only 10 percent or less of the town's population.

The general store was open for business already, and as soon as they entered, Berlin spotted Chandler and Travers commiserating near the meat area. Chandler had a cut lip and some scratches on his face and Travers must have mentioned it because the reverend touched his face and winced, playing it for all it was worth. Berlin knew they were discussing him and Sarah Longwood. He could almost hear them, had heard them on a number of occasions at the tavern, the entire council discussing the absolute evil of the witches.

All of the council members believed that the witches had conspired to bring about the death of the previous magistrate, who certainly would have ruled against the women. And all of them, at least in his book, were sociopaths whose psyches chafed so deeply at the sexual restrictions imposed by their culture that they had projected these feelings onto women who didn't conform to the customs of the time.

"They can't see us," Nora reminded him as she touched his arm, hurrying him past Chandler and Travers. "I'll get Sarah's clothes and meet you back here in . . . what? Five minutes?"

"Let's stay together. We don't know what will happen to the time effect if you go in one direction and I go in another."

"Good point." She pointed at a stack of straw baskets. "If I grab two of these for us, what will it look like to other people?"

"I don't have a clue." He glanced around, saw that no one was looking in their direction, and quickly picked up two baskets, handed her one. "Let's make this snappy."

Up and down the narrow aisles they went, selecting foods and supplies that Berlin thought he would need. Apparently no one saw anything unusual; from the perspective of other people, the baskets weren't floating. They didn't seem to be visible at all. The time effect definitely had parameters of distance. How much distance? In the jail, there had been moments when Nora had been as close to him as she was in the wagon. So why hadn't the time effect claimed him then? He didn't know. There were so many things he didn't know about any of it that the label Nora had given him—gate-keeper—suddenly seemed silly.

In the women's clothing area, Nora combed through dresses and skirts and bodices, caps and boots and undergarments, and picked out items she thought would fit Sarah.

Within a few minutes, their baskets brimmed and they headed back to the front of the store. Light the color of cur-dled milk was visible in the windows. More people had ar-rived. Chandler and Travers had been joined by two more of their council cronies and were huddled over a piece of parchment. Berlin and Nora looked at each other and she grinned.

"Yes, let's eavesdrop," she said.

"If we get close to them, though, will they be sucked into the time effect or something?"

"When Sunny and I took on Chandler and his thug, we were up close and personal and they didn't know what hit them. I think it's connected to my intentions."

Let's hope so, Berlin thought, and they moved up behind the group of men. The time effect distorted the sound of their voices, just as it had distorted the sounds outside. But he could clearly see the piece of paper Chandler held.

I, Sarah Longwood, confess that I . . .

The bastard had forged it. He snatched it out of Chandler's hand and he and Nora hurried toward the door. He glanced back just once and saw Chandler and his boys glancing around, confused, puzzled, apparently trying to figure out what had happened to the confession.

Outside, they paused, checked both ends of the street. The time distortion continued. Nothing moved the way it should. Even the snow seemed to fall more slowly. But on the way back to his place, the process started to reverse itself. Sounds penetrated first—the sudden clatter of a wagon as it emerged from a patch of fog, someone shouting, horses neighing. They were intermittently visible to others and Berlin was sure they were sighted by people in one of the wagons that went past.

He and Nora broke into a run, their baskets banging against their hips, their boots slipping and sliding through the snow. As they dashed into the house, the time effect broke down completely. Berlin, seized with urgency now, latched the door, dropped the basket onto the table, and hurried into the bedroom to check on Sarah. Still unconscious, but her vitals were strong.

"I'll get her dressed," Nora said from the doorway. "Then Sunny and I will help you load up the wagon so you can get out of here."

"I'll bring the wagon around back."

Sunny hesitated, looking from him to Nora, then decided to accompany Berlin outside. Berlin suspected Chandler had been at the store to drum up support from his council members to override the magistrate and take matters in their own hands. Berlin could imagine him stoking the fires of fanaticism and lying about how he had sustained his injuries. *The doctor conjured Satan's minions and they attacked us. . . .*

Now that Chandler's so-called evidence had disappeared, would it make a difference in the outcome? Probably not. He worried that an angry mob would show up at his house before he could get Sarah out of town. And if they found Nora and the dog here, too, the mob would lynch all of them.

As preposterous as it seemed to his twenty-first-century mind, the likelihood terrified him.

The fog was still thick when Berlin pulled up behind the house, but not as thick as it had been earlier. He tied the horse to the porch railing, and while Nora loaded the baskets into the back of the wagon, he hurried inside to get Sarah.

Nora had cleaned her up a little and dressed her in fresh clothes, boots, even a cloak. He wrapped the quilt around her and carried her out to the wagon. He set her down carefully, in the space Nora had cleared among the supplies, and hastened back inside the house. His bag. He needed his bag, his extra chip.

Moments, it only took moments, but before he was finished, he heard shouts outside, the pounding of hooves. *They're coming, sweet Christ.*

Berlin raced outside, dropped his bag in the back with Sarah and Sunny. "They're nearly here," Nora said urgently and threw her arms around Sunny and then around Berlin. "Sunny has chosen to go with you. Take care of each other. We'll find you." Then she ran over to the post, untied the reins, and handed them to Berlin. "Go! Fast! The fog should cover you!"

Berlin directed the horse toward the river and the woods, where the fog loomed like a huge white and porous wall, their haven, their refuge. When he glanced back, he could no longer see the town.

Nora watched until the wagon vanished in the fog, then spun around and ran in the opposite direction of the noises: shouts, horse hooves beating the frozen ground. But as she started across the road to the stable, she stumbled and couldn't catch herself and sprawled into the hard-packed snow. Her feet struggled frantically for purchase, boots sliding and slipping against the snow, but she was so terrified that her legs didn't work right.

Then they were on her, men on horseback surrounding her like goblins in a fairy tale, everyone shouting, two men leaping down, grabbing her by the arms. They jerked her upright, her head spun, the world seemed to roll, to list, everything blurred. Hands tore off her cloak, the frigid air grabbed her.

"Her clothes," shouted one. "She dresses like a man."

"Put her in the wagon," Chandler demanded. "Restrain her. Take her to the gaol. The devil is afoot, my friends, and it falls on us to do battle with him. Francis, we will go with two men to find the other witch and her consort."

They shoved Nora forward, she stumbled, and then they lifted her and threw her into the back of a wagon. Someone—Travers? Rowe?—restrained her hands and feet with metal bracelets connected to hooks in the wagon wall. The cold bit into her exposed skin, gnawed at her cheeks, and she huddled as best she could, struggling to draw her body into itself. There was straw in the wagon, and even though it clawed and scratched at her, she tried to sink into it, down deep, where it would be warmer.

But one of the men grabbed her hair and jerked her head back and she saw his face—Travers, it was Travers, the owner of the general store—and he grabbed her chin and leaned in close to her, his eyes bright with excitement. "You will suck me, wench."

With one hand he struggled to open his breeches. The fingers of his other hand tightened around her neck, pushing her head down, down toward the hay, toward his crotch, but Nora managed to jerk her one leg upward, sinking her knee into his groin. His face lit up and, groaning, he fell back, writhing in the hay, his hands pressed to his crotch.

"If you try that again, Satan will bite it off," she spat, and pushed back as far as she could against the edge of the wagon, begging the chip to trigger the time effect again.

But Travers suddenly reared up, eyes wild, madness transforming the topography of his face, and struck her across the face with the back of his hand. She felt the hardness of his knuckles as her lip split open, the force of the blow as blood gushed from her nose. Stars danced in her eyes, the world tilted, bile surged in her throat. She knew she was seconds from passing out. He struck her again and again, with his fist, his open hand, his fist again, each blow worse than the one before it, and she was swept away, into blackness, a strange, blissful silence, and beyond.

17
The Lighthouse

The universe is a quantum computer.
—*Seth Lloyd*

Aruba, March 2007

Suddenly the cell connection went dead and his father just wasn't there anymore. Mike clutched the cell more tightly and hissed, "Dad, c'mon, don't do this, please. Please come back."

He even called his father's cell number again and, no surprise, got the voice mail: "Hey, this is Eric. I'm outside working on my tan. Leave your name. I've already got your number."

Mr. Cool, Mike thought. *Mr. Fucking Cool.*

He disconnected, slid the cell into his back pocket, and flexed his hands against the steering wheel. His dad sounded like he had it all together, but the truth was that his life had started collapsing around the time of the divorce. Legal troubles. Job problems. Money problems. Not that his dad had mentioned it to *him.* The only reason he suspected anything was that sometimes during dinner his mother and stepfather, Frank, referred to his father's "challenges"—that was

Frank's word for it—but in a veiled way, as though certain words and phrases were a kind of code that meant something else. They talked like Mike had an IQ a few points above that of plant life. Most of the time he pretended he didn't hear them. But when he asked his dad how things were, if he was okay, his dad was always Mr. Cool.

Mike squeezed his eyes shut and struggled to shove all the shit to the back of his head, where he could lock it up and throw away the key. When he opened his eyes again, they went to the dashboard clock. 8:55.

He was parked in front of the lighthouse restaurant, the Beemer just one car among a dozen. Below it, the Caribbean seemed to stretch out forever, a blue so blue that he thought this color had been born at the same moment as the universe. He picked up his bag, with the laptop and his few belongings inside, slung the strap over his shoulder, and headed toward the restaurant. He figured he would be safer surrounded by people.

And there were plenty of people inside—most of them tourists who were dressed as casually as he was, all of them here for the sumptuous brunch set out on the long serving table. After twenty-four hours of cold ravioli and canned tuna fish, Mike's mouth watered just from the mixture of delicious aromas.

"How many in your party, sir?" the host asked.

"Two," Mike replied. "My friend is on the way."

"That will be forty-five dollars, sir."

Just for two brunches? On the other hand, it was worth it for safety in numbers. Mike handed him the cash and a waitress showed him to a table along the massive picture window that overlooked the Caribbean. Gulls pinwheeled through the hot, brilliant light, half a dozen kite sails bloomed like colorful flowers against the vast canvas of the sky, and, more distantly, windsurfers sped across the blue glass of the sea.

When he turned his head to the left, he could see across the dining area and, beyond it, the parking lot. He spotted an old VW Bug, late sixties, just nosing into a parking spot. Beige. Nicked. Dented fender. A very tall man—well over six feet tall—unfolded himself from the Bug and turned slowly, checking things out. Even though he wore dark shades and a cap pulled down low over his forehead, Mike recognized Ryan Curtis. He had a cell phone pressed to his ear and Mike's own cell sang softly from his shirt pocket. He flipped open the lid. "I'm inside, a table at the window."

Curtis strolled into the restaurant like a tourist, in shorts and a cotton shirt with sailboats on it. He looked much different than he had on the laptop photos—a little heavier, bearded, his hair blonder and longer. He spoke briefly to the host, who nodded, and when he glanced toward the window, Mike held up his hand, a quick, unobtrusive gesture. Curtis gave no indication that he'd seen him. He continued to check out the room and made his way through the buffet line.

After a few minutes, he came over to Mike and set two plates on the table. "Mike," Curtis said.

"Ryan Curtis," Mike acknowledged.

Curtis removed his cap and pushed his sunglasses back into his blond hair. "You could've gotten my photo from the Internet."

"Could've, but I didn't." He gestured at the bag on the chair next to him. "Got it off Lazier's laptop." He dropped one of the buffet tickets in front of Curtis's plate. "Lunch is on me. Well, technically it's on Lazier. He had about two grand in a money clip in his penthouse."

"I'd say he owes you at least that for pain and suffering. Tell me about your dad. Why did they choose him?"

"Probably because you and your people had never seen him. And he had a kid they could nab for insurance and they knew that if they offered my dad enough money, he would consent to do it."

"And when did they take you?"

"Maybe ten days ago. I'm not sure of the exact date. But they got my dad roped into this on Thanksgiving. I didn't see him again until Christmas, when he told me he had a new job and would be gone for a while." Mike eyed his platter of food: a steaming omelet, biscuits steeped in butter, slices of mangos, melon, strawberries, a couple of small pancakes, coffee with a thick, rich aroma. More food than he'd seen since his mother and Frank had left for their cruise.

"How much did they pay your dad?"

"I think the total is about a million. And he's chipped."

"You say that like you know what it means."

"I know what I read and heard. Lazier and his people don't have any chips left. They're calling you and your group terrorists. Why're you still in Aruba?"

"We won't be for long. We're looking for a new refuge."

"In the past?"

"Yes."

"Can you help me get home before you leave? Help my girlfriend and I?"

"She's here, too?"

"She will be around noon today. She's flying in from Caracas."

"Jesus, Mike. You shouldn't have gotten anyone else involved. You don't have any idea how dangerous these bastards are."

"I couldn't stop her. And excuse me, but I know exactly how dangerous these fucks are. They kept me locked up and drugged for more than a week. Can you help us or not?"

"That depends on whether you should even go back home. Once they finish looking for you here, they'll go to your home next."

"Then can you . . . can you take me to my dad?"

"Or take you somewhere safe until we can sort things out. What can you offer me in return?"

Mike unzipped his bag and brought out the laptop, lightweight, thin as a wafer. "Take a look. I have copies of everything on a memory stick."

"You're a geek?"

Mike laughed. "Why? Just because I know how to copy files onto a memory stick? Ann's the geek. She writes code for fun."

"Ann. That's your girlfriend?"

He nodded. Curtis set the laptop beside his plate, turned it on, and clicked rapidly through the files, nodding now and then to himself. For five or ten minutes, neither of them spoke. Mike polished off everything on his plate and got up for a second helping. As he went through the line, he noticed a table of culturally diverse men at a corner table. A short Asian man with graying temples appeared to be in charge, talking animatedly to the others, gesturing at a laptop screen. It made Mike uneasy—but probably because just about everyone in here, except for him and Curtis and a few others, were couples or families.

When he returned to the table, the laptop was shut and Curtis looked smug. "Everything I could possibly need or want is in these files. These people won't be fucking with us or you or anyone else again. I promise you that."

"Look, man, the only thing I need is to get someplace other than here. Can you help me or not?"

"Are you willing to help yourself?"

"I escaped from the penthouse, stabbed the senator with a screwdriver, hit the fire alarm and created all sorts of chaos in the hotel, stole a BMW, a laptop and two grand, hid out in two motels, and figured out enough on my own to contact you. Does that answer your question?"

Curtis laughed. "And you're how old?"

"Nearly seventeen."

Curtis reached into his own bag, resting on the chair next to him, and withdrew something that he folded inside his cloth napkin. He set it in front of Mike's plate. "Take it."

"If it's a gun, I don't want it."

"It's not a gun."

Mike took the napkin and set it in his lap, where he folded back the edges, revealing a small, transparent syringe filled with a blue gel the same color as the waters of the Caribbean. *Shit, this is it. The biochip.* "But . . . I mean . . . what do I do with it? How . . . how do I . . . ?"

"You read the file, right?"

"Yeah, but it said . . . the chip is injected through the nostril."

"That's right," Curtis said, then leaned forward and spoke so softly now that Mike had to strain to hear him.

He latched onto every word, every instruction, every warning. And as he listened, it seemed to him that the heat of his hands began to warm the syringe. "So I just stick the end into one of my nostrils and press the plunger? That's it? Then I can get to where my dad is?"

"Then you're at least ready," Curtis said. "But understand, Mike. As far as I know, no one as young as you has been chipped before. I don't know what kind of repercussions there may be."

Mike's fingers traced the shape of the thing. His dad had done this. How awful could it be?

"Just go into the restroom and . . ."

Fuck the restroom. Mike brought out the syringe, flicked off the cap, and turned his head toward the window, away from the crowd, and slipped the tip of the thing up inside his right nostril and pressed the plunger.

The inside of his nose went numb. The gel not only froze tissues and nerve endings but clogged his sinuses on that side so terribly that he couldn't breathe. He felt the cold shit dripping down into the back of his throat and suddenly his throat, too, went numb. When he swallowed, he couldn't feel anything going down. Couldn't feel anything at all. He knew that he inhaled, but the air didn't seem to be flowing into his lungs and he panicked and shot to his feet.

His chair slammed to the floor, his vision blurred, he groped blindly for something to grab on to. His arms flopped around, knocking dishes and glasses to the floor, and the world around him now moved in a ghastly slow motion, as if his brain were shutting down because of a lack of oxygen. He was vaguely aware of heads turning in their direction, of a gull sweeping past the windows, through the endless blue sky. He had a vivid impression of Curtis, his mouth widening into a huge O, his brows lifting ever so slowly, and how he seemed to grow upward from the floor as he got to his feet. Then Curtis was reaching for him and for Mike's bag, and then the restaurant just wasn't there anymore.

The next thing Mike knew, he sprawled on a tile floor, gasping for air, and Curtis was patting him on the back as though he were an infant with colic who needed to burp. Mike reared up, twisted his body, and shoved Curtis away from him. He fell down onto his hands and remained like that, chest heaving, air hissing through his teeth.

"Aw, fuck, we've got a problem!" a woman yelled.

Mike lifted his head and knew that the woman leaning over him was Kat Sargent, her long raven hair falling over one shoulder. Curtis's partner. If nothing else, he knew the faces, the history, the weird connections. It was all in the files.

"I'm not a problem." The words rushed out with a breath of air. Mike sank back on his heels, palms gripping his thighs. "I may be the solution."

"I doubt it, hon." Kat dropped to a crouch so that they were eye to eye. "But let's hear it."

Now it was a long time later. Nearly noon. Mike thought that Curtis had transitioned them back only ten or fifteen minutes, but he wasn't sure. Wasn't sure of much of anything except that he needed to get to the airport to meet Ann's flight. But there appeared to be something really wrong with this picture. His right hand was cuffed to a hook that protruded from the side of the table. Tyler had done it. Tyler, Nora's brother, Mr. Paranoid, Mr. Oh My God the Sky Is Falling. And it was Tyler who kept leaning into Mike's face snapping questions at him, demanding answers that he just didn't have.

"I think you're a spy for them, Mike. I think you and your old man are in this together," Tyler spat.

"You know what? Go fuck yourself. Stun me now so I can be rid of this chip. I need to get to the airport."

"C'mon, Tyler, leave it alone," Diana said, touching his arm. "He is who he says he is, a—"

"Yeah?" Tyler's head snapped toward Diana. "How do we know that?"

Her expression suddenly hardened and Mike liked what he saw in her eyes. "I'm not going to be infected with your paranoia," she said, then pushed away from the table, came over to Mike, and unlocked his cuff.

Tyler started to protest, but she spun around. "Listen up, Ty." She didn't shout, but it seemed that she did. "I'm not going to live out the rest of my pregnancy or my goddamn life treating everyone like a suspect."

"Calm down," Kat said. "Both of you. He's not a spy. He's a kid who was in the wrong place at the wrong time." She set a bottle of water in front of Mike and leaned toward him. "Now that you're chipped, there are a couple of hard-and-fast rules you need to know, Mike. A stun gun will cause your body to reject the chip and that is *not* a pleasant experience. You can't transition anyone who is unconscious. Your intention, emotional needs, and desires are what propel you to where you want to go. The farther back in time you go, the trickier it is to be accurate. That takes a lot of practice. It's possible to transition into the future, but we haven't mastered that one yet. We're still learning the parameters."

"Jesus," Tyler snapped. "What the fuck are you doing, Kat? We don't know for sure who this kid is, what his . . ."

"Shut up," Curtis said. "You apparently haven't thought ahead, Tyler. Mike Holcomb, Diana's baby . . . they're the new generation of Travelers, okay? We won't be around forever. We may think we will be, but we won't. At some point, we'll die off—murder, sickness, who the hell knows? And then who's going to carry on? Mike has a vested interest in all this. He's shown initiative. He—"

"I get it, Ryan." Sharp edges filled Tyler's voice.

They talked as though he weren't present, Mike thought, sort of like his mom and stepfather. He was beginning to think that most adults were assholes. "Look, if you don't mind, I need to pick up my girlfriend at the airport. She—"

"Your *girlfriend*?" Tyler burst out. "You've got someone else involved in this?" He glared at Curtis. "Did you know this?"

"Back off, Tyler," Diana snapped.

"Yeah," Curtis barked. "Back the fuck off. Di, get him outta here before I rearrange his goddamn nose."

Mike rubbed his eyes and wondered what they would do if he just got up and walked out of here and hitched a ride to the airport. Shoot him? Cuff him? Drug him? They couldn't do anything worse than what Ben had done to him already. He started to say something, but Curtis and Tyler were still arguing, their voices getting louder, more shrill, uglier. It struck something in Mike, all this yelling bullshit, something from his middle school years when his parents had argued all the time. He suddenly leaped up and threw out his arms and screamed, "Enough!"

The men shut up and just stared at him.

"I'll be glad to leave. I just need a car so I can pick up Ann at the airport."

"You can take the Bug," Curtis said.

"By himself?" Tyler exploded. "You're going to turn him loose *alone*? While he's chipped? My God, Ryan, you're a fucking fruitcake."

Curtis spun around and swung. His fist split open Tyler's lip and Tyler stumbled back, his face apple red, blood oozing from his cut lip, his entire body tightened to retaliate, but Diana grabbed his arm before he could lunge at Curtis.

"This ends here!" she shouted.

Silence gripped the air. Mike's arms dropped to his sides. "Never mind," he said. "I'll walk."

He grabbed his bag off the floor, slung it over his shoulder, and headed through the kitchen to the front door. No one stopped him. Pandemonium broke out behind him, but it wasn't his drama. He opened the door and hurried outside, into the hot, desert wind, the burning light. His nostril felt almost normal now, but he was still aware of something up there inside it, of movement, of a difference. He checked his messages and, sure enough, Ann had sent one ten minutes ago.

> Just got thru customs. Where r u?
> Sit tight. On my way.

"Mike," Curtis called.

"Yo." He raised his arm but didn't look around.

Curtis fell into step beside him. "I'll get you to the airport. In the meantime, the others are headed elsewhere to find us a new haven."

"That Tyler's a jerk."

"He's stressed out. We all are."

"Can't you take me to where my dad is? Or show me how to do it?"

"Let's pick up Ann first and then get you two off the island. Is she already at the airport?"

"Landed ten minutes ago."

Curtis clasped his shoulder. "First lesson. We're going back five minutes. I'll target the men's room at the airport."

"You can be that precise?"

"With a lot of practice. And when you're aiming for a particular location, it helps if you've been there before."

"What do I do?"

"As long as I'm doing the transitioning, you don't have to do anything. But if you were doing it, you would conjure the most vivid mental image possible of the place and time. You would reach for it emotionally, and then release the desire. *Reach* and *release*. Since it's Ann you want to get to, you would reach for her and then release the desire. And if you're transitioning someone who isn't chipped, you have to be touching the person."

"So when you transitioned me in the restaurant, you reached for your home here."

"Yes. Most Travelers have a place they can get to with hardly any effort at all. For years, Kat's spot was Woodstock the day that Jerry Garcia played."

Mike was starting to see just how incredibly cool this was going to be. "All right, I'm rea—"

He finished his sentence on his ass on the floor of the airport men's room. "—dy. Oh my God."

Curtis grabbed his hand and pulled him to his feet just as a heavyset man came out of a stall. The man glanced at them, went over to the sink, and Curtis tilted his head toward the door. They stepped out into a busy corridor, bags over their shoulders, passengers and cops everywhere. "You okay?" Curtis asked.

"I feel kind of nauseated and I have a headache."

"That's normal. You'll feel better in a few minutes. Keep your cap on, don't look at any of the cops, act normal." He pulled a bottle of water from his bag and passed it to Mike. "Take a few sips. It's important to stay hydrated. And call Ann. Find out exactly where she is. It's risky to spend too much time here."

Mike quickly punched out her number. "I'm in a bookstore, where the duty-free shops are," she said softly.

He repeated what she said and Curtis pointed off to the right, to a bank of escalators and elevators. "Almost there," Mike told her. "Stay where you are."

"In the event that we get separated or something," Curtis said, "you should target Nellysford, Virginia, the Monroe Institute, and ask for Lea Cuthoney or Russ Berlin. Late April or May 2006."

"I've never been to Virginia. How am I going to know how to get there?"

"Look, nothing's going to happen. I'm just a big believer in redundancy. But whenever you're targeting a place you've never been, get pictures off the Internet. Or go to the location in your own time, so you get a feel for it, and then target the time. That's for accuracy. These new chips—like the one you have—seem to be connected to each other in some way. Like a unified field of energy. So if one of us has been to a place, it's possible for the rest of us to get there just by focusing our intentions on that location."

They rode the escalator down to the next level and headed for the duty-free shops just ahead. Dozens of shops, their windows glistening with jewels and china, wines and coffees, stuff from all over the world. Curtis stopped just outside the bookstore. "I'll wait right here for you. Hurry."

Mike entered the bookstore—and spotted her immediately, at the magazine rack, her beautiful hair a pale river that flowed down her back. Khaki slacks hugged her narrow hips. Her short-sleeved shirt, that same fantastic shade of blue as the Caribbean water, left her lovely arms exposed. He came up behind her, whispered, "Your dad's really going to hate me now."

She whirled, light dancing in her eyes, her mouth lifting into a smile that he could feel in his toes. And when she slid her arms around his waist, her body pressed into his, he wanted nothing more than to get somewhere fast and peel away her clothes.

"My God," she murmured, and ran her hands up the sides of his face and nudged the cap back farther on his head, then slipped her fingers into his hair. "Pretty good disguise, Holcomb. Really short hair, glasses . . . but I'd know you anywhere."

He kissed her then, loving the taste of her mouth, the way her tongue teased his. She pulled back and took his hand. "Let's get outta here."

As they turned away from the magazine rack, an Asian man with his cell pressed to his ear hurried between Mike and Ann, forcing them apart, and Mike flashed on the Asian guy in the lighthouse restaurant. *Is that him?* He glanced back, certain the men were one and the same, his mind stumbling to calculate the odds, and when he turned again, half a dozen cops surrounded him and Ann, rifles pointed at them. Wade stood out in front of them in his impeccable Mafia clothes, turning the diamond stud in his ear.

"Mr. H junior," he said, smiling like they were all old friends. "And this lovely young woman must be Ann Lincoln, who got here via Caracas. A clever move, Ms. Lincoln, but we've had you under surveillance for so long now that any deviation in your routine threw up all sorts of red flags."

"I . . . I . . . I haven't done anything," Ann stammered.

"Let her go," Mike said. "I'm the one you want." He reached for her hand, wanting only to touch her so that he could transition them somewhere.

But Wade lunged forward and stunned Mike in the neck, and suddenly Mike had no control whatsoever over his body. He writhed and twitched and moaned and knew that he was falling, that Ann was screaming, that people were scrambling away from them. Then he felt a rush of warmth pouring from his nostril, a torrent of blood.

"He's hurt! He's hemorrhaging!" Ann shrieked.

"Shut her up," Wade snapped and stooped over Mike, his face a blur. "Looks like your body is rejecting a chip, Mr. H junior." His soft, slippery voice curled and twisted like smoke through Mike's diminishing awareness. "You're going to tell me all about it. Because if you don't, Ben will have to hurt your girlfriend." Mike felt a sharp prick in his neck, felt the blood drying on his mouth and chin, and then he floated away.

PART THREE
COUNTDOWN
February 12–13, 1695

Where is it, this present?
It has melted in our grasp, fled where we could
touch it, gone in the instant of becoming.

—WILLIAM JAMES

18
In the Belly of the Beast

We are deep within ourselves and shifting from time-to-energy awareness and back again.

—Fred Alan Wolf

The sounds echoed inside Kincaid's dream, as if he were locked inside his own heart listening to the rhythmic rush of blood through arteries and veins. And then a voice intruded, caught in the silence between heartbeats, and Kincaid struggled upward from the abyss of sleep. It took enormous effort to open his eyes into the anemic light that filtered through the dirty, frosty windows, the light from another time. Nora's side of the bed was empty, Sunny was nowhere in sight, the fire had died. The room was so cold he could see his breath when he exhaled. He sat up and rubbed his fingers against the frosted glass so that he could peer outside. A rising river of fog rolled through the town.

Pounding at the door, then James Cory's voice: "Magistrate, we have a problem. Please open the door."

Just *one* problem? That was welcome news. "Just a minute, Mr. Cory. I'll be right there."

Kincaid threw off the quilt and glanced quickly around the room to make sure that nothing from his own time was in sight. He swept up the PDA that Nora had left next to the bed—he'd read its files thoroughly—and dropped it into his bag. He dressed quickly and hurried to the door. Only as he opened it did he realize he was completely out of costume: twenty-first-century jeans, a sweatshirt, wool socks. Cory, in fact, didn't hide his surprise at how Kincaid was dressed, but he didn't remark on it, either.

"Your wife, Magistrate, has been accused of freeing Sarah Longwood and facilitating her escape from Blue River with Dr. Webber. She was captured as she fled that area around the doctor's home. She has been taken to the gaol. We are prepared to help you in any way we can."

Kincaid couldn't get beyond the accusation. He thought it was just after two when he and Nora had made love, and now it was . . . what? Seven or eight? At some point in the last five or six hours, Nora and Sunny had left here, met up with the doctor, freed Sarah Longwood from the jail, and the doctor had taken her out of town. But what connected these events?

"Magistrate?" Cory said.

"While I put on proper clothes, could you fetch Mr. Ivers? As the governor's emissary, he represents the highest legal voice. I suspect we may need him to find the truth about these events and to keep the reverend from doing something we would all regret."

"Certainly. We will meet you in the stable in twenty minutes."

Kincaid shut the door and leaned against it, pressing his fingers against his eyes, his thoughts scrambling around like mice in a maze searching for a bit of cheese. Chandler had no doubt taken enormous pleasure in accusing and arresting Nora. Not only was it the ultimate "fuck you" gesture to the magistrate, the man who had challenged Chandler's authority, but it also sent a message to the town: even the magistrate's wife is not immune from accusation. He thought of the filth in the cells, of the scars and sores on Sarah Longwood, and knew that his biggest challenge would be freeing Nora without killing someone.

He dressed in clean era clothes and his body instantly screamed to be free of them. But he couldn't very well act like a magistrate if he didn't look the part. He pulled on his boots, then went over to the cabinet, brought out Nora's bag, and dumped the contents onto the bed.

Her jeans and sweatshirt were missing. Why would she venture outside wearing her own clothing? The only answer that came to mind was that Sunny had to go out and it was easier for her to dress in her own clothes. She probably had thought that since it was dark no one would see her.

If you touch her, you sick fuck, if you torture her, if you, if you . . .

Kincaid cut off that line of thought and forced himself to focus on the items strewn on the bed. He picked up the bulging velvet pouch that had been tied to Nora's wrist when she had transitioned back to the beach from Aruba. Inside were an array of items that might prove useful in the hours ahead: stun guns, glow sticks, a pair of handcuffs, an extra clip for their weapons, matches, and a packet of firecrackers. He had the uneasy feeling that they might have to use all of them.

He slipped the stun guns and matches into the pockets of his cloak, divided the glow sticks and firecrackers and slipped half of each into the pockets, along with the Glock, a Swiss Army knife, and the cuffs. Everything else went into his bag. He dug out the extra syringes from the snow on the roof, put them into the insulated pocket of his bag, and hoped they wouldn't warm up.

He packed up Nora's bag, returned it to the cabinet, and brought out the last bottle of water from his own bag. Sipped. River water. He stuck it inside his cloak and glanced quickly around the room to make sure he hadn't forgotten anything. But the image that exploded in his head was all that he saw: Nora on the strappado, lifted upside down by some crude system of pulleys, and Chandler screaming at her to confess, to confess, and then lowering her down until her hands and arms vanished into a pot of boiling oil.

His knees suddenly buckled and he sank to the foot of the bed, bag in his lap, hands covering his face. He struggled against the crushing waves of despair and fear that paralyzed him. Chandler would be after blood, spectacle. Robbed of one witch, he now had another. He needed a gruesome extravaganza that would stoke religious furor and hysteria in Blue River for weeks and months to come.

He *reached* for Aruba, *reached* with everything he had, *reached and released.* But it wasn't enough. He couldn't break through the barrier of whatever prevented them from transitioning, couldn't find that place within himself that would allow him to stop time, speed it up, change the frequency, whatever the hell he had done on Cape Cod months ago. His frustration was so extreme that he gripped his thighs to keep from throwing something. He realized he was caught in the loop of this era, entrenched in it, immersed so deeply that the months of training for this particular transition had created grooves so deep in his unconscious that he was stuck until he completed what he'd come here to do. His only alternative was to find solutions through ordinary means.

The moment he resigned himself, he suddenly was in the front room of the jail. The glowing fire was the only source of light. It was as if his acceptance of his situation had released him, set him free. He wasn't sure how far back he had gone in time—minutes or hours—but since blackness swam in the only window, he figured he had gone back at least several hours before sunrise.

No sign of Davies or Chandler.

Kincaid brought out the strap for the shoulder bag, looped it over his neck, then fitted the bag snugly against his hip. Next, his weapon. He moved quickly but carefully up the corridor to the heavy wooden door that opened into the cell block. His senses strained, but he detected nothing immediately threatening. He pulled open the heavy wooden door, wincing as it scraped noisily against the floor, and stared into an abyss of darkness, of silence. No torches, no lanterns, not a single goddamn glimmer of light in here.

He pulled out the glow stick, bent it, and the green light illuminated enough of the cell block so that he could see his way to the first cell. Sarah Longwood's cell, the door open, the cell empty. He moved on to the next cell. The door was shut, but not locked, and he opened it, peered in. Empty. "Hello," he called softly. "This is Magistrate Goodwin. Is anyone here?"

His voice echoed through the cell block. He heard soft rustling, like the wind through leaves—*rats*. But that was all.

Chandler had moved them. But to where?

Kincaid continued to the end of the cell block, pushed open the door, and entered a small, claustrophobic room— the torture chamber. The strappado pulleys hung from the ceiling. Torture tools were strewn across the table and floor. He stepped around the pulleys, his head pounding with vivid images borrowed from history, from the lecture he and Nora had listened to the day they had visited this place in their own time.

He stopped under the pulley, which was in front of a large iron pot in which oil had cooled. His imagination didn't have to supply details. That sick fuck Chandler had been torturing someone here. *Nora? Please, God, no*. Had the window gotten broken during the torture session? He picked up an instrument that looked like a branding iron, dropped the end into the oil, and fished out a skirt, a bodice, underclothes. Not Nora's.

He flung the clothes across the room, and they smacked the wall and dropped to the floor. He slammed the branding iron into the pulleys and hooks of the strappado again and again until the entire contraption collapsed at his feet. He stood there, breathing hard, his fury a beast without remorse, and went after the table next, pounding it with the branding iron until the wood cracked, a leg snapped, the remaining tools spun to the floor. He moved through the room, swinging the iron from one side to the other, smashing chairs, the remaining legs on the table, a wooden contraption that resembled a rack.

And then he attacked the torture implements themselves, hammering and pounding at them until sparks flew, until some of the tools flattened like dimes. He swung the iron at the jagged pieces of glass that still stuck up from the window frame and shattered them, shards flying out into the cold darkness. He kept swinging until the wood splintered and the stone beneath it chipped.

When Kincaid was done, sweat poured off him, and he stank of fury, panic, terror. He turned slowly, looking for anything he had missed. He shoved the iron pot onto its side and the cool oil poured out, a dark river of blood and sadism, of burnt flesh and agony, oozing across the stone floor. For a moment, he thought he heard voices, shouting, but when he listened closely, he heard only the breeze, strumming at the splintered wood around the gaping hole where the window had been. Fog now drifted through it, into the room.

He desperately wanted to hurry back into the cell block and set the filthy hay on fire, torch the atrocity to its foundations. But if there was some hidden chamber in this building where Chandler had taken Nora and the other women, they might die before they were found.

Is there such a chamber somewhere?

Kincaid dropped the branding iron and moved quickly along the walls, his fingers running over the cold stones, seeking an irregularity that would indicate a secret door. He didn't find anything unusual. If a secret chamber existed, the most likely place would be *under* the jail, in a cellar of some kind. He didn't recall any historical reference to a secret room, chamber, or even a cellar, and Nora had never mentioned it. If it existed, she would know about it because of her access to the building while she had taught at Blue River.

Yet, Chandler had moved the women and Kincaid doubted he would risk taking them *out* of the building to some other location. So where were they?

He ran through the cell block, certain there was nothing in any of the cells that would provide an exit for a prisoner— no trapdoors in cell floors, no hidden doors in the walls. Any entrance to a secret chamber would have to be in the front room. When he reached it, he stood near the fireplace, turning slowly. When he and Nora had come here . . . yesterday? today? three days ago?—he didn't know yet—Davies had been sitting in that chair near the fire. But where did he go when he wasn't in here? Where did he take a leak, stretch out to rest his eyes, eat his own meals? Kincaid opened the door to the cell block again and held the glow stick up higher so the light was more evenly dispersed.

To his left, just before the row of cells began, was a dark vestibule that he hadn't seen when Davies had brought him and Nora into the cell block. It was hidden so deeply in shadows that it was practically invisible. Kincaid moved toward it, the glow stick casting the stone walls in a ghastly green against which his shadow loomed, larger than life. What he thought was a vestibule was actually a narrow corridor that he didn't recall seeing in his own time. How many other details about this building would be obliterated by history?

He reached a door, opened it, and stepped into a small room with a pallet and quilt on the floor, an unlit lantern, a chamber pot against the far wall, an unwashed wooden plate on a small table, and a pewter mug with liquid at the bottom. He sniffed at the mug. Beer. You'd have to be half drunk all the time to work in this place, Kincaid thought. Up near the ceiling were two tiny square windows, the glass so caked with snow and ice that he could barely make out the darkness. The air stank of piss and filth, just like the cell block.

It didn't take him long to run his fingers over the walls, checking the stones and the seams between them for anything irregular. He found nothing. A kind of sick despair welled up inside him, and he pressed his fists against his eyes, trying to shake it off, but his frustration and fear were too great. He had to let the emotions run their course, like the flu. He told himself he had faced worse than this, a bald-faced lie. Even the worst moment of his life—when Nora and Jake McKee had stood on that Cape Cod beach and exchanged marriage vows—didn't compare to this.

Based on what he knew historically and personally about Chandler, a secret chamber was the only thing that made sense. And if it existed, its doorway would be much more apparent. After all, Chandler's torture room wasn't hidden. Open enough doors and you eventually reached it.

He suddenly wished that Sunny were with him. The dog would sniff out Nora, track her down, dig her way to wherever she was if that was what was required. Kincaid lit the lantern, stuck the glow stick in the waistband of his breeches, and examined the floor under the table. Nothing irregular leaped out at him. He grabbed the quilt, snatched up the pallet, tossed both to the side.

Something clicked against the stones. Two clicks, like a kid's marble bouncing away. Kincaid dropped to his knees and turned, set the lantern down, and saw it. Crawled toward it. His eyeballs throbbed and burned. He leaned forward, his hands dropped to either side of the object, and he brought his face down to within inches of it, stared—and nearly wept.

The digital watch that Nora wore around her neck, that round little thing that faithfully recorded the time and date regardless of the era to which they transitioned, had a cracked face. A piece of the gold chain on which it hung was still caught in the little gold eye. Either she had torn off the watch on her way in here, leaving proof of her presence in this room, a bread crumb that would lead to her location, or it had been torn off by someone else.

This last possibility triggered several vivid, horrifying

images of Davies or Chandler or another man in their tight circle of lackeys groping at Nora, tearing at her clothing. . . .

Kincaid grabbed the lantern and scrambled to his feet, the watch still clutched in his hand. He felt its shape and hardness against his skin, his joints, and forced himself to look at it.

Still ticking. That was a good sign, right? *Right? Tell me it's a fantastic sign. Please.* It was 3:21 A.M., but it was February 12, 1695. He had transitioned forward a day. But how? And why? It meant that Nora had been incarcerated for . . . what? Eighteen hours in this place? Longer? No telling what horrors Chandler had committed in that time. Something about this date nagged at him, something he knew he should be remembering, but it escaped him.

He crouched at the area the pallet had covered. And there it was, the trapdoor, outlined in the stone as if someone had taken chalk to the shape of it. He dug his fingers into the outline of the door seeking a way to open it. Along the edge closest to his feet, he found a loose stone, pulled it free, and worked his fingers under the thick wooden door and began to lift it.

It creaked and moaned and the stench of human waste washed over him. He nearly gagged on it. His hands flew to his face and pressed against his mouth and nose until his nausea ebbed. Kincaid rocked back onto his heels and turned his head to the side and breathed deeply—fetid air, yes, but better than the shit radiating from the hole. Then he picked up the lantern and brought it down closer to the gaping black abyss and saw the stairs.

He turned around, his feet found the top step, and he began his descent. The stairs seemed to go on forever, the chamber was so deep. In his time, the jail that represented the darkest period of Blue River's history didn't have a cellar. So where and when in history had it ceased to exist? When he finally reached the bottom of the stairs, he raised the lantern high above his head. "Nora?" His voice was a pathetic rasp. He cleared his throat and called more loudly this time, his voice echoing, rising and falling and bouncing against the stone walls.

"Alex . . ."

Sweet Christ, she sounded as if she was barely alive. "Keep talking. Can you see the lantern?"

"Yes, okay. Keep moving forward. That bastard . . . no light, food . . . water . . ."

"Help us!" another woman called. "Help us!"

"Over here!" a third voice said. "Keep moving toward our voices. . . ."

Kincaid moved slowly, the lantern held way above his head, the flame hissing, flickering, threatening to go out. The ceiling sloped downward suddenly and he had to lower the lantern and hunker over to keep from smacking his head against the stones. The smell of earth, dampness, mold, and shit swirled into his nostrils, suffused his senses. He felt as if this cellar was where Chandler's real atrocities were hidden away, a secret grave.

His heart nearly broke when he finally reached her—Nora—inside a small, filthy, zoolike cage, hands and feet shackled. Dirt smeared her swollen, bruised face, while bits of hay stuck to her skin. Her liquid eyes reached for him, begged him, spoke to him. He fired at the lock, the explosion echoing, echoing, as he fired again and again and again. He slammed in a fresh clip, but the door had sprung free and he ducked his head and rushed inside.

The cage was so small that only a midget could stand upright in here. He set the lantern on the floor and wrapped his arms around her, lifting her head from the filthy floor, combing his fingers back through her hair. Metal bracelets encircled her wrists so tightly that he couldn't even slide his thumbnail under them. Both bracelets were attached to the bars of the cage with small, thick metal hooks. Another metal bracelet was attached to her right ankle and it, too, was hooked to a bar of the cage. Her left ankle was bound with cord to her right ankle.

"That fuck, that sick fuck . . ."

"I . . . didn't think you would find us down here . . . I . . . I tore off the watch . . . hoping you would . . ." She choked up, her swollen lip quivering. "I saw . . . Chandler torturing Sarah Longwood. I . . ."

Kincaid pulled out the bottle of water, spun the cap, then held her head and brought the bottle to her mouth. She sipped, coughed, sipped again, paused, and took a longer drink. She went on, stumbling for words as she described the events that had led her to Berlin at the Monroe Institute and to Berlin here and his flight from Blue River with Sarah Longwood and Sunny.

Berlin, the legendary Berlin And our dog went with him.
"Take another sip." He brought the bottle to her lips again.

She sipped, turned her head to the side. "Save some. For the others."

He couldn't transition her out of here while she was restrained and he didn't dare try to shoot the bracelets off her wrists. "I can't get these bracelets off without another tool, but I can at least get this goddamn cord off." He put the cap back on the bottle, brought out his knife and sliced through the cord. It fell away from her ankle, revealing a deep slice in her skin.

"Get the others first, Alex. They're only tied."

"Who hit you?"

"It doesn't matter."

"It matters to *me*."

"Travers. He wanted a blow job." She emitted a sound— half laugh, half sob. "Kneed him in the balls. Told him if he tried that again Satan would bite it off."

Kincaid barely clung to his sanity. It was an effort to speak. "I'll try to transition the other women to the stable.

Then I'll come back for you. I think the Cory brothers and Fry will help us."

"Hurry," she said. "When Davies came down here . . . hours ago, he . . . he said they would burn us tomorrow."

He couldn't bring himself to leave her side, not without one more stab at freeing her. Kincaid slammed the handle of the Glock against the hook that held one bracelet to the bars, hoping he could knock it loose. Three more blows weakened the metal, but didn't free her.

"Just *go*, Alex. One of them . . . could come back any second."

"I think I can free your left arm." He slipped the flat edge of his knife between the gap he had widened and pulled it toward him, straining to widen it just a little farther. The hook, apparently weakened by the pounding, suddenly snapped and her arm fell free. Nora gasped at the abrupt cessation of pressure. He started on the next hook, but she flung her free arm around his neck and pulled his face toward her, kissed him hungrily, desperately. Her voice was choked and soft when she spoke. "They took . . . my gun. My cloak. Free the others. Now. I'll be okay."

"I can do it—"

"*No. Go now.*"

He pressed one of the stun guns into her hand and left a glow stick next to her on the floor. "As soon as I blow open the other doors, I'll leave you the gun." He picked up the lantern and fled the cell before he could change his mind. He loped down the corridor to the fourth cell, where a woman with long, matted gray hair was tied to the bars of another cage. Rebeka—this had to be Rebeka Short. He set the lantern on the floor, blew it out, and brought another glow stick out of his cloak pocket.

Kincaid blew open the lock with two shots, the explosions echoing, and had her free in under sixty seconds. He helped her out of the cell, shocked at how frail and thin she was, her wrinkled face a testament to the hardness of life in this time for the elderly. And "elderly" was relative. He knew she was seventy, but she looked a hundred.

Rebeka sank to the corridor floor, too weak to walk or stand. He held the bottle of water to her mouth and she sipped, then pulled back, her eyes darting from the bottle to the glow stick. Before she could ask him what they were, he gave his standard answer: "They are from Europe. Wait here while I free Lucia."

She was the youngest of the accused, and when he blew open the door of her cell, she rattled the bars and cried out, "Hurry, please!"

Lucia's clothes hung in dirty tatters and she radiated a powerful, gagging stench—of urine, vomit, blood. She seemed too thin to be three-dimensional, but as soon as he cut her free, she lurched from the cell like a toddler who hadn't quite mastered the art of walking, her bare feet slapping the cold stones, and ran over to Rebeka.

Kincaid hurried over to them, gave Lucia the bottle of water before he realized it was plastic, from his own time. Too late now. He ran back in to Nora's cell, crouched in front of her, pressed the Glock into her free hand. "Three bullets are gone. Don't hesitate to use it. Not with these fucks. I'll be back in a jiffy."

"Alex, the date. What's the date?"

"February twelfth."

"Historically, the real magistrate is supposed to arrive today."

Of course. That was what had been nagging at him. "He won't be here yet. It's too early. See you in—"

A voice upstairs silenced him. "Reverend? Are you down there?"

Davies. Kincaid motioned at Rebeka and Lucia to move to the other side of the cell block, deeper into shadow. He shut the door to Nora's cell, tucked the glow stick into his cloak, and moved quickly and silently to the small, cramped space under the ladder. He pressed back into the shadows until his spine was up against the wall and brought out the stun gun. He set his bag to the side, then waited, head pounding.

"Reverend?" Davies called again.

Silence. No one here in the belly of the beast made a sound.

Davies started down the ladder, one hand holding a lantern, the other gripping each step as he descended. Kincaid realized that he had miscalculated. If he stunned Davies as he came down the ladder, he would drop the lantern, the glass would shatter, the oil would spill, and the flame would start a fire. He would have to wait until Davies set the lantern down or hung it from one of the wall hooks and then come up behind him. But suppose he kept holding the lantern? Kincaid couldn't risk stunning him as he was entering a cell, where the dry hay would burn faster than money.

And so he conjured a bright, vivid image of what he desired, *reached* for that image, *released* it. Nothing changed. Time didn't slow or stop, Davies kept on descending, and as he reached the last few steps, the glow of his lantern stopped just short of where Kincaid was hidden. He could see the jailer's handsome face clearly—clenched jaw, narrowed eyes— and then Davies reached the bottom of the ladder and turned, slowly, the lantern held just above his head, and shouted, "Wenches, we will begin building your funeral pyres at dawn!"

"Mr. Davies, please," Nora called. "We need water."

Kincaid knew that Nora was intentionally drawing Davies toward her cell, that she had realized what he had— that Davies couldn't be shot or stunned while he still held the lantern. Sure enough, Davies headed toward her cell and paused long enough to hang the lantern from a hook on the wall—and Kincaid ducked out from behind the stairs and rushed at him, the stun gun clutched in his hand.

Davies spun a heartbeat before Kincaid reached him, but seemed so shocked to see him here, now, that he was slow to react. And by the time his hand went for his pistol, Kincaid had tackled him and they crashed to the floor, rolled down the corridor between the cages. Davies was stronger than he looked, outweighed Kincaid by at least thirty pounds, and pinned Kincaid beneath him, punched him in the ribs, the face, struggled to knee him in the groin. But Kincaid was quicker, more desperate, and the moment he stunned him, Davies flopped around like a headless chicken.

Kincaid struggled to his feet, ribs shrieking, breath exploding from his lungs. He backed away from Davies, panicked that when he came to, he would take out his rage on Nora. So while Davies writhed and gurgled, while spittle balled in the corners of his mouth, Kincaid quickly patted him down. Keys. He had to have the keys that would unlock the metal bracelet that kept Nora imprisoned in the cage like an animal.

No keys. How could a jailer not have keys? *Because Chandler took them.* Kincaid dug out the glow stick, held it between his teeth, gripped Davies by the forearms. He began dragging him around to the front of the ladder.

"Lucia, help him," Nora shouted. "So you can escape this place faster."

Lucia, huddled against the wall with Rebeka, shot to her feet and ran over. She lifted up the jailer's feet and, together, she and Kincaid carried Davies over to the wall, where a hook protruded. "I must get my bag," Kincaid said to Lucia. "Stay here."

He loped back to the area under the ladder, dug out the handcuffs, lifted the bag, and ran back to her and Davies. Kincaid handcuffed him to the wall hook, pulled a small cloth from his bag, stuffed it into Davies's mouth.

"What manner of device is that?" Lucia asked, pointing at the handcuffs, her voice riddled with suspicion. "And the bottle. And the green torch. Why is it not hot?"

"Europe," Kincaid said. "Everything is from Europe."

"What did you do to him?"

"I hurt him before he could hurt any of you."

"He wet himself, he salivates, convulses, twitches. I think Satan possesses him." And she kicked him savagely in the side, kicked him with her bare feet, her skinny toes, kicked him again and again until Kincaid grabbed her foot.

"Enough."

She glared at him, her soft, dark eyes suddenly defiant, enraged. "He *hurt* me, Magistrate. *He hurt me bad.*"

"I know. And unless we flee, he will hurt you again." Kincaid grabbed her small, bony hand. Her body odor was so overwhelming that he had to turn his head so he could breathe without gagging. "Who has the keys to the gaol?"

"Satan's minion," she spat. "Where can we go? The town now knows what has happened, that your wife helped Dr. Webber flee with Sarah. They will be building our pyres, they . . . We cannot escape this place."

"The Lord will help us," Kincaid said, nearly choking on the lie, and led her over to where Rebeka huddled in on herself, legs drawn to her chest, cheek resting against her knees.

"What about Mrs. Goodwin?" Lucia asked. "We cannot leave her."

"I'll be back for her."

"Go with him," Nora called. "I will join you shortly."

Kincaid dashed back to the ladder, scrambled up the stairs, and lowered the trapdoor. Then he hurried back to the women, dropped his left hand to Rebeka's shoulder, gripped Lucia's hand, and *reached* for the rooms above the stable, *reached* with the certainty that the chip would take him where he needed to be. And then he released his desire and the crushing pressure grabbed him, shook him like a dog with a bone.

Chandler's secret chamber vanished.

19
The Burning Times

If something is real, it can be put to use even if we don't understand it very well.

—*Dean Radin*

Holcomb bolted awake, his head throbbing, his bladder aching, his blistered feet complaining. The odors in the air told him everything he needed to know about where he was. The faint stink of manure from the stable downstairs seemed to permeate the walls and to drift upward through the chimney. The Cory brothers and Fry were asleep in the next room.

Oriented now, he sat up and instantly recalled what he had read on the PDA that Kincaid had left behind in a bag: *Someone who claims he was abducted by Lazier's people has gotten in touch with us through our website. The kid is supposedly Lazier's insurance to make sure his father will do what Lazier hired him to do. . . . He allegedly escaped and is hiding out somewhere here on the island. One of us will check it out.*

Mike. Holcomb squeezed his eyes shut trying to imagine his son escaping from Lazier's penthouse prison, hiding out on the island, tracking down Nora and Kincaid's group. How had he done all that? And now what? Would they help him?

He dropped his feet to the cold floor, heaved himself up, hobbled over to the fireplace. The embers glowed, radiating enough heat to take the chill off his bones, but not by much. Holcomb added more wood and fanned the embers with his hands until the fresh wood caught fire. He filled the pot on the fireplace with more water, then went over to the chamber pot and relieved himself.

Jesus, the indignity of it all. Just the basics in this era consumed so much time and energy that it was miraculous people had time for anything else. How he longed for electric light, a hot shower, a stove, a coffeemaker, a fridge, a real bathroom, a CD player, a toaster oven, a microwave, a car, a computer, satellite TV, the Internet. And that was just for starters. He was so homesick for his own time and so eaten up with anxiety about his son that he didn't know how much longer it would be before he went stark raving mad.

When the water in the iron pot felt marginally warm, he scooped some into the basin and quickly stripped off his smelly clothes, shivering in the chill. He ran a wet cloth over his body and added Dove soap and real shampoo to his wish list.

At dusk last night, after an exhaustive search for Kincaid, Nora, and the other women—at the jail, the general store, and many of the other buildings downtown—he, the Cory brothers, and Fry had convened here. They had tossed around ideas and plans and plots, but in the end, all their talk had come to nothing. The bottom line was that Kincaid had mysteriously vanished in the minutes after James Cory had announced that Nora had been hauled off to jail for aiding and abetting the escape of Sarah Longwood. And according to Jacob Nash, the inn proprietor, Chandler had taken Nora and the other women to a secret location and left town with a mob of vigilantes to track down the doctor and Sarah.

Since Kincaid had left behind one bag that he and Nora

had brought to this time, Holcomb suspected he and the dog had transitioned suddenly, without warning. The boomerang, that was how Holcomb thought of it. His own boomerang experience had lasted all of what? Ten minutes? Twenty? Was that the norm? *Was* there a norm? Probably not. Kincaid had been gone for nearly twenty-four hours now, and if a boomerang was behind it, then he would reappear here, where he had vanished. Or maybe not.

The bag contained some useful treasures, including the PDA, but until Chandler returned and was forced to reveal the location of the women, there wasn't much that anyone could do. *Force him how?* Holcomb doubted if Chandler would be intimidated now by his alleged authority as the governor's emissary or by Cory's threats to stop delivering food to Blue River. Probably the only thing that might prompt Chandler to divulge where he had hidden the women was hard evidence about what he really had been doing in this town. It had to be the sort of evidence Holcomb could hold over Chandler, something he could threaten to present to the deluded masses who still believed in Chandler's supreme authority as a representative of the Almighty.

Torture wasn't a crime; it was accepted as a necessary means to extract a confession. Was assault a crime? Was homicide? Murder probably was, but he couldn't see Chandler killing someone outright. His methods would be more covert, insidious—murder by starvation, dehydration, or extreme torture. At any rate, he suspected the most likely place to find such evidence would be in Chandler's cellar.

When Holcomb was finished washing, he dried himself with the tiny cloth that passed as a towel. He couldn't stand the thought of putting on era clothing, the breeches that squeezed his balls, the boots that kept his toes immobilized and had resulted in blisters on the soles of his feet. So from his bag he brought out clothes from his own time. Jeans, a soft, long-sleeved T-shirt made of organic cotton, a thick sweatshirt, wonderfully warm wool socks. He pulled out his hiking shoes, tied the laces together, slung them around his neck. Fuck whoever called him on it. He was done with pretense.

Holcomb selected items from his bag and Nora's that he could use, filled the pockets of his cloak, then hid the bags inside the cabinet. He turned the lantern down low, picked up his cloak, and slipped quietly into the front room, where the Cory brothers and Fry snored on pallets. The stairs squeaked softly as he descended. At the bottom, he put on his hiking shoes, wrapped his cloak around him, and stepped out into the darkness.

He wished for yesterday's fog, the cover under which the doctor and Sarah had escaped. But there was only a very low ground fog and the night was crystalline, the moon just setting, and the sky lit up with hundreds of thousands of stars. He had never seen so many stars. Orion's belt looked close enough to touch. The Milky Way was a jewel-studded road to Oz.

Thanks to the brilliance of the stars, he didn't need a glow stick until he entered the first of several alleys. Then he kept it partially hidden by his cloak so that it wouldn't be visible to anyone behind him. Not that anyone was out and about. Too dark, too cold. But once the sun rose, Chandler's fanatical followers would be visible in droves, hauling in wood for the pyres.

This particular deviation from history troubled Holcomb. Most of the accused in the colonies were hanged, but one man in Salem had been pressed to death by boulders. In fact, Holcomb couldn't remember a single instance of burning in the colonies. Had his presence—and that of Nora and Kincaid—*changed* history or were they creating a *new* history? Or none of the above? Maybe this was just some weird glitch with the chip. Maybe this, maybe that. Shit, shit.

Whatever, he was about to complicate the historical picture. If he didn't *find* evidence that he could use against Chandler, then he would *create* evidence. And that evidence, he thought, would resonate throughout history, so that Chandler would be depicted not only as a despicable sadist but as the monster that he truly was.

The door to the reverend's home wasn't locked. Holcomb slipped inside and stood for moments with his back to the thick wood, breathing in the residual smells of Chandler's life. Smoke, ashes, food, urine, herbs, beer, spices. And always, everywhere he went, the body odor—sometimes faint, often strong, and occasionally so overpowering that he nearly gagged on it. He stepped forward, the glow stick held above his head, and made a beeline into the bedroom, where the trapdoor was.

In Holcomb's time, Chandler's home, like the jail, was a historical monument. Holcomb had seen photos of it on the Internet, taken a virtual tour of this very room, where all the furnishings for this era had been recreated. But nowhere on that site, he thought, had there been any mention of the cellar into which he now descended. Did that mean that somewhere in the next three hundred years the cellar would collapse? Get lost in time? What?

The glow stick cast a ghostly light against the walls. Claustrophobia swept over him again, threatening to paralyze him. He stopped midway down the ladder and forced himself to breathe deeply, to focus only on the act of breathing, in and out, deeper and deeper, slower and slower. And pretty soon, he started to descend again, one step at a time, but he smelled his own fear, seeping through the stink of his sweat.

Finally, with both feet planted firmly on the floor, he let go of the ladder and turned. The ceiling of the cellar sloped down sharply just a foot in front of him and he hunkered over and moved forward with slow deliberation, aware of the shrieks of panic in some back room in his head. The claustrophobia pounded against the walls of that mental room, screaming to be freed. But as long as he could keep it trapped inside that room, it didn't belong to him. If it didn't belong to him, if he refused to acknowledge it, then it couldn't affect him.

Holcomb hastened to the cabinet from which Chandler had retrieved the poppets. The door was locked. Several hard kicks caused it to spring open, revealing several dozen small drawers in rows of six. It reminded him of his ex-wife's jewelry chest except that hers was hand-carved walnut, studded with diamonds and emeralds, had come from someplace in Asia, and had cost thirty grand. That bit of information had come to him courtesy of Mike.

Dad, you know what he bought Mom for Halloween?

A yacht?

That was her birthday present. For Halloween, he got her a jewelry box that cost thirty thou. Probably because it had some diamonds in it.

The first drawer was labeled CLAIRE and held two rings, a necklace, a hair clip carved of bone. The second drawer had no label, but contained this era's version of a comb and brush. And on it went until the third row, where he discovered several poppets and a copy of Increase Mather's book *An Essay for the Recording of Illustrious Providences,* an inflammatory treatise on the Puritans' fight against Satan for dominion over the New World. In the fourth row, he discovered the bound book he had noticed during his first visit.

He paged through it, scanning the entries. They ranged from snippets of dreams to prayers, to sermons and visions of Satan and the Lord battling in some ancient field, to Chandler's mad ramblings on how to live righteously. Then, in the middle of the journal, there were dated entries:

4 August 1694
    My wife screemes like the possessed, she writhes and drools, her eyes roll back until only the whites showe. Her mouth moves and I must lean closer to hear what she sayes. She names names. Lucia Gray. Rebeka Short. Sarah Longwood. And the new woman, Catherine Griffin. They consort, they enchant, they appeare to her, demanding that she join them. Stuffe exudes from

Claire's skin. It is damp, like water, but solid, colored. I know not what it is. I wipe it away with a wetted cloth, but it returns and when it is present, she raves, screemes.

19 August 1694

I cannot allow others to see her. They would think I am like her, that I am given to fits, to strange tongues, that I am consorting with Satan. I have created poppets. Claire has instructed me how to make them, where to obtain the fabrics and bits of hair that give them a human appearance. Sometimes at night in the light of the lanterns her fingers move quickly, braiding this bit of hair, attaching the beads for the poppet's eyes, stitching on the little dresses. It is as if she is a child herself, my wife, but a stupid child with just one talent, to imbue the poppets with life.

5 September 1694

Forgive me, Lord. I confess that I am beyonde my ability to care for her, that I cannot endure another day of her ravings, her madness. On this eve I added lantern oil to her porridge.

16 September 1694

She cursed Francis Travers. He is my witness to her madness. Her vomitus spewed from her mouth while Travers was presente. He staggered from her room and later confided that he saw Satan, descending over Blue River, infecting everything. He will tell the others on the council, I know he will. They will look at me first with pity and then with suspicion.

28 September 1694

The physician bled her two days ago. She screemed that he was Satan's consort. She is a witch, my Claire is a witch. I continue to feed her the oil. On this eve she tears off her own clothing and begs me to come to her, to enter her, begs as she writhes and cackles and runs her hands over her own flesh. I am disgusted, fascinated, I screem that we must pray, but she refuses. I demand that she recite the Lord's Prayer, but she would not. And she screems for me to come into her, she offers her breasts, her wetness, and we move into the long, dark river of sin and desire and oh Lord, forgive me, forgive me, but I am elsewhere when inside of her. I am in Satan's grip, under his Spell.

   I plunder.

1 October 1694

   The physician is dead. His wife claims that Claire's curses killed him. Today she was cursed by Lucia Gray. So when Claire dies from the oil I continue to feed her, I can accuse Lucia. And I will put poppets in her bedroom. I will triumph still. The Lord has forgiven my trespasses and guides me in what I do.

5 October 1694

   She feels no pain when I stick the pins into the devil's mark on her breast. I want to take her to the river, to dunk her, to see if she sinks, but I dare not remove her from the house.

9 October 1694

   She dies. My Claire dies with only the whites of her eyes showing. Tomorrow I will put the poppets in Lucia's bedroom. Two days from now, I will accuse Lucia and the others.

Holcomb slapped the journal shut, struggling not to rage through the cellar smashing everything in sight. The fucker had poisoned his wife because her behavior eventually would

cast suspicion on him as the spouse of a witch—and there-
fore, a consort—and then framed Lucia Gray and the others.
He had used his wife's death to fan the fires of religious fanaticism, thus cementing his grip on this town.

Holcomb felt like he had the night Wade and his buddy
had appeared in his home with all that cash. *Follow us. Do
our bidding. And we'll solve every fucking money problem
you've ever had.* But Wade never mentioned that Mike
would be held as ransom. No one had told him that the chip
in his brain was defective, that once he was here he might be
here for good. Unless he stunned Kincaid, Nora, and got
their extra chips—oh praise the Lord, yes siree.

Holcomb hid the journal in his cloak, scooped out the
poppets just in case he might need them, shut the cabinet
door. But with the lock broken, the door swung open again.
Chandler would realize the cabinet had been broken into the
moment he came down the ladder. *Well, so what,* Holcomb
thought. With any luck, he would be long gone by then.

As he started back up the ladder, the tightness returned to
his throat and chest. He heard the screams and pounding in
that room in his head. He focused on the pale green light that
radiated from the glow stick, focused and breathed and
struggled to ignore his rising panic. When his head popped
back up through the trapdoor, he scrambled out on his hands
and knees, gulping at the air.

He heard commotion outside—the clatter of wagons,
shouting, the beating of hooves—and quickly shut the trapdoor, dropped the rug back over it, and ran to the front window. The street out front was empty, so the racket had to be
coming from the main road through downtown. He couldn't
see anything, not from here, and hoped it didn't mean that
Chandler and his mob of vigilantes had returned with the
doctor and Sarah Longwood.

Out the door, fast. He tore toward the closest alley,
backed up to the wall to catch his breath, and suddenly his
right nostril exploded with pain. It felt as if a hot metal rod

had been jammed up into his sinus cavity and an invisible hand now twisted it, as if to probe into his brain. He gasped, and his hands went to his nose—and came away bloody.

Fuck. No. Tell me this isn't happening. His body was rejecting the chip. *Why?* The pain ratcheted up another few notches and then burst with such excruciating agony that it knocked his legs out from under him and he sprawled onto the ground, blood streaming from his nose and blooming in the snow like some exotic rose. Through this haze of anguish, a memory surfaced of Wade hemorrhaging in the elevator in Aruba in the moments after Holcomb had stunned him. And then that hideous ticklike *thing* falling onto the elevator floor.

Moaning, he clutched his arms to his waist and rocked back and forth on his heels, then fell onto his hands and knees again, eyes squeezed shut against agony that stole his breath and emptied his mind of everything except the pain. The urge to claw at his face, to dig the chip out of his nostril, nearly overwhelmed him.

When the spent chip finally dropped into the snow, he stared at it, writhing on its back, glistening with blood, its body still thick, grotesque. In seconds, the cold killed it, the chip went flat. A sob burst from Holcomb's mouth. Without a chip, his lifeline to his own time was severed and he wouldn't be able to get to Mike. The only two people who might be able to help him were missing.

Torn between grief and rage, Holcomb slammed the heel of his hand down over the chip, twisting it down into the snow. Weeping softly now, he rocked back onto his heels again. He wiped at his nose with the back of his hand and it came away bloody. He tried to wash off the blood with snow, then scooped up a handful and pressed it to the side of his nose, hoping the cold would stem the bleeding.

Stuck. Trapped. Never see Mike again.

He sat there in the shadowed alley for what seemed a long time, fists pressed into his eyes, his sobs gradually subsiding. The din he'd heard earlier seemed louder and closer now and drove him to his feet. He stumbled out of the alley and across the street and into another alley, anxious to return to the stable, to show the Cory brothers and Fry what he had found.

But when the main road through downtown Blue River became visible, Holcomb quickly stepped back against the nearest building and fell into a crouch, watching in horror. Several hundred people moved through downtown, their flickering torches held high, fists beating the air as they shouted, *"Burn the witches! Burn the witches!"*

The firelight spilled over them, turning their breeches and their linen shirts, their bodices and skirts, and even their faces a hideous orange. Scattered among them were horse-pulled wagons—empty wagons that would be loaded up with wood as soon as the sun rose. Even children were among them, hurrying along dutifully beside their parents, their fists pummeling the air.

He poked his head out from the edge of the building and looked down the street, appalled that several hundred more people followed. Dogs trotted along the edge of the crowd, barking. He felt the growing madness of the collective, the mass energy that would gather momentum until the moment of release—the burning of the women on the pyres that would be built throughout the day.

Holcomb ducked behind the safety of the building and darted back the way he'd come, searching for a better spot to cross the main road. Only half a mile later did he realize that he now clutched his twenty-first-century weapon, that he was ready to fire it, that it might be all that stood between him and the gathering madness. The burning times had arrived in Blue River.

20
Pushing the Envelope

There will come a point where the chip will be more coveted than oil.

—Mariah Jones

Aruba, March 2007

Mike, Mike, Mike. The voice pushed persistently against him, stirring him from his dream, demanding to be acknowledged. Awake now, he couldn't quite reach full consciousness. His head was filled with cobwebs, his eyelids seemed to be stapled shut. He tried to roll over onto his side, but something held him back.

His eyes snapped open.

No bed. He was strapped in a chair, in a room that he recognized. His penthouse prison. An IV needle was inserted into the back of his hand, tape covering it, but no tube was connected to it. Canvas straps held his arms immobile, while duct tape kept his ankles pressed painfully together. The inside of his mouth tasted like dust, as if he had ground his face into desert sand and then eaten his way into it. His tongue felt thick, deformed, and when he tried to speak, the words were unintelligible.

"Don't try to talk," Ann whispered. "They had something

dripping into your veins, but it's been turned off for a while now, a couple of hours. No telling what kinda shit it was."

Mike drank in the sight of her, taking in the liquid blue of her eyes, the soft trembling of her mouth, the long, graceful curve of her neck. He also noticed that no IV pole stood next to her chair. No drugs for Ann. Of course not. She was plan B. They would use her to make him talk.

Both chairs faced the picture window, where the sweep of blue sky promised a freedom they didn't have—but that they might earn. Okay, he got the message.

"Mike, you with me?"

"Yeth. What time ith it?" He sounded like a toddler learning to speak. His tongue felt sluggish, like a fat worm.

"I'm not sure. Maybe three or four, something like that. You've been out of it for about five hours." Her voice remained soft, dilatory. "Some black guy was in here a couple of times much earlier, adjusting the drip. He also brought me food and water. He made a point of telling me how you'd stabbed the senator with a screwdriver and that made you a terrorist or some shit like that. A *terrorist*, right? *They're* the terrorists. Another time, the senator came in with that jerk Wade. They asked you a lot of questions, but they were all, like, 'Hey Mike, ole friend, ole buddy, where'd you get that chip the stun gun dislodged? And where's Curtis? And McKee?' You were so out of it that you just laughed and laughed and that pissed them off big-time. That's when they turned off the drip."

"Thorry," he said, struggling to make his tongue work, to force his lips to form words normally. "For involving you."

She bit at her lip, the first sign that she wasn't as together about this as she sounded. She looked down at her thighs, whispered, "They can hear what we say. Their cameras watch constantly. One to our right, the other behind us."

"Let 'em watch."

Unless Lazier had hired some other people, which Mike doubted, no one maintained constant surveillance on the images the cameras captured from this room. He didn't hear any noise from the other part of the penthouse, either, and guessed the senator and his buddies had left to look for Curtis and his group. Curtis, that bastard prick, had gotten the laptop with all the info and had talked a great line. But he'd split as soon as there was trouble. Mike still had the memory stick zipped inside his pocket, though. He could feel it.

"Need to get looth. No one home." His tongue seemed more manageable now, as long as he thought about what he needed to say before he said it. "They're out looking for Curtis and his people and the chips."

"I've got a knife. Taped to the side of my leg. Before you got to the airport, I bought it in the gift shop. They didn't find it. If we can move closer to each other, maybe you can get it."

With what? His teeth? His nose? His goddamn chin?

Ann pressed her bound feet against the floor, thrust her hips toward him, and her chair slid sideways a couple of inches. Then she swung her feet hard to the right and her chair tilted toward him and slammed against the floor, the vibration exploding upward through his feet.

She didn't move. The side of her face was pressed against the floor, her arms were still strapped to the armrests of the chair, her feet were still taped. The details hadn't changed, but everything else had. Mike bolted forward and back, again and again, turning his chair until it faced her. Eyes shut, body motionless. Was she breathing? Was her chest moving? *Is she dead? Please no . . .*

And whatever held him together snapped. He screamed, adrenaline coursed through his muscles, and his legs suddenly popped free of the duct tape. The unexpected freedom shocked him. He kicked his legs out, stretching them, then heaved forward, his knees smacking the floor. The chair felt like a block of concrete against his back. But his face was near hers, his chin mashed against the floor, and he managed to inch even closer to her.

When he heard her breathing and realized that she wasn't dead, that she only had been knocked out, he flipped onto his side, and the chair fell with him. All his weight was now on his left side and left arm. He used his feet to propel himself closer to her and started gnawing like a rat on the tough nylon restraints that kept her arms trapped. Useless. At the rate he was going, he would still be doing it a month from now.

He kissed her forehead, cheeks, eyelids, willing her to come to. And when she did, she looked at him as if she were surfacing from a dream and sort of smiled. "Holcomb, this is really pushing the envelope."

"I . . . I thought you were dead."

"I'm not dying in *this* place."

"Which leg is the knife taped to?"

"Right. Just below my knee."

Perfect. Her right leg was exposed. "Stretch it out. I think I can get to it."

Once again he used his feet to move his body—and the chair that felt like it was growing out of his back like some hideous appendage. When he had positioned himself, he extended his right leg and his toes nudged her slacks upward until the knife was exposed. A switchblade. He turned again, bringing his face up close to the knife, and chewed at the masking tape. Then, using his chin, he pushed the top of the knife to the right, the left, the right and left again. As it began to loosen, he closed his teeth around it and wrenched his head back. The masking tape tore, the knife clunked against the floor, and Mike turned again, like a lazy Susan, and moved it toward her with his feet. She didn't have the use of her hands, either, but apparently had a plan.

"Mike, can you use your feet or toes to flip it over?"

"I think so."

His toes twitched and moved as if they knew exactly what to do. Once the knife was on its other side, Ann maneuvered her own body and pressed her chin against the knife.

The blade popped out.

"Damn," he breathed, genuinely impressed.

"If you can steady the knife between your feet, I think I can get the restraints against the blade."

He did and she went to work, maneuvering her right hand so the nylon was pressed up against the blade. The muscles in his feet and toes ached and tightened, and it seemed that hours passed, that the shadows in the room lengthened, that light collapsed into darkness and gave way to light again. Even though he knew it was the aftereffect of the drug they'd given him, it disoriented him.

Ann's right hand suddenly snapped free. She grabbed the knife, cut through the nylon around her left wrist. In moments, she had sliced through the tape around her ankles. She pushed the chair away, sprang to her feet, freed his arms. She shoved the chair away from him, and Mike rolled onto his back, arms flung out at his sides, his body screaming for food, water, a bathroom. But Ann leaned over him, her hair falling at the sides of her face, a curtain of pale gold, and as her mouth opened against his, Mike's body shut up. His arms came around her, time screeched to a complete standstill.

He lost himself in the softness of her mouth, the taste of it, the deep warmth of her breath, the caress of her hair against his face. He ran his hands over her shoulders, reading the little protrusions of bone, the valleys and indentations, then slipped his hands under her shirt against the sweet warmth of her breasts. They had been sleeping together for a couple of months, and right now he wanted nothing better than to make love to her here, immediately. But if they didn't save themselves from their captors, they'd be dead.

He broke away, sat up. "We need to get out of here."

"How?"

"They've probably got a dead bolt on the door now, so I think the window is our best bet."

"You're joking, right?"

"You see any other way to get out?"

"Didn't you tell me we're on the fifteenth floor?"

"We are."

"So you have wings? A parachute stashed away some-where?"

"I wish." He got to his feet, pulled her up as well. "Let's push the bureau in front of the door, buy us a little time, just in case. Then let's bust those cameras."

Within moments, they had shoved the heavy bureau up against the door and pushed the bed against the bureau. It might buy them four or five minutes. Ann hurried over to the floor lamp, jerked the cord out of the wall plug. "Perfect. The metal base should do the trick." She removed the lamp-shade, tossed it onto the bed, unscrewed the bulb, passed him the lamp. "You get the first swing."

"With pleasure." He went over to the camera in the left corner, shot a bird at the ubiquitous eye, then swung the metal base into the front of it and smiled as it shattered. He passed the pole to Ann. "Your turn."

One hard swing and pieces of the second camera rained down to the floor. They ran over to the picture window.

Mike figured the wall of glass was eight or nine feet wide, perhaps six feet tall. On the right was a small window about three feet square. He opened it, punched his fist through the screen, tore it away from the frame, and he and Ann stuck their heads outside. The afternoon heat beat against their faces, the hot wind drying their eyes and filling the room with the smell of heat, sea, desert.

"Okay, so let's sum this up," she said. "We're going to climb through this window and use a sheet to parachute down fifteen stories."

"We're going up. To the roof."

"Is it possible?"

"I think so. See those metal bars?" He pointed to the right and she craned her neck to see. "I think there are more of them. That's how we get to the roof."

He stuck his head out a little farther, glanced down. The outside ledge was fairly wide and extended about two feet beyond the end of the window. Five or six feet beyond it was the balcony of the penthouse, which was off the living room. In between was a series of metal bars, like steps, that climbed the wall in a perfectly straight line, neat as a ladder, and vanished under the eaves of the roof. And then what? Was there an opening to the roof that he couldn't see from here? Had to be. Otherwise, what were the bars for?

Mike peered down, studying the surface of the wall below them. There were metal steps here, too, but they appeared to be randomly spaced, separated by three feet, six feet, ten feet, and spread at various intervals across the face of the building. He suspected there had been others that had rusted and been removed or fallen out. *Up* it would have to be.

Insanity, whispered his mother's voice.

Go for it, whispered the voice of his father.

"Anything in here we should take with us? That we might need?" Mike asked.

"We've got each other. What else is there?"

He loved the sound of that. "Then let's—"

Voices in the next room eclipsed the rest of his sentence.

"Shit," Mike hissed, and climbed onto the sill, thrust one leg through the opening, and his foot touched the outer ledge. He now straddled the window frame, a rider on a horse bent into the wind. He suddenly didn't know which direction they should face as they made their way along the ledge. He tried to determine how easy or difficult it might be to turn and quickly decided that the ledge was too narrow, that movement of any kind might prove fatal.

But remaining in the room was out of the question.

The voices on the other side of the door were louder now. Terrified that one of the men would get into the bedroom before he and Ann could escape, Mike motioned frantically at Ann, urging her to hurry. She quickly joined him, straddling the window frame, one foot in, the other on the outer ledge. She and Mike both faced the metal bars between the window and the balcony off the penthouse living room.

"There's a strip of molding that looks like it runs to the end of the ledge. We'll hold on to that. Facing inward."

"You go first," she said.

"Don't look down. Listen, if I slip . . ."

"I'll never forgive you," she muttered, then squeezed his shoulder and kissed the back of his neck.

Mike pivoted his right foot against the outer ledge and slowly brought his left leg through the window so that his back was now to the sky, the ocean, the vast blue nothingness. As he stood, he gripped the upper part of the frame, where bits of screen still remained and bit into his hands. He moved sideways several steps, making room for Ann, who now duplicated what he had done. She looked scared shitless.

The wind whipped his shirt up in back and whistled around his head, drowning out every other sound. When he looked over at Ann, he couldn't see her face. The wind blew her hair to every point on the compass. With his left hand still holding on to the frame, he released his right hand and brought it up to the molding. Concrete molding. Warm to the touch. His left hand joined the right and he started inching along, away from the window. Ann followed.

Don't look down, don't look down, don't . . . he thought.

The heat pounded against the back of his head, radiated from the concrete face of the building and up into his bare feet. How many shoes had he lost since he'd been nabbed the first time? The day his mother had left, his last memory before he'd been grabbed the first time, he'd been wearing shoes that cost nearly two hundred bucks. When Curtis had taken him, he'd been wearing sandals from the senator's closet that probably cost six hundred bucks. At the airport, when Wade had found them, he'd been wearing thongs he'd bought here in Aruba that had cost him a buck.

There was a message in this for him about the sort of money that enabled him to live in a caretaker's cottage on a five-acre estate on an island where everyone was someone. He knew there was another message about the privileges that came with this kind of money—not just the boats and the planes and the cars, but the network of *people.* In just the three years since his mother had married Frank the Zillionaire, Mike had shot baskets with Magic Johnson, had dinner with the owner of the Marlins, and had talked with Angelina Jolie about Buddhism. That was just for starters.

All told, he would like to have his old life back, when his parents had gotten along and they'd divided their time between Miami and Key Largo as a family who had brought along the dog, the cat, the bird.

If one of us slips . . .

The thought nearly panicked him. *Breathe, keep moving, don't look down.* One baby step, another, then another and another. His hands grew slick with sweat. Perspiration rolled down the sides of his face, into his eyes. He kept blinking to clear his vision and struggled not to think about the men on the other side of that door, perhaps throwing the dead bolt now and discovering that the door wouldn't budge. He did not look down.

He turned his head slowly toward Ann and saw that she stood very still, her forehead pressed to the wall, chest heaving, beads of sweat glistening on her cheeks. He said her name, but the wind swallowed it. He slowly extended his right arm and touched her shoulder, squeezing it gently, just to let her know he was here. He wouldn't allow anything to happen to her.

Once again, he was aware of the bones in that shoulder, its intimate topography. She raised her head, looked over at him, biting at her lower lip, her eyes bright with terror. Her mouth moved, but the wind gobbled what she said. He pointed to his ear and shook his head. *Not much farther,* he mouthed.

He began inching along again, Ann moving with him. Sweat streamed from his pores, his feet slick with it. Nearly there. Two more baby steps, that was all. And then the sill ended and he stopped.

The first bar was a foot away, almost even with the sill. The second bar was just above it. But right now, one foot might as well be a hundred. The bar looked corroded, beaten by the elements, and he hoped to hell it could bear his weight. If he could grab on to that, he could get his foot to the first bar. *If.*

Mike felt Ann beside him now, her arm brushing his, her body so close that he could hear her hyperventilating. He turned his head to look at her. "Breathe normally," he said. "We're okay. We're nearly to the bars."

"I . . . I feel like I'm going to puke. I . . . the height . . ."

"Don't look down."

She squeezed her eyes shut; a sob escaped her.

"It's okay," he kept saying. "It's okay. Once I'm on the bar, you can grab on to my hand."

"Just hurry," she said breathlessly.

He clutched the edge of the building with his right hand, reached out with his left, leaned forward slightly. He couldn't quite reach it. Another inch or two, that was all he needed. But with his feet already perched at the edge, he couldn't move any closer. His only option was to jump and try to grab the bar.

His breath lodged like a lump of food in his throat, his eyes ached to look down. He rubbed his sweaty hands against his shirt and leaped. While he was airborne, the world slammed into a strange slow motion, as though he were outside of himself watching the hot, dry wind rush up at him from the ground, filling his shirt, watching as the sky reached down to touch him. Blue melted into deeper blues, everything blurred. Then his hands found the bar and he hung there, feet kicking wildly, grappling for purchase against the face of the building.

His right foot landed on a metal bar, his left foot followed, and for moments he didn't move. Couldn't move. His muscles had frozen up. When he finally was able to turn his head toward Ann, she seemed to be plastered against the face of the building, as if the wind were holding her there. She had tucked her hair into the back of her shirt so that it wouldn't blow into her face, but already, the wind was pulling strands free, flinging them across her throat, her eyes.

He tucked his left arm up under the bar, securing himself in place, then leaned out as far as he could toward Ann, and extended his right arm. "Take my hand!" he shouted.

"I . . ."

"Take it!"

She grabbed his hand and leaped for the first bar. Her foot missed it and she dangled against the face of the building, clutching his hand and forearm, her feet wildly treading air, her head thrown back, mouth open in a silent scream. The muscles and tendons on the right side of his body—his shoulder, arm, hand, even his fingers—strained with her weight and started shrieking. His heart thumped and pounded. Blood thundered in his ears. The wind whipped his back. Her hand, slick with sweat, began to slip from his, her grip on his forearm loosened and he yelled, "My leg, grab on to—"

But she slipped away from him, her screams pounding the hot wind. Mike twisted around just as she grabbed onto his legs, nearly pulling him off the bar. Air exploded from his mouth and he clutched the bar with both hands, struggling to stabilize himself, his mind in a blind, white-hot panic.

Gates slammed open inside him, energy rushed into him, through him, and he reached down and seized her arm and pulled. She pressed her bare feet against the building, providing enough leverage so that she could clasp the bar on which he stood. He kept pulling and her feet climbed the face of the building, so that they created a kind of human pulley. Push, lift, climb. Push, lift, climb.

And when her feet were on the bar, when she was upright beside him, he drew her into the circle of his arms, his feet planted on either side of hers, their sweaty bodies pressed together, both of them breathing so hard they couldn't speak. Mike rested his forehead against the back of her neck, no longer certain they would ever reach the top of the steps, much less get to the roof or anywhere else that was relatively safe.

But they couldn't remain immobilized against the face of the building.

"Climb," he said, his voice close to her ear. "I'm right behind you."

And she did—hesitantly at first, then faster and with greater confidence, as if her brush with certain death had instantly changed something deep inside her.

As they climbed, he kept his eyes glued to her. Her hair was drenched in sweat and clung to her skull. Her wet blouse looked like part of her skin, as though she had been tattooed with exotic colors and patterns. At every step, the voices of his parents battled for dominance. *Insanity, go for it, insanity, go for it.* He finally managed to shut out both voices and to hear the silence within himself and a new voice that said, *You can do this.*

As they neared the roof, he glanced back and down, and there, on the penthouse balcony off to his left, stood two men: Lazier, decked out in white, and another man—dark, short, compact. The Asian from the restaurant and the airport? He couldn't tell from here, and right now, didn't give a shit who the guy was. If either man looked up . . .

They climbed faster, faster. Ann reached the top step, flashed a thumbs-up, and vanished into whatever lay beyond the last step. Mike grabbed on to the last step and heaved himself up. He could see a deep hollow in the shadows under the eaves, a place with a concrete floor and sloping concrete walls. He climbed onto it and collapsed next to Ann, gasping for breath, sweat pouring off him, rolling into his eyes, down his cheeks and onto his mouth.

For the longest time, they just lay there, silent, hands clasped, the stifling heat sucking at them. Mike finally broke the silence. "You scared me."

"I scared myself."

"No, you don't understand." He rolled onto his side and lifted up on his elbow. "I can't live without you."

Ann stared at him there in the shadows, her mouth quivering, her eyes brimming with tears. Then she wrapped her arms around his neck and pulled his head against her chest and he listened to the beat of her heart, the rushing of blood through her veins.

"We can't ever go home," she whispered.

"You're my home."

"We're . . . we're going to be living on a fucking rooftop."

"My dad will find us."

"And then what?"

He shook his head. "I . . . I don't know."

"They'll always be looking for us."

"And we'll always be one step ahead." He kissed her and she clung to him and they somehow drew strength from each other.

She finally sat up, stretched out on her stomach, and snaked her way forward to peer over the edge. Mike crawled up beside her. He could see the penthouse balcony from here and Lazier and the other man were gone now. It scared him. "We need to look for a way onto the roof," he said.

"Look where? I don't see shit up here."

Just as she said this, he noticed a wedge of light to his left and shifted his body around, rolled onto his knees, and crawled toward it—and then into it, a tight, narrow space that appeared to angle along under the eaves. Pigeon shit and the carcasses of insects littered the floor. With the sound of the wind blocked by the walls, he could hear the cooing of pigeons and, more distantly, the shriek of gulls.

Ann scrambled after him. "Can you see where this goes?"

"Not yet. But it turns just ahead. You okay?"

"It's solid. I'm not dangling in midair. Yeah, I'm okay, just thirsty. You think that they'll figure out we're up here? That they'll come looking for us?"

"I don't know. But they probably would need permission from the hotel."

"He's a senator, Mike. Lazier can probably do whatever the hell he wants."

They kept crawling, Mike in the lead, Ann right behind him, neither of them speaking. The corridor curved; the pigeon shit got deeper and thicker. When they came out of the curve, Mike could see that a metal grate covered the end of the corridor. Sunlight shone through the tiny holes. The corridor widened at the end, too, enabling him and Ann to sit side by side on their heels, peering through the grate.

The roof lay on the other side, and from here, he could see several AC units, phone boxes, satellite dishes. How wonderful it would be, he thought, if they found a fire escape that would take them down the side of the building. They leaned back on their elbows, brought their knees up to their chests and looked at each other. "Remind me never to go on vacation with you, Holcomb."

"After this, I may never leave home again." And that was assuming that either of them would get home at all. "You ready?"

"Ready," she said, and they simultaneously slammed their heels against the metal grate.

21
Truth or Consequences

Answers? Who has answers? I don't even know the right questions.

—*Nora McKee*

Kincaid emerged on his feet, in total darkness, the glow stick dead in his hand. Since the air didn't smell of horse shit or hay or of any other familiar odor, he figured he had missed the stable and the rooms above them. If anything, the air smelled stale but clean, as if this place had been shut up for several days. It was cold, too. He blew into his hands to warm them, reached into his cloak for another glow stick, bent it. The stick glowed brightly, revealing Lucia and Rebeka slumped on the floor to his right. The transition had knocked them out.

He raised the glow stick a little higher above his head and saw that they had emerged in some sort of storage room where tables and chairs had been stacked. On a cabinet against the wall stood several empty basins and pitchers and a pile of books. He went over to the door, pressed his ear to the wood, listened. He heard noise, but it wasn't coming from the other side of this door. It sounded more distant.

Kincaid opened it and stepped into a room where two dozen small tables and chairs were lined up in three precise rows. In front of them was a single larger table and chair with another stack of books off to one side.

The schoolhouse. He had overshot his target by just one building.

Behind the teacher's table was the front door and two windows through which he could see torches and people on foot, on horseback, and in wagons, all of them on the move. Their shouts rang out, and even though he couldn't understand the words, the sight disturbed him. Any sort of mob in this town had to be connected to the witches.

"Magistrate?"

Rebeka's terrified voice startled him and he whirled around. "Speak softly. Something is going on outside. I believe it is about you and Lucia and my wife."

"We . . . we are in the school." She rubbed one bare foot against her leg. "But . . . I remember being in the gaol. How came we to be here? I do . . . not understand. And your wife. How will she . . ."

"I will try to explain later, Rebeka." He struggled not to think about Nora, about what might be happening back in that abyss under the jail. "We need to rouse Lucia and escape this building. Is there a back door? Another way out?"

She didn't seem to hear him. Fixated on the window, on what was happening outside, she moved past him, her bare feet whispering against the floor. Kincaid hurried after her. She and Lucia would need shoes, warmer clothes. "We cannot risk being noticed," he said.

Rebeka stopped, but seemed unable to tear her eyes away from the spectacle outside. And in those moments of silence between them, the mob's shouts echoed clearly. Perfectly. *Burn the witches.* Her jaw tightened, her wrinkled mouth went as flat and straight as a dash, and when she looked at Kincaid, her blue eyes had darkened with raw terror.

"They will *burn* us. All day, they will build the pyres in the town square. They will bring wood from the forest. They will build three pyres—four if they bring Sarah back, five if they also find the physician. And they will celebrate with ale and food and the preacher will preach, his voice rising so high and mighty to the heavens." She threw up her hands, as if to indicate the direction of heaven. "And . . . when the people are drunk on his madness, when the sun is close to the tops of the trees, he . . . he will have Davies put us in wagons, Magistrate, and the wagons will move through town . . . and the people will jeer . . . and hurl snow at us. They will curse us, whip us as though we are animals. They . . ."

"I understand." The picture was too vivid, too real, *too goddamn possible*, and filled him with terror for Nora. The sooner they got the hell out of here, the sooner he could get back to Nora.

Yet, at the back of his mind, the disparities between the events happening here and the official history of Blue River nagged at him. He couldn't recall anything like this from history. Was history flawed? Flat-out *wrong?* Censored? Or was it because history was changing due to their presence? To Nora's arrest and incarceration? Did it matter?

He touched Rebeka's arm, urging her back toward the rear of the room. Now she was staring at his glow stick. *Christ, oh Christ.* He had done so many things wrong on this transition, revealed too much so recklessly, that it was miraculous any of them were still alive.

"You must tell me about this magical light you hold."

Right. Well, see, it's chemical. Hydrogen peroxide is combined with tert-butyl alcohol and a fluorescent green dye. The combination creates a chemical reaction that releases energy. Electrons, which you won't know about for . . . oh, at least two centuries, get really excited, sort of like Chandler does when he talks about the witches. And that excitement causes the electrons to rise to higher energy levels. As those levels drop back to normal levels, the result is light. Aren't you glad you asked?

"Later, Rebeka, I will try to explain all of it."

"It is not hot to the touch?" she asked.

Nope, nope, nope. "The colder the temperature, the paler the light." And since it was maybe twenty degrees in here, the glow stick looked anemic. "Is there a back door?" he asked again.

"Once there was. I do not know now."

"Where was it before?"

She frowned, then padded into the storage room and pointed at the cabinet. "Here. Behind this."

Kincaid grabbed on to the edge of the cabinet, but it was solid oak and he couldn't move it alone. He asked Rebeka to pull from the other side, and she immediately grabbed on to the edge with her bony hands, and together they pulled the cabinet away from the wall.

Lucia moaned and Kincaid said, "Keep her quiet. I'll find the door."

He squeezed between the cabinet and the wall and found both a door and a small window covered in years of grime. Kincaid unlatched the door and leaned into it, pressing his shoulder against it, but it wouldn't budge. He suspected a foot of snow was piled against it.

How long had the transition taken? How long had they been in here? What time was it? *When will the sun rise?*

He fished out Nora's digital watch. It had stopped at 4:17. *Stopped.* In all the months she had owned it, the watch never had stopped. It wasn't supposed to stop. It had become their grounding, their compass, their North Star. And now it was dead. Kincaid shoved it back into a pocket in his cloak, grabbed a chair from those stacked against the wall, and whacked the window. The glass fell away. He used the handle of his weapon to get rid of the jagged shards stuck in the window frame.

"Come, fast." He motioned at the women. "We are going to the livery."

"The livery?" Lucia balked. She was leaning into Rebeka—or the old woman into her. It wasn't clear to him who was being supported. Lucia raised her skinny arm and jabbed her finger toward the livery. "They *hate* us. They are terrified of us. They . . ."

Kincaid's patience snapped. "If you want to burn, then stay here. If you want to live, climb through that window."

Lucia looked down at her bare feet. "We have no shoes."

"I will get you both shoes and warm clothes when we are at the livery."

Through the window they went. Kincaid scrambled after them and landed on his hands and knees in a three-foot drift. The glow stick fell out of his hand and struck the snow, sending up tufts of white powder, and nearly blinked out. He scooped it up and rocked back onto the balls of his feet and took it all in, orienting himself. The sky toward the ocean had turned dove gray, revealing a low scudding of clouds. A fog drifted from the nearby woods, obscuring the lower trunks of the trees, and swirling like some strange life-form toward downtown Blue River. It wouldn't be long before the sun would burst over the horizon, which meant that the 4:17 at which the clock had stopped had been some time ago. Gun and glow stick in hand, he stumbled toward the livery, the women in front of him.

As they moved through the snow, the women lurched and fell and lifted themselves up. By the time they reached the livery and he heaved open the door, Kincaid's heart strained as if it might quit at any second. The stable workers, seated around the fireplace with their bowls and mugs of whatever, regarded Kincaid and the women as though they were ghosts that suddenly had materialized in their midst. The welcoming stink of horse shit and hay both humbled and buoyed him.

"We need your help, gentlemen," he muttered. Then his knees gave way and he dropped to the floor, bent forward at the waist like a yogi seeking redemption or blessing. It stretched his aching arms, his tired spine. When Kincaid raised his head again, James Cory stood to his right, a hand on Kincaid's arm, helping him to his feet. The other men had helped Lucia and Rebeka over to the fire, and handed them bowls of food. "My wife," he said. "She's restrained in the gaol. I must return to her."

"Not yet, Magistrate," Cory said. "First you must warm yourself. And eat."

Kincaid left his bag where it was, away from the fire, where the heat couldn't warm up the chip in the insulated pocket and activate it. He weaved over to the fire, sank into the chair, set his bag at his feet, and shrugged off the cloak, glad to be rid of it. Fry brought him a bowl of hot porridge and the Cory brothers pulled chairs up on either side of him.

"The women will need warm clothes, shoes," Kincaid said in between bites of porridge.

"We will find them what they need," James Cory said. "Do you know what is going on outside?"

"A mob."

"Led by Rowe," said the younger Cory. "He has inflamed the madness in this town, he and Travers. And as soon as they enter the gaol and find that the accused are gone"—his eyes darted to the women—"they will hunt all of us down and hang us."

"It will not come to that," his brother said. "We will take them out of town." His eyes locked with Fry's. "Paul, would you ready the wagon? And find warmer clothes and shoes for the women—surely there must be something in our supplies."

Fry nodded and hurried off toward the horse stalls.

"Take them where?" Kincaid asked.

"Someplace safe," Edward Cory said. "I will take them, James." He glanced at his brother. "You and Paul should remain with the magistrate. To help him." To Kincaid: "Nothing will happen to your wife until the reverend returns. There is time yet."

But James Cory looked worried, Kincaid noticed, and that worried him. He suddenly wondered how the hell he would get into the jail if he couldn't transition there. And if he *could* transition, what would he do with Cory? "The mob may not wait for Chandler. We cannot anticipate what they might do."

No one said anything. The hissing of the fire and the snorting of horses in the nearby stalls filled the silence. Edward Cory turned to his brother. "He is right, James. We must take the women out of Blue River as soon as possible. I am going to get the supplies."

He hastened away, leaving Kincaid alone with James Cory. "May I ask you a personal question, Magistrate?"

Ask away, pal. "Of course."

"May I address you by your first name?"

Kincaid almost laughed out loud. He had expected something else altogether. "I believe we have reached that place, James."

"Indeed we have, Alexander."

"Alex. And where I come from, James is often shortened to Jim. That nickname seems to fit you."

"Jim," he repeated, nodding, half smiling. "I like that very much." Another nod, then: "How did you get into the gaol, Alex, past the jailer?"

Shit, that was your real personal question, right, Jim? "Long story." Kincaid finished his porridge and set the wooden bowl in front of him. "Right now, I need some sort of tool that can cut through a metal band. My wife is restrained in a cage in a secret chamber beneath the gaol. She has metal bands around her wrists that are attached to the bars of the cage."

"You cannot shoot them off?"

"Not without shooting her hand."

"Is it possible to apply fire to the metal?"

"The metal is tight against her skin."

James pressed his fingers together, forming a steeple, which he touched to his bearded chin. "It needs a key?"

"Yes, and Davies did not have it."

Kincaid wasn't sure when scissors had been invented. He remembered reading that da Vinci had invented scissors, but also recalled that scissors had been around since ancient Egypt, some fifteen hundred years before the birth of Christ. So it probably was safe to assume that the concept existed in this time.

He thought a moment, then leaned forward and in the ashes that had spilled onto the stone drew a pair of scissors. "But they must be powerful enough to cut through metal."

"I will show this to the blacksmith. Perhaps he made the

bands for the gaol. If so, he may have the key. Can you find us a way inside the gaol, Alex?"

Not without revealing more than I already have. "I hope so."

"And Mr. Davies. Where is he?"

"Restrained. Unable to free himself or to shout."

James chuckled at that. "This I must see."

"If I cannot get us into the gaol, do you know of any other way in?"

"There is a maze of tunnels under some of these buildings that have been used in the past by escaped slaves. Paul Fry knows more of these things than I do. I will ask him how to get in."

It was news to Kincaid and appeared to be one more instance of history deviating from the reality. "But first, the women must be taken out of here."

Just then, Fry returned, carrying clothes and shoes for the women. He handed everything to Cory, gestured rapidly, and Cory nodded. "Paul says the wagon is ready and he and Edward are getting the supplies. The women can change upstairs."

"I will take them," Kincaid said. "Thank you."

Cory handed Kincaid the clothes and shoes and Kincaid went over to the women and explained what was going on. They were too worn out to ply him with questions and eagerly followed him to the foot of the stairs. "Change up there. And hurry."

"Thank you, Magistrate." Rebeka took his hand between hers and squeezed. "We will never forget your kindness."

"Never," Lucia echoed.

"But someday you will have to tell me about your magical light," Rebeka added, with a quick smile that threw her face into a chaos of wrinkles, creases, folds, each with its own story.

"I will," he promised, then hurried back into the stable.

The doors were thrown open now to the lightening sky and a thickening fog that swirled around the hooves of the horse hitched to the wagon. Fry was leading it in on foot, the wagon's wheels clattering. Just as he signaled to the stable hand to shut the doors, someone darted inside, cloak flapping.

It was the governor's emissary, Ericson Ivers. *Wearing jeans.*

Kincaid stared, struggling with the implications, the possibilities, but there was only one conclusion: this guy was from their own time, which made it likely he had been sent back by Senator Lazier and his gang of mercenaries.

Ivers—or whatever his name really was—spotted Kincaid and hurried toward him. Kincaid's feet uprooted from the floor and he ran to his cloak, dug out the stun gun, and whirled around as the man breathlessly called, "Magistrate . . ."

Kincaid held up his hand so that Ivers could see the stun gun. He stopped, his face seemed to come unhinged, and he shook his head. "It's not what you think." He spoke quietly and glanced around quickly, furtively, making sure that no one was close enough to hear them. "It's . . ."

"Don't tell me what *I think*." Kincaid moved toward him. "What's your real name?"

"Eric. Eric Holcomb." Whispering, he added, "My body rejected my chip half an hour ago. I'm no threat to you."

"You're a threat just by being here. Who hired you?"

"Lazier and one of his lackeys, a guy named Wade, a mercenary. I . . . I was supposed to come back, stun you and Nora, then transition one of you and . . . and broker a deal. Your chips in exchange for transitioning the other one home. But Lazier . . . abducted my son. As insurance so I would cooperate." His voice broke, his face caved in, and he sat down heavily in the nearest chair. "I . . . I just want to get the fuck out of here and back . . . back to Aruba. That's where he's holding Mike. My son."

"Aruba." Kincaid lowered his arm, strode over to the chair, and leaned in close to Holcomb. "Were you part of the group that attacked us?"

Holcomb hesitated, then nodded slowly. "Yes."

"One of you sliced Curtis, you fuck." Kincaid struggled not to deck him here and now. "You blew our cover and now we've got to find some other place to hide. You try living a life where you're constantly pursued, always looking over your shoulder, never quite sure whom you can trust so you don't trust anyone but your group. *You* try it, Holcomb. In fact, that's what you'll be doing if you ever get back. You'll be running as fast as you can with your son. And if you don't get back, you'll be stuck here in the fucking dark ages and, oh well, too bad about your son." Kincaid started to turn away, but Holcomb grabbed his arm.

"Please, you've got to help me. I—"

"I don't *have* to do squat for you." Kincaid wrenched his arm free. "You think I'm a goddamn idiot? Now I understand why you've been so willing to help, why you wanted to listen to the testimony from the women, why—"

"If I'd been able to transition out of here on my own, I would have," Holcomb snapped. "But my chip was flawed. Just once, I . . . boomeranged back to Key Largo."

Boomeranged back. Just like I boomeranged forward.

"And my son . . . my son got through to me on a stolen cell phone. He had escaped from Lazier's penthouse and was on the run . . . in hiding. Somehow, he'd gotten in touch with your group and was supposed to meet someone at the lighthouse. He had Lazier's laptop."

When Kincaid didn't say anything, Holcomb rushed on. "I'll do anything you ask. Anything. I'll help you free Nora from the jail, help you bring down Lazier, help you—"

"You've done enough already. I don't need your goddamn help."

Kincaid hurried away from him, anxious to get the women on their way, to talk to James Cory and the blacksmith about some sort of tool to free Nora. But Holcomb rushed after him, shouting, "Wait! Hear me out!"

His shouts brought unwanted attention from the other men: the stable hands, the blacksmith, Fry. Kincaid knew that he already had tipped his hand one too many times, that even James Cory had begun to suspect he wasn't a magistrate. He was afraid that Holcomb's outburst would blow everything wide open. So he did what he'd been wanting to do since he'd seen Holcomb in jeans. He swung, struck Holcomb in the chin, and Holcomb stumbled back, arms pinwheeling for balance, and slammed into the wall. Kincaid ran over to him, grabbed the front of his cloak, jerked him forward.

"What do you have to offer *me,* Holcomb, besides bull-shit like this that could blow everything?" He kept his voice low. "You see how those guys behind me are watching us? I need their help, I need my cover, and you need yours. So don't fuck this up."

In an equally quiet and surprisingly humbled voice, Hol-comb said, "I'm . . . sorry. I lost my head." He reached into his cloak and brought out a bound book. "This is Chandler's journal. I took it from his cellar. He poisoned his wife and framed Lucia Gray by planting poppets in her bedroom. His entries are in the middle. As the magistrate, you can charge him with murder and I, as the governor's emissary, can de-mand that he release Nora. That's the first thing I can offer you in return. The second thing is that Lazier and his group are out of chips. So they aren't a threat to you. And there's some sort of protection around Lazier's penthouse that makes it impossi-ble to transition in or out. I want my son back, Kincaid, as deeply as you want your wife. Please, let's help each other."

It was probably the most honest thing anyone outside his group had said to him in months. Just the same, Kincaid was reluctant to trust Holcomb. His plea for help could be just another ploy.

Kincaid opened the journal to the middle, and as he scanned Chandler's entries, his revulsion for the man be-came so palpable that his stomach turned sour, as if he'd eaten a bucket of limes. "Too bad we can't get this to the real magistrate. That bastard Chandler should be in prison."

"All we have to do is turn people against him. Maybe the best way to do that is through the guy who owns the inn. He seemed sympathetic."

"He removed himself from the town council out of disgust for Chandler."

"Here comes James Cory," Holcomb whispered.

"I am pleased we reached this understanding, Mr. Ivers." Kincaid spoke loudly enough for Cory to hear.

"As am I, sir," Holcomb replied.

"Alex? Mr. Ivers? I trust you have, uh, resolved your disagreement?"

Kincaid nodded. "Indeed we have, Jim. Mr. Ivers has brought some incriminating evidence to my attention concerning Reverend Chandler. I was merely objecting to the way he procured this evidence."

Cory looked pointedly at Holcomb's jeans, but didn't comment. "And that evidence would be . . . ?"

"That the reverend poisoned his wife," Kincaid said, then handed him the journal. "And made it look as if her death was caused by Lucia's alleged witchcraft. His entries are in the middle."

Cory flipped through the pages. "Extraordinary. But hardly surprising."

"As magistrate, I will accuse and incarcerate him," Kincaid said. "As soon as he returns to town."

"And that will end the madness," Cory said. "But until then, the women must be in a safe place." He gestured toward Lucia and Rebeka as they appeared, decked out in their clean clothes. Except for their matted hair, they looked like completely different people, Kincaid thought. Edward Cory and Fry joined the women. Fry, and the younger Cory helped the women inside the wagon. James Cory instructed them to stretch out amid the bags of rice, potatoes, corn, and other supplies and cover themselves with the quilts.

Fry gestured some more and James Cory nodded. "Good idea. Paul thinks he should ride with you, Edward, to make sure you reach the road to safety. The fog is thick now and should cover you."

The road to safety. What does that mean? Kincaid wondered.

Moments later, the wagon clattered back out through the stable doors, Edward Cory on the bench, Fry on horseback beside him. The fog embraced them, and for moments Kincaid could see only vague shapes within it, spectral images, and then the swirling fog swallowed them completely.

Kincaid and Holcomb pulled the heavy doors shut, and when they turned around, James Cory stood there with his arms crossed against his chest. "Gentlemen, we can go no further without answers. I need to know who you are and why you are really here. You"—he pointed at Kincaid—"are not the magistrate. And you"—he pointed at Holcomb—"are not an emissary of the governor. If you cannot be truthful with me, I will not show you the location of the slave tunnel and the blacksmith will not give you the tool he has found that will cut through metal."

Kincaid looked over at Holcomb, who shrugged and said, "Truth or consequences. It seems to be a virus that's going around."

"I need to get my bag," Kincaid said.

"The answer is in your bag?" Cory asked.

"Yes." Kincaid swept it off the floor and carried it over to the fireplace. He sat down and Cory and Holcomb claimed chairs on either side of him. He opened the bag and began removing its contents, setting everything on the wooden table in front of him. Next came the contents in his cloak pockets.

Cory leaned forward, eyes wide with wonder and curiosity, and ran his thick fingers over one of the PDAs, a cell phone. He examined the firecrackers, a pack of matches, the digital camera, the iPod and its portable speaker. On down the line—and up through time—Cory's fingers traveled.

Minutes ticked by, each one excruciatingly painful for Kincaid, who just wanted to get back to Nora. At one point, he even tried to do so, *reaching* for the cellar under the jail, *releasing* the desire, reaching and releasing, but nothing happened.

"What . . . what are these treasures?" Cory breathed.

"Here's one of the simplest." Kincaid struck a match and held it up. "Instant fire."

"Sweet merciful God."

Kincaid blew out the flame and handed the pack of matches to Cory. "You try. Strike the red tip against the side of the box, away from your body."

The first two matches snapped, but on his third try, Cory got the match lit. He held it up, the flame reflected in his astonished eyes.

Holcomb reached for the cell phone. "Smile, Jim," he said, and snapped the photo as Cory looked up, then showed it to him on the screen.

On it went, like a show-and-tell with a preschooler. When Kincaid hooked his iPod up to the portable speaker and Cory heard "Imagine," emotions danced like sunlight across his face. "The words, the music," he breathed. "All beautiful." He sat back. "These . . . these marvels . . . They come from another world? You are from another star?"

Yeah, we're aliens who dropped in. "We come from another time, Jim," Kincaid said.

"The *future*?"

Kincaid nodded. "More than three hundred years in your future." He unzipped the insulated pocket inside his bag and brought out the syringe. "And this is what makes it possible."

The blue gel inside the syringe glistened in the firelight and Cory leaned forward, studying it, entranced. "What is it?"

"The most coveted invention in our time," Holcomb said softly, reverently. "My son was kidnapped for this. People have been killed for it."

"And men have been corrupted by it," Kincaid added, looking pointedly at Holcomb.

"I wasn't *corrupted*," Holcomb corrected him. "I was desperate enough to be *seduced* by it."

Maybe, maybe not, Kincaid thought. "I may have rocks for brains"—he held out the syringe—"but I believe this has your name on it, Eric."

Holcomb wrapped his fingers around it. And with all pretense gone, spoke freely. "Wade said you have to wait a week after a chip is rejected."

"Put it in your other nostril," Kincaid said.

His fingers tightened around the syringe. "Still cold. The chip should still be dormant, don't you think?"

"Yes, the new chips activate at a higher degree," Kincaid concurred.

"The new chips. Mariah's chips? The ones that old Senator Aiken was going to buy from her before you and Nora and Curtis . . ."

"I see that Wade filled you in on the history."

"You speak like men who were once rivals," Cory observed.

"We came here to find Catherine Griffin," Kincaid said. "The woman who escaped."

A deep frown crossed Cory's face and an emotion Kincaid couldn't read flooded his eyes. "Why?"

"Because she's Nora's mother, taken by our government when Nora was just a child, and brought to this time, this place."

Something inexplicably strange happened to Cory's expression, his very essence. He pushed to his feet. "We must hurry." He gestured at everything on the table. "And all of this, we must bring it with us. I must speak to the blacksmith." He hurried toward the other side of the table, where the blacksmith worked, and then Cory vanished.

"We either blew it or he knows Catherine," Kincaid said.

"Or both." Holcomb flicked off the cap on the syringe, tilted his head back, slipped the syringe up inside his nostril, and pressed the plunger.

22
In the Cellar

Since time and space are treated like a piece
of rubber band that can bend and warp,
Einstein worried that the fabric of space-time
would warp so much that time travel might
be possible.

—Michio Kaku

Nora could hear them scurrying through the filthy hay, their claws scraping and tapping against the stone floors. Emboldened by the dimming glow stick, the rats kept edging closer to her cage, and now and then one of them emitted a high-pitched sound like a battle cry.

She held the glow stick between her teeth and with her free hand slapped a branch against the floor to keep them away from her. She had found the branch buried in the hay, a forgotten remnant of autumn, which was probably how long it had been since the hay had been changed. And who knew how many autumns ago that was. She had snapped it in half and had been sharpening the end of the shorter piece by rubbing its edges against the floor. She hoped she could get the point small enough to fit into the locks on the bracelets. The task seemed futile. Every time she stopped banging one stick to sharpen the end of the other, the rats came closer.

Rub and turn, rub and turn, a mindless rhythm. Pretty soon, the end of the branch grew warm, then hot. Afraid that it might break off, she paused, stretched out to rest her screaming muscles or to bang the other branch against the floor. Then she started all over again. Rub and turn.

She became aware of the grunts and muffled screams from Davies, whom Kincaid had handcuffed to the ladder some thirty or forty feet from her. He alternately shouted and rattled the cuffs until she yelled, "If you keep that up, I'll shoot you, Mr. Davies!"

She didn't know whether it was her voice or the threat that silenced him. But she welcomed the silence. She rubbed the end of the branch faster and harder, and suddenly, the sounds of the rats were louder, closer. Nora dropped the branch and twisted around as far as she could, holding the glow stick high above her head, searching through the strange green light and the deeper shadows beyond it, hoping they would show themselves.

Then she saw one of them, a rat the size of a house cat. It paused in the glow, eyes burning like hot coals, its mouth drawn back as if it were grinning. Its hideous teeth gnashed together. Images from dozens of movies raced through her head: Willard with his plump pet rats, rats the size of small trucks in New York sewers after a nuclear holocaust, thousands of rats in *The Last Crusade*, mutant rats in some mad scientific experiment gone awry, rats in space, in hell, in Medieval Europe during the plague. In her mind's eye, she saw the open, festering sores on Sarah Longwood's feet.

Nora waved the glow stick around behind her, but the rat squeaked shrilly, as though it were laughing at her, and dived under the hay, out of sight. Its companions scurried after it and vanished, one by one, the hay moving as they burrowed beneath it, less than two feet behind her. Nora's heart slammed into overdrive and she twisted until her spine, her body, just couldn't twist any farther, and slapped the branch repeatedly against the floor.

The rats remained hidden and kept squeaking, chattering. When she raised the glow stick again, the hay a foot behind her trembled and rustled as the rats scrambled closer to her, stealth fighters who approached from her right, her left, and directly behind her. She caught sight of a thick tail as long as a snake whipping back and forth, like a signal to the others. Seconds, she thought. In seconds, they would be all over her.

She scooped up the weapon Kincaid had left her. One of the Glocks, a new clip in, thirteen shots. Why thirteen? Why not twelve or fourteen? What nutcase had decided on that number? Then she remembered that Kincaid had fired three shots from this clip already. That left ten.

She tried to turn her body so that her back would be against the bars, but her shackled arm and leg prevented it. Her back was still to the rats and the rats knew it. Nora leaned forward and tried to lift up, thinking she might be able to peer under her own butt to see them, a yoga position that, years ago, she'd been able to do. Not now. Not like this. The hamstring in her shackled leg suddenly cramped, and the cramp sped up her leg and she gasped and fell back to the ground.

One of the rats squeaked once, loudly, the attack cry, and leaped onto her back, sinking its claws into the fabric of her twenty-first-century sweatshirt and ducking its head under her hair. Nora's shriek ricocheted against the walls, shrill and loud enough to wake the dead, and she kept on shrieking as she dropped the gun and glow stick, and groped wildly behind her, clawing at her own back, trying to reach the bastard rat. But it was too high on her spine now, and the only thing that prevented its claws from piercing her skin was the thickness of her Old Navy sweatshirt.

The rat bit at the collar of her sweatshirt, its steel claws clinging tightly to the fabric, its mouth so close to her skin she could hear it gnashing its teeth. *If it bites me . . .* Nora threw herself back against the floor, the metal bands rattling against the bars, panic imbuing her with shocking strength and flexibility. The bands strained against her wrist and ankle, slicing into the flesh, drawing blood. But it didn't matter—she didn't feel the pain, didn't feel anything except the *thing* on her back.

She bolted forward, slammed back against the floor, forward and back, again and again, the rat's shrieks so strangely human that she nearly faltered, nearly stopped. Her head pounded, her mouth went desert dry, drier than it had been before Kincaid had arrived and given her water, drier than anything she could recall in her entire life.

And then the rat made no more sounds. She felt it drop off her back, heard it thump against the stones, and the other rats squealed and scrambled forward, closing in. Nora pushed as far forward on her butt as the bands would allow, scooped up the gun, twisted and fired. Twice, three times, four shots. The deafening explosions lifted two of the rats into the air and sent the rest diving for the shadows. Nora wrapped her free arm around her free leg, pressed her forehead to her knees, choked back a sob.

Already, she heard the rats' hungry buddies closing in to cannibalize their bodies, and it would be only a matter of time before they would attack her again. They would sneak from the shadows, scurry from the other cages, burrow through the crevices of this terrible place to surround her, and then all of them would leap at once and that would be it—she would be done.

Nora placed the glow stick between her teeth, grabbed the branch, and kept rubbing the end of it until it was small, sharp, and so narrow that it fit into the lock. She worked it hard, fast, and the point broke.

"Fuck, shit, fuck." The glow stick dropped to the floor. *Start over again. Get the other branch and do it fast.*

Sputtering from Davies's side of the cellar, then, "Witch." And a familiar litany: "Satan's consort."

Go away, you don't exist, you're a flea on the back of time.

She stuck the glow stick between her teeth again, grabbed the remaining branch, rubbed and turned, rubbed and turned, sharpening, whittling the end.

"Witch, you will burn, you will burn, you . . ."

Nora dropped the branch, scooped up the gun, and fired it into the air, silencing Davies. *Five bullets gone plus the three that Alex fired. Eight gone, five left.*

She started rubbing the branch again, grinding the point small enough to fit into the keyhole. It had to work. Would work. Because eventually the glow stick would go out and she would be trapped here until she burned. And long before then, the rats would move in and she would be a raving lunatic.

"Witch," Davies repeated. "Witch, witch." Like the neighborhood bully.

She removed the glow stick from her mouth, set it on the floor beside her. "Minion of Chandler," she shot back.

"You are wrong."

"You watched him torture Sarah Longwood. And when you left, he dropped his breeches and tried to defile her. That makes you like him."

Rub, turn, rub, turn. And back there, behind her, she heard the other rats coming for their fallen comrade, coming to devour him and then feast on her.

"I . . . I went for the physician and the physician, he . . ."

"Did Sarah ever harm you, Mr. Davies? Did she harm your wife? Your family?"

"No, but . . ."

"But what? How can you justify what you allowed to happen? She did nothing to you personally."

"Reverend Chandler said . . ."

"Chandler made you an accomplice. He lied to you. He turned you away from God, toward Satan. He—"

"*No.* Lies, lies, lies, all of it. Satan lies. He . . ."

"Yeah, whatever." *Rub and turn, rub and turn.* "I am not here to save your soul. Believe what you want."

The silence stretched like a canvas on which their collective futures would be painted. That scared her. She kept rubbing the branch against the stone floor. She heard the rats chattering in the darkness behind her. Planning.

"Catherine Griffin spoke like you," Davies said finally. "She, too, called me a minion of Chandler. When he . . . put her on the strappado, when he shouted at her to confess, when he brought out the boiling oil, she . . ." His voice broke. "Dear God. What . . . what have I become?"

The easy answer was that he had become more of what he always was. But she suddenly understood how the repression and superstition worked on the collective psyche of this era. To survive, you had to rationalize the horror because if you didn't, your spouse or your children, your mother or your father, your brothers or your sisters might be torn away from you, put on the strappado, branded, stuck with pines, hanged or burned. So you did what you had to do to prevent that from happening. You lied, cheated, aided and abetted, and your guilt ate away at you like an insidious cancer. Here, you drank the Kool-Aid of self-deception—or you and everyone you loved perished.

"Tell me about Catherine." *Rub and turn.* "Why was she accused?"

"Because she . . . she refused to lie down with Francis Travers. And Travers . . . I believe he told the reverend and he . . . he decided she should be accused. The reverend made Lucia confess that she had seen Catherine's specter while she was working at the store. Even though spectral evidence was decreed unlawful after Salem, the reverend said that the law of God was higher than the law of man."

"Mr. Davies, Chandler is no more a preacher than you or I. You do not have to call him *reverend.*"

"But that *is* his name."

"His name is *Walter* Chandler. He has long since violated his right to be called a reverend."

"He promised me . . . a better job. A place on the town council. But none of that came to pass."

"How did Catherine escape?" Nora transferred the glow stick to her shackled hand, held up the end of the branch, examined it. Nearly there.

"Late one night, Chandler arrived at my home, woke me, and said we were going to do the Lord's work. I . . . I knew what that meant. I knew he intended to put Catherine on the strappado again, to make her . . . confess. I did not want to be a part of it. But I was afraid of him, afraid of what he might do to my wife, my children. He could accuse anyone, at any time. Such is his power. So I went with him. But I . . . I put several large stones in my pocket. When he told me to fetch her, I gave her the stones and unlocked the bands and told her to hit me with them and to flee. To take my horse and run. And . . . she did."

All of this was uttered in a voice so soft that Nora had to strain to hear him. She recognized that Davies had just made his confession and knew that he needed to hear that he had done the right thing, that he had turned the corner from Satan's world. "You did the right thing, Mr. Davies. You saved her life." Behind her, the rats were closing in again, chattering.

"Perhaps. Yes, perhaps. I cannot say for sure that she lives, yet I am hopeful. She was resourceful. But my fear of Chandler remains. And . . . and when he comes for you and finds me here, shackled, and the other women gone, it will be terrible for you. He will parade you through the streets, you will be strapped to the stake, he will light the pyre himself. To keep the people controlled, he must give them blood, and that will further their belief that the battle against Satan is being . . . won."

Yeah, that about summed it up. She examined the sharpened point of the branch and stuck it carefully into the band's lock and began to move it around, praying that it would do the trick. "Where are the keys to the band?"

"Ever since Catherine escaped, he keeps all the keys."

"Is there any way to get them off without a key?"

"Can you shoot your weapon at the hook that connects to the cage?"

"Not without shooting off my hand. I have a branch with

a sharp point that I am trying now. What about one of those pins that Chandler stuck in Sarah's birthmark? Would one of those work?"

"*Yes*. Yes, I believe so, Mrs. Goodwin. But I, too, am restrained."

Progress. He had referred to her by name rather than as "witch." Unless it was a trick, a deception, a ruse to get her to toss him the gun. *Can I trust him?* She didn't know. But she was fresh out of options. "I am going to throw my weapon to you, Mr. Davies. I believe you can shoot off the handcuffs with it. But I ask that you return it before you leave, so that I can defend myself against the rats and against Chandler if he arrives before you return."

"You cannot throw it between the bars of the cage. If you can open the door fully and throw it hard . . ."

"I am not sure I can reach it. I will try."

Nora set the branch on the floor, next to the Glock, and balanced the glow stick upright against the bars. She laid back and stretched her free leg out, then slid her butt closer to the door and kept sliding even when the bracelet bit into her wrist. Thanks to the way her ankle was shackled, she had a little leeway before the bracelet tightened painfully around her anklebone. When she had moved as far as she could without breaking her wrist, she lifted her head from the floor and raised her foot slightly to gauge its distance to the door.

An inch or two.

If she kicked the door and it opened only partway, it would be out of reach. She would get just one attempt.

Nora shut her eyes and visualized her foot connecting just right with the door so that it would swing all the way open. She focused her remaining strength, such as it was, in that leg, those muscles and tendons and bones, and altered her breathing so that both hemispheres of her brain came into alignment, techniques that Curtis had taught them during their training. And when she kicked out, her foot struck the door, and it opened like a giant, gaping jaw and didn't swing back.

Davies let out a non-Puritan whoop. "You *did* it, Mrs. Goodwin! You *did* it!"

Nora slid back again, her wrist and ankle burning with pain, and sat up. Behind her, around her, rats chattered. "Now if I can just get the gun to you, Mr. Davies."

She held the glow stick out in front of her, trying to get a sense of how far and how hard she should throw the gun. Her original estimate of his distance from her—thirty or forty feet—was probably fairly accurate. She hoped it was closer to thirty. She grasped the Glock at the barrel and, once again, focused on her desired outcome, just as they did whenever they transitioned. "Here it comes," she called, then hurled it across the floor.

The gun spun like a top, then skittered across the stones.

"I can reach it," Davies reported, and she saw him straining against the handcuffs, reaching out with his leg. "I have it. But how do I use it? I have never seen such a weapon."

Nora explained step-by-step and held the glow stick up and out as far as she could. "The noise will be loud, almost deafening. Your ears may ring for a few moments afterward. Hold the gun back a little, be sure your aim is exact, and then squeeze the trigger."

"I am ready," he said, and fired.

The explosion filled the cellar, echoing and ringing even after Davies shouted, "I am free!"

When he reached her cell, he handed her the gun—*four shots left*—then stepped quickly behind her and stomped his feet and shouted and slammed a branch against the bars to scare the rats off. He finally crouched in front of her. "You will not burn as long as there is a breath left in my body, Mrs. Goodwin. This much I promise you. You are my penance. My redemption."

Just get me outta here.

"Allow me to look at the keyhole on this band." He touched her foot, saw the blood seeping from where the band had cut into her skin, and wiped it away with the cuff of his shirt. "The pin will fit. But I have never heard of a pin unlocking one of these."

"I can do that."

"This magical stick of light that you have. Where did it come from?"

"Europe."

"How long will the light last?"

Not long enough. "A while. It depends on the temperature of the air. Do you need it to find your way upstairs?"

A small, resigned smile tugged at the corners of his mouth. "I have worked here for many years, Mrs. Goodwin. I am the blind man who can find his way through these rooms. Upstairs, I will get a torch."

As he stood, he stared down at the rats she had killed, then quickly stooped over, grabbed them by the tails, hurled them out of her cage. "I will be back shortly."

"Thank you so much, Mr. Davies. You saved Catherine's life and now you are saving mine."

Moments later, Davies vanished through the trapdoor, leaving her alone again with the glow stick, the sounds of the rats gathering in the shadows that drenched the cage behind her, and four bullets.

23
Gatekeeper

I dwell in Possibility.
—*Emily Dickinson*

Their second day in the woods dawned with thick fog curling through the trees. A layer of ice covered the wagon's wheels and the river was frozen so solid that Berlin couldn't break through it to replenish the diminishing supply of water. He, Sarah, and Sunny sat by the fire he had built, shivering despite the quilts wrapped around them. Only the horse, with a quilt over her back, seemed comfortable. She grazed on the hay Berlin had put on the ground in front of her.

Sarah had come to yesterday morning and, other than plying him with a thousand questions, seemed completely healed. She ate the porridge he'd made with undisguised gusto, the wooden bowl balanced in one bandaged hand, the other hand gripping the spoon. He dished up two more bowls, one for himself and one for Sunny, set them on the ground to cool, and brought out the loaf of bread he'd bought at the general store. Hard as a rock.

"Put it in the porridge," Sarah suggested. "It will warm quickly."

He dropped it into the iron pot over the fire. "Do you have any idea where we are?"

"In the woods."

Well, yes. But relative to where? Maybe, though, it was just that simple. *In the woods.* They had enough food to last several more days, and this deep thicket of trees was probably safer than being out in the open. "But how far from Blue River?"

"I have only been to Boston and that journey took many days, along the coast. I do not know how far we are from Blue River. Tell me again why you helped me. I have been thinking on this and cannot find a logical explanation."

"I'm a doctor, okay? You had been badly tortured. I couldn't let you go back to the gaol. The magistrate's wife helped us to escape."

"I liked her. And him. And the dog." She looked over at Sunny, who had raised her head at the sound of her name, and now barked. "But tell me, why is the dog with us and what is *'okay'*?"

Shit, he was speaking in contractions, and using other words she never had heard. But what did it matter at this point? "It means . . ." How to explain the nuances of twenty-first-century lexicon? There was okay as in, "You got it, moron?" Or okay as in, "Do you understand?" or "Do you agree?" And okay as in, "Is this all right with you?" And . . . yeah, whatever. " 'Okay' means many things. The dog chose to join us."

"Where are we going?" she asked.

"I don't know."

"You speak so strangely sometimes."

"In what way?"

"Don't. I'm. Couldn't. Okay."

"It is how they speak in Europe, where I went to school."

Berlin picked up his bowl of porridge and concentrated

on eating. If his mouth was full, he wouldn't dig himself a deeper grave with the English language, circa 1695. If his mouth was full, he wouldn't have to talk at all.

Yesterday, their first full day together, it had been easier to avoid slips like this. They had spent most of the daylight hours gathering wood, looking for a place in the river where the ice was thin enough to break, and taking stock of their supplies. They had pretty much avoided talking at any length until it got dark. Then they had huddled around the fire and she had poured out her heart about her captivity. Chandler's barbarism. The accused who had died in jail.

According to Sarah, fourteen women and four men had been accused since last spring. Three had met the gallows, two had been burned, the rest either had died in captivity or escaped, and all of this deviated from historical fact as he knew it. He didn't have any idea what *that* meant. To even contemplate it was the equivalent of trying to solve the ultimate conundrum about time travel.

The fog continued to slip and slide through the trees, spiraling insidiously around the trunks, upward into the lower branches, swirling across the frozen river. Sunny suddenly lifted her head from her bowl of porridge and growled. Then she moved closer to Berlin and dug her nose under his arm until he wrapped his arm around her back.

"What?" he whispered, and she growled again.

"She hears what we cannot." Sarah put her bowl on the ground, looked back, and moved closer to Sunny and Berlin.

"Animals seeking shelter from the cold." Kincaid hoped to hell it was true.

"Do you have a gun, Dr. Webber?"

"My name is Berlin, Russ Berlin, Sarah. I had to use another name while I was in Blue River. And yes, I am armed."

"But since I am healed, you must really be a doctor."

"Yes."

"You must be a very good doctor. My hands no longer hurt." And with that, she unwrapped the bandages from her right hand and then from her left and turned her hands this way and that in the pale morning light, staring at the fresh pink skin that covered them, the perfect skin of a young child. "But . . . but I remember they were burned. By the oil. How can they be healed so quickly?"

"The burns weren't as terrible as you thought."

She raised her eyes to his, and in that moment, *he* knew that *she* knew he was lying, that her burns had been crippling. "I know what boiling oil does. I saw the injuries on Catherine's hands. Her left hand was so badly burned that the skin had blackened. She could not bend her fingers. She . . ."

Sunny growled again, a deeper, more menacing growl this time. Berlin strained to hear something, anything, and when he didn't and Sunny's growls grew more insistent, he whispered, "Sarah, hide in the wagon."

Sarah rose quickly, the fog wrapping around her legs to the knees, darted over to the wagon, and climbed inside it. Berlin and Sunny quickly followed her, and moments after they had hunkered down in the quilts, he heard the beating of hooves against the ground, horses snorting in the cold air, shouts.

Terrified that it was Chandler and his mob, Berlin crawled to the front of the wagon, his weapon ready. Sunny remained close to Sarah, her guardian, friend, consort, and the girl's arm rested across the dog's back. Berlin stretched out on his stomach and peered through the space between the bench and the upper edge of the wagon, his feet touching Sunny. If the dog transitioned, so would Sarah, and now, so would he.

A dozen figures rode out of the fog, dark silhouettes in the milky light, the thickening fog, and formed a half moon around the wagon, but at a distance. "Hello," a man called.

"Identify yourself, sir."

"Lucas," the man called back. "Aaron Lucas."

"We mean you no harm," Berlin called back. "But we want no company."

"From where do you come?"

"From where do *you* come, Mr. Lucas?"

"The Mystic Hills."

"Sarah," Berlin whispered. "Do you know of this place?"

"It is just legend," she whispered back.

Sunny had stopped growling. Kincaid hoped that was a good sign. "That is just a place of legend," he called back.

"It is a true place." A woman's voice now, soft but firm. "We are looking for James and Edward Cory and Paul Fry. Do you know of these people?"

The merchants. "They are in Blue River and were trapped by the blizzard." Still peering through the space beneath the wagon's bench, Berlin watched as one of the riders trotted forward, head held high but hidden beneath the hood of a cloak. Only when the rider dismounted did Berlin realize it was the woman who had spoken, her arms raised, empty palms visible, as if someone held a gun to her back.

"I am unarmed," she called. "We only wish news of the Cory brothers and Fry. We have heard that a madness has gripped the town, that the burning times are beginning in Blue River. Is this true?"

"Please stop where you are," Berlin warned. "Come no closer."

She slid the hood back, revealing a tumble of luxurious black hair that reached her shoulders. The pale light spilled across her face as if across time itself. He nearly choked on his own spit. Catherine Griffin Walrave. She looked just as he remembered her during that time at the institute, a woman whose beauty was so simple and yet so complex that you could study her face for days and never understand it.

Sarah suddenly bolted upright, vaulted out of the wagon, and ran toward Catherine shouting, "It is me, Sarah Longwood! You *live,* Catherine, you *live!*" And she ran into Catherine's arms.

Even Sunny, who always seemed to know what to do and when to do it, was perplexed by all this. She whined and pawed at the floor of the wagon and looked at Berlin, head cocked slightly to one side, as if to say, *Hey, guy, what the hell's going on here?*

Berlin ran his fingers through her fur. "It was after you ran away from Mariah. It's okay, Sunny." Like she would understand every word.

He slipped his weapon inside his cloak and climbed down from the wagon. Sunny leaped out and stayed close to his side as he moved toward the embracing women, who stood between him and at least two dozen men on horseback. All of them appeared to be armed.

The forest seemed to be holding its breath, not a noise anywhere. Even his footsteps were soundless. The fog continued to eddy into the clearing, mysterious and ancient, like something on the Scottish moors. He almost expected Mel Gibson to gallop into the midst of this surreal landscape, waving his sword and shouting for freedom, *Braveheart* centuries too late.

And then the women broke apart and Catherine saw him. *Really* saw him. Identified him. She made a sound—gasp, hiccup, choked confusion, he couldn't define exactly what it was—and suddenly it was all there between them, their brief, shared past at the institute, that week or ten days that had set the course for the rest of his life—and hers. They ran toward each other like separated lovers in some Shakespearean tragedy. But they never had been lovers. They were just two people from the same time who understood the broad strokes that had brought them together in *this* time.

He had no idea how long they stood there holding each other, he and Catherine. His concept of time had been warped so long ago that he now seemed incapable of judging the validity of the smallest details: the passage of moments, the weight of flesh and fabric, the smell of her hair. It might all be some intricate hallucination, a trick of the chip, fantasy. He might actually be on a street in some unknown city en route to a movie, fugitive from his humdrum, stable, and predictable life as a janitor at the institute. Life was as simple or as complex as you believed it to be, he reminded himself. And the chip, if nothing else, acted on this belief and amplified your deepest intentions.

Catherine finally stepped back from him, breathtaking in her beauty. "How . . . how can you be here, Russ?"

"We came back to find you."

"Tell me Joe Aiken isn't hidden in that wagon."

"Daddy Joe is dead, Joe Junior is in federal prison. My life went on, Catherine. Right into the twenty-first century."

"But you . . . you look the same. You haven't aged. How's that possible?"

"The chip seems to retard aging. I'm not sure how."

She squeezed her eyes shut, clenched her fists, looked at him again. "And Mariah?"

"Adrift. Somewhere."

"Lydia Fenmore?"

"Gone. I don't know where."

"Ian?"

"Dead."

"And SPOT?"

"Collapsed."

She bit at the corner of her lip. "Are we dreaming, Russ? Is it all just some vast and complex dream and we don't know how to escape it? Is that it?"

"I don't know," he admitted.

"How's the dog fit into all this?"

Sunny nudged Catherine's hand, asking for recognition, a pat hello, then rubbed against Berlin's leg, whined, and seemed to fade from view, like something in a dream. But when he blinked, she was still there, as solid as the nearby trees. If Catherine noticed, she gave no indication. Berlin hoped it was just a trick of the light, a by-product of fatigue and shock. "The only dog Mariah ever used in her experiments."

"But . . . that means the dog must be . . . what? Forty years old? More?"

"Something like that."

"That's impossible, Russ."

"I know. It's all impossible."

"You're both chipped?"

He nodded. "But we can't seem to get back."

"I don't understand."

"Me, neither."

Catherine crouched in front of Sunny and ran her fingers through the dog's fur. "You're gorgeous." In response, Sunny rolled onto her back, offering up her tummy for a rub.

While they had been talking, the men had moved closer to the wagon, to the fire, and Sarah invited them to help themselves to whatever food there was. Some of the men dismounted and now warmed themselves by the flames. Berlin didn't know what to think of this. He didn't know what to think about anything. But this was Catherine Griffin Walrave, mother of Nora and Tyler, the woman he had come back to find. Now that he had found her—and Sarah Longwood—would he be able to transition back to his own time?

"What was the exact date to which Lydia disappeared you?" he asked as they settled near the fire, slightly away from the others.

"July 1694. I'm not sure of the exact day."

"July?" Another of Lydia Fenmore's lies.

"What date did you think?"

"According to Lydia's records, it was January sixth, 1695."

"Big Joe Aiken always said that the prime directive where Lydia was concerned was to never trust anything she said. She dropped me inland somewhere. I . . . I was in a state of shock, I think. I wandered for several days, hid every time I saw wagons, people on horseback. At night, I slept in the trees. By the third or fourth day, I was sick, out of water and food, and then I took refuge in a barn and the family who owned it found me and felt sorry for me and took me in. I told them I was on my way to Blue River when I was ambushed and robbed. After a week or so, I asked if I could borrow a horse and rode off toward Blue River. I . . . I think a part of me believed that if I got to the town, everything would magically become normal again. Well, that fantasy was crushed pretty quickly. I got arrested in October and escaped in December."

Sarah came over with mugs of hot cider. When Catherine took hers, Berlin noticed the terrible scars on her hands. Chandler's boiling oil, he thought.

"Your people have so much food," Sarah exclaimed.

"And I want you to eat as much as you can," Catherine told her. "You are much thinner."

"But I have not forgotten how to cook. I will fix us a feast."

Sarah hurried off and Catherine looked over at Berlin. "She told me that Chandler put her on the strappado, that you healed her burns. That was the day before yesterday, right? But the skin on her hands looks untouched."

"A gift from Mariah. I'll treat your hands when we're alone."

She held her hands out in front of her. The scar tissue from the burns was so thick that the nubs of her knuckles barely showed. It had deformed the pinky and ring fingers on her left hand, the third finger on her right, and the palms weren't much better. "You're lucky you didn't lose your hands," he said.

"I'm lucky that Chandler's little torture session was interrupted by Davies or the damage would have been much worse. The second time he intended to torture me, Davies helped me escape. And I returned to the family who had lent me the horse. They treated my hands."

"And now? Who are all these people?"

"Friends who understand what monsters Chandler and his vigilantes are. We got word that they're after escapees. That must be you and Sarah."

"Word from whom?"

"We have spies in town, Russ. Not just in Blue River, either. The hangings and burnings have been happening all over. We do what we can, free whom we can without killing or harming others. But we're a small group. Our settlement has less than a thousand people. This rampant religious fanaticism is like some sort of epidemic and it's spreading us thin. We heard that Chandler's followers are building pyres—presumably for Lucia and Rebeka and whoever else is imprisoned. Chandler likes to do his burning at dusk."

"Your settlement. What's it called?"

"Why?" Her tone indicated that just because they had a brief, shared history, he wasn't entitled to everything she knew.

"It's called Mystic Harbor, right?" he asked.

"Yes. But . . . how could you possibly know that?"

"Because certain parts of history are changing. Look, Catherine, there are two, possibly three others here from our time."

"*Your* time, Russ. It's not my time anymore. Once I understood what had happened, where I was, I knew my only chance for survival was to make this time my own. I had to forget my kids, my husband, my . . . my life."

Uh-oh, he thought.

"Who are the others?" she asked. "And if you're living in 2007 . . ."

"I'm hiding out in 2006, at the institute. I work there as a janitor. A lot has changed in all these years."

"Do you have any idea what happened to Nora and Tyler? And to my husband?"

Here we go. "Your husband passed away eight or nine years after you were disappeared. Tyler got married and divorced and had a prosperous computer company. Nora went on to become a professor of psychology at Blue River College. She got involved with a librarian who was also the brilliant inventor of a hy—" He started to say "hybrid car," but realized she wouldn't have any idea what that meant. He suddenly understood just how far the world had moved in the decades since she had been disappeared. "A new type of car. Anyway, they split up and Nora ended up marrying Jake McKee, an English professor at the college. Five years into the marriage, she realized it wasn't working. The day she intended to tell him she wanted a divorce, he was arrested while they were having lunch. It was a repeat of what happened to you. SPOT agents hauled him off."

She looked stricken. "When did this happen?"

"In October 2006. And then they started looking for her and she went on the run. Long story short, she and the inventor, Alex Kincaid, helped bring about the collapse of SPOT. And now she, Alex, and Tyler, along with Tyler's wife and two rogue agents from SPOT, are on the lam. Nora and Alex came back to find you. She helped Sarah and I get out of town, and I'm afraid that she was arrested by Chandler's people while Sarah and I were fleeing."

The horror that gripped Catherine's face was a perfect reflection of what Berlin had felt ever since he had arrived in this dark pocket of history. "My God," she whispered. "Nora . . . grown? And Tyler . . . married? Both of them *chipped*? And Nora *here*? But if she's chipped and in the jail, she can transition, right? She . . ."

"We haven't been able to." He explained his theory.

"That bastard isn't going to burn my daughter." She shot to her feet. "We've got enough people and weapons to storm the town and stop this madness once and for all."

"Wait." Berlin got up. "How far is Blue River from here?"

"Four hours on horseback. We can get there before dusk, hide on the outskirts of town."

"He's got hundreds of people in town who believe in what he's doing, who follow his absurd Laws of Righteous Living. We're maybe two dozen."

She rolled her lower lip between her teeth and looked around slowly, assessing their numbers. "What do you suggest?"

"A much smaller group. And you would be chipped. I have an extra."

"Chipped? But I don't remember how . . ."

"You don't have to remember how. These chips are light-years ahead of the ones we used at the institute."

She sat down again and spoke quietly. "And we would . . . what? Transition into the jail?"

Sunny, stretched out by the fire, kept watching them closely. Berlin had the distinct impression that she was listening to them and understood what they were saying—maybe not word for word, but certainly the general gist. "Yes, but from a location close to Blue River. If we can. If we succeed at transitioning, it'll be easier if we're closer to town."

Catherine pulled her knees to her chest, wrapped her arms around them, and sat that way for a while, watching everyone around them with the same quiet intensity with which Sunny watched him and Catherine. It was what she used to do at the institute, he remembered. Catherine the observer, Catherine the only one in the group who could recall what everyone had eaten for breakfast three days before.

"All right, let's do it. Just you and me," she finally said.

"I can't leave Sunny."

The dog heard her name and raised her head, regarding them both with unveiled suspicion.

"She won't be able to keep up with the horses."

"I'll carry her in my saddle."

"C'mon, Russ, that's ridiculous."

Sunny suddenly stood, shook herself, and barked. She loped toward the wagon, stopped, glanced back at them—and then disappeared.

"Oh, shit," Catherine murmured, glancing quickly around to see if anyone else had witnessed the dog's disappearance.

"I think Sunny just made it clear that she isn't riding on any horse for a couple of hours," Berlin said.

"But where'd she transition *to*?"

"My first guess is that she went to . . ."

Sunny abruptly reappeared in the exact spot where she'd vanished only moments ago. She loped toward them, tail whipping from side to side, inordinately pleased with herself. Berlin realized she carried something in her mouth and quickly went over to her. "Good dog, fantastic dog. Could I see that?"

She dropped a PDA into his cupped hands, then sat back, tail thumping the ground, and barked, as if expecting a treat. Berlin turned on the PDA, navigated to the Word documents, and brought up seven files. He clicked the one entitled READ FIRST:

> Sunny will get this back to u—whoever *u* are. Nora, Ryan, Tyler? This is Alex Kincaid. We're trapped inside the livery stable in the middle of town. Hordes of people fill the streets, most of them armed, all of them shouting to burn the witches. We're trying to get outside, to a tunnel once used by ex-slaves that leads into the cellar of the jail, where Nora is imprisoned. Eric Holcomb, whom we've known as Ericson Ivers, is with us—and one of us—and so is James Cory. Paul Fry and Edward Cory managed to escape town with Lucia and Rebeka. I was able to free the women earlier, when I transitioned into the jail. But now we can't seem to get back.
>
> We could use some reinforcements.
>
> Nora, if you're getting this, do whatever you have to. If Sunny returns, I'll grab on to her before she can transition again.

"What's that thing?" Catherine asked, joining him, gesturing at the PDA.

"One way in which the world has moved on since you were disappeared. Read this."

She cradled the PDA in the palm of her hand as though it were a sacred object of some kind. When she glanced up again, her face looked egg white, flat, the features gone, erased, like a censored image on TV. She thrust the PDA back into his hand. "Can you get that chip, Russ? And keep

Sunny here until we're ready? I need to talk to my friends. They'll be sure to get Sarah to our settlement. I'll be right back."

She moved quickly away from him and he glanced at Sunny. "Treat, girl. I've got a treat for you for your incredible work."

She knew that word, *treat,* and fell into step beside him. He plucked his bag from the wagon, flipped the shoulder strap over his head, and dug out the syringe. He checked his weapon and filled the pockets of his cloak with some of the treasures from his own time that he might need. Sunny barked, asking where the promised treat was.

"I'm getting it, just hold on." He brought out a piece of raw meat wrapped in cheesecloth that he'd taken from the general store. He peeled off the cloth and handed it to Sunny. Never mind that it was frozen solid. She took it between her teeth and dropped to the ground, gnawing at it. That would keep her busy for a few minutes, he thought, and opened the other files on the PDA.

The note from Nora's brother suggested that he had written it while she was here and he was in Aruba in 2007. As far as he knew, text messages couldn't travel more than a year in either direction. That meant Nora had transitioned to Aruba or Tyler had come back here—or Sunny had acted as the messenger.

Is that it? We each have a specific archetypal role in this drama and Sunny, like Mercury, is the messenger?

Then what the hell was he? Healer? Gatekeeper? Or both? *Can I be both?*

And Catherine? Nora? Kincaid? Mariah? Chandler? James Cory? Sarah, Lucia, Rebeka, and all the ones who had gone before them?

His head ached with questions. But that was business as usual for him. Eventually, most of his questions would find answers and he would be almost incidental to the process of discovery.

"How do we do this?" Catherine asked when she returned.

"We start with this." He pressed the syringe into her hand. "Tilt your head back, press the syringe up into a nostril until you feel discomfort, then press the plunger."

"What's this blue goo shit in here? I don't remember that."

"It keeps the chip cold, dormant. Once it's inside your sinus cavity, your body heat activates it, and the chip takes care of the rest."

"And Sunny?" she asked.

"She'll do her part."

Catherine dropped her head back, stuck the syringe up into her nose, and Kincaid turned off the PDA and waited for fifteen or twenty seconds. Then he handed Sunny the PDA, closed his fingers around her fur with one hand and grasped Catherine's wrist with the other. "Deliver the message, Sunny."

She made a strange sound deep in her throat and the woods vanished.

24
On the Roof

We have to look at it as an adventure.
Otherwise, we're done. Cooked. And they
have won.

—Alex Kincaid

Aruba, March 2007

They pounded at the grate for a long time. The skin on the soles of their feet broke open and started to bleed. They had to stop frequently to catch their breath, to lick the sweat from their own skin to keep their thirst from overwhelming them. Beyond the grate, long, narrow shadows now fell across the roof and it seemed to Mike that the air had begun to cool, however slightly.

Gradually, at dusk, one screw gave way, then another and another. They finally were able to pry the grate open and crawled out onto the roof, into the Caribbean dusk. He was so beat that he didn't know if he would make it—where? He had no idea where to go from here.

He and Ann moved slowly along the wall that surrounded the roof, looking for a way down. No fire escapes. No more metal steps. The only way down was the route they'd taken to get here and that would get them only as far as the penthouse.

Everything below them looked impossibly distant, dwarfed. He could hear cicadas, the distant crash of waves against the beach. Venus popped into view, and within moments, the sky burned with stars, so vivid and bright enough so that they could make their way away from the wall without tripping over anything. They found a metal door on the far side of the roof, but it was locked, lacked both a handle and a keyhole on their side.

"Now what?" Ann asked. Her voice held a note of desperation that he understood completely.

"I don't know yet."

She sat down in front of the door and pressed her hands against it, as if she were seeking to communicate with it or begging it for a miracle. But they were fresh out of miracles.

Mike moved restlessly across the vast expanse of the roof, navigating through the many humps and protrusions that were air conditioners, transformers, satellite dishes, telephone boxes. Here and there he found depressions in the concrete where water had accumulated. From rain? Drippings from the AC units? He didn't know, didn't care. He leaned forward and lapped at it like a dog, certain that a few hours from now he would be puking from intestinal bacteria. He called to Ann, urging her to at least wet her tongue, her lips, but she would have none of it.

One sure way to draw attention from the hotel management, he thought, would be to start twisting the satellite dishes so that the signals would be lost. Get enough guests complaining about the lack of TV and someone would be up here very quickly to check things out. Ditto with the transformers and phone lines. But if technicians came up here, they would have plenty of questions about his and Ann's presence. It would be their word against a senator's and it was a no-brainer who would be believed.

So maybe all they needed to do was get someone up here so they could make a break for the open door.

He started with the satellite dish closest to him, then

moved on to the closest telephone box. He crouched in front of it, popped open its door. He didn't know a damn thing about phone lines and didn't have anything to cut them with, but what the hell. Pulling the suckers out couldn't be a good thing, he thought, and started jerking wires out of the panel. Ann joined him and started pulling, too. "Once we've disabled some stuff, we'd better figure out where to hide when that door opens," she said. "We'll have to make a run for it."

"My thoughts exactly."

"Great minds and all that, Mike." They moved on to the next phone box, the next satellite dish, the first electrical transformer.

Locked. "I need a rock or something heavy to smash this sucker with."

"No rocks up here." Then she snapped her fingers. "But I stubbed my toes on something in that corridor. Be right back."

He sat down in front of the transformer, his stomach rumbling with hunger, his mouth screaming for water. At least the blazing sun had gone down and a warm wind blew across the rooftop, drying the sweat on his face. This same wind blew Ann's hair around as she limped back through the starlight.

"How about this?" She held out a chunk of cement twice the size of a brick. "It was just lying there against the side of the wall, half buried under pigeon shit and feathers."

"Perfect." He rolled onto his knees, slammed the cement block against the lock. Three blows later, the lock surrendered and he pried the door open with his fingers. He knew even less about transformers than he did about telephone boxes and there wasn't enough light to see where all the wires fit and to read which switches went to what. So he pounded the wires and the switches at random. Wires fell away, switches were knocked loose, sparks flew, and suddenly he heard something deep within the heart of the transformer—

a rumbling, a ferocious growl. He leaped away from the box, grabbed Ann's hand, and they loped toward the door.

Seconds later, the air filled with the explosive sound of gunfire and the transformer blew, sparks lighting up the darkness like a swarm of fireflies. Way below, the parts of the building that he could see were plunged into darkness.

They ran over to the door and Mike pressed his ear to the metal, listened, hoping to hear voices, footfalls, something. Then Ann grabbed his hand and pulled him back against the wall to the left of the door, so that when it opened, the door would hide them. He kept a tight hold on her hand and whispered, "We wait until they're out on the roof and then we make a run for it."

"And keep running until we're outside?" she asked.

"Or keep running until we find a place to hide."

Minutes passed before they heard voices on the other side of the door. Ann's nails bit into the back of his hand. The door swung open and several bright beams of light swept across the roof. Half a dozen men poured out, speaking a language he didn't understand. Dutch? The local dialect?

The wind kept the door open and when he was sure no one else would appear, he gave Ann's hand a quick squeeze. They darted out from behind the door and exploded through the doorway.

"Hey, you two, stop right there!" one of the men shouted.

Mike slammed the door shut, threw the lock, and they tore down a narrow flight of stairs illumined by a dim emergency light. They went down eight floors, well below the penthouse, before they paused on the landing to catch their breath. And that was when he heard the shrill, rhythmic shriek of an alarm—not the fire alarm he had tripped days ago; this was different. He didn't know if that was good or bad, but suspected that any second now, evacuating guests would fill the stairwell.

He opened the door and peered into a corridor where several emergency lights blinked off and on, painting the walls and carpet in a weird, surreal glow. People hurried through the hall but headed away from him and Ann, toward the EXIT sign at the far end. He guessed these stairs were used only by maintenance personnel.

"Let's go," he said, and they slipped out into the corridor, conspicuous in their bare feet, their dirty clothes.

He was afraid that Lazier and his people had figured out by now that he and Ann were behind this disruption in power, phones, TV. If they alerted the hotel security and the local cops, no telling what might be waiting for them at the foot of the stairs in the lobby or in the parking garage or even on one of the lower floors. So at the first juncture in the hall, they turned left, following signs that read TO THE BEACH AND THE POOL. He hoped there might be another staircase that would take them down. Instead, the hall ended at an elevator, the doors shut, the buttons unlit. No power.

"Shit." Mike looked over at Ann, who was biting at her lower lip and glancing around anxiously.

"Hey, over there." She pointed at a supply cart—and the partially open door just behind it.

They ran over to it, pushed the cart out of the way, ducked inside, closed the door. Even in here, an emergency light glowed from a corner near the ceiling, but it was considerably smaller than the ones in the corridor. Shelves lined two of the walls, piled high with neatly folded stacks of linens and towels, pillows, uniforms and shoes, bathroom supplies. Against the third wall stood a small utility room sink, a locker, a small fridge filled with bottles of water and someone's lunch or dinner, and a door for the laundry chute.

Mike helped himself to four bottles of water. He and Ann gulped down a bottle of water apiece, then split the turkey sub, a bag of chips, and a banana. In the hall, the alarm kept shrieking.

They hastily went through the uniforms looking for clothing that might fit them. Mike settled for a workman's jumpsuit and a pair of shoes that fit pretty well. Ann couldn't find a woman's uniform that fit, so she zipped herself into a jumpsuit, too, then opened the locker, picked up the tennis shoes inside, and slipped them on her feet. A perfect fit, like Cinderella's slippers, he thought, and plucked a baseball cap from the hook inside and dropped it on her head. She twisted her hair around her hand and drew it up and repositioned the cap on her head so it covered her hair. She tugged it down over her eyes.

"Do I look like a guy now?"

"Never." He tilted her chin upward and kissed her. Everything else melted away from him. Only her mouth and the fragrance of her skin and hair existed. He didn't know how long they stood there, arms around each other, hearts beating together, but suddenly she broke the embrace.

"Voices, Mike."

"I don't hear anything."

But then, in between bleats of the alarm, he did hear something. A radio crackle. "We're searching the seventh—" The alarm swallowed up the rest of it.

Mike moved to the door, to lock it, but the lock was on the outside. He heard the crackle of the radio again, more voices, closer now. "Check those three rooms!" a man shouted.

To come this far only to be captured again? Or killed?

He swept up their old clothes and shoes, hurled open the door of the laundry chute, and peered inside. It looked like a slide at the local carnival, but steeper. He didn't see a light at the end, but maybe there weren't any emergency lights in the hotel laundry room. Although he felt warm, gentle currents, he couldn't tell whether they came from above or below them. He tossed their clothes down the chute and motioned for Ann to go next. "I'll be right behind you," he assured her.

"I don't know about this, Mike. We're . . . what? Seven stories up? For all we know, that chute ends on floor five. Or we land on solid concrete in the basement and break our legs."

"Even dressed like this we can't step out into that hallway right now."

She ran her tongue over her lower lip, thinking, glancing from the door to the chute. The alarm kept bleating, voices intruded again, much closer now. "Okay," she said. "I'll whistle when I reach the bottom."

While he held the chute door open, she scrambled onto the top of the pint-size fridge, a bottle of water in one hand, the other hand gripping the edge of the chute until she positioned her legs directly in front of her. Her eyes held his for a moment, then she let go and vanished.

Mike leaned over the chute, listening hard for her whistle. How long would it take for her to get to the end of it? Seconds? Two minutes? What? As the seconds ticked by, his anxiety deepened. Then he heard it: two short whistles.

"I'm going to check the storage closets!" a voice outside the door shouted.

Mike scrambled onto the top of the small fridge, climbed into the opening, positioned himself on the slide, shoes braced against the surface as he lowered the door down so that it rested on top of his head. *Here goes.* He straightened out his legs so that his shoes were no longer touching the surface of the slide, pushed off with his hands, and shot down into the darkness.

The chute curved at one point and he leaned too far to the right and nearly went over the side. Then it straightened again, and moments later, he landed in what felt like a mountain of fabric and sank into it. The air was the color of tar, impenetrable, impossibly dense, and hot. But it smelled good, of soaps and detergents.

"Ann?" he whispered.

"Right here." Her voice sounded muffled. The fabric around him fluttered, moved, and he felt her hand on his arm. "It's official, Mike. We're in the laundry room. And the alarm either stopped or we just can't hear it down here. Now what?"

"We get out of here and upstairs to the lobby. Or find a

door in here that leads outside. Are we in a giant laundry basket or what?"

"It's a bin of some kind. When I sank to the bottom, I felt metal."

They crawled through the fabrics to one of the giant bin's walls. When he stood, the upper edge reached to his throat and he had a sudden image of a gigantic aluminum bowl with walls that were nearly as tall as he was. He still couldn't see shit, and he and Ann had to feel their way over the wall, navigating like the blind. Once they were out of the bin, they moved side by side, clutching each other's hands, their backs against the bin to orient themselves.

They reached the edge of one wall, felt the corner, and he realized it wasn't a bowl at all, but was shaped like a square or a rectangle. They kept taking small, uncertain steps, shoes whispering against the cool, slightly damp concrete floor. On the other side, he detected an orb of anemic light that seemed to hover in the darkness, a miniature UFO. The closer they got to it, the more certain he was that the orb was some sort of emergency light.

It gave off enough of a glow for him to detect the vague shapes: huge squares along the closest wall that he guessed were industrial washing machines and dryers. The rectangular shapes directly in front of them appeared to be a row of large sinks. Way off to his left stood counters piled high with folded linens. Off to the right was another mammoth bin, positioned right under one of the laundry chutes.

"Where's the freakin door?" Ann whispered.

"I . . ."

Shouts rang out, radios crackled, and all of it echoed through the laundry area. Mike lurched toward the row of giant washing machines, flipped open one of the lids, and knew that neither he nor Ann would last five seconds hidden in one of these things. He raced toward the closest bin and they scrambled inside. They burrowed down under soiled bedsheets, towels that smelled of suntan lotion and sand, bath mats trampled by the feet of strangers, blankets that had covered bodies large and small, fat and thin, and everything in between. When they reached the bottom, the metal cool against their bodies, they went completely still, his arms around her, their heads turned toward each other, their bodies creating a fortress against the pressing weight of the fabrics so that they could breathe.

Her breath, warm and moist, was erratic, labored. Mike felt and heard the hammering of her heart, smelled her sweat and her terror, and his arms tightened around her. "I love you," he whispered, his mouth moving against her neck. "I just want you to know that."

She brought her mouth to his and he felt her stifled sob. "Me, too."

Then, beyond them, a door crashing open, more shouts, but everything sounded muted, distant, as if he and Ann were underwater, hidden in some deep crevice in an ocean floor.

"Check the washers, the dryers, those fucking bins!" someone shouted.

Mike heard the words, but they sounded drawn out, chopped up, like flawed audio in a movie. Ann's mouth was still pressed against his, not in a kiss, exactly, but as if they were becoming one body, her skin melting into his, her breath becoming his breath, her bones fitting themselves to his.

"Don't move," he whispered.

The weight of the linens, the towels, the bath mats; the lack of fresh air; the oppressive heat—he suddenly felt as if he were dying. Any second now, he would shoot up through the fabrics shrieking like some fucking crazy, and these pricks would open fire. And he *would* die. He could see it happening, could see the bullets slamming into his chest, his face, his head, could hear Ann screaming.

Don't breathe, don't move.

"They were just sighted outside!" someone yelled.

Mike heard a door slam shut and then silence settled like dust through the air. Ann stirred, her mouth slipping away from his. He tightened his arms around her and whispered, "We wait. It may be a trick."

For the longest time, neither of them spoke or moved. Then she said, "If we get out of this alive, I don't think either of us is going home again, Mike."

"We'll bring home to wherever we are. And it's not *if*. It's *when*."

She tightened her arms around him and pressed her forehead against his chest. Minutes ticked past. Hours seemed to unroll in slow motion. They finally climbed out of the bin, found the door, and made their way slowly and carefully up a flight of stairs. The air in the stairwell smelled damp, moldy. Their footfalls echoed softly. They paused in front of the door on the landing and pressed their ears to it, listened. Music, that was all he heard. Shoplifting music, like what you heard in hotel lobbies all over the world.

"Lobby?" she whispered.

"I think so." He cracked the door open and peered out. Bellhops, tourists, families, guys with briefcases—all of them moving through the strange glow of emergency lights. No one seemed to be in any particular rush, though, and he could no longer hear the alarm. Did that mean the emergency had been declared over? "We walk fast but not too fast."

In the quiet, he heard her swallow. "Okay."

Mike opened the door farther. The lobby loomed before them, as vast as a continent, with the revolving front door so far away that he nearly lost his nerve. "Let's go," he said, and they stepped out.

They kept their heads down as they started across the shiny floors. Two little kids scurried past them, laughing. Several businessmen swept by them, chattering away in Spanish. Tourists were lined up at the registration desk. He suddenly craved the chaos into which he had disappeared several days ago, throngs of people pouring across the lobby, escaping what they had believed was a fire. He checked the distance to the door. Too damn far. *Keep walking, don't look around.*

Suddenly, a man fell into step beside Mike and another guy came up alongside Ann. The man next to Mike gripped his arm. "End of the line, kids. Now just come quietly with us and we'll—"

Mike wrenched his arm free, slammed his elbow into the man's ribs, and grabbed Ann's hand. They raced for the door, shouts ringing out, echoing. "Stop them! Don't let them get through the door!"

Pandemonium broke out behind them, but they kept on running, shoes slapping the floor. Someone lurched toward Mike on the left, and he swung around behind a baggage cart and shoved it. It crashed into the guy, knocking him off his feet. Suitcases tumbled to the floor, creating an obstacle course for the men behind Mike. When he checked the front door again, he saw that it was blocked by a row of men in suits. Hotel security people? Lazier's men? *Does it matter?*

"Need another exit," he gasped, and he and Ann spun around—and faced a half-moon of local cops armed with rifles, all of them aimed at him and Ann. Wade and Ben stood in the middle of the men, smirking.

"Jig's up," Ben said.

"We're American citizens," Ann burst out. "We—"

"You're terrorists," Wade snapped. "And under—"

"These men kidnapped us!" Ann shrieked. "We were running for our lives. Someone help us, *please*. My name's Ann Lincoln. My friend's name is Mike Holcomb. We live in Palm Beach, Florida. Call the embassy . . . ."

Wade's smirk faded. Ben's hands tightened into fists and he moved toward them. "Shut up," he snarled. "Or . . . ."

"Excuse me!" shouted a man hurrying up behind the cops. "Excuse me!"

The cops parted like the Red Sea, Ben stepped back quickly, and he and Wade gave the man their full attention.

Mike guessed he was the hotel manager. "Mr. Wade, this is not a detention center. You told me you were looking for terrorists, not a couple of teenagers. I would like you and your group to move over to the registration desk and we will discuss this."

"Mr. Visser, we have the full cooperation of your—"

"You and your group have disrupted business here for the last time," Visser snapped, then turned to the local cops, barked out something in the local dialect, and all but two of them dispersed. The pair left behind fell in beside Wade and Ben, making it abundantly clear that they were taking their orders from Visser.

Wade's face tightened, his mouth pursed as if he'd bitten into something horribly sour. "Mr. Visser, you're interfering with the business of the United States federal government. And that is—"

"Must I remind you, sir, that you are no longer in the United States? We have a call in to the American embassy and will sort this out. Now please. Move this entire fiasco to the registration desk. We will wait there for my boss and an embassy representative. If you create any more trouble before they arrive, I'll have you escorted off the grounds."

"This is the same young man who assaulted the senator," Wade burst out, stabbing his finger at Mike. "You saw it on the hotel video yourself. He—"

"We are not arguing about this," Visser said tersely, then nodded at the two cops, who promptly raised their rifles and gestured for the four of them to follow Visser.

Mike took Ann's hand and they fell into line behind Wade and Ben, with the two cops bringing up the rear.

25
Choices

Which thought feels better?
—Esther Hicks

They were everywhere, moving like a village of insects, hundreds of them, mindless in their collective mission. Despite the daylight, they didn't extinguish their torches. Their fists thumped the air. Their voices rose as one voice: *Burn the witches.* Whether Holcomb looked up or down the street, the view out the stable window was the same.

Burn the witches, burn the witches . . .

Horrified, he watched until James Cory pulled him back. They couldn't transition to the jail or anywhere else, and although they were armed, they didn't have enough ammo to take out thousands. They could probably escape from the stable on horseback, but that would leave Nora inside the jail's cellar, a sacrificial lamb. But that wasn't his problem. All he wanted to do was rescue his son.

We are so fucked.

Stones rained against the glass, shattering it, and Holcomb scrambled back, hands flying instinctively to his face. Cory and Kincaid immediately rushed forward with a large piece of wood and nailed it over the window. Then they retreated to the center of the stable, next to the fireplace, their silence an eerie backdrop to the rising madness outside. Upstairs, a window broke.

They all glanced toward the door that led upstairs; it was nailed shut. "Is the front door taken care of?" Cory asked.

"I did it when I got my bags," Kincaid said.

"We'd better reinforce those stable doors," Holcomb said, his voice betraying urgency, fear.

The blacksmith, flanked on either side by the two young and obviously terrified stable hands, said, "They want the witches. But the witches are gone. If they do not get their burning, their bloodletting, they will begin burning buildings."

"It sounds like they are doing that already," Holcomb remarked as more stones struck the boarded-up window.

"The burning of buildings happened before," the blacksmith rushed on. "You know that, Mr. Cory. You seen it with your own eyes. It is not safe to stay here."

Cory nodded, his face bright with sweat. "Last winter. Yes. And the crowd out there is many times the size of the one last year."

"There are a dozen horses in the stalls," the blacksmith went on. "There are six of us. If we release the horses all at once, they will stampede through the crowd in the back and we . . . we can escape."

Kincaid was shoving one bag inside the other, trying to consolidate his belongings. He flung the shoulder strap over his head. "I was hoping reinforcements would arrive," he said, referring to the appearance of the dog a while ago, something only he and Holcomb had witnessed. "But that seems to be wishful thinking. Where is the tunnel in relation to the gaol, Jim?"

"Far enough from the crowd for us to reach it once we are out of here."

"Then let's get our shit together, people," Holcomb said, clapping his hands together loudly, twice.

Cory, the smithy, and the two stable hands looked at him.

"An expression," he said. "Let us do it. Let the play begin. Onward. Forward. *Let's move.*"

Cory snapped instructions at the stable hands, who took off, and he and the blacksmith followed them. Holcomb loped over to one of the windows and peered through the space between the window and the board that covered it.

The human tide had multiplied, like the loaves and the fishes, people spilling through the streets, chanting, shouting, black smoke spiraling upward from their torches. Across the street, a building now burned furiously, flames leaping for the sky, a breeze fanning the tongues of fire. *Get me the fuck outta here. . . .* He needed to find Mike.

And Holcomb suddenly appears in the middle of a conference room table in the penthouse where Lazier—Wade at his side—is conducting some sort of emergency meeting with a racially diverse group of men. An Asian, a Hispanic, a black, another white guy. Tension crackles in the air, is evident in their faces. Time is critical; it's all critical; it's a critical mass.

What happened to the energy field that kept him from transitioning before?

"Hello, gentlemen," Holcomb says, and raises his arm and points his weapon at Lazier. "This fucker has kidnapped my son. And if he has promised you chips, it's a lie. He doesn't have any chips. I've got the last one he had."

The Asian goes Zen, the Hispanic wrenches back and hastily makes the sign of the cross on his forehead, the black man looks like he has seen his father's ghost, the white guy manages a polite laugh, like a cough, Wade seems to have swallowed his tongue. And Lazier just stares and stares, his eyes as bright as a radioactive field.

"Mike!" Holcomb shouts.

"He isn't here, Mr. Holcomb." Lazier pats the air with his hands, as if he is trying to calm a wild beast. "Now why don't you—"

"Don't patronize me," Holcomb snaps, then *fires just to the right of the senator's elbow, shattering a water glass.*

Lazier wrenches back, Wade goes for his weapon, and Holcomb fires again. Wade leaps to the side, his gun clunks against the floor, and he stumbles back, his eyes burning with rage. Holcomb moves back to the edge of the table, jumps down, and glances quickly at the other men. But none of them move. They hardly breathe. If they are armed, they are wise enough not to pull their weapons.

"Mike!" he shouts again.

Silence.

As he backs toward the hallway from which Ben brought Mike lifetimes ago, the Asian and the Hispanic stand slowly and deliberately, and the black man says, "You can't take on all of us."

Holcomb fires three times at the huge picture window, where the sunlit island stretches in all its strange splendor. The glass explodes and the hot trade winds rush inside, whipping shards around the room, filling the curtains until they flap and billow, and then everyone is shouting, scrambling to get out of the way. Chairs crash to the floor, papers blow everywhere, and Holcomb spins and runs into the hallway and throws open the first door.

Empty. The room is empty. An IV pole stands near the empty bed. His son hasn't been moved. He escaped, just like it said on that PDA. He . . .

And just that fast, he was back in the stable, Kincaid exclaiming, "You can *do* it! You can transition!"

Holcomb backed up to the wall, his equilibrium destroyed. He still clutched the Glock and threw his arms out at his sides, grappling for something to grasp, to steady himself. He tried to focus his vision, but couldn't. The room spun, turning upside down, inside out. Colors ran together; smells got all mixed up; the air felt like rough wool.

Kincaid grabbed him under the arms, holding him up, shouting, "*Breathe,* man, *breathe!*"

Holcomb hadn't realized he'd been holding his breath until it rushed out of him. He blinked, and Kincaid's face snapped into clarity. "How long?" Holcomb asked breathlessly. "How long was I gone?"

"I don't know. Thirty seconds, a minute, two minutes. No longer than that. Not long enough for anyone but me to notice."

Two minutes, two lifetimes. "Lazier's ramping up the stakes with foreign governments. My . . . my son is gone. He escaped, just like it said on your PDA. But . . . how . . . how the hell am I going to find him?"

Kincaid grabbed his shoulders, leaned right into his face, his eyes bright, intense. "Listen to me, Eric. Your emotions are key. If your love for him is great enough, the chip will find him. Do you understand what I'm saying?"

Holcomb jerked back. "My *love* for him? What the *fuck* is that supposed to mean? You think I don't love my son, Alex?"

"Jesus, calm down. It's a figure of speech, okay? It's . . ."

Something weird happened to Kincaid's face just then, his expression changing, mutating. "What?" Holcomb snapped.

When Kincaid spoke, his voice was quiet, but edgy with surprise, shock, as if he had been fooling himself. "Maybe you didn't love him enough when you accepted Wade's proposition."

Rage swept over Holcomb, deafening him, and he swung. But Kincaid's reflexes were like lightning. He grabbed Holcomb's wrist and forced his arm to his side. Holcomb blinked; Kincaid's eyes burned like comets. "Take a deep breath, Eric. Because if you don't, I'll break your fucking hand."

And all his rage drained out of him. "You don't know what kind of mess I was in. In debt to my eyeballs, a foreclosure notice on my house . . ." And to his utter horror, the rest of his story spilled out, the abbreviated version, just the plot and the players, words sliding into chaos, his emotions collapsing into a moiling river, everything coming undone.

"Wade offered me a million bucks and I took it. That doesn't have anything to do with my love for Mike."

"Yeah? You're not going to tell me you did it for him?"

"Don't stand there pretending you know what I feel, what I think, why I did what I did. You're not me. You're not inside my skin. Let go of my goddamn wrist."

Kincaid did and Holcomb rubbed it. "The night that Wade made his proposal, he wanted an answer in ten minutes. I told him I couldn't make this sort of decision in ten minutes. So he said he'd give me a taste of what was involved. Up until that point, I didn't know it was connected to time travel. I didn't know anything except this prick and his buddy Ben had appeared in my living room. He transitioned us to a field of stampeding dinosaurs in the Jurassic era. I didn't think twice. I told him to sign me up."

Kincaid wondered if the field in the Jurassic era was Wade's safe spot. "And now? Knowing what you know, would you do it again?"

Incredulous, Holcomb threw his arms out at his sides. "For *this*? For the kidnapping of my son and *this*?" He tried to laugh, but it sounded choked. "Fuck you," he spat.

Kincaid stepped back, smiling. He grabbed Holcomb's bag off the floor, put the strap around his neck, patted it. "Good. Use that indignation and rage to find him, Eric."

Holcomb realized that Kincaid had goaded him deliberately, to propel him onto an emotional roller coaster, which in turn triggered certain hormones or chemicals or whatever in his brain. He sank his index finger into Kincaid's chest. "You missed your calling, you sly fuck."

Kincaid's eyes locked on Holcomb's. "You want to find him? I just showed you how to do it."

"But . . . but I don't know what time or date it was when I emerged in the penthouse. I don't even know how the hell I did it."

"The chip records every transition, Eric. Your intention and emotions are what take you there." He reached under his cloak for something, then pressed it into Holcomb's hands. "Get your son. Then join us, Nellysford, Virginia, April 2006. The Monroe Institute. *Go.*"

Holcomb felt a weirdness in his skull, as if the bones were being elongated, stretched, as if his cranium were some giant rubber band being pulled in opposing directions. When the tension was released, he shot forward like a photon.

He emerged in a hotel lobby lit by emergency lights, emerged behind his son and Ann, who faced two cops with assault rifles. Wade stood off to the side, arguing with a guy in a suit. Ben saw him and gaped and suddenly shouted, "Shoot him! Shoot that guy!"

Around them, clerks and tourists and families with kids were scrambling out of the way, and Holcomb felt as if he had appeared suddenly on a movie set, a character whose role didn't exist, had never existed. Yet, here he was, a ghost in the machine, holding lit firecrackers.

Kincaid must have pressed them into his hands before he transitioned, but he didn't remember lighting them. He hurled them into the air and shouted, "Happy Independence Day, guys!" Just as the cops raised their rifles and fired, he flung one arm around Ann's neck, the other around Mike's neck and, just in the nick of time, transitioned.

He slammed down against something hard, the explosion of firecrackers and gunfire still echoing in his ears. His breath rushed out of him and he just lay there on his back struggling to breathe, his bag like a load of rocks against his chest. He gradually became aware that the air smelled vastly different—fresher, sweeter. He heard his son's groans, his eyes snapped open. He tore the strap off his neck and rolled toward Mike and gathered him in his arms, lifting his head.

"You're okay, you're okay," he said over and over again, smoothing Mike's hair off his forehead, running his hands over his son's face, certain that if he repeated the words often enough they would be true.

"You're both okay, but I'm not sure I am."

Holcomb raised his head and looked up at a woman with a blond braid draped across one shoulder, arms folded at her waist. She looked familiar, but he didn't know why. She also looked pissed.

"I know you," she exclaimed. "You're the guy in the elevator who only went to the penthouse. In Aruba. And this young man must be your son. But who the hell is she?" The woman pointed at Ann, who was pushing up on her elbows, frowning, confused.

Holcomb's eyes darted about frantically. White, plush carpet. Walls decorated with serene landscapes. No furniture. An unlit fireplace. He tore off his heavy wool cloak. "Where are we?"

"Wrong question," the woman said, then stooped down so that they were at eye level. "What's your name?"

"What's *yours*?"

"Lea Cuthoney. And let me guess. You're connected to one or all of the following: Russ Berlin, SPOT, Nora McKee, Alex Kincaid, Mariah, biochip, time travel. Does any of this ring a bell?"

He pressed the heels of his hands into his eyes.

"I take it that's a yes?" she asked.

"Is it April 2006?" he asked.

"The twenty-sixth of April, to be exact," she said.

"Dad? Where are we?"

Ann started laughing. "Firecrackers? They weren't ready for firecrackers, Mr. Holcomb."

"They apparently weren't ready for the two of you," Holcomb said. "Are you okay? Intact?"

Ann rubbed her hands down her arms, over her legs. "Yes. Intact. I mean, thirty minutes ago we were hiding in a giant laundry bin, five minutes ago we were in the hotel lobby facing a firing squad, and now . . . here."

"If we're in April 2006, then one me is in Palm Beach, right?" Mike asked. "How's that possible?"

"I don't know," Holcomb admitted.

"It doesn't matter how it's possible," Ann said. "It is what it is." She looked at Lea Cuthoney as if she had all the answers. "Right?"

"Beats the shit outta me," Lea said. "But let me guess. You two"—she gestured at Mike and Ann—"transitioned here from Aruba 2007, right? And you"—she pointed at Holcomb—"transitioned from Aruba 2007 via Blue River 1695. Do I have my facts straight, people?"

"Something like that," Holcomb managed to reply. "Alex Kincaid told me to come here."

"Kincaid." She nodded slowly. "Okay. I haven't met him yet, but I'm sure that's coming. Can you stand?"

"Yeah, I think so. I'm just feeling disconnected," Holcomb replied.

"And you two," she said to Mike and Ann. "Are you all right?"

They nodded and got to their feet and closed in on each other with the ease of lovers who had been through so much together that they no longer had to speak to each other to communicate. A telepathic connection. Holcomb recognized it for what it was, appreciated it, and was profoundly happy that his son had found this connection so early in his life.

"What place is this?" Mike asked Lea, his arm around Ann's shoulders.

"Nellysford, Virginia," she replied.

"Are the others here yet?" Holcomb asked.

"Which others? Kincaid and Nora? Russ Berlin? Be specific, Mr. Holcomb. Right now, I really need specifics. I need details."

"Kincaid said the others would be here. Ryan Curtis, Tyler . . ."

"If they're here, I don't know about it," she said. "Look, in about five minutes this room is going to start filling with people." She picked up Holcomb's bag. "Let's get outside."

She hustled them through another room and outside into

the spring air, where the view stole Holcomb's breath away. Rolling hills, green so rich it looked as if it had been painted on, the sky a fragile blue, like glass. He glanced back at the building they had left and saw a cluster of other similar buildings, white with green or dark red roofs, some stone set into the exterior walls, and a widow's walk at the top of one structure. "Is this your home?" he asked.

"Home away from home. It's the Monroe Institute. I work here."

Kincaid had mentioned it, but Holcomb had never heard of it. "So it's a school?"

Lea laughed. "Not exactly. People who come here are trained to enter altered states."

"Altered states," Mike said, nodding. "Like in the movie?"

"You *saw* that movie?" Lea asked.

Ann and Mike exchanged a glance and laughed and Ann said, "In American Lit. From the Paddy Chayefsky novel."

Huh? Holcomb had no idea what they were talking about. "What happens in these altered states?" he asked.

Lea's smile hinted at an entire universe that he hadn't explored yet. "Well, we're not shape-shifters yet," she said, with a laugh, looking at Ann. Then her eyes went back to Holcomb. "Here, people discover that they are more than their physical bodies. In fact, that's our litany."

"Is that how I can be in two places at once?" Mike asked. "In April 2006 while another me is in 2007? Because I'm more than my physical body?"

"Hon, I'm basically clueless when it comes to time travel. And the guy who would be able to answer your question isn't around. C'mon, my car's parked out front."

Moments later, they were in Lea's car, speeding along a dirt road, past more rolling hills and pastures. Holcomb's body molded itself to a leather seat as soft as butter. Fragrant air drifted through the open windows. His eyes begged to close; his body craved sleep, normalcy, a greasy hamburger with all the trimmings, an AriZona Iced Tea. But the instant he started to relax, anxiety forced him to sit up straighter, to pay attention, to plan.

They were going to need money. In his bag, he had about five grand from the original fifty that Wade had paid him. The rest was hidden in his Key Largo house in 2007. The money Lazier had paid him was in an offshore account in 2007. Two stops. And they would need a place to live. Here? Would they be safe here? Or would it be safer to go farther back in time?

Lea pulled into a long, curving driveway, and there, hidden behind the trees, was a split-level house with a small cottage off to the right. As they got out of the car, Lea said, "Make yourselves at home in the guesthouse. You'll be safe there and it's got everything you'll need."

Half a dozen cats suddenly scampered out of the woods and Mike and Ann paused to pet them all. Lea and Holcomb walked toward the guesthouse and the cats followed them, with Ann and Mike hurrying alongside them.

"What's going on back there?" Lea asked. "In 1695?"

"Nothing good," Holcomb replied.

"Are you going back?"

"It would be suicide."

"You have to go back, Dad," Mike said.

Mike and Ann had come up behind them and Holcomb looked at them—they were innocent, but perhaps not as innocent as they had been weeks ago. "This wasn't my battle to begin with, Mike. I got roped into it, I—"

"That's a *lie*," Mike burst out. "You think I don't know what was going on with you? I know about the foreclosure, Dad, about your financial problems. I know all that. Wade offered you a ton of money and you took it because you thought it would get you out of a mess. So you can't just say you're not going back. Your presence in that town three hundred years ago helped screw things up. You *owe* those people."

"I paid my dues and you don't know what the hell you're

talking about. Kincaid is chipped. Berlin is chipped. Nora is chipped. They'll get back, just like I did."

"Your word never means *shit,*" Mike spat, then whirled around and quickly walked away from him. Holcomb just stood there, feeling small, shamed, and cheap.

"He didn't mean that, Mr. Holcomb," Ann said. "It's just that a lot's happened to him in the last few weeks."

She hurried after Mike and Holcomb jammed his hands in the back pockets of his jeans and stared down at the ground, struggling with himself. *You owe those people . . . Your word never means shit.* True, it was all true.

He rubbed his hands over his face, wave after wave of self-loathing washing through him. One of the cats slipped between his legs, purring, and Holcomb reached down and drew his fingers through its fur.

"Do you have any wire clippers?" he finally said to Lea.

Lea hadn't uttered a word during the entire exchange with Mike, and she sort of smiled now, as if she understood exactly what he felt. "Sure. In the basement. Should I even ask why?"

"Nora's imprisoned in a cellar under the jail. The town is rampaging to burn the witches. Berlin fled with one of the accused and no one is sure where he is. Kincaid and some other guys are holed up in the town stable. Mike's right. I can't abandon them."

"It sounds like you need an army, not wire clippers."

"An army of about five thousand would do it."

"Can't do the five thousand," she said. "But I've got wire clippers in the basement, flashlights, a couple of rifles that belonged to my dad, a motorcycle that belonged to my brother . . ."

"What kind of motorcycle?"

"A Harley."

His heart sang. "What model?"

"Beats me," she replied. "My brother just stores it here."

Could he? Was it possible to transition something as

heavy as a Harley? Had anyone ever said it *couldn't* be done? Had anyone ever tried it? "The Harley. I'd like that, the wire cutters, and one of the rifles. Would it be okay if Mike and Ann stayed here until I get back?"

"Absolutely."

"Thank you. I really appreciate this." Holcomb glanced toward Mike and Ann, now disappearing behind a bank of trees in the distance.

"He'll come around," she said.

"Everything he said—it's true. My word doesn't mean squat and I'm terrified of going back there."

"*Was* true," she corrected him. "C'mon, I'll show you the stuff. But eventually, someone has got to explain all this to me, okay?"

"Eventually, you'll have to explain to *me* what you were doing in that elevator in Aruba nearly a year from now."

"It's a date," she said.

Holcomb went back to the car and got his bag, and he and Lea walked over to the house. What she had referred to as a basement was actually a spacious room with sliding glass doors that faced the woods. The Harley stood in the middle of the room, all shiny black and glistening chrome, polished to perfection, a machine that put his old, neglected Harley to shame. This beauty was a 2002 FXDXT Dyna Super Glide T-Sport, with a dry weight just under 650 pounds and a top speed fast enough to do the job he had in mind. It looked spanking new, the tank was full, and the machine had about three thousand miles on it.

"Are you, uh, going back on the Harley?" she asked.

"If it can be done."

"You mean, you don't know for sure if it's even *possible*?"

"Do you know for sure that we're more than our physical bodies?"

"I do now. But I didn't fifteen years ago."

"I'm where you were fifteen years ago. No one ever told me it *can't* be done."

He started pushing the Harley out of the room, into the yard and up the slope to the driveway. He swung his leg over the seat, turned the key in the ignition, and the Harley roared to life.

Lea hurried out with his gear. She passed Holcomb his bag, cloak, and the rifle. He slung the rifle and cloak over one shoulder, the bag over the other. He was beginning to feel like Wesley Snipes in one of those vampire movies.

"The wire cutters are in the bag already, with a couple bottles of water and some snacks," Lea said.

"Thank you," he told her again.

"Hey, I figure it's all for the cause. Get back here in one piece. All of you."

He turned the bike around, revved the engine, and the machine flew through the spring grass and out onto the dirt road. It rode like a dream, smoothly, flawlessly. The wind whipped over him, around him, and he tore into a field bursting with green, with the smell of spring. Hills loomed in the distance, lost in a pale blue haze, and exhilaration filled him. And he knew this emotion was as strong as the fear for Mike that had flung him back to Aruba and as powerful as the need to get someplace safe that had brought them here.

He gained speed, the Harley racing through light and shadows, under trees and out into the open again. Then he *reached* for Blue River on February 12, 1695, and *released*, turning the rest of it over to the chip. The Harley hit the edge of a rise and suddenly was airborne, the bike reaching for the cerulean sky. Joy filled him like helium in a balloon—and then everything below him simply wasn't there anymore.

26
High Strangeness

Your intentions act as the chip's booster rocket.

—Mariah Jones

The blacksmith flung the stable doors open, slapped one of the spooked horses on the rump, and the entire herd of horses tore out into the fog and the cold, neighing and snorting, hooves pounding the trodden snow. Kincaid, huddled forward in his saddle, gripped the reins in one hand, the horse's mane in the other, and struggled not to fall off.

Horses galloped on either side of him. The crowd shouted and pointed and seemed to careen toward them, en masse. But when the crowd of lunatics realized the stampeding herd wasn't going to stop or swerve, they moved apart and the galloping horses tore through them.

Kincaid's ass slammed against the saddle, one of his feet slipped out of a stirrup, and suddenly he was sliding to the left, could feel the saddle sliding with him. Cory drew up alongside him, shouting, "Follow me into the trees!"

Kincaid threw his body to the right and his horse raced after Cory. They broke away from the pack and headed for the pines. The blacksmith, stable hands, and the rest of the horses continued on toward the other side of town, forcing the marchers out of the way. Kincaid didn't raise up until they were inside the pines, and he was surprised to glimpse the shimmering blue Atlantic through the trees just beyond them.

They stopped just short of some fallen trees and a tangle of dried brush, snow, and ice and dismounted. Kincaid's bag, with Nora's stuck inside it, now felt like it contained a dead body. He adjusted the strap around his neck, let the bag fall to one side, against his right hip, and hastened over to Cory.

They had escaped the stable, but Kincaid was beginning to think this option sucked. They were at least a quarter of a mile straight out from the jail and any tunnel between there and here wasn't going to be anything like a tunnel in his own time. No concrete holding back the dirt. Nothing wide enough for a man to walk upright inside it. Probably so narrow, in fact, that he would be shimmying through on his goddamn belly. It could take hours.

Nora didn't have hours.

"Jim, this isn't going to work. It's too far to the jail."

"Jail?"

"The gaol."

"I think not. The . . ."

Wild, frantic barking erupted behind them and Kincaid spun around. Sunny loped toward him, ears flopping, tail whipping from side to side. She barked again, and when he threw his arms around her, she covered his face with sloppy kisses.

"Where'd you go? How come you're alone?"

Sunny ran her tongue over his face, his hands.

"Dear God," Cory said softly, urgently, and pointed. "Alex, look."

A man and woman stumbled out of the far line of trees, the last barrier between them and the beach. Kincaid didn't recognize them, but Cory did. "Catherine," he cried and loped toward her with all the desperate passion of a man who had not expected to see the love of his life here, now.

Catherine? As in Catherine Griffin Walrave? And *Cory? Sweet Christ, how?*

She broke away from the other man and she and James Cory came together in such a way that it left no doubt in Kincaid's mind that she would not be going with them. Cory's hands vanished into Catherine's thick, black hair, and she dropped her head back, her mouth meeting his, all of it so intimate that Kincaid felt like a voyeur and looked away.

Her companion hurried over to Kincaid, a tall man with salt-and-pepper hair and a beard threaded with gray. "I'm Russ Berlin."

Language failed Kincaid. Inside his head, probabilities collided, collapsed.

"You look much different from your photos, Mr. Kincaid."

"Probably because I'm decked out in breeches that are squeezing the blood from my balls."

Berlin laughed and the two men shook hands. Sunny paced anxiously in front of them, reminding Kincaid of the urgency of Nora's situation. "We got your PDA, Alex. Where's the tunnel?"

"Somewhere around here. But it may take too long to get in there. I don't think Nora has much time."

Berlin nodded. "They're burning Blue River. They torched the stable. That's where we emerged first. Then Sunny brought us to the beach."

"I couldn't free her. Chandler cuffed her with these metal bands to the bars of a cage. I've got a crude tool that supposedly will cut through the bands, but I . . . I can't seem to transition back to the cellar."

"Maybe Sunny can. Maybe that's her role. The messenger who takes us to where we can't go ourselves."

Kincaid glanced out toward Catherine and James Cory, who were still embracing.

"Let's give Catherine and James Cory a few minutes," Berlin said, then added: "I've been a fan of yours ever since I bought one of your early hybrids," Berlin said.

Now *that* was something he understood. The hybrid. *His* hybrid. "What model hybrid did you drive?" *In our other lives?*

"The AK Jupiter. On the highway, I was getting a hundred and twenty miles to the gallon. In the city, it was about a hundred to the gallon." He spoke fast, his hands moved restlessly through the air, as if to pull in words at a lightning pace. "I modified the engine somewhat after the first year, so I could use a combination of alternative fuels, and boosted the mileage to two hundred miles to the gallon. Two twenty on a good day."

What? Kincaid's tiny group of engineers had spent two years trying to modify the engine of the AF Jupiter and had failed at every turn. Who the hell *was* this guy? "And you did this how?" he asked.

Berlin started explaining, his language as technical and precise as Kincaid's when it came to the hybrid. And his summary amounted to about fifty words. Stunned, Kincaid's mind lit up with the schematic of the AK's engine. "That's brilliant. And I never thought of it. Jesus."

"I had help from Mariah."

Ah. Right. Of course. The original design for the hybrid had come from Mariah. "Did she ever tell you where she got the idea?"

"She told me a lot of things. I didn't know what to believe. I still don't."

"She's *alive*?"

"I last saw her in April 2006. As you know, she doesn't disappear on your timeline until October 2006."

"So where did she get the design? Did she ever say?"

Berlin sat back on his hands, straightened his legs out in front of him. "In one version of her story, the design came from twenty or thirty years in our future, when the oil is nearly gone. In another version, the design came from 2012, right before the end of everything."

"What's that mean? The *end of everything*?"

"It means whatever she wanted it to mean. Supposedly, in the early days of her chip experiments, around 1966, she inadvertently transitioned to 2012 and what she saw horrified her as such a deep level that it set the course for the rest of her life. She was determined to change that outcome."

Kincaid was almost afraid to ask. "What'd she see?"

"Devastation, drastic climate change, nuclear ruin in certain parts of the world, a vastly changed planetary geography." Berlin paused. "Beyond that, I don't know. I can't even say with any certainty what that meant for her."

Images leaped to mind, snippets of dreams, a collage of facts and figures that he had collected over the years, a picture so grim that a shudder rippled through him. Toxic air. Melted ice shelves. Rising seas. As eastern coastline that extended inward to the base of the Smokies, with Florida, Louisiana, parts of Alabama and Georgia and Mississippi reduced to nothing more than a string of islands. New York City gone, Philadelphia gone, Nova Scotia underwater. And to the west, a coastline that began at Billings, Montana.

Kincaid looked at him, really looked. He saw the underlying sadness in Berlin's eyes, a personal tragedy, he guessed, that had changed the landscape of his life forever. And beneath that lurked another layer of emotion, the deeper layer where all men were connected, where all shared a collective fate. Both had driven him into Mariah's life, into her arms. "What do *you* believe?"

Berlin drew his legs up against his chest and wrapped his arms around his legs. He stared out at Cory and Catherine Walrave, evidence of the high strangeness that had invaded their lives. "I'm not sure. Once, in the early days of our relationship, she talked about how there were seven, eight, maybe a dozen historical events which, if they were changed, would alter what she had seen in 2012. I don't know which specific events she was referring to."

Kincaid mulled this over. "Atomic fusion would be pretty high on my list."

Berlin shook his head. "If that never had happened, it would change too much. No bombing of Japan. For the same reason, preventing the assassination of JFK or MLK or RFK probably wouldn't work, either."

"It doesn't make sense. If you mitigate large historical events, wouldn't you just be creating a new timeline?"

"I don't know," Berlin replied. "That's the whole thing. *We. Don't. Know.* The technology is too new and it's been improved so many times that we're basically writing the script as we live it, Alex. None of us knows what the rules are, where the parameters lie, what we're doing or supposed to be doing. It's a brand-new universe. The exploration drove Mariah."

"And what drives *you*?" Kincaid asked.

"Hope."

"Optimist."

"Fear."

"Uh-huh."

"Despair."

"Why?"

Berlin breathed in. Out. "My son died when he was four. Can I change that? And if I do, am I changing timelines? And what does that mean, really? That I die on one timeline and continue on another? That he dies on one and continues on another? What's real? What isn't? It all comes back to that silly argument you have in college, when you're so stoned you can't see straight, it's four o'clock in the morning, and all the weed's gone. Illusion versus reality. It's the oldest philosophical argument in the history of man."

"Yeah. It's called, *Who the Fuck Are We*?"

"Right."

He could like this man. "So we're all stumbling around in the dark."

"Even Mariah," Berlin replied. "She acts and talks like she's on top of it all, but she isn't."

A kind of spiritual malaise seeped through Kincaid and he briefly shut his eyes, as if that act alone could shut out the reality of what Berlin had said. *We're blind men. Clueless. Groping in the dark.*

Cory and Catherine hurried toward them, his arm around her shoulders, hers around his waist. She was several inches taller than Cory, but not as tall as Nora, and wore pants, a real no-no for women in this time. And she was stunning, just a few years older than her own daughter, a complete mindfuck.

"And after this?" Kincaid asked. "If we survive? What then?"

"I don't know. But I'd like to be a part of whatever you and your group are doing."

"We don't really know what the hell we're doing."

Berlin laughed, stuck out his hand. "That's the most honest thing anyone has said to me in three centuries."

When they shook hands, Kincaid felt as if they were being initiated into a secret society, into something that might sustain him, sustain the group, for a very long time.

"Catherine came to rescue Nora," said Berlin. "But I don't think she'll be going back. She and Cory live in a settlement of the disenfranchised. They're rogues who go from town to town, rescuing those accused of witchcraft."

"This settlement. Is it called Mystic Harbor? It's a real place?"

"Apparently. And Lydia Fenmore's records are lies. Catherine has been here since July of 1694. She survived her transition, Alex, because she adapted to this time."

And then Catherine and Cory stood right in front of them and she just studied his face, the edges of her cloak fluttering like dark wings in a slight breeze. "Thank you for everything you've done, Alex," she said finally. "Thank you for coming back to look for me. Is she in the jail?"

"In the secret chamber, the cellar, in a cage, restrained by metal bands. Davies is handcuffed to the ladder. And gagged."

A horrifying shadow swept over Catherine's beautiful face. "Rats," she whispered. "As big as toy trucks." She paused, breathing through the memory of that place. "Davies helped me escape. Let's hope he can do something for her."

"Hoping won't get us in there."

"Sunny will." She dropped her hand to Sunny's back, her fingers combing through her thick, luxurious fur. "She got us this far. She'll take us the rest of the way."

Cory, who had gone to the line of trees that hid them from the town, now hurried back and crouched on the other side of the dog, one hand covering Catherine's. "We must hurry," he said. "Dozens of buildings are burning."

Kincaid leaned close to Sunny, who was now sitting up, attentive, waiting for instructions. Around them, the pines sighed in a cold, salty breeze and that same breeze carried the stink of smoke from the burning town and the shrieks and hollers of the crowd.

He brought out another PDA from the bag and held it toward Sunny. "Can you deliver this to Nora, girl?"

Thump, thump went that tail, a drumbeat of battle, then Sunny took the PDA in her mouth and all of them made sure they were touching each other and Sunny. Kincaid whispered, "We're ready."

When the glow stick began to fail, the rats closed in on Nora, squeaking, chattering, their tails thumping against the old stone floors. She shot two of them and was down eleven bullets when the rat closest to her leaped.

She whipped up her branch with the sharpened point and thrust it at the rat as it was in midair. It impaled itself on the branch and Nora flicked the rat away, its warm blood spattering her face, clothes, hands. She thought she screamed, but maybe it was the other rats screaming, as they scurried, moving in for the kill. She lunged to the right and felt the stick sinking into a second rat, heard its hideous squeals, and saw it twitching and bleeding before she hurled it away from her.

Minutes, her glow stick had minutes of light left. It was too damn cold down here and it had been lit too long. How long had it been since Davies had left to find a pin in the torture chamber that she might use to jimmy the lock on the bracelets. Minutes? Hours?

Her only measurement of time was the noise of the rats converging from every direction in the cellar. The call had gone out, the light was failing, the prey was alone, down to just two bullets and a single, blood-drenched stick. She could almost decipher those squeaks and scratches, that tapping of claws against the stones. The rats knew. They knew.

She shut her eyes and rested her head against her shackled arm. She hurt. She hurt everywhere and nowhere, a non-specific pain that seemed to move randomly around her body, like a virus seeking a place to call home. The belief that she might die here began to work its way through her and despite her best intentions to banish such a thought, it remained, coiled close to her heart like a cobra, ready to strike.

Behind her, more noise, more scratching, more squeaking, and she twisted around and fired. She would rot in animal hell for her slaughter of the rats. But she vowed to become a complete vegetarian, to rally for animal rights in her own time and every other time, too, if the animal gods kept the rats away from her.

Down to three bullets. No, down to two. The third was further, if it came to that. She talked to herself out loud. "Breathe. You will live through this. Breathe like you mean it." Then she shouted, "Breathe, dammit!" and her voice echoed against the walls, a mockery.

A rectangle of light spilled into the cellar. The trapdoor had opened. Davies had returned. *The animal gods heard me.*

Voices. Someone climbed down the ladder and a second person followed. Their torches cast strange shadows that slipped down the walls and eddied across the floor, gobbling up the erratic orange and yellow pools of light. "Mr. Davies!" she shouted. "Hurry!"

The figures approached her cage—and her heart seized up, hammering. Despite the stale cold in the cellar, beads of sweat rolled down the sides of her face. Her stomach tightened in horror. It was Chandler, his cane tapping the way toward her cage, his other hand gripping a torch.

"You see, Magistrate Goodwin? She bewitched Mr. Davies. He opened the door for her. She took your wife's name. And look at her, covered with the blood of the rats she has been eating. She . . ."

Nora didn't hear the rest of what he said. She was stuck on the other man's name. *Magistrate Goodwin*. The real guy had arrived, that much was historically accurate. The magistrate slipped his torch into a holder and then stood beside Chandler with the uncertainty of a ghost, his cloak drawn up so far against his neck that his head seemed to vanish into it. And she suddenly understood that this man, this magistrate, this idiotic puppet would help to perpetuate Chandler's superstitious madness.

"Can she recite the Lord's Prayer?" the magistrate asked.

"No, she cannot, sir," said Chandler, looking smug.

"Excuse me, but you can speak to me directly, Magistrate. And I *can* recite the Lord's Prayer."

The real Magistrate Goodwin drew his eyes toward her slowly, reluctantly, as though to look at her—a woman accused of witchcraft—might somehow *infect* him, *contaminate* him, *entrance* him. The horror in his expression told her more than she wanted to know about how she looked to him, her lip swollen, her face bruised and swollen and splattered with blood. "Then do so."

"Our Father Who art in heaven, hallowed be thy name, thy kingdom come, thy will be done . . ."

"What kind of Lord's Prayer is that?" the magistrate asked.

"You have some other version?" she asked.

The magistrate wrenched back as though her words, the volume of her voice, her insolence at challenging him was proof positive that she was possessed and the possession was contagious.

"Who is your Lord, woman?" the magistrate demanded.

"Ask that asshole beside you who *his* Lord is. He tortures the women he accuses. He sticks pins into them, thrusts their hands and arms into boiling oil, and when they pass out, he defiles them. Do you understand what I'm saying? He *rapes* them. Do you understand that word, Magistrate? It means to force a person to have sex. He rules this town, ignoring the *governor's* laws, ignoring *your* laws. He admits spectral evidence."

Chandler slammed his cane against the bars of the open cage door. "Silence! You are nothing more than a mouthpiece of Satan, of—"

"*You* be silent," Goodwin shouted at Chandler. "Unlock her bands. I wish to speak to her outside of this . . . this black and terrible place."

"But . . . but Magistrate. If she is not restrained, she will enchant us, trick us. The people . . . you have seen what they are doing outside. They are demanding that the witch burn. Look at her. See the dead rats she has been eating? And her clothing. She wears pants. Like a man. And that stick of light that she holds . . . what is that? It comes from Satan. She helped Sarah Longwood escape. She—"

"*The keys,*" Goodwin snapped, and held out his hand. "Quickly."

Chandler slapped the keys into the magistrate's hand and Goodwin moved toward her, his clothes rustling, his steps uncertain. Nora clutched the gun in her right hand, hiding it against her leg. *Three bullets*. The inside of her mouth flashed dry, she heard the rats retreating into the hay, then Goodwin stooped in close to her, rattling the keys, trying to find the one that would fit the lock for the band that encircled her left wrist.

"I . . . I cannot allow this, Magistrate Goodwin," Chandler stammered, and his cane whistled through the air and slammed across Goodwin's back.

Goodwin cried out and fell against Nora, his weight pinning her to the floor, her hand and the gun trapped beneath her. The keys flew from Goodwin's grasp and landed somewhere in the filthy hay behind her. Nora no longer saw Chandler—Goodwin's shoulder blocked her view—but she could hear him, the mad mutterings, his cane swinging from side to side, his boots shuffling against the stone floor, through the hay.

Nora managed to lift her right hip just enough to free her hand, whipped the gun up and fired blindly. *Two bullets left.* "Stay back or the next bullet will be to your brain, Chandler!" She twisted, shoved a moaning Goodwin to one side, bolted upward.

Chandler stared in disbelief at the blood pouring from his hand, the broken cane at his feet. He had dropped his torch and bits of hay just outside the cage were now engulfed in flames.

Jesus God. "The torch!" she screamed. "Pick up your torch! The hay caught fire!"

Chandler was oblivious. "You . . . you shot me, witch!" he hollered, then stumbled forward.

The magistrate suddenly reared up and threw himself into Chandler, knocking him backward. They crashed to the floor, shouting, moaning, cursing. More hay caught fire, and in another moment the flames would leap the divide of stone and dirt that was free of hay and the inside of the cage would go up so fast that Nora would be cooked before she could free herself.

Her fear ruptured like an appendix, spewing toxins. She scrambled back, back, slapping the hay with her free hand,

and suddenly felt them. The keys. Nora scooped them and fumbled through them, her fingers searching, reading the shapes of a dozen keys, looking for the smallest one, the one that would fit the keyhole of the band around her wrist.

The hay inside the cage now burned brightly, crackling, spitting smoke. Nora could feel the heat of the flames. Her eyes watered from the smoke that rolled through this horrid place, she could hardly breathe. Coughing, her eyes watering, she fit the smallest key in the lock and nearly wept when it clicked and her hand fell free. Now, her ankle. She scooted closer to her shackled ankle, turned the band so she could see the keyhole, jammed one key after another into it, trying to make it fit. Nothing.

So she brought the Glock to the bar of the cage to which the band was connected, moved it up slightly so she wouldn't shoot her foot off, and fired. Her ears rang, new pockets of hay burst into flame. Her ankle was still shackled.

The shot had torn away the upper part of the bar, but she couldn't lift her leg high enough to slide the band off over the top. Nora gripped the gun by the muzzle and slammed the handle against the lower part of the bar. The bar's structure, weakened by the gunshot, began to succumb. She jerked her leg hard to the right and it snapped free.

Coughing again, her eyes tearing terribly, Nora pushed to her feet. Through the thickening smoke, she saw Goodwin sprawled facedown, unmoving, one leg of his breeches already smoldering. Chandler was nowhere in sight. She stumbled over to the magistrate, grabbed his arms, dragged him away from the cage. Nora hurried over to one of the half-full buckets of water left here from when Davies had brought water to the accused for bathing. She poured it over his breeches, then his head. He raised up, sputtering, coughing, and Nora screamed, "The cellar's on fire! On your feet! Fast!"

Please, oh please, get up, now, immediately.

Nora scrambled up the ladder, pushed on the trapdoor,

but it wouldn't open. She pressed her shoulder against the wood and heaved. The trapdoor wouldn't budge.

"Burn in hell, witch!" Chandler shouted from the other side.

The prick had gone topside and probably was sitting on the trapdoor, holding it down, preventing her and the magistrate from escaping.

"Dear God, dear God," the magistrate muttered from the foot of the ladder. "The stories about this madman are *true.*"

Nora quickly climbed back down the ladder and clasped the magistrate's shoulder. Then she reached for the room where Chandler was, *reached* for it thirty minutes ago, *reached* and *released. . . .*

And remained exactly where she was, at the foot of the ladder. *Shit.*

"The buckets, we need the buckets of water!" Nora shouted. They ran from the ladder and grabbed up the buckets. She ran over to where Goodwin had been sprawled, while he hurried into another cage, and they hurled the water onto the burning hay. It hissed and spat, spewing smoke, but at the back of Goodwin's cage the hay still burned, flames leaping, dancing, mocking them as the hay in the next cage now exploded with flames.

"More water!" Goodwin yelled.

But there was no more. Their buckets were empty. Dry. Done.

"Under the ladder, to the farthest corner!" Nora shouted, and they ran, Chandler's hideous taunts rising and falling around them as the flames cackled and consumed, taunting them. Laughing at them.

27
And Then Some

The chip will outlive us all.
—Mariah Jones

They emerged in the front room of the jail, Kincaid, Catherine, Cory, Berlin, and Sunny. It shocked Kincaid, who had believed that Sunny would transition them to the cellar. The shouts and chants of the people outside reverberated against the building, a testament to how deeply Chandler's religious superstitions had poisoned the town. When he peered out the grimy window, his heart nearly stopped.

Thirty yards from the front of the jail, in the middle of the street, wagons filled with logs were being unloaded by dozens of men, women, even children. The pyres they were constructing were impressive already, three of them with logs stacked several feet high, each with a narrow path leading to the thick pole that served as the stake. Kincaid suspected that once Nora was secured to the stake, the path would be filled in with more wood, the pyre would be lit, and the bystanders would party until the witch was dead.

But it won't get that far.

Kincaid moved quickly away from the window and ran

toward the doors that opened to the cell block, the others racing around him. Sunny shot past all of them and took off up
the left corridor, where Kincaid now smelled smoke and
heard shouts, pounding. The dog jumped at the closed door,
and it swung open. Chandler was on his knees, smoke curling up through the floorboards and around his head so that
he looked like some madman sniffing the vapors at Delphi.
He hammered his fists on the trapdoor. Blood seeped from a
bandage around his wrist and stained the floor. "Die, witch,
die!" he shouted.

Sunny snarled and leaped at him, knocking him back and
pinning him to the floor. Kincaid ran over to them, grabbed
Chandler by the front of his shirt, jerked him upright, and threw
him against the wall. Chandler's head smacked against it and
he slumped to the floor and lay there, a deflated balloon.

"Get him out of here!" Kincaid shouted to the others.

He jerked open the trapdoor and clouds of hot, thick, greasy
smoke rolled out. He started down the ladder, shouting for
Nora, but the farther he descended, the harder it was to breathe.
He swept one edge of his cloak across his face, breathing
through the damp wool, his eyes watering so badly that he could
barely see. Before he reached the foot of the ladder, the heat
became almost unbearable, a raging furnace of vivid orange
tongues of fire that were eating through the wooden ceiling and
scorching the stone walls. The only reason the ladder hadn't
gone up yet was that the floor around it was clear of hay and
the fire hadn't found a way across the stones yet.

Coughing, a muffled voice: "Here. We are here."

Kincaid dropped to the floor, blinking rapidly to clear his
vision, and a rotund man stumbled out from under the ladder, one hand pressed over his mouth and nose, the other
waving his cloak through the air, trying to clear away the
smoke. "Back there. She is in the corner. Help her, dear God,
help her."

"Get to the ladder!" Kincaid yelled over the roar of the
fire. "My friends will help you!"

He ducked under the ladder where he had hidden from Davies hours ago, and found Nora curled up on the floor, face buried in the curve of her arm. She wasn't conscious, but she was breathing. Christ, still breathing. Still alive. He shook her, but she didn't respond. He tore off his cloak, covered her with it, slid his arms under her and lifted her. His lungs ached, his eyes burned. When he turned, flames snaked up one side of the ladder, greedily devouring the wood.

No fucking way we're dying down here.

He shifted Nora to his shoulder, carrying her like Santa with a bag of toys, whipped the cloak off her, and slapped it against the flames on the ladder, smothering them. Then he started climbing, his head spinning, his coughing so violent he couldn't catch his breath.

Before he reached the top, hands reached down through the opening and grabbed hold of Nora, pulling her to safety, and another pair of hands latched on to his forearms and helped him to the top. Kincaid collapsed against the floor, alternately gasping for air and wheezing like an asthmatic, then rolled away from the opening and someone slammed the trapdoor shut.

"Alex, quick," Cory said, pulling him to a sitting position. "The fire is now weakening the floor. We must leave this place. Your wife is in the other room. We found the jailer, Davies, in the torture room, dead. The doctor tied up the madman."

That would be Chandler. Kincaid wiped his arm across his eyes, got to his feet, and weaved toward the door. Cory caught his arm, steadying him. Suddenly, behind them, flames burst through the trapdoor and the floor around it and huge chunks of wood simply collapsed and fell into the cellar. The fire leaped upward, tendrils bursting outward in every direction, seeking something solid to consume. The two men broke into a run and raced up the narrow corridor and into the front room of the jail. Kincaid shut the heavy wooden door and leaned against it, sucking in air that was still relatively free of smoke—but wouldn't be for much longer.

"We need to get out of here," Berlin said, turning away from the window, anxiety evident in his face, his eyes. "That crowd out there is large and those people want blood. But Nora isn't conscious yet."

So they couldn't transition her, that was what he was really saying.

"She breathed in . . . much more smoke than I did," the fat man said.

"And you are who, sir?" Kincaid asked.

Catherine, sitting on the floor with Nora's head resting on her thigh, said, "He is Magistrate Goodwin."

Uh-oh, Kincaid thought, then reached inside a pocket in his filthy breeches and slipped out Chandler's journal. "This is for you. It is Walter Chandler's journal, in which he confesses to murdering his wife and making it look as if Sarah Longwood was a witch. I have been impersonating you, sir, in order to rescue my wife."

Goodwin didn't have a chance to reply; a hail of stones struck the windows and rained down over the roof.

"Time to split, people!" Berlin yelled. "They're starting to converge—"

Shots rang out, the windows shattered, and lit torches sailed into the room. Cory and Goodwin swept them up, hurled them into the fireplace, and stamped out the tiny fires that burned through bits of hay scattered across the floor. The chants outside rose to a frenzy. *Bring out the witches, burn the witches, the pyres are ready.*

Bodies now crashed against the heavy wooden door, the chanting ratcheted up another notch. Kincaid slung his pack over his shoulder, dug out his Glock, and joined Berlin at the window. They fired simultaneously into the air and the crowd moved back, en masse.

"We will shoot the next person who approaches this building!" Kincaid called out.

Francis Travers edged away from the crowd. "Bring them out! They must burn!"

The real magistrate waddled like a penguin over to the window, moving as quickly as his short legs would carry him. "I am Magistrate Goodwin. This man is my assistant. I sent him here to investigate the activities of Reverend Chandler." He waved the journal at the crowd. "And here is the evidence that your reverend killed his wife, defiled the accused, that he himself is possessed by Satan."

"Lies!" Travers hollered and motioned the crowd forward.

As men and women and children surged around Travers, a living tide of madness, Kincaid and Berlin opened fire.

A man at the front of the line keeled over. A woman shrieked and threw herself to the ground beside her wounded or dead husband or brother or son. Kincaid looked on, horrified. It wasn't ever supposed to come to this. "Russ, get them out of here," he snapped. "*Now.* I'll stay with Nora until she's conscious."

A roaring filled the air and it seemed to be everywhere—here in the room with them, outside with the crowd, echoing from the heavens, pounding against the cold, resounding across the hard white snow. The surging tide opened up, people scrambling to either side of the pyres to get out of the way, and when the view was clear, Kincaid thought he was dreaming. He blinked, but it was still there.

"Are you seeing what the fuck I'm seeing?" Berlin whispered.

"A Harley. Eric Holcomb on a Harley."

It roared straight toward the jail, Holcomb leaning slightly forward, into the wind, the engine revving. He made a fancy turn just past the pyres, the front tire skidded on the snow, and Holcomb stopped just shy of the door. His feet dropped to the ground, he withdrew some sort of rifle from the pack on his back, and fired it into the air. "Get back and stay back." His voice echoed through the cold air and the crowd withdrew, as if it were of one mind, one heart, one soul, a collective, and the collective was terrified of the Harley, the rifle.

Holcomb dismounted and backed toward the building, the rifle ready. Cory threw open the door and Kincaid and Berlin rushed out and pushed the Harley into the room. Cory bolted the door. "We have minutes, no more, before they rush forward again," Cory breathed.

"And smoke is now coming through the floors," Catherine added.

"Your son," Kincaid said. "Did you rescue him?"

"He's in Nellysford, with a woman named Lea. What happened to Nora?"

"Smoke inhalation," said Catherine. "She can't be transitioned unless—"

"Yeah, I know." He looked at Kincaid. "You know how to drive one of these machines?"

"Yes."

"If we can get Nora on the backseat and tie her to you, you can get her out of here."

"If the bike can fit three, we can prop her between us," Catherine said. "And I can direct you to our settlement, Alex."

Kincaid glanced at the real Magistrate Goodwin. "You can stay here or go with my friends, Magistrate, and leave the reverend and the rest of this town to its destiny."

"I will go with you," Goodwin said quickly.

"C'mon, c'mon," Berlin said urgently. "We're running out of time."

Sunny, obviously agitated, paced and whined, licked at Nora's face, grabbed on to Kincaid's cloak and pulled on it, and finally sat in front of Berlin, peering up at him.

"The fire," Berlin said. "The fire scares her."

"The fire scares *me*," Catherine said, and moved her daughter's head to the floor and got up. "Are you sure three will fit?" she asked Kincaid.

"It may slow us down, but we'll do it. We have to push the bike back, so I've got the full length of the room," he said, and all of them started pushing. "How far is this Mystic place, Catherine?"

"How fast does the bike go?" she asked Holcomb.

"If there's a road, it can do between sixty and seventy."

"Then by the road, it should take two to three hours." She said. "We will all met there. Is there enough gas?"

"This baby gets fifty miles to the gallon, two hundred and fifty or so to the tank," Holcomb replied.

"Perfect," Catherine said. "That'll get us there and then some."

Outside, the chanting started up again. Cory, standing near the window, called, "It is starting. They are moving forward again. Hasten, do what you need to do."

Chandler screamed into his gag and thrashed from side to side until his chair fell over.

Kincaid wasn't taking any chances that Sunny would transition elsewhere. He slipped a rope under her collar, tied it. "You're going with Russ." He passed the rope to Berlin, who tied it around his wrist. "What's the local mean time?"

"Five past one," Berlin announced.

"Then you and Eric should target three hours ago, Mystic Harbor. Magistrate Goodwin, are you joining them?"

Three torches sailed through the window, struck the opposite wall, and fell to the stones. Goodwin looked scared, his face the color of sour milk. "Yes, that is the wisest course. But how will we travel?"

"Chandler suddenly screamed through his gag. "On their brooms!"

"On the winds of time," Berlin replied, then helped Catherine lift Nora and carry her to the Harley.

Kincaid straddled the bike now, his bag snug against one hip. "Russ, if you and Jim can cover us as we're leaving . . ."

"Done," Berlin said.

"When you say so, Alex, I will open the door," Cory said.

More torches flew through the window. More stones pelted the door. *Burn the witches, burn the witches,* the crowd cried.

"Take the rifle," Holcomb said and tossed it toward Kincaid. But Catherine caught it.

Kincaid turned the key in the bike's ignition. "Russ, is the door clear?"

Berlin squeezed off two shots. "It is now. If you go behind the pyre on the far right, the other side of it looks pretty clear."

The engine revved to life, a beast hungry for the open road, and the roaring suffused the room, the world. Cory threw open the door and Kincaid steered the Harley forward. It shot out into the cold February air.

The first few moments were bad. The cold air sliced through Kincaid's lungs, his eyeballs, the skin on his face. The tires skidded in the snow as he leaned into a turn, around the back of the pyre to the far right, but he came out of it effortlessly, the Harley hugging the ground like a bug.

He knew the crowd surged behind him—he could feel the people, the weight of their collective madness. He heard gunfire and the crowd retreated, buying him sixty seconds, and then he came around the pyre and saw that some of the people in the crowd had broken away from the others and were racing toward him, shouting, waving their arms and their torches, guns and tools until they formed a wide half-moon, cutting him off on three sides.

Kincaid considered barreling straight through them, but there were so many of them he couldn't risk it. They were like insects— bees, ants, beings controlled by their mass beliefs. And if the bike went down, they would swarm all over them, devouring them in seconds. So he swerved into a sharp right turn and tore away from them, headed for the beach. If Nora came to, he might be able to transition the three of them and the bike to Nellysford. Except he'd never been there. And he'd never tried transitioning on a Harley.

Catherine fired the rifle half a dozen times. Then the Harley tore across an empty field, sped through a scattering of pines, and finally hit the hard-packed beach. And he opened her up wide.

The speedometer needle climbed to sixty, sixty-five, seventy. The tires kicked up sand, the waves broke against the beach, and when he glanced back, the crowd looked like an army of toy soldiers. Kincaid leaned into the wind, the cold air slapping his teeth.

Catherine shouted, "Alex, she's coming around! Let's do it!"

"We're gone!" he shouted back.

Then the beach disappeared.

Berlin fired until the clip was empty, until the Harley vanished in the pines and he could no longer see it. Even though the crowd had kept its distance from the jail, they had lit the middle pyre and it burned hot, bright, the long, orange tongues curling around the logs, spiraling steadily upward, pursuing the lantern oil they had splashed on it. And now others in the crowd surged forward, grabbing sticks and logs from the pyre as they chanted and shouted, inflaming those who hung back. If ever there was a case for mob mentality, this was it.

Berlin moved back from the window and hurried over to Holcomb, Sunny, Cory, and Goodwin. Smoke from the burning cellar now swirled through the front room, a black, putrid smoke that wrapped around them like a heavy cloak, making it difficult to breathe, to see. Even the open window wasn't large enough to draw out all the smoke. There was simply too much of it.

A hole opened up in the middle of the floor, the wood crumbling beneath the heat of the fire.

Berlin grasped on to the end of Sunny's rope with one hand, clutched Goodwin's arm with the other. Berlin and Holcomb locked eyes and Berlin knew they were thinking the same thing. Holcomb took Cory's arm and Berlin looked down at Sunny and said, "Get us out of here, girl." The door of the jail burst open, the crowd poured in, and all of it vanished.

28
Home

It's where the heart is, right?
—Nora McKee

Nellysford, Virginia, June 21, 2006

They walked beneath a summer sky so blue that it seemed luminous. Fields of bright yellow wildflowers rustled in the breeze. Trees swayed like dancers. The grass against Nora's bare feet felt as soft as a baby's skin. The picnic basket she carried swung at her side.

"All those years you were gone," Nora said, "I always wished we had had a picnic."

Her mother slipped her arm around Nora's shoulders, and for a while, they walked without speaking, content to simply be together, beneath the warm sun, in a place as beautiful as the Virginia hills. "You and Jim could move here," Nora said suddenly.

"And fight your fight?" Her mother shook her head. "We have our own fight, Nora. Even though Chandler probably will burn—or has burned already—there are other nutcases, all over the colonies."

"You could be a snowbird. You could have a second place here, a refuge from the cold winters. You could have a hot shower."

Catherine threw her head back, laughing. "Now *that* is tempting."

Just ahead, Nora spotted her brother, standing in the shade of a massive oak, waving a bottle of wine. Nora grabbed her mother's hand and they ran toward him, laughing, and the three of them settled in the shade and had a picnic that was many decades overdue.

Shadows lengthened across the field, the surrounding hills. Nora realized that her bond with this woman would never be broken, regardless of who lived where or when. The chip would enable them to visit each other, to make up for all the years that SPOT had stolen from them. She and Tyler now had the best of all worlds, a chance to know their mother separate from their need for her, from their childhood anxiety about what had happened to her. They had their lives, she had hers, but their lives would intersect, rub up against each other like spoons in the same drawer.

Kincaid and Diana joined them, and Catherine promised to be back in time for the birth of the baby sometime in the late fall. They made plans. But when Catherine finally got up to leave, to transition back more than three centuries, Nora threw her arms around her mother, this beautiful woman who now was only a few years older than she. And all of the heartache and angst her absence had created in Nora's life now rose up inside her. She was no longer thirty-three; she was ten and losing her mother all over again.

"Don't go," she whispered, burying her face in the curve of her mother's neck, in that scent of lavender, lemon, love.

Catherine's arms tightened around her, holding her. "Nora, Nora," she whispered, then flung her other arm around Tyler, pulling him close. "We'll overcome what Mariah took from us," she promised, and then she was gone.

Nora and Tyler stood there with Diana and Kincaid, none of them speaking. Kincaid took her hand and the four of them walked toward the road. The warm summer sun spilled over them, the trees rustled in a breeze, the odors of earth and green suffused her senses.

"Hey, you hear that?" Kincaid said suddenly.

"What?" Nora asked.

"That noise."

"It's a Harley!" Tyler said, and they raced through the grass, the wildflowers, and out into the middle of the road.

It came into view, a tiny dark smudge against the trees, and behind it was a second smudge. Both Harleys screeched to a stop in front of them. "Hop on," Eric Holcomb called.

"Yeah," Mike said from the second Harley. "We've got room."

"Where the hell have you guys been?" Nora asked.

Holcomb grinned and lifted the leather satchel that hung around his neck. "Collecting what's ours." Bills poked through the top. "A million dollars, enough to see this extended family through a long, long time."

"And we had to pick up his old Harley," Mike chimed in.

"We had a score to settle with Lazier and his people, too," Holcomb added. "He won't be bothering us again. Hop on, guys, two and two. We'll fit."

Nora and Kincaid got on behind Mike, Tyler and Diana, with her bulging belly, straddled Holcomb's bike. They raced along the road, climbing the hills, the tires kicking up pebbles, dirt, until they turned into a long driveway with a ceramic Buddha at the end, arms held out, as if to greet whoever arrived.

Sunny, snoozing in a patch of sunlight on a wide front porch raised her head and shot to her feet, barking, alerting everyone else. The front door flew open before they had dismounted from the bikes and the rest of their extended family poured out. Curtis and Kat, Berlin and Lea, and Ann Lincoln, Mike's girlfriend.

Including the dog, they were twelve in all.

Not an army in the cosmic scheme of things, Nora thought. Not even spit in the bucket. But big enough for her right now, in this place, this time, big enough to call home.